CHILDREN OF THE GODS

NEEN COHEN

CHILDREN OF THE GODS

Edited by Lyndsey Ellis-Holloway

Cover Design by Greg Chapman

For everyone who ever felt trapped, there is a family for you, don't give up looking.

A NOTE FROM THE AUTHOR

Children of the Gods has had a long journey.

From the initial ideas, to two novellas, to the longest book I've so far written.

I am so excited to finally be able to tell Adie's story to its fullest. Children of the Gods is the story I always wanted to write, and I hope you enjoy the journey.

I have so many people to thank for their contributions to this book.

To my ever patient and supportive partner and my fiercest cheerleader and ideas lookout kiddo, everything I do is dedicated to and possible because of who you are and who you encourage me to be.

Without the found family I have that surround me in life and in the writing community, both local and sapphic, I wouldn't be continuing to move forward in all that I've found myself doing.

To my incredible editor and Teapot Britch, your comments kept me chuckling. To my amazingly talented cover artist, Greg thank you for letting me share your talent. Chloe, my fearless proofreader who didn't once criticize me for continuing to using Aussie language and idioms.

To my fellow authors and sprinters who got me out of bed at stupid o'clock in the morning thank you for being my external accountability. Special thanks to AJ, Maggie, Sarah, Ames, Katie, Sel, and Liz. What rockstars you continue to be as you inspire and push me to be my best.

Lastly, because I couldn't write a note without thanking you, dear reader, for giving my book a go. It means the world to me.

Be Safe
Be Brave
Be Kind
Neen x

CHILDREN OF THE GODS

PROLOGUE

"No more pushing dusty old books around your bloody library." Mikayla Smith nodded with determination despite the shaking in her hands.

Her dark curly hair bobbed around her head and cascaded down her back. It was just one of the many actions of rebellion she'd embraced since this morning when she'd decided enough was enough.

A smile, unfamiliar and long overdue, stretched wide across her lips. She knew she'd made the right decision.

Her hair shouldn't have made her feel so brave, but it did. Working in that library had slowly taken away *everything* she loved. About herself, and life in general. But it was the only place she could get work. But the questions were never-ending.

Why isn't your hair up?

Why are you flirting with patrons?

Have the books been re-shelved?

Why aren't the meeting rooms reset?

Never the praise for what she *did* do.

Besides, why couldn't she keep her hair down? It had only got caught in the printer once.

"If I see you again, Openfields, it'll be too god damned soon."

From the risen path on the edge of town, Mikayla could see the long shards of light stretch over the place in pinks and oranges. They faded like day-old bruises. Purple smudges that would soon darken to black.

She was getting out. Before this town put any more of its nasty bruises on her.

As she continued to watch, the fingers of light pulled away as the sun slipped further behind the buildings and sank over the horizon.

Night claimed its rightful place and Mikayla Smith took a deep breath. She gave the town the middle finger and turned her back on it for good.

She stepped over the last boundary of the town, indicated solely by the sign that screamed in large red letters: *You are leaving Openfields. Come Back Soon.*

"Not bloody likely," she muttered.

Three steps beyond the sign and Mikayla paused. She closed her eyes and waited for the inevitable. It would come, she knew it would.

While the only man-made indicator of the town's limits was the sign, there were others if you knew where to look.

One moment her steps had been cushioned against soft, moist, nutrient-rich grass, and the next, browning blades crunched beneath the soles of her shoes.

But the liquid lightning continued to run beneath her skin.

She reached her mind out toward the surrounding earth. The dead grass unfurled, growing plump and healthy once more as it softened around her black, thick-soled boots.

The magic lingered.

It buzzed beneath her skin just as strongly as if she stood in the centre of town. Hope bloomed inside her chest. Could she *really* keep the magic, even outside of the town? She had been told it was impossible. They had all been told that.

"Don't get too excited yet." She *tried* to calm the hope that refused to quell within her. "A few more steps and then we'll see," Mikayla muttered as though trying to placate an overly excited child.

She had accepted the price of satiating her wanderlust. Her connection to the magic would end at the town's borders.

They had all been taught this truth, they had always known the price of leaving. Several had left, promising to keep in touch, to return at some point. But none of them ever did. The life they found too good for them to return to the trappings of Openfields.

The magic fizzed out of her, through her, as it continued to feed her surroundings. Green luscious grass sprang up from where the magic left her feet. The grass cradled her steps as she moved further away, as though coaxing her to change her mind and return to the soft safety it provided.

It was the same sensation of static that raised the hair on her body when she dragged her feet through the carpet in the town hall. But town hall was the hub of all Openfields' activity, it was the concentration of the magic. Why would she feel it here?

She gasped as a shadow, tall and featureless, detached from the ragged shrubs at the side of the road.

"Hello?" Mikayla's voice cracked; her heart raced beneath her chest.

The shadow moved toward her, smooth and soundless.

Her breath caught, her heart pumped faster, and the magic thundered to an aching pulse beneath her skin. She turned on instinct, back toward the safety of her town.

The spotless sign beckoned: *Welcome to Openfields.*

Run!

The shadow's presence, black and sharp like metal on the back of her tongue slowed her steps.

Mikayla had never been in quicksand; she'd never before considered how it might feel being trapped in it. She did now.

Beads of sweat collected on her forehead as she forced another step toward home and safety.

And another.

So close. She was so close to the protection that had always been promised to her.

With trembling legs and aching arms, she collapsed on the soft ground just inside the sign welcoming her home.

She'd made it.

The green grass in front of her face swayed in the wake of her breath. Tears stung the corners of her eyes.

She had made it.

Her lips twitched at the corners, but exhaustion stopped the smile from growing any further.

The night noises of the town were drowned out by the roar of blood in her ears, while her nose was filled with the richness of wet dirt and summer heat.

Time was irrelevant.

It could have been ten minutes or two hours before Mikayla finally pushed herself back to her feet. She breathed slow and easy once more, despite the spider legs of anxiety creeping slowly up her spine.

She turned around. She didn't want to. But she *had* to know.

Using the edge of the town's sign to keep her unsteady legs from collapsing once more beneath her weight, she stared out past the boundary and its safety. And she saw nothing.

No detached shadows or spikes of adrenaline rose the hairs on the back of her neck.

If she could have, she would have put the entire experience down to an overactive imagination. But she was born and bred in Openfields. She wasn't stupid or delusional. She knew the touch of magic all too well.

With a small shake of her head, a shudder in her shoulders, and a small laugh that sounded like a scream in the still darkness, she turned around to head back home. She had failed again. But this time she had gotten so much further. Still, she really thought this would be the time she finally snapped that last cord. But the fear had found a new way of pulling her back.

With a sigh, she reluctantly accepted she would wake at least one more day in her bed in Openfields. Perhaps all she really needed was a nice warm soak in the bath. And maybe a haircut.

The scream didn't *quite* make it out of her mouth. Instead, it choked her, sticking in her throat.

The shadow now stood in front of her. *Inside* of Openfields.

"No!" The word came out small and rough while her head moved back and forth as though the movement to the negative might somehow affect the truth of what loomed.

The black cowl that covered the head nodded slowly up and down, counteracting any hope her own head movement might have given.

Death?

The Grim Reaper?

He didn't *belong* in Openfields. He had no power here!

But the cowled figure stepped forward, oblivious to this fact. The blades of grass parted at the pressure of their boots.

No. This wasn't Death then. Nature did not bend to Death.

Hands, pale and soft in the moonlight, reached out toward Mikayla.

Run!

Before she could move a step, her legs gave way beneath her and she fell to the ground once more.

A coldness, deeper and sharper than anything she had experienced before, washed over her. It started at her hair and splashed down her neck. It bit into her skin and seeped into her blood, threatening to freeze the very marrow of her bones. Her breath froze in her lungs, and her body sent her brain paralysing signals of pain as sharp tipped icebergs pierced her insides.

Life and colour drained away from her surroundings. She reached for the grass, green and perfect. The blades withered as she reached with trembling hands to grab them.

Not-Death stepped forward, and those white skeletal looking fingers fluttered in the air.

As though dragged by some outside force, Mikayla rose to her feet. She kept her head down, staring at the ground, begging for it to save her.

The ground ignored her pleas.

Then those hands, cold and thin touched Mikayla's chin. A whimper escaped her lips, but she could do nothing more. Fear had paralysed her.

With minimal force, Not-Death pinched her chin, forcing her eyes up until she looked into the vast depths of the darkness within their hood.

Unshed tears pricked at her eyes as the hands moved to cradle her head, palms coldagainst her skin.

The roar of blood screamed in her ears and Mikayla didn't notice the sudden stillness of the world around her.

With a strength belied by the softness of those hands, they tightened against her face, and with a sharp jerk snapped Mikayla's neck.

The hooded shadow watched as the life spilled from the girl, draining back into the land of Openfields, where it belonged. He waited, grip growing tighter as her body mass shrunk in his grip. He sighed, mesmerised at both the beauty of her stillness and the sadness at her loss.

Another one lost, another one gained.

He swung her empty body into his arms as though carrying a sleeping child to their bed and turned toward the moon that lit the town in tones of silver and black. Beneath the dead body and the shifting cloak, pale skin peaked through as Not-Death headed back toward the centre of town.

Death might not have any power here, but *they* did.

And *they* had arrived in Openfields.

PART ONE

CHAPTER
ONE

ADIE

Magic existed in Openfields. And that magic was a drug. Adie knew this fact as sure as she knew anything in her life.

It was an ache in one's jaw bones, as though sugared syrup had been held in the mouth too long before it dripped acid sweetness down the back of the throat. Cloying and sickly, but addictive.

Once a person tasted OpenFields' magic, the craving belonged to them. Or they belonged to the craving. Either way, it remained inside of them from that instant onward, always. The sting and the ache faded away in the euphoria of the power and the rush. Nothing in the world could compare to it, except for the next hit.

And people did stupid things for that next hit.

Adie loved the town, her town. It was home. The fresh air and the views from Dedication Rock created solace and helped centre peace within her. She revelled in the familiarity and the vibrations beneath her feet when she stepped into the centre of town.

She loved it, she must have. Because why else would she still be here?

There were so many reasons to hate it. So many reasons to leave.

The people, the church, the magic she craved every minute of every *single* day. They were all good reasons to get the hell out. Even the fear that filled her in equal measure to the cravings weren't enough to give her the courage to leave Openfields.

She'd stopped investigating. About the magic, about the town. Even about where she had come from. A past lost. She'd hoped that would help. It didn't.

She'd stopped begging and pleading for another taste, just one more taste. And then just a hint of it, a small glimpse or display or power. Anything please.

But they wouldn't let her stop completely.

She scowled and gave the finger to the camera they didn't even bother to hide. It mocked her, whirring as it moved left and right and zoomed in and out from the room's top corner.

They used it to watch her sleep, and eat, and not do anything else. Because anything else was why she'd ended up in this place to begin with.

She shifted her gaze to the wall of books. *Her* wall of books.

They were piled up on top of each other, a tower of stories and strength. Most of them were second-hand volumes pilfered from wherever she could find them. Some were even acquired in less nefarious ways, but never new and never truly gotten with her in mind. But she was alright with that, as long as she got them.

Those pages were responsible for stopping her going entirely insane.

Some were filled with adventures of heroes, while others told amazing stories about the common people, the apparent nobodies. But it didn't matter who the story was about, in the end, they were all far braver than she could ever be.

Hope, a child's hope, had always lingered deep with her. Even before her relocation. If she read enough, maybe one day the courage scratched into the pages might leak out and help her escape.

She had wept tears and promises to characters. These imaginary people meant more to her than any of the town's residents. It hadn't always been that way, but it might as well have been. Forgiveness was a rare commodity in Openfields.

All of her promises were the same. One day she would find the strength she needed to finally leave, and to accept the consequences of those actions.

She wasn't sure what this place, this prison pretending to be her home, had originally been used for. She doubted it had ever been intended for someone to actually live in.

Perhaps it had been an office once upon a time, in a story long, long ago. A story so unlike the ones she read about. There were no heroes here, no common people who were moments from breaking free. Despite her promises to the pages, she couldn't leave the magic.

Maybe one day she would find peace enough to accept the place as home, but she couldn't imagine it.

The kitchenette was barely enough to make toast, brew a coffee, and heat microwavable dinners. But she had learned there really wasn't much more she had the energy, or inclination, to do when it came to feeding herself.

The only room with a door was the bathroom. A simple toilet and a bath she could sit in with her legs out straight. Luckily, at just over 5 foot, she wasn't even average height. On the bad nights, the ones where sleep called but she refused to answer, she would sit in the bath, tempting her own resolve as the water filled to the lip. But before she gave in to the idea of ducking her head beneath the water level, she found herself back on her feet, the sudden movement sloshing water onto the bathroom floor. The sound a wake-up call of its own.

Adie had tried to make the place more bearable, more her own. She had painted the door to the bathroom; it had taken a while and some acetone scrubbing of mistakes before she was happy with the field of bright yellow sunflowers. In the centre of the field stood a gnarled chocolate-brown climbing tree. The trunk was thick and twisted. Layers of leaves in autumn colours, green, gold, and red, created a rainbow hanging over the sea of sunshine below. She was proud of it, and having found little to be proud of over the years, it was her pièce de résistance.

There was nothing else to make this place hers. No photographs or artwork hanging on the wall. No knick-knacks to express her individuality. Just the books and the painting.

Time ticked by, and soon her alarm would let her know if she didn't get her arse out of bed that she'd be late for work. The sound, a high-pitched shrill, Adie imagined reminiscent of a harpy's scream filled the space around her and between her ears. It was the only noise that had ever been guaranteed to get her out of bed.

Groaning, Adie pushed the blankets away and instantly regretted it. Her skin prickled in the cold air. She grabbed the folded azure blue throw rug from the end of her bed and wrapped it around her shoulders. Not that it did much as she continued to shiver beneath layers of blanket and nightmare sweat.

Always the same *bloody* nightmare.

She scurried to the kitchen; her socked feet whooshing along the wooden floorboards. Adie flicked the kettle before shuffling back to shut the window near the closed bathroom door. Twelve steps, kettle to window. Counting. A coping mechanism she didn't remember starting but one that was as natural as breathing.

She reached to pull the window closed but stopped halfway, entranced by the tendrils of light reaching out over the horizon. The cold bit, bone-deep, but the colours were so vibrant. The pinks and oranges swirled with the purples and yellows, pushing away the darkness. The colours danced in front of her as she watched, reminding her even more of the magical flames she had never learned to control.

A bittersweet joy filled her as she continued to admire the bright colours even as they contrasted with the bleak path her thoughts threatened to take. Adie scanned the horizon, still smiling at each reaching flame, each tendril.

Along the horizon, her rainbow view was interrupted by a figure of darkness. Adie blinked; certain it must be nothing more than a trick of the light. But the figure remained, looming in the new daylight, a new stain upon the horizon.

She knew it had to be a tree. It was crazy to think it could be anything *other* than a tree. But she also knew she was wrong.

She stared at this view every single day.

It was the only view she had, and she'd memorised it long ago.

There *was* no tree. There was nothing except her daydreams of walking beyond the horizon and leaving Openfields behind her.

The figure moved and Adie's breath caught in her throat as she gasped.

While she couldn't see clearly with the distance between herself and the figure, she knew it stared in her direction. It stared at *her* and it *saw* her. Slowly it lifted an arm, and then once it reached its zenith, it waved wildly, as though caught in the gust of a strong wind.

Adie's hand rose in automatic response, fingertips pointing to the sky and palm facing the figure. Her fingers danced in a wave as familiarity nudged at the edges of her mind.

The sound of the kettle clicked, and Adie blinked, her eyes stinging from staring so long, mixed with the bite of the cold.

The figure vanished. Not slowly fading, but poof in an instant. The very instant of her blinking. Though there was silence, she imagined the disappearance as a finger snap, audible only in her mind.

She shivered against more than the weather, and pulled the window closed with a reluctant creak.

Wrapping the blanket tighter around her shoulders, she found the clear plastic water bottle on her bedside table. After a sip to moisten the sudden dryness of her mouth, Adie glared back down at the small opaque bottle that still sat on the table. With a resigned sigh, she shook out two small white pills and placed them on her tongue. Turning back toward the camera she stuck her tongue out at it, the pills beginning to dissolve, leaving their bitter bite behind. She gulped down half the remaining water but the bitterness remained. A reminder she didn't need about her place in this world, and her feelings about it.

It wasn't as though the pills had bothered to work last night. Thankfully the cameras couldn't catch her dreams or nightmares. But she no longer let them miss the fact she took the bastard things.

The magic continued to buzz beneath her skin. It shouldn't, not with the pills in her system. She was certain it was the reason she woke in the first place. That, and the damn nightmare.

Adie took a deep breath, closed her eyes and remembered it was Saturday. She didn't have to head into town. Not today. A small smile stretched her lips as she let the breath out.

A day of peace. As much peace as she could *get* in Open-fields, at least.

The magic continued to buzz beneath her skin, and it would have been unbearable had she needed to go into the library for work.

It wasn't that the magic pulled stronger or crawled with more intensity beneath her skin. It was never the magic that was the problem. Not really. She had never been ignorant to the conversations that filled the otherwise peaceful air. The Chosen Ones, it was always about them in the end.

The excitement of their magic buzzed in every corner of the town. Even if it wasn't one of them talking about it, it was a conduit or a hopeful. It was everyone else.

Almost everyone else.

Lisa was different. She had always been different. Even if only in secret.

She only had to touch Adie's hand or brush her fingers along her arm as they crossed paths, and there was relief. An instant balm that smoothed over the bumps of the bad days. It didn't stop them *being* bad days, though it did make them far more bearable.

And today was definitely a bad day. The mornings after the nightmare were always bad. Even with Lisa's help, and her understanding.

But Adie knew today would be different. The figure hadn't been her imagination. She had felt it's presence as surely as the vibration beneath her skin. But who had it been? Adie knew death had waved at her, why the hell had she felt inclined to wave back?

Debating whether or not she would tell Lisa made her stomach tumble uncomfortably, the way it hadn't in a while. When they had first gotten to know each other, when Adie had first taken the job, even knowing it had been offered with strings and pity attached, she had been wary. Lisa's mother had been Adie's least favourite person for a while now. But Lisa had turned out to be nothing like her mother, and though part of Adie wondered at Lisa's angle, she'd allowed herself this small piece of relief. To have someone, anyone to talk to had become an addiction all on its own, in a town where addiction to the magic was paramount.

But things were shifting, Adie felt it in her stomach.

"Or you're just hungry, you moron." Adie sighed, trying to shake the lingering heaviness that lay on her shoulders like a cloak of mist. There, but not really, when she turned her head and tried to look. Like she stood in the very middle of it all.

The last few months, a storm had steadily built around the town, the tense atmosphere simply waiting for the deluge to break through. Now it felt as though it was building inside of Adie as well.

Shivering again, Adie wished the pressure came with some heat, or at the very least humidity. It was Queensland after-all, and this cold was more than just a little uncommon, it was previously unheard of.

"Weeeeell," Adie dragged out the word. "Gotta love bad omens on a morning that feels like the Ice Age is making a comeback." She shook her head and rolled her eyes at herself.

Winter hadn't even officially started, and yet each morning she wrapped herself tighter with the blankets she had scattered over her place.

Step five from her bedside table, she grabbed a wine-red throw blanket and threw that one over the azure blue one that had been enough yesterday morning. Three more steps and she was back in the kitchenette space. She made her cup of chai tea and, eleven steps from kettle to table, sat at one of the mismatched chairs in the corner opposite her bed.

Her favourite chair. It was scarred wood with a thick red

cushion she had tied to the seat. She never used the other two, she often thought about getting rid of them, but in the end, she couldn't be bothered. And just in case anyone did bother to visit, she would happily direct them to sit at the straight-backed torture chair, or the black metal one with one slightly bent leg that wobbled back and forth with the tiniest of movements.

She sipped her brew, savouring the sweet milky spice with its hints of cinnamon. The warmth spread to her fingers, making them tingle.

She pushed the image of the waving shadow from her mind, knowing she couldn't tell anyone about it, not even Lisa. The decision wasn't hard to come to, though she felt a knot form in her stomach. The same knot that tied itself whenever she and Lisa had to pretend that they weren't even friends, let alone anything else.

She scoffed and sunk further into her chair. Just imagining giving the town another reason to ostracise her would surely cause even *more* trouble for her, and for Lisa. Hallucinating would be another mark against the suicidal dark creature they barely tolerated but couldn't get rid of.

This *was* her home, after all.

Except it wasn't and it never really had been.

CHAPTER

TWO

ADIE

Adie was an orphan as far as she and everyone in the town knew. She had shown up at the edges of Openfields when she was just six years old. Before that, there was nothing.

She had no memories, no life, no heritage.

Just a name.

Adeline.

It wasn't even a very good name. In fact, she hated it. Adie was acceptable *most* of the time. But not exactly something she would have chosen. Her full name was an entirely different situation altogether. It filled her with emotions she had no idea how to name, let alone understand.

But at six years old, they had all loved her. Adults and fellow children alike.

She had stepped over the boundary into the town and the electricity had hummed beneath her skin. It made her smile. They adored her. At least she had thought it was her. But it all came down to the magic, and how easily it came to her, as though it were drawn to her. The magic was a magnet, and she was made of metal.

It presented in a way they were all fascinated with as she described it more articulately as she grew older. An aural sensation that vibrated in the very air. The magic created colours around all that she saw. And the heat. The heat was always present. A thread weaved through her body, her very existence.

And all before she had become a conduit.

But they told her she was unique. She was a gift from the Goddess. *Their* gift.

Who wouldn't accept such adoration and love? Especially as a six-year-old who understood just enough to know she was alone without them. So, she embraced the town, and the magical history interwoven so seamlessly with school lessons about Maths, English and Science. And every single resident was taught the truth of their town, over and over again.

Magic came from the sacred earth. The sacred earth that was Openfields. This was the resting place of the bones of the first Goddess. She had returned to her most faithful when it was time for her to become one again with the natural elements.

The most faithful of her people were honoured and blessed for that unwavering dedication. And their descendants were those who now filled the town of Openfields. But they were responsible for maintaining the beauty of their town, and their commitment must continue if they wished to keep the magic the Goddess blessed them with.

Engraved images of the Goddess adorned the town and were tattooed on the people alike. No one could say the Goddess was ever forgotten.

Their town leader, Mr Kenjins, had been blessed with direct correspondence to their deity. He communed with her through sacred rituals. The Goddess gave him guidance and direction to choose those most dedicated to becoming direct conduits of the magic. Only the strongest of her followers, those strong enough to *contain* it and share it with the other residents of the town were chosen.

Each conduit's powers manifested differently when receiving the essence of the Goddess. But no matter how it presented itself, the one thing that remained consistent for all was that the root of the magic stemmed from nature and the elements.

Some fire conduits could ease the wrath of the flames, while others could only create a spark with little to no control over where it would burn.

Adie loved to watch the earth conduits as they helped flowers bloom, guiding roots to the most nutrient-rich soil. There were also those who could manipulate water where others could create it, and while clouds could be summoned by almost all elements, not all conduits could force them to weep.

She had once asked why they couldn't stop the drought ravaging towns outside of Openfields. After being scowled at, she was told the will of the earth, and the will of the Goddess was not theirs to question.

She had only been eight years old, and she already sensed what a crock of shit this was. Their entire existence stemmed around them changing what the earth did without their magic. At least, within Openfields' borders.

But whatever had happened to Adie before she could remember had created indelible caution within her. Until she became a teenager, and she was finally chosen, as everyone told her she would be.

She was sixteen, and the darkness the transition brought out in her was unbearable. The power had flooded her, while flames danced on the tips of her fingers. She had laughed to feel it until she couldn't *stop* feeling it as it burnt within her.

It was beautiful until it became too strong, and she set things alight without control.

Her understanding and acceptance had been replaced with her nightmares and fear.

A nightmare.

It was just the one. Over and over again.

The cave was dark and veined with colours she couldn't quite catch or name. The open space around her was little more than a mirage, the trapped and foreboding feelings pressed against her chest. She sensed the tunnel behind her and knew there was no other means of escape.

In front of her stood the beast, dripping someone else's blood from fangs that pushed his top jaw over his chin. The eyes were wide open, burning flames flickered from within their depths.

Dream Adie focused on the face. It had distinctly canine features; long snout, pointed ears and a wide smiling mouth. But the body reminded her more of a bull, muscular and powerful. Ragged, bristly fur shuddered under his movements, his raging as he flexed unseen muscles.

But the stomping and huffing were nothing more than for show.

His back hooves were chained to the wall behind him, and dried blood coated his legs and cuffs alike. Sores and scabs were half hidden beneath the shifting manacles and his hair had been worn away. When the metal cuffs shifted and clinked against the chains, she noticed how dirty the skin beneath was.

Against the walls of the large area, figures carved from dark glistening rock surrounded him.

Whatever fear Adie would feel about the beast at this time was nothing compared to what overtook her when she took in the figures. None of them had recognisable faces. They were warped, as though she saw them through a wall of ice, fractals running like rivers through the wall. And while the features couldn't be picked out, she knew they all wore identical silent screams, frozen as solidly as the warped wall between them and Adie.

To add to her terror, a glowing red pulsed within the chest of each figure. The only movement to them was this strange beating heart. And the contrast made it all the more visceral to Dream Adie.

They were trapped by the slobbering beast. The crimson pulsing colours trapped the slobbering beast. No. Adie always grew confused at this point, and the horror became internal just as much as it radiated outside of her.

Still, she couldn't stop Dream Adie from drawing closer. With each step, her body threatened to collapse, until the sharp jerk as her foot drooped into a groove in the earth that she hadn't noticed.

Squinting closer in the intermittent light, Adie realised that she stood in an indentation. The beast and the statues remained on the ledge on the other side.

The beast and the fear his presence caused came and went like an image flickering in a damaged celluloid strip of a movie reel.

One moment the beast snarled and pulled against the chains that had no more give in them, stretched to their limit.

With a flick, a snap of unseen fingers, he became a man; malnourished and chained to the black rock wall by his wrists. His chains were thicker than his neck. The man's clothing had turned into little more than strips of dirty, decaying rags. The original colour had been lost beneath age and grime. The colour of his skin, hair, and eyes were hard to be certain of between the dirt and the gloom.

Her attention was drawn to the raised white welts that covered much of the man's skin stretched too tightly over his bones. Beside the man sat a lidless stone coffin. This alone caused Adie's body to shudder. Her heartbeat roared in her ears and her breath came in short audible gasps.

This was worse than the beast and the man combined.

The image flicked back and forth, a voice begged for help while another voice, unseen and unknown, screamed for mercy.

The screaming and the begging bled together, mixed and grew louder until she staggered back; out of the cave, into the tunnel, and returned to the waking world.

Adie looked around herself and took a deep gulp of air as though she'd forgotten to breathe. She blinked at the bright light that flooded in through the small window of her kitchenette. She didn't remember standing up and walking back from the table. She didn't remember the last gulp of her tea, though the cup now sat empty beside the kettle. Streaks of cinnamon lined the inside of the mug. Remnants from that morning's first cup relieving Adie of fears of having not actually woken at all.

It would have been nice to have put the waving figure down to an extension of the nightmare. But she knew, without any proof, that it hadn't been that. The tingle beneath her skin assured her she was right on this matter.

Reliving the nightmare always crashed down upon her. Her limbs heavier than at any other time. The exhaustion one that went bone deep and her desire to sleep fought against her hope to never dream again. Adie had as little control over these reactions as she did with having the nightmare in the first place.

She slipped her fingers beneath her wrist bands, her touch trailed over the raised flesh as she grounded herself in reality. She never took the bands off, not anymore, not even to shower, refusing to look at them as she washed beneath the bands, or closing her eyes when she swapped them for clean ones, in order to wash them regularly.

But the sight of the scars always proved that little bit more than she could bear.

Yet, she would seek them out as a form of comfort for her

fingertips whenever the nightmares, or the waking world felt too heavy. It didn't make sense, not even to herself. But no matter how much she tried to resist, it was as though she was as addicted to her failure and the evidence of her weakness as she was addicted to the magic itself.

The feel of them would help catch her breath, slow it down, and ease the pounding of her heart.

Normally, the tablets were enough to push the addiction back and keep the magic dormant.

They were enough to keep her and other people safe *from* her.

They kept her mind intact.

Not having the tablets made her feel like she would shatter into a million pieces and every single one of them would be a dangerous weapon pointed toward all those she knew. The pills not working as they should made Adie feel as though she stood at the edge of a precipice. One that she couldn't step off of, not again.

She had to see the Doc soon and get this shit under control. Seeing the Doc was *almost* as bad as having the tablets not work, almost.

Fear threatened to rise up her oesophagus and out of her mouth as though she were a dragon.

The latest nightmare brought that fear closer than ever.

Adie waited for the kettle to boil again for her second cuppa of the morning while she made toast.

Food, maybe she just needed some food to help the tablets work properly again. She had been neglecting it recently, her appetite diminished in the unusual cold weather. All she wanted lately was her chai.

She slathered the near burnt piece of bread in butter then cut thick chunky slices of tomato. She sliced the last piece of tomato, her stomach growled in anticipation of the salty tart combination. The unexpected knock on her front door made her jerk, and the knife slipped. It cut deeply into her left hand, three fingertips on her left hand now stinging.

"Fuck."

The blood flowed quickly, splashing over her breakfast. The crimson river flowed over the lighter red of the tomato leaving it glistening before soaking into the ruined bread beneath. She pulled her eyes away, blinking rapidly as she raced to the sink. Her stomach churned, the hunger instantly gone at the sight and smell of her now blood-stained food.

Adie looked toward the front door as the knock came again.

This was her sanctuary. Monitored or not, she was given relative freedom here and she savoured what little she had.

Despite the enjoyment she entertained herself with making guests uncomfortable at her uninviting chairs, they weren't welcomed.

She had never sent out invitations. Not to anyone.

"Coming!" Adie growled out reluctantly as she rifled through the crap drawer in the kitchen for some bandaids, or more accurately the off-brand version she could actually afford.

Pulling the door open, she stood for a moment wondering if she really had woken up, or if the nightmare had continued. First the waving figure, and now *Billie*. Even the woman's *name* in Adie's thoughts was a snarled hiss.

This nightmare came from real life. The pressure within her chest made Adie far too aware of that.

It had been years since she had seen her old friend up close. She often saw Billie from a distance; their small town made sure of that.

"What the hell are *you* doing here? And what the hell are you *wearing*?" Adie found her voice and, refusing to feel any weaker than she already felt in Billie's presence, snapped out before Billie opened her mouth.

The last few years had been kind to the other woman. Adie couldn't help but feel a little woe-is-me over that annoying fact. Where was karma now?

Adie's thighs and waist had thickened, and her dark dense hair became wilder and more unmanageable as the years charged forward. It didn't matter what she tried.

Billie, on the other hand, grew more Barbie-like, her figure the perfect hourglass.

Of course it would be Billie at the door. No one else would brave it.

Adie bit back the scoff of her internal thoughts. For a town screaming at her for her own weakness and fear, they still managed to move out of her path and away from her whenever she approached.

Once upon a time, Billie and Adie had been inseparable.

But Adie's life wasn't a fairy tale, and she didn't get a happy ending.

"What do you want, Billie?" Adie repeated.

CHAPTER
THREE

ADIE

Billie looked like some kind of '80s reject. Wrapped in an oversized pink jacket and a pair of old dusty jeans with colourful green patches over the knees.

So maybe karma had a better sense of humour than Adie expected. The left side of her lip quirked up in a smirk.

Adie hadn't thought about Billie knowing where she lived. She supposed the whole town had been told, as a warning so they didn't stray too close.

"Adie, something's happened in town." Billie's voice was thin and watery.

"And?" Adie's anxiety was lightning beneath her skin, desperate to find some patch of ground to release to, but Billie didn't need to know that. She'd lost the right to know *anything* about Adie six years ago.

"Get dressed, everyone's being called to the great hall."

"Get fucked, Billie. I'm not running at your heels like a dog."

"Please, Adie?"

Please?

Adie bit her top lip.

"Please?" Bille asked again, eyes pleading. Who the fuck was this? Even when they were friends, Billie had never been the kind to apologise for anything, let alone say please. She was a bully. It had just taken Adie some distance to see it.

Adie sighed. Bully or not, that look still worked. She wished it didn't. But for now, she simply chalked it up to another reason to hate herself and her own weakness.

"Fine. Come in while I get dressed."

Billie shook her head and stepped back, away from the door's threshold. The corner of Adie's top lip curled, barely containing the growl that built in her throat.

"Sure, wouldn't expect you to be brave enough to actually step inside. Must have taken such an effort to even knock," Adie muttered, not caring if Billie heard or not. Okay, she cared, but she felt a little more satisfied as it pushed down the self-loathing that lingered.

Her eyes flicked to the camera as she closed the door, flipping it the bird once more.

She wasn't sure who had to watch the footage, if it was recorded or not, but she used every chance she could to make sure all sets of eyes knew she understood how fucked up this was, and how much she didn't approve.

She walked to her cupboard, which was nothing more than a 16-cube China white bookshelf that served its life having clothes unceremoniously thrown into it. Sometimes they were folded. Sometimes.

Adie jammed a shirt over her head and shoved her feet ruthlessly into sneakers. She pulled the laces too tight and had to undo them and try again. As she buttoned up her jeans, she shook her head. Facing the townspeople on the weekend was not her idea of a good time. And the buzz beneath her skin was like fire ants crawling on every nerve.

She scoffed as she straightened the hem of her shirt, pulling it more out of shape. There weren't any mirrors in the house, too dangerous a risk for her. They could all imagine what she could do with broken glass. Some even remembered other times. The outfit would do, no matter how out of shape it had become from her tugging and pulling at it, covering up her body as if that would somehow make her invisible. Her tongue ran over her teeth as though checking their cleanliness, but it was nothing more than a habit that had, in the past, helped calm her. Now it was just another thing that wasn't working.

On a whim, Adie grabbed her work backpack and flung it on before walking to her front door. Its weight dropped comfortably on her shoulders as it settled, the bottom of the bag pressed gently into the small of her back.

Leaving right now, going to where she didn't want to be, felt uncomfortably like a final goodbye. She didn't know how, but at least she had finally learned on some level that trusting Billie was all kinds of stupid.

She pulled her door open and revelled at the sight of Billie shivering on the pedestrian footpath at the front of her place. She supposed even being on the property rubbed little Miss Openfields the wrong way. White dragon breath puffed from Billie's mouth. *Dragon, right.* More like a common brown lizard playing dress up. *Serves you right.*

Billie hopped from foot to foot, hands rubbing up and down her arms through the thick puffy highlighter-pink jacket.

Adie almost burst out laughing. But the morning took too much entertainment of the situation away.

She doubted anyone in the town had ever seen Billie in anything even remotely crumpled. Until now. The look should have given her more satisfaction, but despite herself, she ached for the past and the long-lost friendship they had shared.

With a huff, Adie turned back to the door and locked it. The lock snapped with a nudge from her hip. She supposed it was habit more than anything else. Because the old weathered wooden door could probably have been blown open with the gentlest of breezes. And what would anyone take? It wasn't as though they didn't have access to every part of her existence already.

Following a step or two behind Billie, Adie found herself disturbed more than amused at Billie's unbrushed hair, pulled back haphazardly into a chunky ponytail.

"So, are you going to tell me what the hell is going on?" Adie really hadn't cared earlier, but now? Now she wanted some idea of what she was walking into.

Billie shook her head. Sunflower blonde locks bouncing along, flying left and right.

Adie stopped and turned around, heading back toward her home. "I'm not playing your games, Billie."

Billie grabbed Adie's arm. The sensation sent a warmth directly to Adie's cheeks. She clenched her teeth and looked pointedly down at Billie's long, slender fingers.

Billie released Adie's arm and mumbled an apology. "Dad asked me not to say anything, just to get everyone to the town hall."

"So," Adie smiled. A grim one. "You drew the short straw in getting me. I'm still not going until you tell me what the hell is going on."

"Dr Simms."

"What about her?" Adie's words came out between clenched teeth. She needed to see the Doc, but it would be on her terms. Adie wouldn't be dragged by the Doc's summoning, not again.

The last time Adie had seen Dr Simms hadn't gone so well. Adie needed a new script and getting it from the good ol' Doc had felt akin to pulling teeth. Adie had yelled, while Dr Simms had remained perched nonchalantly on the edge of her desk, her slight frame hidden behind the starched white doctor's coat. Adie had yelled more. The Doc's smile simply grew smug as the door opened and Sheryl, her secretary, barged in, all heroic and worried. Adie had to go two days without pills before the fresh bottle had been left in her letterbox.

During those 48 hours, the electricity had returned in full force beneath her skin, much like this morning. Her blood had run like lava and the nightmares were walking hallucinations. So vivid, she had taken the rest of the week off work. She remembered all too clearly sitting in the corner of her room, screaming at the camera. She had also screamed at the tree on the bathroom door as it swayed in the non-existent breezes, mocking her sanity. She had sworn to herself in her half-crazed state that she would paint over it as soon as she got more pills. The withdrawal from the magic, once she started on the tablets again, was almost as bad.

Once the pills had finally re-balanced her mind and body, she couldn't say goodbye to her tree or the sunflowers.

"Sheryl found her this morning when she went to open the surgery." Billie's voice wavered, emotion even Billie couldn't control seeping through.

"Found her what? Spell it out, Billie." But the clenched fist in Adie's stomach, the thickness of her tongue, told her what she didn't want to know.

"She's dead." Billie met Adie's eyes, and for a moment they were friends again.

Blinking, the illusion disappeared, and Adie breathed easier. She didn't need the complication of Billie in her life again.

"How?" Adie pushed the word out through her suddenly dry mouth. Memories of the shadow waving at her that morning bloomed in her thoughts. But no. It couldn't have been the good doctor. She would have recognised her, more than just some familiarity she couldn't name. Surely?

"It wasn't a natural death." Billie's words were steady again and Adie wondered how she ever thought so much of the woman. She had slipped her performer voice back on. The one she used to get people's attention as she told salacious stories.

"Suicide?" The idea made Adie's breath quicken. Her own dark thoughts were never far from her mind, and no one, not even the Doc deserved to feel that hopeless.

A quick shake of Billie's head to the negative calmed Adie's breathing slightly. And then the realisation of what Billie was saying sunk in.

Murder.

Someone had murdered the good doctor? Adie shook her head and focused as much as she could as too many thoughts raced through her mind.

"Who?" Adie asked.

"No one seems to know." Billie dropped her eyes and the fist in Adie's stomach twisted.

Her body felt as though a creature had buried itself inside of her and was now eager to crawl back out. "I have an alibi, Billie," Adie said darkly. "You know that. *They* know that." Adie's arms waved around, refusing to move another step and be dragged into another witch trial.

"You aren't a suspect," Billie whispered.

"Then *why* am I being summoned?"

"*Everyone's* getting brought to the town hall. I don't know what is happening, but I can feel it in the earth. Something's not right. Something more than Dr Simms' murder."

Murder. That word again.

But this time it brought a bubble of laughter up Adie's throat.

Murder didn't happen in Openfields. Hell, *death* didn't even happen.

The magic protected them. All of them. That was why they stayed, why they cared for the earth. It was a symbiotic relationship.

The image on the skyline, arm lifted as if in greeting, flashed across Adie's memory once more. She mentally placed an image of Dr Simms over the misty figure. The image was almost amusing. They definitely didn't match. She had been right. It wasn't the Doc, but then who?

Billie was right, something was wrong. Long before this morning, Adie had been feeling the build-up of tension. The calm before the storm.

Even when the tablets had been working properly, Adie had sensed it.

No, that wasn't right.

She had *felt* it. Why could she feel it?

She shook her head and then turned it into a nod. Standing here arguing with Miss Perfect in her most imperfect image wouldn't get Adie any of the answers she wanted or needed.

They turned in silence, together, and headed back toward town.

3793 steps of counted silence before Adie stood in front of the town hall. For a moment, Billie stopped and stood beside her.

The town hall featured a large clock tower that didn't even pretend to be anything but a phallic symbol. With a front facade of large rough-hewn stone, it was weathered and grey no matter how many times they used the gurney on it. It stood out against the more modern designs of the surrounding town.

Which she supposed made sense. According to the town's

histories, everything had sprung up around the hall, and Adie had never found any reason to doubt it. The contrast did nothing but reinforce this truth.

The hall looked across the road to the town square, where the mumbling of almost four hundred people was a buzz against Adie's ears.

The square was all but filled, the green overrun by a mix of dark and far too bright clothing.

"I thought you said we were meeting in the hall?" Adie accused.

"We were." Billie sounded genuinely surprised, and Adie decided to let it go in light of more important things.

"Has anyone spoken to Lisa?" she asked, failing once again to keep her breath steady.

Billie's eyes narrowed at Adie before leaving her and making a beeline toward her father.

And of course, her father was the one and only Mr Kenjins, Town Leader. He was tall and lean with large strong hands and a crooked nose that always made Adie wonder how he broke it.

Far too many times, she had imagined incrementally more hideous events—a clenched fist from the first girl he asked out, a horse's hoof to the face, a trip over his cocky arrogance in front of the entire town—and wishing she had footage.

He stood up on the small gazebo, talking to someone whose back faced Adie. She knew with all certainty the person was female, and it wasn't a woman from the town.

For a town filled with magic, they could be insanely petty about spreading the most mundane of events as though they were hot topics. The haircut this woman wore was far too short for the rumour mill of Openfields *not* to have grabbed a hold of.

If someone had decided on such a dramatic change, it

would easily have been big enough news that even Adie would have heard about it.

She scanned the crowd. Everyone's arms were waving as their mouths flapped.

But Adie saw no signs of Lisa. Her chest rose and fell a little faster and she scanned again, slower. Desperate to have been wrong on the first look.

The town square was Adie's favourite place to be. The grass and earth were grounding.

She would sit during her lunch breaks from the library and take off her shoes, feeling the power in the earth. So similar to the power she no longer felt vibrating beneath her skin every waking moment.

It calmed and it terrified in equal measure.

She loved watching as others focused on different plants and trees and had them bend to their will. It was addictive in its pain. Just as the magic itself had been for her. But watching the others had been like worrying a sore tooth with your tongue. The pain of not being able to touch the magic was worth seeing it. It was better than being cut off completely.

In the town square no one hid it from her, as though she weren't unworthy of its touch.

But she knew she was.

The centre of town was little more than a main street with houses surrounding it like a barrier from the outside world. The town had only one of everything. A bookshop, a hairdresser, and a laundromat lined up like a pub joke on the right-hand side of the town hall. To the left were the library, the post office, and the pub itself. The public toilets were set slightly back and next to them were the clothing store, the doctors' surgery, the shoe shop, and the bakery. The rest of that side of the street was filled with the town's grocery store. Adie could walk from the roundabout near the bookshop all the way to the end of the grocery store in little more than ten minutes.

1392 steps.

1000 steps exactly to the start of the doctor's surgery.

With a start, Adie remembered why everyone was there.

The town square would never be the same again. It was taken over by the murder of the doctor.

CHAPTER
FOUR
ADIE

Murder. In Openfields!

The very idea still held a small bubble of laughter within Adie, but the worry she saw on the scrunched eyebrows of every face in the square quickly sobered her. Tears streaked through make-up on women's faces who had never let their own *husbands* see them as less than perfect. Protective arms wrapped around children; hands gripped their shoulders to pull them closer than comfortable.

Nausea roiled in Adie's belly as she focused harder on the swarm of residents. Every third or fourth set of eyes glistened. But not with tears. Nothing so humane as that. There was an excited buzz, like a swarm of wasps emanating from these people within the crowd.

A woman had been murdered by someone in their town, and what they focused on was the *thrill* and the *excitement* of something new and different. It was as obvious as though they had speech bubbles over their heads. And sure, Adie had imagined unpleasant things happening to the Doc, but not this. Never this.

Adie shook her head. She couldn't look at any of them anymore. The scared or the excited. No matter how much she had hated them in the past, for the consequences of her own decisions, she had never felt so disgusted by these people.

She had never really thought of them as separate from herself before either.

She sighed and shook her head. Nope, there were already too many untethered thoughts running around causing havoc in her mind. She wasn't adding this to it now.

Resigned, Adie focused on what Mr Kenjins pontificated. Because the man never just *spoke*. But her eyes wouldn't linger on him, her attention pulled instantly to the strange woman who stood beside him. She had turned around and looked out over the crowd.

Adie's breath caught in her throat. Had her mouth dropped open, she wasn't sure.

The woman *was* a stranger, not that she needed the confirmation.

A stunning stranger, but it was more than that. There was a familiarity, not individual features but with the woman as a whole. The idea itched at the back of Adie's mind.

She couldn't have been much older than Adie, a year, maybe two. A sharp chin, big eyes, and skin so smooth Adie's finger itched to stroke it.

Adie crossed the road, not bothering to check left or right. Who would be driving past to hit her? Almost everyone in town stood in front of her.

The woman's eyes flicked to Adie's as she stepped onto the grass. Her head had jerked in that moment and Adie's stomach clenched as it did a small flip. What the hell was that about?

The woman gave Adie the smallest of nods before her eyes continued to move, drifting over the crowd once more. Those eyes were familiar in a way that was impossible. Adie knew she had never seen this woman before in her life and yet the feeling wouldn't be shifted, no matter how logically Adie tried to present the facts.

"We will be holding a memorial service for Doctor Simms this afternoon at Town Hall. In the meantime, I have promised Detective Tala that everyone in town will willingly and happily answer her questions and assist in anything she and her team need. They will be staying in town at The Inn."

Detective? Staying?

There was no way she was old enough to be a detective.

And staying? *No* one stayed in their town except during the Celebration of Flowers. It was the only reason The Inn had even been built. But the celebration wasn't for another three months and six days. The countdown was impossible to ignore. It was displayed in every moment of them hiding their magic in plain sight. It had kept the town from being looked at too closely over the years. Except, of course, for that one reporter.

Adie's eyes met Detective Tala's again. The itch she couldn't scratch caused a small buzz inside her head. But she had somewhere else to be.

She turned and walked away from the crowd, heading toward the library. 48 steps.

Adie looked back over her shoulder. But no one seemed to take note of her departure. Not even the mysterious Detective Tala. She supposed that was a good thing, but her usual joy at being ignored held a sadness that made no sense.

The townspeople were all mesmerised by her. Even Mr Kenjins' eyes were narrowed on the detective, as though unable to look away from whatever she was saying. For a moment, even Adie forgot what she was doing, caught up with the strange sensation that danced beneath her skin when she looked at the detective again. She *really* had to stop doing that.

Shaking her head, Adie pulled her access card from her backpack and slipped inside the front door of the library.

"Lisa?" Adie called softly as she opened Lisa's office. She hadn't been sure what to expect. Perhaps a distraught Lisa, dishevelled and broken?

Instead, the room was empty of her boss, or anyone else. What she did find made Adie freeze at the threshold of the office.

Papers littered Lisa's desk, her pristine piles tipped and flowing onto the floor. Her drawers were open, and the chair Adie usually sat on during staff meetings lay on its side. Tentatively, she took a step forward and stepped through the door. But her legs had other ideas as they gave out beneath her. She collapsed to her knees, looking at the mess without truly registering the information that filled the papers that covered the carpet.

"What the hell is going on?" Adie's voice echoed around the chaotic but otherwise empty office.

"That's what I'm here to find out." The voice was a low rumble that sent Adie's heart pulsing against an unfamiliar pressure. As though a rubber band, too small for her body, had been slipped around her chest.

She swivelled around on her knees and stared up, as the detective pulled on some cream-coloured latex gloves.

"Have you touched anything?"

Adie shook her head and watched as the woman walked around the room, commanding the very air to pay attention to her presence. She touched nothing, even with the gloves on. She did however lean closer to a book that sat open on the windowsill behind Lisa's desk.

"Why did you come here?" Detective Tala asked.

It took a few moments for Adie to realise an answer was both expected and waited for, from her.

"I didn't see Lisa in the crowd. She's my boss and Dr Simms' daughter. I just wanted to check to see if she was okay." The words came out too fast and hitched in Adie's throat at the end.

"So, you work here?"

"Yeah. The last few years."

"Who else does?"

"I think she has some casuals on the books. I rarely see them; they work weekends mostly. The turnover's pretty high, usually just town kids waiting for something better to come along, usually out of town."

Despite the addictive pull of the magic, Adie had known of residents who had left Openfields behind. There weren't many, usually only a couple a year. Sometimes as many as four, but that had been rare for so many to leave in such a time frame.

Adie had seen many of the casuals unable to hack the workload of the library, leave. She hadn't realised how proud she was to be the only long-term employee of Lisa's until that warmth filled her chest. The only person who had stuck around for longer than just a few months. There were some that barely lasted a few weeks. Most of them tried their hands at other places in town, and a few had been the ones to have gotten away.

Yes, Adie was impressed at her ability to follow through with this job.

But every time Lisa mentioned that someone had left town, whether it was one of her casuals or someone who had never stepped foot in the library before - Mrs Jones' middle boy, or Mr Peters' youngest girl - envy would curl around Adie's chest.

"How many of you are there? Detectives, I mean," Adie asked.

"Just me for now. The rest are on their way." The detective's eyes flitted away as Adie tried to meet them again. They had a strange pull all of their own. She watched as the woman began opening drawers quietly and gently.

"What about your partner, Detective Tala?"

Detective Tala's head snapped up from looking in the drawer she had just pulled open and glared at Adie. She could have sworn there was movement in Detective Tala's eyes. A skittering away.

No, it was the dance of a flame.

Adie had stared into fire enough times to know the pattern. But that was before the pills. When the magic had been so easy to reach.

"I... I just mean, don't you guys always come in twos?" Adie filled the lingering silence.

"Ah, he had car troubles. Should be here soon."

It was the first time Adie saw Detective Tala smile. It lit up her face, and Adie was reminded of a movie star she couldn't remember the name of.

"Detective Tala?" Adie wasn't even sure which question she wanted to ask first.

"Just Tala."

"Oh." Adie blinked, struggling to remember any of the questions she had been trying to decide between just seconds ago. "Okay, Tala. What happened to Doctor Simms?"

"What do you think happened?"

"I have no idea." Adie's pitch was higher than she liked. "I just got told that she died, and it wasn't natural."

"Who told you that?" Tala jumped on the information as though it was some kind of major lead.

"Well, don't you kind of confirm it just by being here?"

Adie didn't know why she felt the need to protect Billie. It wasn't like they were close anymore; all of that had changed years ago. But here she was diverting any dirt from flicking up onto her old friend, as though what Adie did still mattered to anyone in town.

Tala's smile flashed Adie's way again and made Adie forget all about Billie. She focused on Tala, and only Tala. The woman was gorgeous.

And before she could reign herself in, images of Tala with far fewer clothes on flashed into her mind. The woman's legs were eye-catching. They weren't long but the shapely curves couldn't be hidden behind the dark dress pants she wore. Her flat stomach beneath the white shirt was easily noticeable as well. And, in the right light, Adie was almost certain sun-kissed skin half hid beneath.

But for all the lecherous feelings Adie became increasingly and uncomfortably overwhelmed with, she kept being drawn back to Tala's face. Adie wasn't the type who usually leered. She was relieved to focus once more on Tala's facial features. It would have blended in among the rich and famous that smiled out from glossy-covered magazines.

Adie's stomach flipped a few more times. She hadn't noticed in the distance and the gazebo's shade, the touch of red that streaked through Tala's hair. Adie imagined it being described as strawberry blonde, but it reminded her of the bark of her favourite tree trunk. The one in the village green she would tuck herself up against, back moulding to the comforting coolness of the trunk, and read until she felt calm enough to spend another day in Open-fields. Another day in this life that felt anything other than living.

At best, it felt like nothing more than merely surviving. Trying to convince herself the hope of being connected once again, one day, might end up being worth this grey, not-living existence.

"I guess so." Tala smiled, glancing at Adie.

"So, are you able to tell me?" Adie suspected she was

pushing her luck, but she wanted to know. She *had* to know. And she had her suspicions that while every rumour the townspeople came up with would reach her, they would shroud the truth and she would be left wondering, without any answers.

"We aren't completely sure yet. There was a lot of blood," Tala said.

The word made Adie grateful she had never ended up eating. Her crimson-covered tomato toast still sitting on her bench at home, untouched.

"Where would Lisa be, seeing as she's obviously not here?" Tala asked, commanding Adie's attention again.

"I don't know her that well." Adie was terrible at lying, and the rise of Tala's left eyebrow told her she had failed to pull this one off as well.

"Educated guess?" Tala asked, a smirk on her lips, though she seemed to let Adie slide for the lie. At least for now.

"She lives down behind the green. Close to the overhang of Dedo Rock, near the old gold mining tunnels."

"Wanna show me?" Tala asked, the smirk still hinted at the corner of her lips.

Like a fish out of water, Adie's mouth flapped around, looking for a viable way to say no. But she knew it wouldn't be worth being dragged in front of the town council if Tala mentioned her lack of assistance.

She wasn't a good liar, but she was good at bottling up the anger. Her life was controlled by this town, by the town leaders, and she felt betrayed and hard done by. She wasn't even born to this magic, but somehow being dragged here so young it had leaked beneath her skin and taken control.

And nothing had been right since.

Her right fingers slipped beneath the sweatband on her left wrist, grazing over the raised lines, like braille only she could read. Adie pulled out a bottle from her pocket and dry swallowed two of the small bitter pills before nodding and heading out of Lisa's office.

While they were in the library, the town meeting had finished, although small clumps of people continued to natter about. She felt all their eyes turn to her, but no one dared speak until Adie and Tala had moved beyond what they must have considered hearing range.

It disturbed Adie, the excitement that continued to radiate off far too many of them.

"So, is it just me or are some of your fellow townspeople nodding like I've already got the culprit?" Tala asked with a small V forming between her brows.

"It's not just you." That left eyebrow rose again. "I don't exactly fit in."

"I'm not sure that's a bad thing."

Adie smiled. Out of the corner of her eye, she took in this stranger walking beside her. Tala had only been in town mere moments and had seen beyond the perfect image of the town. The smile faltered. Adie didn't want the warmth that spread through her chest. She liked it too much, and soon Tala would leave and take the warmth with her. But the smile returned. It had been so long since she had been *seen*, even if it was incidental to Tala's concerning insight of the town.

CHAPTER

FIVE

ADIE

The air was sucked from Adie's body as she stepped up to Lisa's front door.

The deep brown wooden door had always reminded Adie of the woods. It was raw, unpolished and gave the slightest hint of the respect Lisa held for nature. Now, it peeked open just enough for the tang of Adie's nightmare to float out from the house. Adie shuddered, unable to move closer to the threshold. That smell didn't just sting her nostrils with its sharp tang. It burned and crawled beneath her skin as the taste of copper sizzled on the back of her tongue, making her stomach churn. She wanted to scream and cry. Anything but step over that threshold and find a real-life horror lying within. And if her fears came true, would it be the last time she would ever step over it?

The first time Lisa had brought her home, Adie had laughed at the sight of this modern marvel with its clean sharp lines and perfectly rendered facade. It stood out like a sore thumb. Old weatherboard Queenslanders dotted the area and squatted on either side of Lisa's home. Her only concession had been that door.

"Stay behind me." Tala's voice was rougher than earlier. Her arm pushed Adie back as though she weighed little more than the breeze. Adie wasn't huge, but she wasn't that little either.

In the back of her mind, she wondered when Tala would pull out her gun. The idea threatened to entice her, but the smell grew more pungent as Tala nudged the door open wider. The gap now big enough for them to step through one a time.

Adie wasn't sure Tala even *had* a gun. She hadn't noticed one, she hadn't even thought to look for one. And she had no idea if cops in Australia, let alone Queensland carried them at all. She didn't know much about the real world outside of Openfields. But Tala looked so much like the detectives in the shows Adie recorded all week and binge-watched on the weekends.

When she wasn't here, at Lisa's.

She closed her eyes and tried not to breathe through her nose.

Her mind wandered off in different directions, and she knew better than to try and stop it. She pushed aside the self-loathing that called her heartless. As she had gotten older, and the tablets taken a deeper root inside of her, she understood her own need for self-preservation. Detachment had been the only way she had survived this town.

Billie had called her heartless so many times, Adie couldn't even put a roundabout number on it. And once Billie screamed it enough times in public, along with Adie's macabre obsession with real life crime books and shows, the entire town had an easy list of words to mutter whenever she walked past. She shook her head, shaking loose the memories of name-calling and betrayals.

Lisa would not let that slide. While their rendezvous had been kept in the shadows, building resentment at times, Adie admired and appreciated Lisa's ability to still defend her. Lisa wouldn't let anyone be bullied in her presence. Not even Adie.

Images of Lisa filled her mind. They were nicer memories, but they hurt her heart so much more. Lisa was Adie's library mouse. With her shoulder-length platinum blonde hair that Adie loved running her fingers through. She had even plaited it one night when they lay in bed, the room smelling of sweat and sex, while Lisa talked about the latest books she had ordered for the library.

Lisa was the one who had gotten Adie interested in those crime shows and just as obsessed with reading true crime books. Not that anyone would believe that.

They didn't know anything about the two of them. They didn't know Lisa, not the Lisa that Adie knew. It would have been dangerous for Lisa if anyone found out. Adie knew that, but it didn't stop it from hurting. It didn't stop her from aching inside her chest as she finally stepped over the threshold and into Lisa's home.

Adie forced out a breath and stared at the floor in the living room. The carpet was a thick cream plush. Sense memory tickled Adie's toes inside her boots.

"What are you doing?" Lisa had asked the first time she saw Adie standing in the middle of the living room.

"Making fists with my feet." Adie had laughed at Lisa's confusion written all over her face.

"Fists with your feet?"

"Oh, please tell me you have seen Die Hard?"

"No." Lisa shook her head, her lip not quite hiding her disgust at the idea.

"Well, you are definitely missing out. Plus, it's nearly Christmas. I just might insist on you watching it soon."

"I thought it was an action flick?"

*"A **Christmas** action flick, thank you very much."*

"You really are as strange as they think."

"Yeah." The *light-heartedness of the conversation fell away instantly. Until Lisa wrapped her arms around Adie's body and pulled her close.*

"Thank the Goddess. We don't need any more normal and boring arseholes in this town."

"You mean like you mum?" Adie tried to make the words light-hearted, but the pain seeped through, regardless.

"She's stuck in a pretty shit situation."

"Aren't we all?"

"Well," Lisa took a deep breath and met Adie's eyes, and with a self-deprecating laugh continued. "Yeah. But she likes to play bitch a little more than she really needs to."

Adie had laughed and they had wandered back to the bedroom.

Adie blinked and the dim light of that evening was replaced with the harsh reality of late autumn light spilling over that same carpet.

One night, when she had been walking and making feet fists, she had turned, not realising Lisa was behind her, carrying two glasses of red wine. The wine had spilled. Despite their best efforts, the stain had remained. The red turned a rusted brown but beyond that, it had refused to budge.

Now that stain was the least of their problems. More than half of the white plush carpet in front of the couch was covered in a dark blackish spill. Including evidence of that accidental collision.

The new stain glistened in the weak light. Adie had felt guilt about the wine stain every time she thought about it. She would have traded just about anything to have that on her mind, instead of fear of not knowing what had happened to Lisa. Of losing Lisa.

Even a secret friendship, a secret relationship, was better than having no one.

"Lisa?" Adie called out before she could think better of it. Her voice wavered and reached a pitch far too shrill.

Movement beside her pulled her back to her senses. Tala stared at Adie; anger flashed in those fire-flickering eyes. God, the woman was gorgeous. More guilt twisted Adie's stomach. She had flirted with this woman, and had entirely inappropriate thoughts about her. All while Lisa was in danger? Had she been fighting off the attack while Adie eyed Tala up and down as they rifled through Lisa's office?

"Shh." The word was short and sharp from Tala as she flashed Adie another glare. Adie was extremely grateful the woman didn't have a gun drawn after all.

She bit her top lip, her hands shaking and her legs moving on auto-pilot as she followed Tala's lead.

The house was beautiful but not big. Two bedrooms, a kitchen, and the living room. The bathroom was big enough to swing a cat in, a joke Adie made often as she danced around the spacious area.

It felt as though several lifetimes passed as she followed Tala's search.

All cupboards and doors were peered behind, and beds were looked beneath.

"She's not here." Tala's shoulders dropped slightly.

"Is she, I— Is she dead?" For years Adie had been building up her armour against the people of Openfields. But she didn't care anymore. She acted tough, but she had always been soft-hearted beneath it all. And right now, she was too scared and too tired of acting.

"Blood spreads a long way." Tala rested warm fingers on Adie's cheek.

She tried to hide the shiver that ran across the back of her shoulder. She shouldn't be having thoughts like this about another woman, in Lisa's living room. Especially when Lisa was Goddess knew where missing, bleeding or possibly dea... Adie stopped the thought before she could finish it. No. She had to find Lisa.

"There's no telling just how much blood was actually spilt, but from my educated guess, she was alive when she left."

Adie blinked, realising she hadn't expected Tala to answer her question. Perhaps she really had seen too many cop shows.

"So where to from here?" She needed to find Lisa and found she didn't mind asking this out loud, in the hopes Tala once again answered her.

Adie didn't know how Lisa had categorised her in her mind. Did. She didn't know how Lisa DID categorise Adie in her mind. She wasn't dead, she couldn't be dead.

For Adie, Lisa was the closest person to a friend she had in the entire town. The only truest idea of one. When she had fucked up, everyone else turned their backs on her. Lisa had been told in no uncertain terms not to hire Adie. She'd been told it many times since, even with Adie standing right in front of her.

She *had* to find Lisa.

"She was your boss, right?" Tala asked.

"Yeah." Adie nodded.

"Just your boss?"

Adie froze, staring at the detective. "Meaning?"

Tala simply raised that damned left eyebrow and looked at

Adie with the patience of someone who could, and would, wait for days for an answer if she had to.

"We were friends, we slept together a few times. But that's not common knowledge."

Tala nodded, and Adie could have sworn there were traces of a smile at the edge of her full dark lips.

"So?" Adie asked.

"What do you know about this town?" Tala asked.

Adie blinked in confusion. How did this woman, this stranger tilt her off-kilter so easily? "I don't really know what you mean." *Please don't mean the magic, please don't ask about the magic.* "I've been here since I was six. It's an old school town that focuses on the old ways." The words tumbled out without thought or feeling. Adie even shrugged for extra emphasis at nonchalance.

She was a hideous liar, but what else could she say? At least these were ones she didn't have to think about.

Everyone in town knew the words. They were learnt for these situations.

Well, not this *particular* situation exactly. But any situation involving outsiders. Adie had never encountered an outsider except during the Celebration of Flowers. She was certain it was the same with many of the other town residents.

"And the cult?" Tala asked as casually as if she had questioned the date.

Shit!

Adie wasn't quick enough to hide the distress that must have filled her face.

"Hmmm." The sound from Tala felt more like a scoff than a thought.

Adie remained silent, knowing even in silence she was shit at lying.

In answer to the quiet, Tala pulled out a folded piece of

newspaper from her pants pocket. With a small flick of her wrist, she handed it over to Adie. By the time Adie took the paper, it had opened just enough for her to recognise the article.

It was Mr Kenjins' current pride and joy. She knew this, everyone in *town* knew this. Because a copy of the same article currently held prime real estate on the bulletin board. Unfortunately for Adie, this prime position was also behind a locked plate of glass. She was certain it had to do with some unknown person defacing the bulletin board in the past. But she couldn't swear to that one.

The article had been in the same place for the last seven months.

Adie looked down at the paper in her hand and narrowed her eyes. It was the same, yet different. It took her a moment to realise what that difference was.

At the top of the article, there were two pictures: one of Mr Kenjins and the other of a woman she had never met but had seen *once* from a distance. Even though the print was black and white, Adie would have sworn the man pictured had makeup on. This was made more obvious because of the natural beauty in the photo next to his. The woman was light-haired with a sharp long face and eyelashes to die for. Adie already knew her to be the interviewer who had come to town a year ago.

Around the woman's neck was a thick chain-link necklace with a pendant shaped like a wolf's head. The eyes looked as though they were jewels or gems.

Adie scoffed under her breath as she reread words she already knew.

Openfields' town leader, Samuel Kenjins, chuckled as he responded to this reporter's questions about rumours of the town shunning those who weren't members of the 'religion'.

"No, not at all. We honour and respect the earth and in return, we are rewarded with the beauty and perfection of our town. We are happy to share it with whoever wishes to live here, as long as they respect what we have created."

This was all that was behind the glass in the town hall. Locked away, safe and sound behind the glass. Adie had indeed imagined drawing many things on the man over the last few months, just as she had defaced previous images and notices.

The article she held in her hand didn't end there though, unlike the one on the notice board.

She read on:

But there have been many questionable actions from Openfields, including their unwillingness to open their books of the town's residents and meeting notes. Openfields has been referred to as a cult on more than one occasion, and there is nothing this reporter has seen to deny these allegations.

Adie bit back the laugh that wanted to escape, a bubble rose from the pit of her stomach. She didn't know what she found so funny, but the bubble kept rising. Whatever Tala saw in Adie's eyes concerned the detective enough for her to snatch the newspaper from Adie's loose grip and tuck it into her back pocket before placing a gentle hand on the small of Adie's back. She guided Adie out the front door of Lisa's house and back onto the street.

Adie leaned back a little into Tala's warm touch. The

giggles gained momentum as her feet moved on a command she didn't give, and the world grew far away, as though Adie currently resided in a bubble separating her from the rest. But she'd always lived in her own bubble. That had been the problem right from the start. One of her problems.

The giggles turned into a laugh.

Tala helped Adie over to the footpath at the front of Lisa's home. Adie's foot barely touched the cement of the gutter when her legs crumpled beneath her.

Tala's hands were rough, but her touch gentle as they helped guide Adie to sit on the raised edge of the gutter, her feet splayed out into the bitumen road in front of her. She looked at her legs and wondered when her feet had gotten so far away.

"Put your head down and when you can, have some of this." Tala placed an open bottle of water on the edge of the curb next to Adie.

Moments passed and eventually, Adie pulled out the small bottle from her pants pocket. With a quick shake of the bottle, Adie sighed at the near lone rattle of the few remaining tablets before tucking it away in her pocket again. Not that they seemed to be doing their job. And she had already taken more than she really should have.

Instead, she stared at the opened bottle of water for a few seconds before picking it up. At first, she took small sips, counted each time as she swallowed down the cool water, relishing the numbness sliding down her throat. But after ten sips, she couldn't remain so conservative and took big gulps. She finished the bottle in five gulps and wished she had more. She hadn't even realised she'd been thirsty.

"What are the pills for?" Tala asked as she settled down in the gutter beside Adie.

"Anxiety." It was as close to the truth as she could get.

"Alright." Tala nodded. "And what did you do to your fingers?"

Adie's felt her eyebrows pull together. Her fingers? Then realisation dawned.

"Oh, I sliced them instead of a tomato when I was making breakfast this morning."

Tala only nodded, and Adie felt an intense desire to justify herself. "I didn't even get to eat it. It's still sitting on my bench at home covered in blood."

The last word sat uncomfortably on the tip of her tongue and was her undoing. Adie leaned forward and retched out half of the water bottle, regretting her eagerness to scull the whole thing.

"So, you're a resident of the town. Did you meet Diana Tracey?" Tala asked, as if Adie hadn't just vomited all over the curb.

"Who?"

"The reporter."

"Oh." Adie couldn't figure out the expression that flitted across Tala's face like a cloud racing across the sun. "No. I don't think anyone else did, except Mr Kenjins. And I'm not sure anyone would technically consider me a member of this town. Not anymore."

A car pulled slowly around the corner into Lisa's street, and drove toward them. Adie felt the air ripple, more than just a memory from when the magic danced hot beneath her skin, as Tala tensed and pushed her shoulders back.

This really wasn't the time for the tablets to stop working. She tried to remember the last time she knew with certainty they *had* worked.

Was it just this morning? Had they worked yesterday?

Why weren't they working now?

Adie's heart raced too quickly, and she felt that liquid fire beneath her skin, the one that led to the dark places of her anxiety. The screaming and the begging bled together, mixed and grew louder.

"A walk will help settle you down a bit," Tala murmured.

Adie flicked her eyes from the car, back to Tala. She had to trust her instincts, and right now she knew she didn't want the car to catch up with her there. She enjoyed being around Tala, too much maybe. Adie knew the woman was lying about something. And she was a stranger, after all.

She nodded and let Tala help her to her feet. Despite her slim appearance, Tala pulled Adie upright as though she weighed nothing more than an abandoned feather she had picked up from the grass.

They strolled down the street, away from the car.

"Hey ladies." The vehicle was beside them too quickly. Adie didn't recognise the voice. It sent a shiver up her spine. She wasn't good at lying, but the vice grip Tala had on her arm made her know she had to at least try.

"Hi! Are you lost?" Adie tapped into that old school charm she had been taught for the Carnival of Flowers.

"Are we that obvious?" The man had a chiselled jaw and Adie bit her top lip, holding back a laugh as she imagined him cast in a B-grade FBI movie. His partner had flicked a glance their way before turning ahead again, hands still at ten and two as though the car wasn't stationary.

"Maybe a little. Everyone in the town knows each other. It's not hard to notice out-of-towners." She laughed, hoping the hysteria didn't reach their ears.

"So, both you ladies are from town?" He looked a little closer at Tala and her dark power suit. Adie would need to get her out of those clothes as soon as possible.

Don't think about getting her undressed.

"Yeah," Tala snarled in Adie's silence.

"And were you just at Lisa Simms' house?" The interrogation in his voice wasn't hidden behind his smile.

"Oh." Adie looked back over her shoulder toward Lisa's house, dried blood hiding secrets she was determined to find answers to. "I'm not sure. I was feeling sick, so we sat down for a little bit while my head cleared. I didn't really pay attention to where we were."

"Are you okay now?" His smile couldn't hide his disinterest in her answer.

Adie nodded and tried a small smile. The less she spoke, the better.

"So where are you looking for?"

"Been told there is an inn somewhere around here."

"Sure is," Adie blurted out. "Just hand a U-ie and take the left at the end of the road. Follow that and you'll get to the centre of town. You can't miss The Inn."

"You give my partner too much credit." The man chuckled but Adie would have sworn not one of them found any of this conversation worth chuckling about. "Thanks, ladies, we'll see you again soon."

"No doubt, Officer." Tala's gravelled voice made the officer blink, as though a camera with an unexpected flash had just gone off in front of him.

"That's obvious too, huh?" He had kind eyes, despite the attempt at an interrogation, and he smiled along with Adie's nervous laugh.

The car turned around in the next driveway and headed back from where they had come from, presumably to head toward town and The Inn.

Adie and Tala walked in silence until they were three blocks away.

"You *aren't* a cop, are you?" Adie already knew, despite asking the question. Just as she had known several things in her life that shouldn't have mattered, that she shouldn't have even known about.

And just like those other times, Adie knew. What surprised her, was hindsight made her realise she had always known the woman wasn't a detective.

"Am I that obvious?" Tala mimicked the square-jawed officer from the car.

"Who are you and why are you here?"

"My name is Tala, that much is true. I'm here looking for Diana."

CHAPTER

SIX

ADIE

"Diana? The reporter? She's missing as well?" Adie's eyes narrowed as she stopped walking. "But why would you come *here?*"

Tala sighed and stopped walking as she turned back to face where Adie stood. "She came back to do a follow-up piece. She'd been invited by your town. They wanted a chance to correct some information my ummm- Diana had written up." Tala's rough voice was softer, her eyes looking everywhere but at Adie. "We lost contact with her a few days ago."

Adie chewed her top lip, thinking through the information as she began to walk toward the outskirts north of the town.

No one had come to town; Diana had never shown up.

Adie thought confidently, because she always knew. Her rundown and monitored idea of a home sat on the outskirts of the town. South from where they now headed.

Her place was so close to the entrance and exit of Openfields. She had more than once assumed they put her there in the hopes that she might finally disappear one day. But of course, they wouldn't want that. Because if she left, her connection to the magic would leave as well.

The pills were only temporary after all. Until Adie remembered why the Goddess blessed her with the magic to begin with. Until she wasn't such a selfish coward. That had been what Billie had called her, screaming the words at her as tears streaked down her face.

But it hadn't happened yet, even though the town continued to apparently live in hope.

This only fuelled her belief that Diana had never returned. Adie rarely missed visitors coming or going.

But then again, she did work in the centre of town, and it wasn't like people couldn't come to Openfields during office hours.

"Did you see her return?" Tala snapped Adie out of her thoughts.

"You love her." Adie ignored Tala's question, feeling sick for having said the words. It wasn't jealousy, at least it wasn't *just* jealousy flipping her stomach.

The sickness washed over her, letting her know in no uncertain terms that she had pried into a place she didn't belong. She knew how that felt. Heat rushed through her limbs. She couldn't let herself be like them. She opened her mouth to take the words back, but Tala spoke first.

"Yes!"

"Are they the real cops? Here to investigate Dr Simms's murder?" The word tasted like the copper smell from Lisa's living room. She wanted to know more. Wanted to laugh and call bullshit on the entire day. This wasn't real. But it wasn't as though she could say any of it was out of the realm of possibility. She lived with magic as a daily reminder of possibilities being blown out of the water at every turn. At least to the world she saw on her shows.

"I guess the flat tyre I gave them didn't hold them up nearly as long as I had hoped." Tala smiled over at Adie as their strides kept easy pace with one another.

Though the wicked grin didn't quite reach Tala's eyes, it sent a laugh, like a rumble of thunder, cascading from Adie's mouth. A shiver ran beneath Adie's skin, centring in her lower stomach. She wanted to laugh more with Tala. She wanted to do a lot more than just laugh with her.

What was wrong with her? Now was not the time to be thinking about anything other than Lisa. And she supposed who the hell killed the doc. Her head spun with her internal flip flop of thoughts.

"Why don't you want the cops looking for her?" Adie asked, wording the question as carefully as she could.

Tala looked closer. The V between her brows deepened as her eyes lingered on Adie. The look might as well have been Tala's hands and mouth exploring her body, tugging her open into a vulnerability she never gave to anyone.

She had to stop this. Whatever this was. Because the Doc was dead and Lisa was missing. It wasn't as though she hadn't used sex in the past to forget the real shit she didn't want to think about. But she couldn't *do* that now, and she had to stop letting her thoughts go there.

"They'll just get hurt. They don't know what they're dealing with."

How did I ever think this woman was a cop? How had she fooled Mr Kenjins?

Adie could feel the threat in Tala's words. It shivered through her, as her fingers played with the small pill bottle in the front pocket of her jeans.

"So, what are your plans?" Adie knew she should just turn around, stop walking and head back to Lisa's to help the *real* authorities.

But Tala wasn't wrong. Adie had no idea what was happening in their town, but the authorities would never be the cops. Not in Openfields.

Tala was in over her head as well, but Adie would do her best to keep her away from it as much as possible.

"I have no idea, honestly." Tala's smile was raw.

It radiated through Adie, and she felt that tug, that draw to help. This woman, whose eyes looked as though Adie might never get out if she were to get lost in them, needed her. For the first time, *someone* needed her.

"Alright, then it's time for Dedo." Adie nodded. She had a course of action. It wasn't much, but it was something.

"Sorry?" Both of Tala's eyebrows raised as she flicked the look over at Adie.

"We'll go up to Dedo Rock. It's the only place you can think in this town. And it's the only place they won't think to look. We can figure out this shit, or at least figure out our next step."

"Our?" Tala leaned her head back a little, as though she planned to argue against Adie's assumption.

Adie knew the assumption for what it was, but she couldn't sit back. There was a tug within her, one that told her she couldn't walk away from this. And while that was terrifying in its own right, she didn't want to do it alone.

"Yep." Her voice was steady, and she thanked the years of showing stillness, despite windblown emotions within her. "We're both missing someone, it'll be easier if we look together."

"You're assuming the two are connected?" Tala asked, giving away nothing of her own thoughts.

"Until proven otherwise?" Adie shrugged, wishing her voice hadn't lifted in a question at the end. It gave away too much of the warring doubt and hope ever present within her.

"You're very sure of yourself." Tala slowly smiled, her

mouth reminding Adie of a flower opening. Before looking away, Tala gave Adie a small wink, and Adie had a sneaking suspicion the woman knew the truth of Adie's doubts.

Adie had never been less sure of herself.

But the wink, the unspoken secret between them, made it easier for her to pull her shoulders back and lift her chin.

"Let's get going then." She nodded and turned right down James Road, leading the way to Dedo Rock.

It wasn't like the idea had come to her in some lightning bolt of cleverness. It simply seemed the best thing to do. They were barely five minutes' walk away and it's what she would have done if she were alone.

Dedo Rock was the only place she felt free. Well, not exactly free. But she did feel less caged when she stood up there, the view of Openfields less overwhelming than when she stood in the midst of the town.

After 798 steps they stopped at the unmarked entrance. In the soft breeze, a low-hanging chain swayed lazily over the ground. It brought attention to the change from bitumen road to dirt track. Tala looked over at Adie, scowling. No traces of her previous smile touched those lips.

Adie laughed and ducked beneath the chain, holding it up to let Tala follow her. The chain had never stopped anyone. It would be unlatched by the time the sun went down. And it spent most weekends laying in the dirt, being run over by tyres that squealed their way onto the track. No one bothered to reattach the thing until Sunday evenings. Always before the evening session of Mr Kenjins' pontificating.

"It's make-out central up here, but it's empty during the day. It's usually interesting to Fielders on weekends. But no one is coming up here while there is a mystery on their minds. And during the week they don't bother until the sun goes down." She wasn't sure why her words kept spilling out of her.

It was as though this woman had some kind of spell over her. But Adie would know if it were magic. She would have sensed it. Even on the pills she had always known when magic was aimed at her.

With a shake of her head, she took the lead and began the slow incline to the peak. She heard the gentle, soft tread of Tala behind her, comforted at the company.

"Aren't you a Fielder?" Tala asked.

Adie shrugged. She refused to turn back, to show her face to answer the question. She had no way to explain the colour that undoubtedly showed in her heated cheeks. Heated because she had no idea how to answer the question.

She was a Fielder, of course she was. Wasn't she?

The town had the pull on her. Was being a Fielder about the town or the people? It had been so easy to deny it, too easy to think of life as a her versus them.

Her skin prickled, and her chest filled with emotion she didn't want to feel. The characters in her books, the strong women who knew who they were, never let their emotions overtake them. They never worried about the fallout because they always knew how it would end for them. They would always win, and they knew it.

Adie had no such knowledge. She barely had a belief in her skills, or in who the hell she was. And she hated that this simple question from a stranger brought up all these doubts and pain in her chest again.

If she wasn't a Fielder, who the bloody hell was she?

It shouldn't matter that she asked herself the same thing every birthday. Because it wasn't her birthday, not really. It was the day she arrived on the edge of the town border. The day she had been brought in and adopted by the town, under the pretence of saving her. But she had been in the room when they fought about whether to keep her or turn her over to the outside world.

She hadn't liked the screaming, and she had curled up into a ball on the floor trying to block it all out. Inadvertently she had made the choice easy for them. She had tapped into the magic, pulling it over her like a blanket protecting herself from all of them.

So, they had kept her. Solely because she could use magic without instruction and had called upon it with a natural ease. They had called her a gift from the Goddess, until they stopped calling her anything at all.

She was just a kid, and she went through the same hormonal teenage hell as all the others. And she knew she hadn't been a gift then.

"Adie?" Tala spoke her name with a gentleness Adie didn't recognise. Her name was never spoken with such a concerned caress. Not even Lisa spoke to her that way.

Adie looked up and locked eyes with Tala.

Tala wasn't a cop. The relief filled Adie's chest. But she was still an outsider. Why should Adie trust her more than she trusted anyone from the town? Still, she found she already did. At least Tala hadn't given her a reason not to, unlike the people of Openfields.

Adie shook her head slightly; words fought each other and tied her tongue. Was she confusing someone to trust with someone she just wanted to sleep with? It had been a while. Lisa had gotten busy, and Adie had never been one to push.

"You okay?"

"Of course. Why?"

"Because you stopped walking." Tala's words held a humour Adie wished she could tap into so easily. She had never wanted to be such a serious person, but what choice did she have, stuck in Openfields as she was?

"Oh." Adie smiled; a small chuckle escaped her lips. "Right. Not much further."

It was still cool in the shade of the overhanging trees. The leaves brushed their tips over the dirt track.

They continued up the sloping incline and the coolness of the town fell away behind them. Adie soon regretted her thick dark green jacket.

Mulch, made of dying leaves, layered the ground in front of them as they reached the open area of the rock.

"This is gorgeous." Tala's voice was filled with a simple reverence as she sat down on the edge of the overhanging rock. Her legs dangled in free air, and she tucked her hands beneath her thighs.

Adie smiled in response to Tala's awe. She couldn't argue with her, Adie had always known the place to offer so much more than a spot to 'go parking.'

Still standing, Adie looked out over the town and tensed at the sight. Her breath caught and her eyes stung from not blinking. The streets were laid out in front of her in a pattern that had meant nothing before, but now it filled her with dread. The very air vibrated dark and heavy.

A line, thick and pulsing, overlapped the roads and pulled her eyes toward the darkness that blotted out the main street of the town. She couldn't see any of it, from the roundabout to the grocery store. Tears stung her already burning eyes.

She had never seen Openfields like this before. Not even when she was a good little conduit. The air had always looked different from up here. Not as clear as one might expect from a town that celebrated and literally worshipped nature, and their manipulation of it. More a crystalised rainbow of colour that shimmered and sparked off sunrays when your eye drew closer to the town's centre.

Now, a grey light glimmered like oil on the road after rainfall.

Pulling her eyes away from that darkness that tugged at her, fear prickling the hair at the back of her neck, she followed the black path back away from town. Her heart beat harder, seeming to bruise the inside of her ribs with its insistent thump, as she followed it, knowing where it would lead even before it stopped in the middle of the field at the back of her home.

She closed her eyes, took a deep breath and steeled a side glance at Tala. The woman looked entirely unconcerned about the view that stretched out in front of them. Adie closed her eyes again, counted to ten and then slowly opened them.

The action proved ineffective. The darkness in the air, and the path's beginning and ending remained consistent. Adie wanted to scream. Why, why should she of all people be seeing any of this, let alone now?

Her breath, too quick and too shallow made her head spin. Before she fell, she sat down heavily at the edge of the over-hanging rock.

"Are you okay?" Tala asked, her voice urgent as she looked up at Adie.

"How are you planning to investigate now the real cops are here?"

"I dunno." Tala's smile held an unexpected self-deprecation as she dragged one hand through her hair. "I'll figure it out. They were always going to arrive eventually."

"I'm not, by the way." Adie's words were soft.

"What?" Tala asked.

"You're question earlier. No. Nothing is okay." Adie shook her head rapidly as though that might clear her vision, like an etch-a-sketch. "Something's wrong with the town. It might not look like much to you, but there is something sinister hovering over it."

Tala's eyes flicked to the view and then back to Adie. The V at the top of her forehead running down to the space between her eyebrows rose prominently as she stared harder at Adie. The unspoken question in her eyes.

"There's a blackness, like a dark rain cloud that is blocking the view. And it's poisoning my town." Adie's words were soft.

"Do you know what it is?" Tala's familiar eyes looked hungry enough to consume Adie.

She shivered, unsure if the sensation was fear or pleasure. Shaking her head again, Adie's mind tried hooking on to where she had seen those eyes before, but Tala had asked her a question.

"I don't know what it is. It makes me feel like I'm suffocating. But the culprit is a snake inside my stomach trying to slither its way up my throat." The silence weighed on Adie's shoulders. She didn't know if she hoped Tala felt it too, or if she were alone in this dread.

"Two people are missing and now there's been a murder. Something isn't right." Adie spoke, unable to handle the silent pressure any longer.

"I can't go back into town, not until I know what's going on with the real cops. I only have so much control." Tala shrugged, a movement Adie caught out of the corner of her eye.

"Control?" Adie's shoulders slumped forward at her lack of knowledge and understanding. What was Tala talking about? Should she already know what this control was about? Was it magical? But Tala wasn't from Openfields.

"Nothing important." Tala looked over at Adie with a small smile and shake of her head.

"I'll go back in." As if on cue, Adie's stomach growled. "And grab some food while I suss out what's happening. Can I leave this here?"

"We'll both still be here when you get back." Tala tucked Adie's backpack protectively under her arm, like a duck with a baby chick cradled beneath a wing.

"Okay, just head back into the woods, off the path, if anyone else shows up."

"Thanks." Tala smiled and Adie walked away before she opened her mouth and said something she couldn't take back, or worse...opened her mouth and said nothing at all.

CHAPTER
SEVEN
ADIE

The air was crisp and chilled as Adie made her way back into town. The air within the circle of houses surrounding the main street was heavy and cold. The same area that had been blacked out from her view on Dedication Rock.

She took a deep breath in, forcing her mind to calm as the fresh air enveloped her. She shivered as she stepped within a stone's throw of the town hall.

Not a bad idea, throwing stones.

"Oh, Adeline dear, it's so good to see you."

Adie stiffened as she exhaled. The nasal voice she never wanted to hear again assaulted her ears. Adie stopped and stared at Mr Kenjins. Billie stood beside her father, staring down at her feet.

"Hello, Mr Kenjins." Adie nodded. "Belinda, *lovely* to see you."

"And you, Adeline." Billie barely flicked a glance up, eyes not meeting Adie's.

"I'm so glad you decided to come pay tribute to Dr Simms. She would have been glad to see you here."

Ah, shit! She'd forgotten about the memorial ceremony. How could she have forgotten about the bloody memorial service?

But that snarky voice in her head had her back.

Maybe because this morning you saw a ghost, the Doc's been murdered, Lisa is missing after losing a shit ton of blood and this strange new woman in town has some pull you can't even begin to understand.

Adie forced back the urge to smile. The voice didn't always pop up when she needed it, but she certainly appreciated it right now.

But she also supposed the chips she had planned to grab from the grocery store would have to wait. She just hoped Tala would as well.

Adie forced a tight facsimile of mourning across her face.

She really should have remembered, and maybe being there would be unexpected by the rest of the town. Part of her hoped it might give her some brownie points. And she hated herself as the warmth of hope spread beneath her breastbone.

She had relied on Dr Simms, but the woman had been no more than a dealer. When the darkness had gotten too much, Dr Simms had been the one to force those first tablets into her.

"Shall we go in, girls?" Mr Kenjins asked in that way of his that Adie knew all too well wasn't a question at all. He placed his hands on his hips, elbows sticking out as though he were in some kind of superhero pose.

Adie wanted to vomit at him being *anyone's* hero.

But she nodded, hoping the correct level of sadness remained plastered in place, and lightly put her hand through the gap between Mr Kenjins' right side and elbow. She touched as little of him as she could, fingers barely brushing against his forearm, while the rest of her hand hovered within the space.

She never liked the man and had hated him ever since *that* night. She looked up at his profile and stumbled as they stepped up to the steps of the town hall. She blinked, but again, the sinister darkness continued to hover around Mr Kenjins' form. Adie regained her footing and forced her eyes away. But it did nothing to ease her increasing heart rate.

Billie clung to her father's other arm and glowed with the same darkness outlining her.

Adie let herself be dragged through the front door of the town hall, giving less resistance than she might have had she not been so distracted. It didn't take long before she stopped looking around at the other residents all pouring into the hall. All of them had the same dark outline.

The walls of the carpeted hallway closed around her. She was pulled past the bulletin board behind its glass and Adie forced her eyes not to lift up and see the half article she knew would still be there.

The town meetings were held in the large auditorium within the town hall. All the important events of Openfields were held there.

Adie watched her feet follow the familiar path, making her cringe at memories she tried daily to convince herself had been washed away. Her body trembled beneath her skin, and she felt the roiling nausea in her stomach warn her away from speaking.

Once inside the auditorium, Mr Kenjins quickly peeled off from her and Billie to converse in hushed mutterings with other higher ranked residents of the town.

The great hall hadn't changed. Adie didn't know why she'd expected it to.

It remained filled with pews that lined up too close together as they faced the large stage and podium.

From the books she'd read, it looked much like any other chapel she might have seen out there in what she had grown more and more to think of as the real world. Few of the books she had managed to acquire had visuals, but there were a few and a small handful of images with chapels in them.

Some were far more elaborate in their stained-glass windows, but still, the resemblance to them all made her balk. Of course, the one glaring difference between the images and the descriptions she had read, were the hundreds of candles that lit the room she stood in.

Flames danced shadows and light over the chattering congregation, and Adie wanted to scream as the flames called to her. Their fingers reaching, begging her to come play.

She shouldn't be hearing the calls, not with all the pills she'd popped.

But why did she think popping more would somehow take effect when the efficacy of the things had been fading more and more over time?

Adie barely had thirty seconds to get too worked up within her own head before Billie directed her to one of the pews for the *unallocated.*

And that was the polite name for them. Unallocated were the residents who were not conduits of the magic and, if this were a regular meeting, would not be receiving any this time either. They might as well be lepers.

Disgust rose like bile to the back of her throat. It wasn't a normal meeting, and yet here they were all still separated into their *rightful* place. They wouldn't want anyone to forget just how important, or not, they were compared to each other. She didn't acknowledge Billie, simply followed behind with her head bowed. But the dark outlines flashed in the periphery of her vision. She curled in her shoulders, hoping that shrinking herself more would ensure her clothes didn't brush against anyone's sins, Billie's included.

Is that what they were, sins? Adie wondered how dark her own outline must be.

The ceremony started with a tribute to Dr Simms.

Adie nodded. She could sit through this easy enough. She closed her eyes and breathed through her mouth, not wanting to smell that familiar charcoal tang from the burning wicks.

Her mind repeated reassurances to herself, ignoring the false words and fake on-cue sniffles from those around her. She would be nice and quiet. No tears or sniffs from her. There was only so much faking she could do for the woman. For anyone in this town. Except maybe Lisa.

It wouldn't take much longer, and then she could get back to Tala. Get back to finding Lisa.

And maybe even figure out some of this crazy that she had woken up in the midst of today. And considering her whole life seemed nothing but crazy, that was probably saying something.

Despite how she worried for Lisa, the mysteries were intriguing. One of those mysteries being Tala herself.

Not too much longer now.

Adie forced her shoulders away from her ears, not quite relaxing but at least finding the pretence of it.

Deep breaths, she counted each inhale 1, 2, 3, 4, 5 and exhale 1, 2, 3, 4, 5.

A calm washed over her as she thought more about Tala. There was something about the woman, something vital that she needed to figure out. But she couldn't deny the calmness the woman lit within her. Not a calmness she was familiar with, but something reassuring after being nothing but a disappointment and a cautionary tale to the young.

But the calm didn't last, and the thoughts writhed away, too slippery to grasp.

The corner of Adie's lips pulled up at the sides, just a touch as her prediction came true. The tribute didn't take long.

But then, without warning, the doors closed, and a town meeting began. Her breath came in faster shorter pants and her head jerked left and right, a trapped animal searching for another way out.

Adie had read about cults. In those books with the rare pictures, and many more with descriptions. Right now, Openfields appeared to be just like any other cult. Adie silently scoffed to herself.

Lisa had originally gotten her interested in looking up religions. She loved to point out the beauty of ancient beliefs in rare books she got into the library. But just like everything else, this was all unknown to the rest of the town. Not just how Lisa would pass the books on to Adie, but that she ever got them into the library in the first place.

As far as Adie could tell, they were all just as screwed as each other. Even if their fuckery were unique in all their own ways. What they all had in common though, was a list of the dos and don'ts.

Lisa enjoyed pointing out contradictions within each cult, laughing as Adie would tuck strands of hair behind Lisa's ear.

The ongoing thoughts of Lisa made Adie's leg jiggle up and down. She didn't want to keep thinking about her as though the past was all she would ever get with her. She couldn't allow herself to think that way.

Kenjins only mention of Lisa had been his condolences and hopes that when she is ready for comfort, they would all join him on being there for her. How had they not found out? Where the hell were the real cops? It had been hours since Adie had talked through the car window to them.

Mr Kenjins continued to hold court, and Adie could no longer focus on the bullshit of his words. Her stomach churned at the mooning calf eyes of the townspeople who surrounded her. Hindsight was always 20/20, but she didn't think she had ever truly been convinced of the man's greatness. The idea of him solely being the reason the town thrived had always felt wrong. She had never been able to shake it, no matter how many times she wished she could be just like everyone else.

The unallocated were the worst of all the residents in their unwavering worship of the man. And Adie understood it, she supposed. They lived in hope of being gifted by his words. They would do anything to be chosen as conduits. First, they had to be recipients of a conduit's magic, and today that was what they all pleaded for silently with their wide eyes and fixed faces. It was almost laughable their desire to be nothing more than drug addicts, begging for a drop of poison that the very fibre of their being thrived to taste again. Because what made them so willing to follow the man, was the first taste everyone received, when they were young and malleable.

Even Adie, who hated and despised every one of these arseholes, couldn't find herself staying detached.

Her eyes were drawn to the larger bulk of the congregation. They all smirked as they basked in their own self-worth.

Heat built within Adie, as though she had walked into a kitchen with all its windows closed and the oven up as high as possible. Her breath became a pant as her insides were placed inside that imaginary oven; cooking, burning.

She found herself unable to pull her eyes away from the congregation, knowing the conduits the moment she landed on them. Her own haunted expression was mirrored in their eyes. Faces unsmiling; teeth clenched and eyes desperate to be anywhere else in the world but there.

Once the mundane notices and announcements were done,

the real meeting would begin, and they would open the doors and make her leave. She wasn't even good enough, worthy enough to be a leper in their congregation.

Her legs jiggled. Soon wasn't good enough, she wanted out *now*. She had to get out now.

Without warning, and without anyone moving, the front doors locked.

That larger group of congregants split. It was a subtle move and shuffle. But the gap was definitive and all without need of instruction Adie could see or hear. They were far more organised than she remembered, she'd give them that.

But the reality sank in.

She had no way of getting out. Her jiggling legs grew faster and faster. She could feel the tightness gripping the back of her neck like a large meaty fist.

If she stood, if she tried to leave, she would bring the attention she had to avoid.

She remained seated, not sure her legs would have taken her weight had she been brave enough to stand.

Mr Kenjins' nasal voice began. They were words no one understood, but everyone felt. They pulled Adie's organs around inside of her like the witches mixing the pot in Macbeth. Mr Kenjins finished the first repetition, nodded, and lifted his arms.

All conduits stood, legs slightly bent, grounding themselves for the purge.

As Mr Kenjins began the second recital of the words, the conduits joined in. Adie mouthed the words subconsciously.

The recipients began chanting in the same vein and rhythm, though the words differed. Adie looked over to the candles as the brightness in the room dimmed.

There was no one near them.

Her stomach dropped when she saw Billie's fingers pinching the air, the lights diminishing at her simple gesture.

Billie had finally received a power. The power of fire. Billie had taken *her* place.

Adie tensed her stomach, weighing down her body as she stayed seated in the pews with the children and the unallocated.

Being chosen to receive the magic from the conduits was another gift and another curse. With the first taste of the magic, the addiction began. But once you truly received the magic, you could never *ever* be free of it again.

You couldn't even dream of a place outside the boundaries of Openfields.

The unallocated had no idea how lucky and precarious their position currently was.

But the tablets helped. Usually. That was what they were designed for.

But everyone wanted to be a receiver of the magic. A conduit was of course the dream. But a recipient would suffice. It could even work in one's favour at times.

When Adie had stopped being part of the true town, she saw what it really took to be one of Mr Kenjins' Chosen Ones.

Bowing down to whatever the Town Leader wanted was primary directive number one. The more you were a 'yes' person, to him and only him, the more hits of magic you received. The more of that sweet drug you got.

Fumbling with the small bottle, Adie didn't count the number of pills that fell into her hand before throwing them into her open mouth. She gagged as a tablet hit her tonsils but swallowed them all dry in the end. With the bottle tucked back into her pocket, Adie shoved her hands beneath her thighs and closed her eyes.

Refusing to mouth the words any longer, Adie forced her teeth and lips clenched.

Still, the chant grew louder. It rumbled around the walls. The ground beneath her feet shook vibrations up her legs. She trembled beneath her skin; the chanting loosening her organs from the one thing holding her together.

But the real fear came from inside.

She wanted to rub away the suffocating warmth in her chest, but she would not let her hands out. They itched to soothe the discomfort within. She fought them, keeping them trapped. Not strong enough to keep them entirely still.

Fear flooded her.

This feeling. This fear. As raw and dark as all those years ago.

The tablets.

Why weren't the Goddess-damned tablets working?

She had once commanded the powers so easily. The magic had danced within her, as she and it became partners in a blissful symbiosis.

Even though something in the tablets had stopped working, and she felt the vibrations of the powers as they swept around the room, that beautiful connection had never returned. It had been severed so long ago.

Before the tablets, and before the darkness had almost swallowed her whole.

Adie didn't know how it had been severed and she had been grateful to be given another chance to find the connection. But the powers weren't the same and the joy no longer bloomed inside of her.

She hadn't wanted *their* version of the magic. But she knew she couldn't live without the one she remembered.

This hell she found herself living in was her own fault. The consequences of her own weakness. And she yearned daily for the power. It created that hole inside of her, that never stopped waving and demanding attention, suffocating her in this half-life.

The scars under her sweatbands itched, and she remembered how helpless life was without the connection to the town. The connection to the power. To the magic.

But she snapped her thoughts back from that ledge, snapped them back as she dug her teeth into her bottom lip. The metallic touch of blood on her tongue was enough to refocus her. To pin her to the now.

None of that mattered. The past was in the past. What did matter were the vibrations in the room and why the fuck she could feel them. The tablets had stopped all her powers.

So why didn't they *now*?

Sweat beaded on her forehead and she looked around. Desperation letting go of the pain and trauma in order to find someone, anyone, to save her. She needed to stop the electricity sparking through her skin, flowing to her fingertips.

The heat burned beneath her thighs.

Memories from that darkest of nights slammed against her, fighting against her present and dragging her back beneath the past. The cold steel pressed against the warm skin of her wrists.

No, no, no, no, no.

Her legs jiggled as she focused on her hands still stuck under her legs. No blade. There was no blade. Not again. Not ever again.

A wave engulfed her, smashing her soul against the rough grains of wet sand. Adie gasped for breath as the chanting reached its crescendo and, in an instant, stopped. Even when she had been welcome, been as much a part of them as she could be, the stopping always seemed too sudden and too clean. The cut itself cauterising the wound.

The hum crackled around her, filled the room. The sound was the magic and the connection of the Chosen Ones standing in the room. They smiled, exchanging small nods and identical expressions of relief. They were all of one mind, one thought, and one goal. And the power had now been dispensed.

Adie lowered her eyes once more, surprised to see her hands had not burst into flames.

She didn't want to see the evidence of the transfer. The eyes of the recipients would shine, and the exhaustion from the conduits would be palpable.

Adie counted her breaths, forcing the taste of bile and blood back down her throat in loud sluggish swallows. Silence pressed on her ears, throbbing. Her body shook. Her hair prickled over her arms and neck.

Adie dropped her head forward, waiting for the shaking to finally ebb. The sobs wracked through her chest as the magic in the room settled in its new places. The ritual now complete, her sense of the power drained away from her with each exhale.

Adie had seen the ritual enough times. But she had never felt this. She had never shared her magic, except for that one time, in private.

It was a horror she had nothing to compare to.

It was a horror she would never live again.

No matter how much the craving gnawed away at her very essence. She would not be put through that ever again. Even the memory had sent her body into panic.

She had known the power and the magic as a child.

But it had been lost to her, until it wasn't.

CHAPTER
EIGHT
ADIE

For years, Adie had felt as though a hole existed inside of her. She'd kept that pain and secret to herself, allowing Billie's excitement and friendship to carry her away. It had been easy to see the upside of being just like everyone else her age. She'd understood the excitement of seeing someone receive the magic for the first time. She'd understood the dreams and chatter of the future. But she had deluded herself into thinking she had ever been like the rest of them.

When the magic left, the two different parties of thought clashed. Did she deserve to be among the Chosen of the Goddess, to be considered one of the children? Adie may have lost the Goddess' gift through her own actions, but she had still been a child, and the other side fought for Adie's protection.

Mr Kenjins held the decision in his hands. Since then, Adie had wished more times than she could count that he had sided with the naysayers. Would being thrown outside the boundaries of Openfields ended up any worse than where she was at now? She doubted every day. Every time she looked up and saw that green light on the camera as it watched her every move. It didn't make sense. Others had left both before and after the debate of Adie's residency. No one else had been given the same treatment.

She had watched so many become conduits. And even more of the townspeople be gifted as recipients. Her resentment grew for the man who ran the town and his ability to keep her here without her ever being one of them.

But when the magic returned, she had run to him, as though his opinion mattered to her. Because of course it had, it must have. It didn't matter how the idea now made her sick. Mr Kenjins had scoffed, not believing the magic flowed within her once again. Why would he. *He* chose the conduits of the town, and those who received the magic from them.

But she hadn't understood the danger, she hadn't believed her own body's warning signs. The raised hair on the back of her neck, the way her skin wanted to shrivel under his touch. She had ignored all of her own instincts and clicked her damned thumb and index finger together.

The snap sounded like a gun shot in the silent office. Moments later, flames danced on the tips of her fingers. The man's eyes had burned black in the shadow of her fire. Without hesitation, without warning, he had held her down, hands rough and careless. As she thrashed against his desk, he chanted the words and pulled, *tore*, and ripped the magic out of her.

Two hours later she had pressed the razors into her flesh. She had hissed between clenched teeth as she bit back the desire to scream. But she didn't stop, she couldn't. Not until the blood flowed. And then she had laughed, high pitched and unnatural. Laughed as she watched her secret waterfall no one else would ever know about.

Somehow, they did know. It remained a question she had

no answer for. But they knew and they found her too soon. They healed her, even after she screamed at them to stop. Even after she had set Dr Simms' hair on fire.

Dr Simms had forced the first tablets down Adie's throat and had kept her on a *suicide* watch ever since. Months piled up into years.

Adie's powers, her magic, had been gone before the next town meeting. Connection to the town and the people she had once called friends, and some even family, were forever impaired.

Dr Simms had told them the power scared Adie and she didn't have enough strength or faith to control it. They all believed the good Doc, even before Kenjins confirmed the doctor's diagnosis that the power had not returned, and Adie's delusion had sent her into her attempt at taking her life. Adie had repeated the story until she found herself in moments of almost believing it.

The power had been intense, true enough. It had welled up inside of her. But the real truth, the full truth had never passed her lips. The truth that he had scared her, that the ritual of the transfer of power scared her. Both of these far more than the magic ever could.

The voices as they returned to normal conversations around Adie meant nothing. She was lost in the past, and terrified about the future. If her powers were coming back, what would stop him from knowing, from taking it from her again and again? From having it *ripped* from her body to be given over to others.

What would stop her from using the razors again?

Noise clashed around her, too loud when she returned to the present. Adie felt a macabre chuckle bubbling up in her chest.

Her body had stopped shaking but tears continued to fall

into her lap, even as several gasps of humourless laughter escaped her trembling lips.

Her chest ached, as though invisible fingers had reached in and squeezed all her organs until they were bruised beneath calloused skin.

Adie's insides trembled; her skin prickled with goosebumps.

The magic was back. It burned and wavered inside of her, the flames of a campfire, flickering her surroundings in and out of view.

"Come on, Ads, let's get you out of here." Billie's hand was its own kind of fire against Adie's shoulder blade.

"No, you don't get to call me Ads. Not ever again. You lost that privilege."

Bilie's lips puckered like a cat's arsehole, but she didn't apologise or remove her touch. Adie wanted Billie's fingers off her, but she would bear that itch to get the hell out of the town hall. She nodded without looking around, standing at Billie's nudge. She let Billie weave her through the mingling crowd, vaguely aware of Billie's soft words to other congregants as they slowed but didn't stop.

She gasped at the outside air when they stepped through the open doors and out into the street. But Billie didn't stop. When they reached the field across the road, Adie fell to her knees, catching herself with her hands just before she landed face first into the earth. The grass soothed something inside of Adie as it cradled her palms. The sobs came again, and she gripped the green blades, digging her fingers deeper into the soil.

When her breath had calmed enough for Adie to sit back, she didn't look up at Billie who continued to stand beside her. Adie's proper shoes, fashionable and stylish, were too much for Adie. She didn't want to see any more.

With trembling hands, Adie tried to undo her shoes. Billie crouched down and with a gentle touch that stung of past rejection, pushed Adie away and slipped off the sneakers for her. Adie took a deep breath and dug her toes into the ground while her fingers gripped at the blades of grass.

"I thought I could feel it again. It feels like it's closer than it has *ever* been. I think I'm going crazy, Billie." Adie bit back any more words. Those were already too much. She had to stop, now, before Billie scurried off to her father.

"Shhhhh, hush now." Billie rubbed her hand in slow circles over Adie's back.

Adie continued to dig her fingers into the grass. The cut fingers on her left-hand touched dirt, and the world shifted.

Catching her breath, Adie opened her eyes.

The nightmare, no not yet. It wasn't quite the nightmare. At least not the beginning of it that she had grown used to. Adie knew the nightmare intimately; and could feel the pull of that horrific familiarity, that same sensation, the tug behind her belly button washed over her. More than that, the veins of her nightmare, the pulsing colours of the cave walls filled the transparent film that lay over the solid world surrounding her.

It was her nightmare. Not anyone else's. Not even the residents who ignored her as they stepped callously through the vision, warping it for a few moments before it settled back into place. It reminded her of a pebble disrupting the still surface of a pond.

Through the wavering air, she could still see the green square she had always known. But now a different landscape existed. It was the same place, she knew it. But it wasn't the now she knew. That lay over the top of what she saw.

To what came before?

Withering flowers filled the space while a forest surrounded her. The trees were gnarled and wide. Some brown, some grey, and a few the mottled colours of autumn. Several of the trunks were so wide she couldn't have wrapped her arms around them. Every single one of them was beautiful and perfect in their own unique twisted trunk and reach of limbs.

Peace washed over Adie, and she breathed in deeply through her nose, her soft breath out tickled her lips. Until the pull behind her belly button yanked hard, dragging her attention toward the main street.

The peace disappeared as a huge mass of darkness stood in the middle of the road she now barely saw.

Adie struggled to her feet and the mass of darkness opened its eyes and stared at her, and she instantly knew it.

The beast.

Her breath came hard and heavy.

Her nightmare. In the middle of the day.

Adie blinked rapidly, wishing away the vision. Begging, screaming inside her mind for it all to leave, to disappear with each blink.

Yet, the beast remained. And those eyes glowed far more clearly than she had ever seen them before.

But she *had* seen them this clearly. The familiarity of them barely a memory, since it had been that morning.

Her breath came faster, her chest rising and falling too quickly. Her head growing light and her legs giving out from beneath her.

"Adie?" Billie's voice was a distant echo, as if she was sitting at the far end of a long corridor.

Adie's thoughts snapped back to her body that remained crouched in the grass, fingers and toes digging into the earth, her body arched as though she had been trying to meet the beast in a similar form.

Adie surged to her feet and ran. She didn't register the cuts and scrapes from loose rocks as they bloodied up the soles of her feet. She moved fast, she *had* to move fast before anyone could think about noticing her. No one could follow her.

She headed towards James Road, bypassing Lisa's place and taking the longer route. She needed to get back, but even with her mind a jumble, her self-preservation was on high alert to avoid that potential danger. The cops hadn't been in town, and no one had mentioned them. What the hell had she gotten herself into?

She shook her head, ridding her mind of the other thoughts as she drew closer to Dedo Rock.

Her mind raced and her skin felt tight. Too tight. As though it might split and tear at any moment. She expected a rendering sound with each footfall. Because now she was running. The moment she escaped the bubble of the main town, she pushed harder with her legs as she lifted her feet, running on her toes. They alone were now being tormented by the imperfection of the streets that lay further away from the centre of Openfields.

With the entrance to Dedication Rock in view, the chain still swayed in the cool breeze. The sound of rustling leaves as the wind increased, whistled in her ears, drowning out her heaving breaths.

Doubts threatened to fill her head, and overtake her thoughts.

Years of being told how worthless she was had not rolled off of her back as easily as she liked to pretend they had.

But she couldn't let that sway her. She couldn't let those doubts win this time.

She knew what she had seen.

CHAPTER

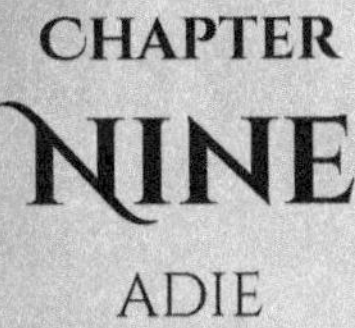

NINE

ADIE

The chain fell apart in a blaze of sparks beneath Adie's touch. She barely heard the heavy metal links hit the hard-packed earth as she raced up the incline toward the peak of the rock. The heat coursed through her veins and her fingers gave off a sharp hiss. They fizzed, crackling with each movement as she opened and closed her hands with the anxiety of this confrontation. The movements hardened her skin as sparks threatened to break through.

The power raged inside her, more powerful than she remembered having felt before. Stronger than it had been on its return when she was sixteen years old. This power was *angry*, but not inwardly, and not angry at her. Its heated raged was targeted at the world outside of Adie. A fury that whipped her insides as forcefully as the wind bent and rustled the trees. It had no intention of letting Adie run away or hide. Not again.

That old horror, filled with fear and darkness, touched against the back of her mind. Still, the power continued to rage through her.

There had been too much. Everything had become just too

much. Not the magic, but the world that fought her and the power that built within.

In that moment, she stopped fighting it. She gave up wanting to be a better person for the town.

The magic breathed a sigh of relief, and a ribbon of smoke escaped from between her lips. This drug, more addictive than anything she'd read about in any of her books, washed through her and for the first time, she found herself remembering what happiness looked like and ached to feel that again.

But not yet. There was work to do first.

Beginning with the uninvited visitor.

"Who are you?" Adie's hand was around Tala's throat as she growled out the words to the shocked woman.

Tala's pulse pounded rhythmically against the webbing between Adie's thumb and pointer finger. The pressure on her wrist band registered enough for Adie to glance down to see Tala's fingers digging uselessly into the material.

"What. Are. You?" Adie's voice was lower, filled with a danger untapped and previously unknown.

"I—," Tala couldn't get enough air for words. Adie threw her to the ground, eyes narrowed on the woman until Tala looked back up at her.

Fear. She saw *genuine* terror in Tala's eyes. It caused Adie to stumble backward a step before she dropped her gaze to her own hands, mesmerised. She had never really hurt anyone else before, only herself. And never intentionally, not even the Doc's hair getting singed had been what she had consciously thought about doing.

It felt good, and it terrified her.

"I'm like you, Adie." Tala coughed between the words.

"Fuck you." Adie's body shook as she tried to contain the

rage without entirely swallowing it back down, uncomfortable in its confinement within her belly. "How do you know the beast? How are you connected? You have his eyes so don't bother lying."

"What beast?"

"The beast from my nightmares. Tell me what's going on!" Adie screamed, but the rage that had driven her to this point suddenly petered out, as though having finally run its course.

Tala smirked at Adie's words.

Adie wanted to hurt her again, wanted to wipe that smile off her pretty face. She clenched her hands into fists, holding back what she couldn't yet understand, and definitely couldn't control.

"My eyes only look like his," Tala stood up slowly, letting the words linger in an anticipatory silence, "because you see us both through *your* magic. It's the same magic that's in *you*, Adie." Tala's voice was velvet as her tongue formed Adie's name.

"What is going on?" Adie asked again, bottom lip trembling. She felt like a stupid child all over again. "The whole truth this time."

"You know what's going on. Deep down, you've always known." Tala spoke so easily, as though she knew it as fact without a single drop of doubt.

"But that's just it. I *don't*." Adie shook her head, hair flying from the ineffective tie she had pulled it up into earlier. "I don't know what you're talking about."

"Where does the magic come from?" Tala asked with a huff.

Adie's breath rushed out of her. She had accused Tala of being connected to the beast, she might as well have accused her of being a witch or an escaped Openfielder. And yet, having Tala ask in such a matter-of-fact way was shocking. Having her say magic and mean it for what it actually was, shuddered Adie's sense of self to her core.

"It's okay. I'm not going to hand you in to the mayor or whatever." Tala's smirk turned soft around the edges. "I just need to know what you do and don't know. And what lies you've been fed."

"He's not mayor. We didn't vote for him. But the magic *is* real." Adie defended this truth with everything inside of her. Despite the shit cards she'd been dealt, especially of late, she wasn't about to deny the truth of this, not even to Tala.

Tala nodded and rolled her hand over, encouraging Adie to continue.

"It comes from the earth. The Town Leader is given it by our Goddess, and he distributes it to those who are deserving, those who will love Mother Earth and maintain her. Those who have pleased the Goddess." The words grew empty and hollow as she finished her learned lesson.

"And you believe that shit?" Tala laughed, hard and angry.

"I don't know, okay? I don't think anyone really knows where it comes from," Adie snapped. It was one thing to feel mocked by the residents of Openfields. Her distrust and anger for them had grown like thick roots into the soil of her soul. But to be mocked by this stranger. She didn't know what it was like growing up with everyone saying the same thing, no one ever questioning the world they lived in. She stalked passed Tala and sat at the edge of the rock.

Several minutes passed as Adie stared down at that looming darkness over her town, her legs swinging back and forth in the open air.

With the sound of loose gravel beside her, Adie flicked a side eye to watch Tala.

"*Someone* knows. The magic isn't given. It's *stolen*." Tala spat as she continued to stand, her shadow cast over Adie, making her shudder from the missing warmth of the sun.

Adie slowly reached up and held out her hand to Tala. Their eyes locked and for a moment Adie swayed a little in time to the flickering flame of Tala's stare.

Tala's hand clutched Adie's fingers and the swaying stopped as though a spell were broken.

With what seemed like little to no effort, Tala pulled Adie to her feet. Their bodies were centimetres from touching. The heat from Tala's body was enough to ignite the sparks in Adie's stomach. And lower. Until Tala blinked.

"Tell me everything." Adie's words were soft, yet raspy.

"I can't tell you everything. I can show you why I'm here, but even that won't answer the questions you probably have."

Adie caught her breath and stepped back when Tala raised her hand, reaching up toward Adie to touch her face.

A 'V' formed in the space between Tala's eyebrows as she stopped, hand hovering in the air between them.

"Sorry. Being touched isn't usually a good thing for me." Adie looked down at the small gap between her bare toes and the front of Tala's boots.

"I won't hurt you," Tala said. "But you will to have to trust me, for it to work."

Adie swallowed hard. She wanted to know. She truly did. So many things had shifted within her and in the town. She had to know what the hell was going on.

But to trust Tala, when she had already lied to her? And for *what* to work?

Trust wasn't something she could so easily grant to anyone. Not anymore.

"I'm not asking for your trust beyond a touch." Tala stepped back a little, hand dropping from where it had lingered in the air between them.

"Oh." Adie's cheeks heated and her teeth pressed into her top lip. She knew how stupid she looked when she did that. Her top lip pulled into her mouth, but the habit was just another thing the people had used to mock her very existence.

Not *all* of the people.

The image of Lisa that had lingered at the edge of her thoughts since she first saw the blood now moved front and centre. They were in bed, her and Lisa. They laughed as Lisa drew sparks in the air. Adie loved to watch the magic, to feel it wrap around her. They all shunned Adie from seeing the magic when they could.

If they knew she could see them when she pretended to read at the park, the scandal it would cause!

But Lisa didn't hide it, she seemed to enjoy showing Adie, just as much as Adie enjoyed watching it. Lisa would let the magic dance on Adie's skin and smile at whatever she saw in the transformation on Adie's face.

Adie hadn't been in love with Lisa, nor Lisa in love with her. That was always clear and open, the communication between them the healthiest Adie had ever experienced.

She did love Lisa though, in her way. As a friend and comfort in a world where eyes either drilled into her or passed through her as if she didn't exist. Lisa had given her what no one else ever would; safety, and a trust that Adie would keep it to herself.

Adie owed her a little trust in order to find her, didn't she?

She had taken the pleasures and freedom that being with Lisa had given her, in a town of supervision and scrutiny. And Lisa had never asked for anything in return. Whatever she got from being with Adie had been enough.

"Okay." Adie had to do this, she would hold on to the snippets of happiness, or near enough, that she'd found with Lisa. She would find the answers to her friend's disappearance.

"Okay," Adie repeated and took a step closer to Tala. "Show me. Please."

Tala didn't smile. She stepped closer, lifting her hand once more.

Adie was mesmerised by the woman's angular face even as Tala's palm pressed gently against her cheek.

"Are you really going back?" Tala asked as she sat cross-legged on the end of the single bed of their hotel room.

She faced the other woman, leg's bouncing as she watched Diana fold a sleeveless shirt and place it in her travel bag. The bag lay open at the end of Diana's single bed, the twin to Tala's own.

The grey and orange comforter on Diana's bed was just as jarring as Tala's pink and yellow one. And neither matched at all with the broken side table that sat between the head of the two beds.

"There's something there, Tala." Diana shook her head as she stared down into the bag, but Tala knew her well enough. Diana wasn't seeing the change of clothes or the other items neatly tetrised perfectly inside. "As soon as I stepped beyond the boundary of that town, I could feel it." Diana shuddered as she closed up the zip.

"But why now?" Tala asked. The whine in her voice reminiscent of older days when the two were much younger. But Tala didn't care enough to push the tone away.

The differences between the two of them had always rubbed Tala the wrong way. But they had bothered her less and less as they had gotten older. Now that twinge of the past was nowhere to be seen as fear clouded all else.

Diana was beautiful. She had long limbs and moved with a dancer's grace. Each shift of her body flowed as naturally as a river dancing over rocks.

Tala and Diana were chalk and cheese. But their eyes were identical. The only thing that indicated the two of them were sisters.

Tala had never dreaded any of Diana's missions before, but the foreboding feeling of this one would not be shaken off. There was something in Openfields, she could feel it even three towns over. She wasn't denying it, she couldn't. But the weight of this mission crawled up her spine and sat unyielded at the base of her skull.

"Please don't go," Tala said, knowing she should have bitten back the words, but she couldn't. Not this time.

"This is what we do." Diana smiled over at her older sister.

Tala saw the sadness in her eyes. "You feel it too. Don't you?"

"Yes." Diana grabbed the backpack and yanked the strap over her shoulder.

"But you're going anyway." It wasn't a question. Tala knew that glint in Diana's eyes. The one no one was capable of dimming.

"It's what we do Tala," Diana reiterated. "If we aren't tracking down the old ones, the forgotten ones, then no one is. You know this as well as I do."

Tala nodded. Nothing Diana said was wrong or false. But this mission felt different.

A heavy pendulous cloud hung over her. It hung over Diana and Openfields and had the moment they had taken on the mission.

Originally, Diana had simply laughed it off when Tala had said as much.

But that did nothing to shift that dark cloud that continued to hover over Tala's mind.

Diana was a brilliant leader, but sometimes she could be a real shit sister.

Despite Tala reminding Diana of her fears and feelings about the mission, Diana still left. Tala couldn't really argue with her. They went into danger with every mission, it was the nature of their work. And despite the sensations that made her stomach squirm as though a pit of newborn snakes had hatched, she couldn't pinpoint a cause.

Three days passed. Three days of pacing. Her neck felt raw from rubbing her hand back and forth over it. Tala's doubts and fears ebbed and flowed like the tide.

Three days and then she woke on the fourth morning covered in sweat with the metallic tang of murder in her mouth. And she knew exactly where that smell and taste of murder had come from. Openfields.

They hadn't been on official business for The Children.

Diana chose to investigate this without Tala.

And now she was missing.

The facts made it easy, even if it pushed Tala outside of her usual place in the unofficial pecking order. Tala had to act. And she would have to go in alone. She couldn't ask for backup; it would take too long to explain everything to them, and that was assuming she would be given help even after that.

Diana wouldn't go radio silent without good reason. Tala just hoped Diana had made the decision to go silent.

But even as she clung to that hope, she threw her belongings haphazardly into her own bag. Shoving it closed and using half her weight in order to get the zipper all the way done up, she cursed herself for not being stronger with Diana. If nothing else, Tala should have at least gone back with her into that town. At least then she wouldn't have been alone.

It had been a while since Tala had felt so alone, and the years between faded into washed-out photographs as she locked the door behind her and headed toward Openfields.

TEN

ADIE

Adie gasped as Tala pulled her hand away from her face.
Adie fell back into her own body, she rolled her shoulders, trying to loosen her tense muscles. Everything felt wrong and overcrowded beneath her skin.

She winced and squinted against the sharp glare of the sun after the dull washed-out colouring of the memory. Tala's memory.

Tala's internal thoughts, filled with doubts and questions, rested behind Adie's eyes for another moment, before drifting away like vapour. She couldn't quite catch them, but the feelings lingered.

"She's your sister." It was the only thing Adie could grab onto from Tala's memory that didn't raise a thousand more questions for her.

"Yes, my baby sister." Tala scoffed; a half laugh that held no humour. Her voice was quieter than Adie had heard it before, though the gruff rumble remained.

Adie wished she was pleased at the revelation. She reprimanded herself. But her mind rarely gave a damn about the impotent scoldings.

"Who are The Children? And the Children of what?" She asked.

"You shouldn't have heard the name." Tala stared at Adie, eyes wide, the deep depths filled with a fear Adie didn't think possible.

"Why not?" Adie didn't like the fear. She liked it less not understanding it.

"They were my thoughts. I only showed you what happened. It's just... dammit, forget the name," Tala snapped. "We need to find Diana and Lisa. And then I'm taking my sister *far* away from this town. Someone else can deal with this bull-shit mess." Tala shivered; Dedo Rock suddenly felt as cold as the town they looked down on.

"And I'm just supposed to be okay with all this? You have magic, you know our town has magic. How?" Adie asked.

"Do you honestly believe your town is special? That magic exists here and nowhere else?" Tala asked in a mocking tone.

Adie opened her mouth to answer and quickly snapped it shut again.

She had questioned where the magic came from until she stopped questioning everything. But she had never asked if it was floating anywhere else in this world, anywhere *outside* of Openfields. The town, her life, seemed too much for her to deal with as it was.

"Look." The touch on her arm made Adie flinch. Tala's hand moved back just as quickly. "Things are never as simple as you think they are. But you don't want to get involved in it. Once you find your friend, you need to get the hell out of here as well."

"I *am* involved in it." Adie's voice was quiet, and for a moment she wasn't certain if she had spoken aloud, or simply thought the words in her head. "I want to know where the magic comes from."

"What the hell has happened in this place?" Tala stood up as she muttered, as she avoided the subject.

Adie had the distinct impression that Tala wasn't talking to her. Fear wormed its way through Adie. Would she be left here again? Alone with a mountain of unanswered questions? Her breath shortened and she turned where she sat, twisting around to watch Tala pacing back and forth behind her.

"Where is the magic stolen from? I've always wanted to know the Goddess. I never understood why the Town Leader got an audience with her, but no one else did; it didn't sound right. But no one would ever listen to me. Please, can't you at *least* tell me where it comes from?" Adie begged.

"You..." Tala stepped back, shaking her head. "You *really* don't know? I thought that was just a town act. Is that why you're shunned, because you want to know?"

"What? No, they hate me because I had the magic, but I couldn't deal with it." Adie plucked at her wristbands as the words rushed out. "They lost my connection when I was no longer a conduit. Looks like I've been replaced now though."

With a heavy sigh, Tala sat back down on the ground beside Adie.

"What do you mean?" Tala asked.

"You mean there's something you *don't* know?" Adie felt the left side of her lip lift in a half grin. A flirty half-grin.

This was not the time for flirting.

"How does Openfields work?" Tala asked, her piercing eyes focused on Adie's face.

Adie looked over the patchwork of a town she loved and hated, despised and cherished, her cage and her sanctuary. "We're all able to receive the magic, but only some of us are gifted enough to become conduits. Mr Kenjins visits with the

Goddess and depending on how pleased she is with us; she gives him the essence of magic. I don't remember when Mr Kenjins gave me the essence from the Goddess, but I have so many moments of blackness in my life it doesn't really matter. Those who receive the essence become conduits. We...no, *they*, transfer the power to the others."

As she spoke, she knew she shouldn't be telling an outsider, yet saying it made her feel freer than she ever had in her life.

"What moments of blackness?" Tala asked, eyes narrowed and pinned Adie, like a dead insect to a corkboard.

"Well, to start with, I don't remember anything from before." Adie shrugged, face scrunching. waiting for an outburst. But of what she didn't quite know.

"Before what?" Tala's head tilted to the side and her eyes gleamed with curiosity.

Adie liked that look. She liked Tala. Too much about Tala.

"I wasn't born here. They found me wandering in the forest when I was six." Adie had never had to say it before. The words were strange on her tongue, like she'd eaten too many furry peaches. But everyone in Openfields already knew her story.

"And it's all blank?" Tala's face was so emotive, Adie could read the surprise in every raised hair of her eyebrows and every small line that crinkled.

"Yes."

"Well, that's convenient."

"I'm telling you the truth." Adie's defences bucked up immediately. She didn't care how cute and intriguing this woman was.

"Not convenient of *you*." Tala shook her head, and then waved her hand indicating for Adie to continue.

Adie stared at Tala in response.

"Sorry. Please. Are there other moments?" Tala asked.

"Some, but just little ones. Nothing important."

"How do you know that? How long has Mr Kenjins been running the town?"

Adie was surprised at the sudden change in the conversation, but the relief was also palpable on her tongue.

"Since before I got here. It's been passed down through his family since the town was established. His great something or other was one of the original miners."

Tala closed her eyes and Adie stared at her, taking the opportunity to examine her features. Her eyes were tilted up, slightly angled, lashes from eyelids to eternity. Adie was drawn to the cupid's bow mouth and had a moment of imagining biting her bottom lip.

Stop it!

"We have to find Diana and Lisa, now. And I have to report back to The Children as soon as we find the source of the magic."

"Children of *what*?"

Tala responded with nothing more than a glare.

"Fine, but where do we start?"

"At the source," Tala replied, the glare vanished. "Close your eyes. Focus on the magic. When you open them again, do it slowly and make sure you keep focusing on the magic. On nothing *but* the magic."

"I told you," Adie couldn't look at Tala's eyes as she tried on the lie. It didn't fit well, but admitting to the magic had never gone well for her in the past. "I don't have the magic anymore."

"Yeah, you do," Tala answered quickly; a small chuckle accompanied the words.

"What? How?"

How could Tala know that her magic had returned when Mr Kenjins didn't even seem to be aware of it? And despite all the signs telling her so, Adie had still hoped it was something else because delusional seemed better than the alternative. Especially as the magic seemed to grow stronger with each passing thought about it. Stronger than it had ever been before.

"I can smell the lavender in the pills you have in your pocket. The herb is covering up the ingredients, and the main ingredient is a pretty standard dampener. It stops you from connecting to the magic. But they aren't working anymore, are they? I'm thinking they must have been infused with your Doc's magic. So, when she died, so did their power over you."

Of course they weren't working. Adie had woken up knowing that with a pure certainty. It didn't matter if she *admitted* it to herself or not. And there was always that part of her that was honest to a painful fault, and no amount of denial would ever drown out its whisper.

But was Tala right about the pills being magically infused? Adie supposed it made sense. It felt right, but so had many things in her life that had proven to be anything but.

It didn't matter. That was a concern for another day. She had to move forward. And that meant doing everything she could to find Lisa and Diana. Besides, what did she have to lose by trying what Tala asked her to do?

"Okay, fine. I'll give it a go." Adie took a deep breath and closed her eyes.

Slowly, she opened them again as instructed. It was like a flashlight piercing the midnight darkness of her mind. Adie yelped and slammed her eyes closed once again.

Tala's hands were a comfort on her forearm. She didn't flinch away this time.

"Slower." Tala's words rumbled through the touch on Adie's skin and filled her with a sense of belief. Adie didn't know who the belief belonged to. "You can do this."

Adie counted to ten and tried again, slower, one eye at a time fluttering before she opened them.

Beginning at the field behind her house, Adie trailed the dark smudge, pushing the magic—her magic? —at it to burn away the black insidious ink. She followed it to the centre of town. As she stared, the mass thinned out and, lit up like a beacon, was the town hall. Fire and ice burned inside her chest as her breath laboured, tears choking in her throat. She wanted to laugh and cry. It was home and a prison cell in one.

It wasn't a surprise, and Adie had to resist the urge to smack herself in the forehead.

Where else *would* it be?

Mr Kenjins had always been so very possessive of the town hall. She had joked, silently in her isolation, at Mr Kenjins acting as though it belonged solely to him. An only child who never learned how to share.

"Please, tell me what's going on?" Adie forced her eyes away from the glow. Tears slipped over her cheeks and ran in rivulets that tickled. Her hands trembled as she brushed gently at them.

Tala stood and started pacing again. It was as though the woman found it impossible to stay seated next to Adie for any real length of time.

Adie watched as Tala took three steps toward her and three steps back again. Adie had to bite back a giggle as she imagined Tala in a ring of residents during a town dance. A demented version of the Hokey Pokey she never wished to witness.

Tala's lower lip pushed to one side of her face, her teeth forcing her lip to stay put.

"Okay." Tala finally stopped pacing and squatted down in front of Adie, excitement in her eyes that made her look crazy or stoned, maybe both. "What if all those old religions were right?"

"What?" Adie scoffed and shook her head.

"Hear me out. Remember. You wanted this."

Adie felt warmth swell in her lower stomach but nodded as she swallowed down the inappropriate thoughts.

"Okay, so let's say there are Gods and Goddesses, but what the religions got wrong was the nature of them. They aren't divine, they're just a different race. Far more in tune with magic, in tune with the *world* and able to wield certain elements by sheer will, through their very blood."

Tala waited for the information to sink in.

Adie nodded, furrowing her eyebrows. She wasn't convinced entirely but she wanted to hear more. "Go on."

"Now, what if humans found out that their Gods weren't immortal or infallible?"

Adie knew that feeling too well, betrayal and anger. Pressure in her chest as the memories from that night rushed to the forefront of her mind.

Mr Kenjins was nothing more than a fraud, hungry and greedy for power. Desperate enough for it to steal it from a child. She had been in the pews with all the rest, looking up at him, this father figure...this *god* of their religion.

"They would feel angry. They would feel like fools. And," Adie tried to rush through the patterns she knew about the human race, rush through the things she had wished in those moments of pure hate for that man, "they would want to get their revenge. And what better way to do that than to steal the power of those they once bowed down to, grovelled to, prayed and confessed their sins to?" Adie knew this with more certainty than she had the authority to.

It was a clenched fist in her stomach.

"And others would fall in love with these beautiful creatures," Tala replied, staring into the mid-distance.

"The Children," Adie gasped. "Children of the Gods."

Tala's eyebrows raised and she looked pointedly at Adie.

"Children of Gods and people? As in together?" Adie said, disbelief mixing with shock.

Tala nodded as she stood back up from her crouch and turned her eyes back to the town. Adie wondered what she saw, but it was quickly pushed aside as she tried to process what she had just learned.

She could believe that people, that humans could and would easily enough fall in love with powerful creatures who manipulated the elements. But would those creatures, those Gods and Goddesses, love the people back? Turmoil mixed inside her.

It was too much, and a cold blankness threatened to wash over her. She forced it back, and for the first time since she could remember, she let a boiling heat, a sizzling anger grow within her.

"So, what *is* the source, then?" Adie dreaded the answer, fearing a truth that lingered at the periphery of her mind.

Tala jumped up quickly and pulled Adie to her feet. "We have to go."

Adie's eyebrows drew together. She had more questions. But the sound of tyres on the dirt road made her understand, made her nod and forget any thoughts of resistance to Tala's pull.

Someone drew near.

CHAPTER

ELEVEN

ADIE

Adie tried her best to ignore the electricity that ran through her fingers as Tala's grip tightened around her fingers. Her feet ached, the cuts and bruises on her soles already making their presence known.

"Okay," she whispered and moved with Tala's pull toward the other end of the overlook.

Magic. Children.

Shit! Tala was a Child of the Gods. A God herself. Did that mean the electricity, the pull and attraction Adie had for her was just the magic?

Adie shook her head. It didn't matter. Once Tala found Diana, they would leave. And Adie would be left to figure out the world with this new truth. She hoped Lisa would be with her, but she didn't even know if Lisa was alive.

And as she tried to imagine a future, it wasn't Lisa she hoped to have beside her.

"Where do we go?" Tala asked, voice tight and urgent.

"Oh." Adie shook her head and forced herself back to the

moment. To the hand that currently held hers, and not a hand in some wishful thinking in an impossible future.

Adie took the lead and smiled when Tala offered no resistance. Nor did either of them let go of the other's hand. Adie hustled Tala and herself further away from the trail they had walked up.

The path they stepped on was barely visible as a track anymore. It had almost been entirely reclaimed by the surrounding bush.

"We're taking the scenic route back to town. This track circumnavigates close to the edge of the boundaries and will eventually lead back to my place. It's only a short walk to town from there. And with the sun setting, no one will look for me."

"I guess that depends on how far the cops have gotten," Tala grumbled back in response.

Adie nodded. She'd forgotten about them.

But in all honesty, she wasn't really worried about any authorities from the outside. She hadn't been raised to fear them, certainly not when they were in her town at least. Despite Mr Kenjins orders, no one would help them find the real truth behind Openfields.

The path grew darker as the sun slipped further below the horizon.

With each step, Adie could feel the pulse of the earth beneath her bare feet. It raced through her soles and vibrated through her entire body, with both fear and excitement.

Her fingers reached instinctively into her pocket, and she gently stroked the plastic bottle of pills. There was no point in them, or the bottle since they had stopped working. Yet, a comforting ease washed over her from the touch of the familiar smoothness.

Too soon they stepped out of the forest and the familiar shape of her prison loomed on the horizon.

"That's my place." Adie jerked her head at the small abode as she walked toward it.

"All on its own?" Tala asked.

Adie couldn't answer, what was the point?

Instead of walking to the front, she skirted around it, far enough away that the sensor lights wouldn't trigger under her and Tala's presence. She sensed the woman's confusion behind her, but still couldn't find any words. It had been easier, up on that rock with distance and the bird's eye view. But back down here the reality bit into her sense of self, her sense of adventure, once more.

She walked quietly past the place she had known as home, without ever having a true definition of the word to hold onto. Instead of looking at it, she focused on the open grass field ahead of her. The same field where she'd seen the misty figure that morning.

Had it *really* been just that morning?

Her world had turned upside down in less than twenty-four hours. She had never thought the stale existence she had been surviving could ever yield to anything, let alone to *everything* so quickly.

"We should go in and rest up. Wait until the dark has fully settled before we head to the town hall," Tala whispered.

Adie wanted nothing more than to go in, have a shower and a cuppa tea. Instead, she shook her head and kept walking.

"We can't wait there," Adie said.

Tala followed silently; a question hovered against the back of Adie's head. She could feel the pressure of it from Tala's gaze.

Adie sat down on the grass behind the house and watched the last fingers of the sun disappear over the horizon. Adie shivered, wondering if they sat in the spot where she had seen her waving figure. She shivered, but even now she wasn't afraid, not of the figure.

It sure had turned into a fucking horrid omen, though.

"Why didn't we stop at your place? Shoes would probably be a good thing." Tala sat down next to Adie as she spoke, the darkness settling around them.

"When I became a conduit, when I first felt the magic, I did the right thing and told the town leader about it. I wasn't happy having to, but it's what everyone did." She felt stupid. Since the moment she woke that morning, the anger and frustration she had over her world had multiplied. And she wondered why the hell had she not pushed back on so many things.

"Shouldn't he have known?" Tala asked. And while she didn't turn to face Adie, Adie felt the side-eye look just as distinctively.

"Well, yeah. But no one talks about the things that don't make sense. No one, even me, ever seems to be able to focus on them."

After a beat, Tala asked in a voice that seemed to hold no judgment, though Adie was certain it was tinged with sadness. She wasn't sure which was worse. "What happened?"

"He tried to force a transfer of power on me. I don't know if that's what he does to everyone. But yeah, he lied. He claimed he chose who received the power. He would never have chosen me, the mongrel of the town even before what was to come. But I could feel it pushing against me, begging me to hurt him. I could see myself using the magic to kill him. I didn't want to kill him, even as I wanted nothing more. But I stopped and let him take whatever he wanted. Everything after that felt wrong and strange. And dark. Above everything else, it was so dark. I got a blade and tried to take the darkness away."

Adie pulled off her wristbands and showed Tala the scars beneath. Tala gasped and Adie lifted her eyes.

Their eyes met.

Tala's gaze slipped down to Adie's wrist and back up. Tala's hands tentatively inched forward. The question in Tala's gaze almost did Adie in, the tears already so close to the surface.

Adie nodded; meeting Tala's hands halfway. Tala's fingers gently ran over Adie's skin. A lump formed in Adie's throat. Those building tears blurred her vision, ready to run over her cheeks.

"Since they took the magic," Adie's voice was a strained choke, "they put me in that house, and they've monitored every day of my life since. Lisa was the only one to give me a chance, the only one who fought for my need to still have purpose in this town. She even fought her mother on my behalf."

"Why didn't you leave?"

The tears came fast and hard. Too many things she had never even allowed herself to think came rushing to her mind. No, *at* her mind. It was as though they attacked the very essence of who she had ever thought herself to be.

"I wish I knew." Adie's laugh was dark and filled with pain. "I've thought about it. Hell, I've even tried a few times. But I could never take that final step. I still want the magic. I crave it every single waking hour. I even crave the wrongness of what I last felt, if that's what it takes to have it back. But the tablets, they've kept it all out of reach. Until this morning. But if I left, I would never get it back again. I would never find a way off the tablets."

The silence held a weight that slumped Adie's shoulders forward.

"That would be it, all gone forever. Nice and crazy, huh?"

Tala's hands finally dropped away from Adie's wrists as she laughed.

Adie roughly brushed away the tears with clenched fists before pulling the wristbands back into place.

She really was stupid, and just as naive as she had often been told.

Adie hadn't shown anyone her scars. Not since the wounds had healed. And now this woman, the one person she had been stupid enough to trust, was laughing at her.

The anger and disgrace of her past actions crowded in on her. She couldn't blame Tala. Adie had known for so long that she was nothing but a worthless cause. Why did she insist on still clinging to that persistent thread of hope?

"I'm not laughing at you. I think what you just described is so beautifully real and human. I'm a little envious," Tala murmured with a gentle smile.

"Of me? I'm nothing to be envious of."

"You are. I wish we had met in some other circumstance."

"If we had met in other circumstances, I wouldn't have been brave enough to talk to the sexy and confident woman who controlled every room she walked into."

Tala laughed again and reached over to touch the back of Adie's hand. Adie watched as Tala slowly intertwined their fingers, giving Adie ample time to pull away, but she had no such inclination.

Tala raised Adie's hand, kissing her fingers on the knuckles, one by one.

"I'm sorry." Adie had a desire to bury herself beneath the ground. It was the magic all over again, feelings so right and so wrong, threatening to overwhelm her. Lisa, she cared about Lisa, she loved her, but not like that. Here was Tala, a stranger who knew her better than Lisa ever had, even after all those years and nights of whispered pillow talk.

"Please don't be."

"What magic do you have?" Adie needed to know. This wasn't her. Since she'd met Tala, she felt both more and less like herself than she ever had before.

"What do you mean?" Tala's head cocked to the side as she asked the question.

"I can't lie to you. I've just shown you what even Lisa hasn't seen. I am saying stuff I never say." Adie quickly closed her mouth, knowing if she left it open, she would simply continue to spew whatever words came to her mind.

Tala laughed, a rich deep sound that lit her face and her eyes. Adie couldn't help but smile. Laughing suited Tala.

"My powers are only in making you see what I want you to see. And I'm not sure I have that much power over you. You knew I wasn't a cop before the real ones showed up." Tala smiled, and met Adie's eyes for the briefest of moments before looking back to the horizon.

"Besides, you aren't the only one not keeping as quiet as you should be."

"Oh." For all she read, Adie had hoped she would be far more articulate in this situation. But then again, she had never been able to dream of anything even remotely similar to this. Whatever this ended up being.

"So, do you have anything useful in that backpack or have we been dragging it around for the fun of it?" Tala asked, breaking the tension and Adie's self-deprecating and spiralling thoughts.

"You mean, you didn't snoop when I was in town?" And there she went again with the flirty eyes, and was that a sexy smirk? Surely not.

Tala smiled back with what Adie assumed, -- or more accurately hoped -- was the woman's version of flirty. For a moment Adie wondered if time could be forced to stand still.

Tala shook her head and they returned to a regular viewing schedule.

"Just the usual stuff. My staff access card, a torch, a bottle of water, wallet, muesli bar. Random things I have forgotten to take out of it. That kind of thing."

"So at least some of it is handy." Tala nodded as she spoke.

"It's not getting any darker than this, we should head off." Adie forced the words over the lump in her throat. "We've got to find Lisa and Diana."

She had never felt this connected before. Not to Billie, or to Lisa.

There was something different between her and Tala. Too many thoughts brushed against her mind. Too much information, too much confusion.

Puzzle pieces were being dropped in front of her, but none of them connected with each other.

Tala helped Adie to her feet.

Adie closed her eyes, unable to watch the trace of lines Tala made as she lingered at Adie's wrist bands.

The magic was back, Adie could no longer deny it. But so was the darkness.

CHAPTER
TWELVE
ADIE

Darkness smothered the town hall.

Billie's home, Mr Kenjins' house, backed onto it, so the chances of being seen, of getting caught, were likely, but the lack of daylight would help conceal them long enough to get inside. At least Adie hoped.

The tension raced up and down Adie's body, electricity and fire flirting dangerously beneath her skin. What Adie couldn't quite believe was how much she loved the sensation. And too soon, inch by inch, excitement replaced the fear.

She silently chastised herself as her mind kept itself occupied in the creeping darkness.

Why had she stopped asking, stopped searching for the truth, for the source of their magic? Adie should have known the town hall stood at the centre of it all. She had never doubted its importance to the town or the magic. But she had stopped thinking beyond that. She had stopped digging to understand more.

She could almost visualise a wall in her mind. Thick bricks and heavy grey mortar barring the way between her thoughts and her knowledge. The wall had been there, unbreachable for years. Too many years.

As she focused harder on it, a strength inside her spread out from her chest and warmed her limbs. There, to the right, were cracks in the wall. And just a little closer to the centre, were not just cracks but crumbling chunks. Brick-sized holes appeared at her periphery, and when she turned to face them, they sat dormant, covered in moss as though they had fallen years earlier.

Her fingers trembled as they touched the bottle in her jeans.

She knew why she had stopped asking. Perhaps not the exact details, perhaps not how it had all happened. But something outside of herself had made her stop. Even before the tablets, her curiosity had been tamped down.

Now, the curiosity had returned in a raging fire of need.

"Break into places often?" Adie's voice was muffled as it pressed up against Tala's ear. Her skin radiated with nerves as she watched Tala pick the lock on the front door of the town hall.

"I have many skills." Tala smiled.

Adie's hand shook slightly, the light from the torch bounced around on the front door. A peek-a-boo show of Tala's skills in action.

"Now hold that thing steady," Tala whispered.

Adie grinned, attraction mixing in with the adrenaline and danger.

A heavy clunk bounced around the empty streets as the lock gave in to Tala's insistence.

They both froze, waiting for a call to halt, a scream, a siren. Anything really. But the echoing clicks died down, and after another thirty-second count, the sleepy quiet of the town returned and settled over the intermittent darkness.

Despite the truths of Openfields, the shops that lined the main street still had security lights which broke up the darkness. A telltale of the town leader's lies of near omnipresence. Adie never remembered him saying he had it, but it sure was implied, over and over again throughout the years.

Tala turned the handle and waved her hand for Adie to go first. She slipped into the internal darkness, the light from her torch a bouncing dot around them. The soft carpet was a warm relief to her feet. Though she had barely noticed the sting of the cold night through the adrenaline of engaging in a misdemeanour.

"Where to?" Tala asked, scanning their surroundings.

Adie took a deep breath. She knew exactly where they had to go. She jerked her head toward the hall and the way to Mr Kenjins' office. The mysterious always locked office. Even when he lurked inside, the door *remained* locked. She had tested it a few times over the years, and Billie had confirmed the same.

A memory strong and visceral rose in her mind like bile to the back of her throat. Billie had hurt her leg; they must have been only twelve or thirteen. Adie never focused on time as much as other people, probably because she had no root in what her *own* timeline truly was. But they couldn't have been much older than that. Perhaps they were younger. But it had been a pivotal point for Adie.

She had watched, hands curling into fists as Mr Kenjins had screamed and chastised Billie for daring to interrupt him during his important tasks for the Goddess. She was bleeding, unable to walk without Adie's assistance. Tears stained tracks down her cheeks and he hadn't given a single shit for the pain of his only child.

Adie hadn't had any personal experience of family but she had read about plenty. From what she'd learned; he *should* have been comforting Billie. He should have been her father and not the fucking town leader.

He had finally ripped open the door, eyes narrowed and hard, like dark pebbles at the bottom of a river. Ten minutes they had stood outside, Billie sobbing and the both of them knocking, had felt like a year.

She remembered her thoughts as clearly as though they were new and fresh in her mind.

If this is what having a family looks like in real life, I'm glad I've never had one.

Her relief had been intoxicating when they had finally been given leave to get away from the reprimands. She'd dragged her friend down the hall, ignoring the last mutterings of scolding coming from behind them, and took Billie to the Doc to have her cleaned up and looked at.

To this day, Billie bore the twisted raised scar that ran up her shin bone, from the top of her feet, stopping just beneath her knee-cap, off centre to the left.

She'd been lucky. That's what the Doc had said.

Adie hadn't considered Billie overly lucky after that day. How could she? Not with her having that arsehole as her father.

Adie filled her cheeks and puffed out her breath. She had to focus on the now. Not the memories this place conjured up. But each step closer to the town leader's office brought other memories. They had lain dormant at the back of her mind and now tasted bitter and insoluble on her tongue. When she had heard the raised voices of residents behind closed doors. The tear-stained cheeks and red-rimmed eyes of people rushing past, their heads down, only making them more conspicuous. All these moments with weeks or months in between. All these moments that had been washed back like the tide. She had never linked them before and now that her subconscious seemed determined to, she felt sick at the links it seemed determined to make.

Had they all suffered at the hands of their tyrannical leader? It seemed impossible. Why would they all just settle for it?

Why did you?

The unhelpful thought in her mind made her shudder.

Tala glanced at her, eyes furrowed.

Adie was about to open her mouth and brush off the movement she had made as nothing more than the chill in the air. But Tala shook her head, and quickly placed her hand over Adie's where she had been about to bring the torch up.

Adie's eyebrows furrowed. What was Tala on about?

They hadn't stopped walking, but they slowed. Lifting her warm fingers from Adie's, Tala tapped her ear twice, quickly and succinctly.

Adie forced her breath and roaring blood to become as much background noise as possible in the hopes of hearing what she had missed while locked in her thoughts and memories.

It was a subtle shuffle, different to their soft footsteps. Adie's mouth formed a small 'o' shape, and she lifted her eyes to lock with Tala's.

The soft sound came again. A soft shuffle, a footstep?

And again.

Definitely a footstep.

Adie's breath sped, her chest rising and falling. Tala's lips, darker in the dim light mouthed a simple word.

Turn.

Adie nodded and Tala's mouth counted silently.

One, two, three.

On the count of three, Adie whipped around, lifted the torch and pinned Billie in the glare of its light.

"What are you doing here?" Billie hissed, even as her own torch bounced with a dull thud onto the carpet, her arms crossed in front of her face, blocking the light of Adie's torch from her eyes.

"Right now," Adie's voice was heavy with her hard breath. "I'm trying not to have a fucking heart attack."

"Adie?" Billie's voice shook a little as she lowered her arms.

"Who did you think it was?"

"Another detective." Adie could just see the thrust of Billie's chin toward Tala as Billie spat out the words.

"No, it's just me. I'm with Tala."

"*With* Tala?" Billie sneered.

Adie didn't even feel guilty about the thrill the interaction gave her.

"So, what now?" Adie tilted her head and put on her best disdainful look. "You going to go report me to your dad, again?"

"I was *trying* to help you."

It was years ago, but Adie still held the anger like a ball of fire within her chest. She had been done; she had been free. But then Billie. She had been the one who knew something was wrong, the one who called her daddy. The one who had dobbed Adie in when she hadn't answered Billie's multiple messages.

She was the reason Mr Kenjins and Dr Simms' had shown up in time. They had brought Adie back to this nightmare of unreachable magic and numbing pills.

"Yeah, well, I don't *need* your help. Just piss off. We'll be out of here soon enough. See if you can get your daddy here on time this time."

"You just broke into the town hall." Billie had the upper hand, and she knew it.

"Yep!" Adie didn't have time for Billie or trying to play nice.

She had never been this brave with her, even when they had been friends. But there was a strength in her spine she had long forgotten about. Right now, their time limit for getting in and out had decreased exponentially.

"So, you haven't heard? Why would you, alone on the outskirts of town..." Billie blushed in the torchlight. "He's *not* my dad."

"What?" Adie's head swam. Was nothing she knew real? Bile rose in the back of her throat. How that man held knowledge to his chest as though it belonged to him and no one else. Did this explain his disdain toward his daughter, or would he have been just as detached from Billie if she carried his blood?

Adie's world had changed forever since the morning. Part of her half expected to wake up and find it had all been some strange dream, a new kind of nightmare to replace the other one. But she wasn't waking up, and it just kept spinning like one of those insane adrenaline rides at theme parks she'd seen and read about.

"Mum had an affair with a visitor during the Carnival of Flowers. It's why he's never trusted me. Why he *doesn't* trust me."

"I'm sorry." Did that mean they had a few more minutes after all? Adie fought down a blush at the thought. She could see Billie was hurt, so she should be nice. But she still couldn't find herself caring as much as she knew she should. "So, what are you doing here?"

"I found this." Billie handed something over to Tala instead of Adie.

"Where'd you find this?" Tala's voice rumbled, barely holding back her emotions. But holding back *what* emotion? Adie didn't know; truth be told she warred about whether or not she *wanted* to know.

"My dad had it." She shrugged. "I think he forgot about it."

"What is it?" Adie asked.

"It's Diana's." Tala handed the heavy silver lump to Adie, pressing it into her hand with a little too much force. Adie recognised the necklace in the article that still sat on the noticeboard, only half visible to those who walked past it daily. The one the interviewer wore. The one *Diana* wore. "And it's her blood on it."

"How do you know that?" Billie looked closer at Tala.

"She knows. She's not a cop, Billie. She has magic as well. And she came here to look for Diana." Tala glared at Adie, who could only shrug. "It's either this or she runs and sets off an alarm."

"I'm not telling anyone you're here." Billie's voice dropped, barely audible. "I know where Diana is."

"She's alive?" Tala's voice cracked and rose.

"Last time I saw her, yes." Billie's answer sent a chill down Adie's back.

A chill they all should have been feeling, but as she took note, as subtly as she could, she realised only Billie was dressed for the evening air. But Tala's hands had remained warm.

"Do we trust her?" Tala asked the question Adie didn't know the answer to.

Billie's eyes blinked in the dim light and Adie remembered a time when she would have done anything for her. When she would have trusted her with her life. The dark bubble of laughter pushed at the back of her teeth but she swallowed it down.

She wasn't even sure she could vouch for her.

"What choice do we have?" Adie knew she had a choice. She could turn around; she could forget it all. She could leave this place. But none of that seemed like a real option. It never had been.

"Come on then, before he gets back." Billie spit the words out.

"Gets back?" Tala asked.

"Town leaders meeting in my house." Billie smiled shyly. The way that won over anyone in the town so that they would do her bidding. The one that *used* to work on Adie. "It's why I knew it would be safe to come here."

Billie turned and Adie followed her. After a few steps, Tala's grip on Adie's arm stopped her.

"Shh."

Adie nodded in response, leaving Billie to keep walking, unaware that they had stopped, or at least she appeared to be.

"She smells of Diana; she could have been the one to hurt her," Tala hissed.

"Billie's a coward," Adie replied quickly, frowning after her old friend as her outline blurred, the darkness encroaching upon her.

"They're often the most dangerous."

THIRTEEN

ADIE

"Does *everyone* know how to pick locks except me?" Adie's words spilled out in a nervous rush once they caught up with Billie, on her knees picking the lock to her father's office.

"Probably." Billie's half smile sent an old feeling of familiarity through Adie's body. It was swiftly followed by sadness.

Adie looked at the woman in front of her and felt nothing but the faint memory of fondness. Her friend had idolised the cruel man apparently parading around as her father. Everything she did was in the hopes of pleasing him, making him proud. She couldn't imagine what Billie was feeling now. To discover the reason for his disdain was something she would never be able to overcome. What would that do to a person? It explained so much, and the guilt gnawed in the pit of Adie's stomach. She should have forgiven her. After all, she had just wanted to save Adie. But even now, she couldn't will that feeling into being.

Billy achieved the criminal act as the lock popped, and Adie almost laughed. It was so anticlimactic. The heavy, smooth wooden door swung open and revealed the most generic of offices that Adie could ever have imagined. There was nothing spectacular about it. She wasn't sure what she'd expected, but nothing so... *normal* had entertained her imaginings. But those were when she was still a curious child of the church, and she'd fantasised about what lay behind Mr Kenjins' door.

Perhaps a big glowing neon sign saying 'yep, I'm the bad guy' or something similar would have been nice though. A candlelit altar with bowls of overflowing blood would have also appeased her.

Instead, she discovered a square box with a desk, a chair, and a filing cabinet all facing the door as they entered. Along the left-hand side of where they stood sat a slate grey two-seater couch.

Tala gripped Adie's arm. It carried a comfort and a strength Adie didn't realise she needed quite so badly. It also reassured her she wasn't the only one sensing the disquiet within.

The room looked normal, sure, but she could *feel* something far more nefarious. Adie noticed the soft plume of cold breath from Billie's mouth. It would seem none of them were immune to the metallic, tainted magic that stuck to her own tongue.

"Where is it coming from?" Adie whispered.

"The couch." Tala seemed confident.

Billie nodded and stepped up onto the cushions; one foot on each seat.

"I haven't been in there for years, I don't know what we will find," Billie whispered.

"Been in there? What the fuck?" Adie muttered under her breath.

"Just open it!" Tala commanded.

Adie looked sharply at the woman. Her words were like thunder in the distance.

Billie hesitated, but a narrowed glare from Tala had her pressing the palms of both hands against the wall.

Nothing happened.

Adie let out her held breath, the tease of a smile pulled at the corner of her lips. Whatever had given her the wiggins wasn't some hidden passage behind the damn couch. What did she think this was, scooby-bloody-doo? If anything, this *had* to be a prank. Though, the idea of the town having *any* sort of humour didn't quite settle right on her shoulders.

She was just about to say something about looking elsewhere, when the wall gave way beneath Billie's hands. It moved back with a soft scraping sound. Adie imagined rock on metal. A feint rectangular light illuminated a door that hadn't been there moments earlier.

"What the fuck is this?" Adie felt the hysteria in her words, trying to bubble out of her. That dark gallows laughter lifted its foul head once more. "I feel like we've stepped into another dimension."

"We've always been in this dimension, Adie. Dr Simms just softened the blow for you." Billie's voice was hard and seething.

"You know about the tablets?" Adie snapped.

She hadn't realised Billie, or *anyone* in town could hurt her anymore. But here she was, heart breaking to learn that Billie had known all this time about the magic-dousing pills. Secrets and lies. The more she learned about Openfields, the more secrets and lies she found.

"Yes."

"And you *never* told me?"

Billie's teeth clenched, and she glared at Adie. "Dr Simms didn't want you killing yourself. My dad didn't care either way, but you became her little obsession."

There was nothing Adie could say to that. She had been used. Even more than she'd known or even suspected.

Why and for what purpose, she had no idea. Was she *just* a guinea pig for the tablets?

That familiar burn sparked in her chest. She should be *used* to the betrayal. Had she really expected anything else?

Her breath shuddered as she pushed it out between her lips. She rubbed her chest, the heat building no matter what she did. How much more could she take before the flames sparked to life and used her bones for kindling?

Mr Kenjins controlled who became conduits and who received the power. That's what they had always been told. Except Adie knew that wasn't always the case. Was it *ever* the case?

Why had the tablets existed? The tablets that weren't as secret as she had been assured they were.

Stolen. The magic had been stolen. That's what Tala had said. But from who? The Goddess? The same Goddess she'd prayed to and screamed at so many times. Did she even exist? Tala seemed convinced. But why should Adie believe her? She should have stopped believing *everyone* years ago.

More Goddess damned questions. And answers that led to more questions.

Adie's mind *teemed* with questions. Challenging everything had been as natural as breathing, once upon a time.

"Adie?" Tala's hand, still warm through Adie's clothing, made Adie blink.

She smiled at Tala. The touch had been what she needed to stop her mind going down further paths of inquiry that only succeeded in making her heart beat increase and her mind fuzzy.

"I'm just like them," Adie confessed to the stranger who had no way of knowing what she meant. And yet she felt as though she could trust Tala more than anyone she'd ever known. "I'm just another sheep, following that man's lead."

"No, you *aren't*." Tala squeezed gently before letting go of Adie and turning back to Billie.

"Tell me what happened to Diana?" Tala's voice held the deep rumble of a war cry.

Adie was impressed Tala didn't have Billie by the throat. The way *she* had with Tala not so long ago. Adie's hands itched to grab Billie herself.

"I heard Dad and Dr Simms fighting the night the Doc was killed. She was screaming at him for being so careless and thinking of himself as the god. She mentioned the reporter and told him the interview was his stupidest move yet."

"Is she *alive*?" Tala growled, her face like granite.

"I don't know. Diana came for dinner. She left." Billie shrugged. "I didn't think anything more of it until I heard Dad and Dr Simms fighting."

"Where did you find her necklace, Billie?" Adie forced the words out evenly. It wasn't adding up. Adie wanted it to, oh how much she wanted it to. She wanted *one* person in this town to be more than the liars and secret keepers she was coming to see them all as.

"It was under his desk when I was cleaning up," Billie answered, waving her hand toward the desk; her legs visibly trembled where she still stood on the couch.

"In here?" Tala's voice sent tendrils of fear down Adie's back.

"I clean once a week, when he's in umm," Billie's eyes flicked to the secret doorway she had just revealed. "When he's working."

"And he didn't see you find it?" Adie didn't like this at all.

"No," Billie snapped.

Adie and Tala looked at each other. Neither of them spoke, but Adie saw the reflection of her own doubts in Tala's eyes.

"How did you know about the pills?" Adie had to know. She wanted this over, but not before she got *some* answers.

"I'm not deaf, Adie. I can still hear things. I live in the house where all the damn meetings happen. You think they'd learn to keep their voices down occasionally, but they don't. They know they're completely untouchable, so they don't seem to care what I do and don't hear."

"Fine. Let's get this over with." Adie's voice was a lot stronger and far more in control than how she felt as she waved her hand towards the door.

Listening to Billie bitch about her lot in life was just a little too much for her to swallow. No matter how much of an arsehole Kenjins was, Billie still had her freedom.

I wonder what it cost you to earn your freedom, Adie thought unkindly.

Adie had never been a fighter, the closest she'd been was setting fire to the Doc's hair, but she'd become increasingly eager to hit something, *anything* since all of this started. Had either Tala or Billie argued with her she might have gotten the chance to scratch that itch.

Instead of arguing, Billie pushed harder against the concealed doorway until it gave way, soundlessly swinging open. The hinges should have squeaked if Adie's books were to have been believed.

The three of them stepped over the couch. Billie, Tala, and then Adie.

From the threshold, Adie was confronted with a deep blackness that cut through more than just her sight. It *burrowed* into her mind and trawled through her thoughts. A sharp sting of metal touched the tip of her tongue. The anger in the air pressed against her skin. Darkness settled over her like a cloak as she stepped entirely into the hidden tunnel. Adie was glad neither of her companions could see her face.

Her fear turned hysterical inside her mind. Memories from every nightmare, waking and asleep, danced on the edges of her sanity.

If she had a mirror, she was certain it would be a look reminiscent of The Joker or other such insane characters. The Cheshire cat on speed, perhaps. She stopped and willed her face back into neutral submission.

Tala turned back and gently pried the torch from Adie's gripped fist.

"I'm going first," Tala spoke, shoving past Billie as she led the way inside the dark unknown.

They walked in silence, their steps the only noise in the darkness. The ball of light in front was a comfort to Adie's nerves, even though the shape of Tala had merged with the darkness before her.

Adie let out a slow breath and blinked as white mist wafted from between her lips.

"It's so cold," she whispered, but the words bounced around the tunnel as punctuation between their footsteps.

"It's Diana." Tala stopped walking and met Adie's eyes over her shoulder.

Adie knew she should have understood what Tala was trying to say. But she had no idea.

"The reporter?" Billie asked, doubt, scorn and disgust evident in her voice. Adie couldn't wait to see Tala smack the butt of her torch into Billie's nose.

What the fuck? Where had *that* thought come from? Adie swallowed the lump in her throat and looked down at her feet.

It had seemed so dark when they had been walking, but now the ground might as well have been the middle of town in the middle of the day. Light flooded around her and every detail was in stark relief.

"Adie, are you sure you want to do this? I can go on alone." Tala's hand was warm and gentle against Adie's skin.

"Seriously? You're fucking the fake cop? She's an intruder, Adie," Billie snarled, looking back and forth between the two of them. "I thought you had better taste than that. At least Lisa was one of our own."

Tala's hand snatched away so quickly, Adie stumbled a little by the sudden imbalance.

"You really are a piece of work." Tala turned on Billie, her body seeming to almost vibrate as she hissed out the words.

"And you are *nothing*," Billie snarled back.

"Stop it," Adie snapped, as surprised as the looks that flashed over both Tala and Billie's face. "How is the cold Diana?"

"She has mastery over the temperature. It's one of the reasons I knew she was still here."

"Oh." There was something scratching at the back of Adie's brain. She almost let the bark of laughter out as it swelled within her. There were so many things clawing at the back of her mind, there was no space left for anything else.

"Come on." Tala turned away and led the way further down into the tunnel.

Adie didn't want to know where they were going. But the fear that she already knew what they would find at the end of the tunnel increased with every step they took.

FOURTEEN

ADIE

Despite what Tala thought, the glamour she'd used on the town *had* in fact worked on Adie. At least to a point. There was no other reason that Adie could think as to *why* she hadn't noticed Tala's specific wardrobe, only to be drawn to it now.

She had noticed Tala, and a vague impression of a suit. And beyond fantasising about what she might have looked like beneath it. That had been the end of that.

Now it had slipped, and with each step Adie followed behind Tala, she noticed more about the woman she hadn't seen before. *More* than just the pull that kept Adie intrigued about her.

Tala wore a long jacket with deep pockets. Every time Tala turned back to check on those behind her, Adie caught sight of the pants and pale blue button-down shirt. The collar stood up a little too much, stiff as though the shirt had never been worn before. Beneath the gloom of the tunnel, Adie might have even believed the shirt to be white, except she knew it wasn't.

She didn't look like a cop at all now. What she *did* look like was a weary private investigator. One of those old school TV ones that was never seen without a cigarette in hand and walked against the wind when they left after a pithy response that left you wondering how you'd missed the obvious.

Adie wanted to laugh again. It was a bubble in her chest that pushed against everything she was.

With practised ease, Tala swept the torch beam back and forth, hitting the tunnel walls and picking out the path in front of them.

Adie didn't trust Billie behind her, but it was better than having any distance or bodies between herself and Tala. She had never felt so like herself as when she was with this stranger. For the first time Adie was the Adie she desired to be. Confident and strong. And above all else, believed.

Forty-nine steps further into the tunnel and Tala stopped walking. Adie wondered, not for the first time, if she would ever stop counting. She didn't even know why she did it. But she stopped, the number still sitting in her mind, her tongue pressed to the roof of her mouth.

Tala held up a clenched fist in the half-lit darkness. With a look over her shoulder, Tala's eyes didn't quite meet Adie's, but she saw the concern in them anyway. Tala walked around some kind of obstacle and looked over the top of it to Adie. From where Adie stood, the shape and details that now stood between her and Tala were nothing but a gaping absence of light. Tala's face tilted down at the obstacle and the look on her face grew stormier by the second.

Counting each step, Adie moved around the object.

One, two, three, four, five.

She turned toward Tala and met her shoulder to shoulder.

Six, seven, eight, nine, ten, eleven.

Adie didn't want to turn and face the thing that cast a shadow across Tala's face. A darkness that made the muddy light around them appear like daylight.

Taking measured, purposeful breathes in and out of her mouth, she forced her head to turn and face what now stood in front of her. The obstacle became the unidentified yellowing whiteness of bones, aged by their years piled together.

Billie joined them without any of the hesitation Adie had carried with her. Her world had crumbled around her. As much as she had detested the life she had been trudging through, it had been safe and known. Now there was a pile of goddamn bones, human bones. She wanted to scream, or vomit, or cry. She wanted to break the world as much as she had been broken. She wanted to heal it.

The three soon stood shoulder to shoulder, Adie sandwiched between the two of them, though her shoulder brushed Tala's alone, keeping her distance from Billie purposefully. Billie added her torch to the light and Adie could no longer try to reason away what she could see all too clearly before them.

A pyramid of skulls stared back at her, with their empty eye sockets and their stolen individuality. The pile held a deliberate nature. Every placement had been exact, and all the skulls faced the same direction. No flesh or skin remained, no hair or tell-tale marks. If there were any cracks or defining individual features, the shadows concealed them. A pyramid of stolen identities.

"They aren't real. They *can't* be real." Billie's voice trembled as she turned off her torch.

Adie knew Billie was hiding something, but the fear of those skulls appeared genuine.

Adie's own fear was buried under a flash fire of red-hot anger.

Death.

More Goddess-damned death.

Were these all murders as well? Had murder been in Open-fields all this time, hiding literally beneath the surface of the town?

"They're real. And so are those bodies." Tala stepped away with the light, walking further into the tunnel, leaving Adie and Billie beside the pyramid of skulls.

Adie shifted, panic filled her, as she failed to shrug off the cloud of darkness and fear, as the blackness seemed to grow legs and crawl over Adie's entire body.

Billie collapsed on to Adie's chest, sobbing as her torch dropped to the ground and rolled away. Adie wrapped her arms around her, making shushing noises because she had no idea what else to do.

"What's going on in our town, Adie? What's that man *really* been doing?"

Adie tensed slightly as something false in Billie's words hit her. She had always been able to tell, if she let Billie talk long enough. She could always hear the hints of a lie. Not what the lie *was*, but if one lingered in Billie's words. She heard that slight uptick now.

"He's your father," Adie said, pushing Billie out of her embrace and stepping back from her reach.

"No, he's not." Billie shook her head, but Adie wasn't fooled by the flick of fingers against Billie's cheeks. There were no tears there.

"He raised you. How do you really not know what's been going on?" Adie asked, wondering what else she had been blind to.

"She does know." Tala's voice was a rolling thunder from the darkness.

"Good girl, Billie. You might prove to be my child after all."

The nasal voice of Mr Kenjins hit Adie's ears moments before his snarling face came into view.

One fist was tangled in Tala's hair, while the other twisted Tala's arm behind her back. Above them, a small glowing ball of light bobbed and lit up the tunnel.

Adie turned to Billie and met with Billie's fist, smashing into her face. The pain in Adie's nose made her eyes water as much as the crunch that echoed inside her head had made her feel sick.

The smell of fresh blood filled the air.

"Better actress than I ever gave you credit for." Adie spat blood onto the floor, her stomach curdling at the taste.

Her legs gave way, and she fell to her knees. Hard dirt and rock gashed the skin beneath her pants. She had fallen beside the bodies Tala had spoken of. She hadn't spotted them before, in fact, she hadn't really registered Tala's words. But she registered them, and the bodies *now*.

White limbs stuck out of rags that might once have been clothing. If the remains were any sign, the bodies had simply been dumped. No rhyme or reason, just excess flesh and bone with nowhere else to dispose of them. A shudder forced its way up Adie's back as her mind, playing tricks, superimposed her own body over the bones. An image of her younger self, blood drained from slashed wrists. Would she have ended up here, just another skull for a pyramid that made every sense and none whatsoever?

"Get her up."

Adie didn't resist as Billie followed her father's command and pulled Adie to her feet. She didn't even try to fight as Billie walked, arrogance in her sway, dragging Adie behind her.

"I'm sorry, Adie. But I don't want to lose the magic." Billie's words showed absolutely no regret or sign of any such apology.

"Fuck *you*, Billie!"

"You'll understand soon enough."

Adie bit her tongue on repeating her witty response. She understood all too well how it felt to lose the magic. It was the waking nightmare of her life. All she wanted was to get her and Tala out. The small hope she had for Lisa faded with each step she was forced to make.

"Okay, so *help* me understand."

An unattractive snort was Billie's only reply. But the anger, the hurt, the years of lies and manipulations all stoked the fire in Adie's chest. It filled her with a courage she hadn't had since the night she'd tried to leave this nightmare behind.

"Come on. You're gonna kill me in the end anyway. So, tell me, why did you help kill Dr Simms?" The silence was worse than this. At least this way she might have *some* answers before they killed her. And she wouldn't lie. She was getting a cruel sort of kick out of making Billie squirm in the discomfort of her own sins. "Why?"

"I didn't lie to you, Adie. I found the necklace when I was cleaning. And I did hear dad yelling at Dr Simms. But it wouldn't have mattered. He came and got me afterwards. I mean, who else was going to clean up the mess?"

Adie's hands curled into fists, her short nails dug crescent moons into the skin of her palm.

She had no choice but to keep up with Billie. The woman's fingers bruised her arm as they held tighter than necessary and pulled with a fierceness that gave a little more insight into Billie's own unhinged mind. The woman had been treated like a slave by the man she called father, and she was *still* his little puppet, begging for scraps of attention from the man.

Adie almost felt the need to tell Billie she shouldn't bother. Not only to hope for Kenjins' good graces, or to hold on and drag Adie for the ride.

Adie wanted nothing more than to move faster. They were falling behind. Kenjins and Tala's footsteps echoed back to them, but they were growing darker around the edges, as the gap between the two parties grew.

Adie clung to the heavy clomp from Kenjins and the subtle press onto the earth from Tala. While they still moved, while she could hear *both* sets of footfalls, then she knew Tala was okay. Tala was safe.

Her own and Billie's footsteps kicked up a dust storm of debris that swirled around their ankles. The soles of Adie's feet stung as rocks cut and scraped the soft flesh. But she didn't hiss or cry out. She couldn't imagine what the point would be.

"You cleaned up and helped him stage Dr Simms' murder in her office." Adie felt vindicated as she saw the flinch and cringe in Billie's face.

Was there still hope?

Adie shook her head and wanted to smack herself on the forehead.

How could she cling to such an idea? She had been shown the darkness of humankind over and over. Yet here she was *still* clinging to those very last frayed threads.

"It was an accident, Adie. Dr Simms was going to expose everyone; she was ranting and raving. And she hit him." Billie spoke with such passion, her face a mask of disgust and horror. Even now, the idea that someone might hit Kenjins still carried more weight than the death that surrounded them. "I'm not a liar, Adie. I *never* lied. I hadn't been down here. Not since I was twelve. The skulls weren't here." Billie's last words were far softer than her earlier list of excuses.

"The skulls and bodies are human beings, Billie! Killed by your daddy dearest. You can't possibly be so stupid to actually think Dr Simms' murder was nothing more than an accident."

Adie shook her head. Her neck muscles tensed. She turned her head away, the idea of having to look at Billie any longer fuelled too many emotions, and not one of them good or positive.

Adie had been wrong. This was far worse than any silence.

CHAPTER

FIFTEEN

ADIE

The tunnel ahead sloped downward, further beneath the ground, and the air grew colder until Adie could see her breath, white and cloudy in front of her. A different energy lurked beneath Openfields. It wasn't the beautiful honouring magic that they were all baptised in. It was dark, it was angry. And above all, it was frozen.

What if hell really wasn't the burning pits everyone liked to think? What if hell was nothing more than a frozen wasteland? Barren and dead, and coming up to claim Openfields for its own?

The thought came to Adie, and the strangest sensation of it not being her *own* pressed upon her.

She shook her head.

She had been faced with so many questions. All while having her entire life turned upside down, in less than twenty-four hours.

There were so many questions. Questions from years ago, ones she'd given up asking, knowing they would never be answered.

And every answer she did get, did nothing more than sprout *more* questions.

Adie craved a moment alone, a moment to let herself fully stop and *try* to process it all.

No. She didn't even want that. She simply wanted a chance to process *any* of it. One part, one second to breathe properly. With each step, breathing itself had gotten harder. The cool air turned cold. Adie feared taking too deep a breath and cutting her insides with the shards of ice that would surely form if she tried.

As they drew closer to another patch of darkness that looked, even from this distance like a pyramid, the hair on Adie's arms stood to attention. She wanted to cry and vomit. She wanted to scream and fight.

Ahead of her, something flickered and caught her eye. She squinted, trying to force herself to look beyond yet another triangle of death that loomed in the shadows.

Again, the twinkle of light. No, not light. But *something*.

There was a smudge in the darkness, that floated before her and the skulls. Adie got the impression of an artist absent-mindedly rubbing the heel of their palm across a pencil drawing not yet set. An artist whose creative mind had already moved on to their next masterpiece.

Blinking away the blurry film, Adie gave her head a small shake. The smudged edges lightened, as her eyes adjusted to the intrusion of the gloom, the figure from her morning greeting floated into view. They were still bleary, as though they stood too far away. But there wasn't a doubt in Adie's mind it was the very same figure. She hadn't imagined it. She had never truly believed she had. But here they were, beneath the town. Waving for Adie's attention.

Adie's head whipped around to see Billie's face. Billie's eyes narrowed in confusion at Adie's look. Perhaps it was a question that lingered in Billie's eyes. It didn't matter to Adie. What mattered was the lack of sight Billie obviously had for the figure.

"Tala?" Adie called out. Fear and hope warring in her chest cavity.

"Yes. I know. Me too." The words vibrated from the darkness and filled Adie with a warm blanket of calm and knowledge.

Tala could have been talking about anything, Adie knew that. There was no way for Tala to know *what* Adie called out to her about. But that didn't matter, because she also knew Tala saw the figure, just as she did.

Air washed over Adie's lips in a shudder of sharp shards.

The pressure in the air that had been building up for weeks now reached so close to its limit. The cold snap that was too early for this time of year. The unseasonal weather that told Adie the exact time of Diana's death. The pit of her stomach rolled like the angry sea.

Her anger, or Diana's? Both?

"Shut up." Mr Kenjins' voice was high pitched and sounded completely unaware of the weight of the simple exchange.

Adie almost laughed out loud.

They came to another, was it the third or fourth pile of skulls?

Adie hated that she didn't know. It was just too much for her to take it all in. All these lives lost. No, not lost. They were *taken*, stolen and ripped away.

This pile of skulls was different.

They were still white; they hadn't yet been given the time to yellow or stain from the dirt of the underground tunnel. The skulls and the triangle they had been arranged into sent a shudder of fear and loathing through Adie.

The magic inside of her reacted to them. She realised now, it had reacted to each pyramid. A little stronger each time.

But the clothes, the clothes and the discarded bodies of bones were far worse for her immediate thoughts.

Bile brought a burning trail up her throat as her eyes pulled out features of less deteriorated scraps of cloth. Soon she found she even recognised some for what they were. A uniform. Though as unofficial as the uniform was, it was the same one she put on every weekday morning.

They'd been disgruntled teens, working just enough to earn their way out of the small town. She'd wondered before what price they had paid to have Kenjins let them leave. But she had *never* imagined that they had failed to escape. The number of times she had envied them their freedom. The number of times she wondered if *she* could pay the same price, if he would let her pay the same price for her freedom.

Her mind screamed to turn and run, but she couldn't. Even if Billie's vice like grip wasn't digging into the flesh on her upper arm. She couldn't turn away now, no more than she could every night when the nightmare settled upon her.

But that didn't mean she was powerless.

Before she could talk herself out of it, she placed a hand on top of the apex skull, the smooth surface settled in the palm of her hand. Saying a silent apology for those she no longer remembered the names of, she pushed with all the strength she could muster. It seemed such a childish, useless act but the relief was instant.

The crash and tumble of skulls down onto the tunnel floor vibrated up through her bare feet. The rumble carried to her chest, entwining with the thrill of taking action into her own hands. It made her body shake, as though a rock band had turned all their amps up to full base.

"Get her under control, *Belinda*," Mr Kenjins snarled from

out of the darkness, though the waver in his voice made Adie cock her head in curiosity.

Billie's fingers dug deeper into Adie's upper arm as she grabbed a hold once more and yanked her forward to keep moving.

Adie smiled, not sure where the sense of it came from. But in the darkness, as she was forced further beneath the town, she felt the rightness of it all. The fear from the nightmares lingered, but in a muted version to what she was familiar with.

The tunnel continued to dip downward and some of the unknown disappeared beneath the familiarity of colours. They flicked into life in thin lines along the tunnel walls.

The ghost waved ahead of them.

Adie knew who it was, and her heart ached for Tala. Then, as much as she wished she didn't, she felt the relief wash over her.

Over the years, she had steadily found herself hardening to all those in Openfields. She had grown heartless and numb from the perpetual torment of her existence.

But Adie felt the pain, raw and real in her heart, as she mourned for Tala's grief. As she lamented the death of a person she would never meet. She remembered fiercely the feeling of love Tala had unwittingly shared with her. Shared when all she'd tried to show Adie had been her memories.

She could think. She just had to push aside the metallic taste that grew stronger as they walked. She had to ignore the chill that sunk into her bones with each step. Her feet were frozen blocks of ice, but at least the stinging cuts no longer bothered her.

Every dozen or so steps, Adie caught glimpses of Diana's ethereal form waving her on. Hope bloomed in her chest, not just wisps of wishful thinking, but genuine hope and belief that maybe, just maybe things weren't entirely lost. Not yet.

But she needed to put the pieces together, she needed to work out what was really going on in this town. Her town? Not anymore. Maybe it never had been.

Another large dip down into the earth and Adie's breath caught in her throat. Hints of the nightmare had already flickered into existence as they walked deeper into the earth. But Adie clung to the differences.

She couldn't bring herself to believe the actual details were real. Something inside of her had been trying to tell her something was wrong with the magic.

But the cave itself, the beast, and the man. They weren't real. They *couldn't* be real.

The differences were.

She had always been alone in the nightmares. The nightmares had seemed so real in every aspect except one.

Not once during those terrible dreams had Adie's claustrophobia played a part. Not once did she ache for the sun and the cool open breeze. It was that knowledge when she woke that helped her remember. Helped her know it was all just a dream.

Now the walls pressed around her. Her hands beaded with sweat, despite her breath still puffing out in white clouds of air. The veins of the pulsing colours increased the pressure on her chest.

This was not the same. She would not let this living nightmare end with questions left unanswered.

She had walked into this. She had known, somewhere inside her, she had known this was how it all happened. How she would find the place of her nightmare.

She couldn't deny any of it anymore.

The nightmare had never been her own imagination. As she accepted this knowledge, knowing she understood so little, she realised she hadn't always believed the lies of the world that had been forced upon her. She had pretended to believe them when they had said it wasn't precognitive. It was easy to imagine beasts and fantastical things in a town where magic existed. It made sense, and she'd allowed herself to believe the lie. And the part of her that knew it wasn't the truth grew quieter over the years.

Adie may not have chosen the path that led her here, she may not even be here of her own free will, but that didn't mean she couldn't make a difference. She had proven that when she'd toppled the pyramid of skulls.

She really did need to know; it burned her from the inside out. She *needed* to know, and she needed to stop whatever hell was happening here.

Despite her fear, she knew whatever Kenjins was doing had to be stopped. It had to be as evil as the man himself. The true man Adie had caught glimpses of before she shrivelled under his cruel and malicious touch.

Even if she hadn't found her strength, found her desire to push back against the existence she had been trapped into, the deaths of all those people could never be justified.

She was putting things together, and she was finding the strength in herself growing, dulling the fear as it did. The triangle had meant something. The anger that had radiated from Kenjins told her that.

The man was evil, but not stupid. He wouldn't have simply placed them where they were, how they were, without a purpose and a reason. The differences between how the skulls were placed and the discarding of the rest of the bodies made that clear.

There were still too many bricks in that wall in her mind, but they were trembling against her thoughts.

Old knowledge that had been trying to make its way to her pushed against it.

She was *so* close to understanding.

She fought to remember the books Lisa had shown her. To remember *anything* that hinted about old Gods. The race of powerful beings Tala had spoken of. Because the words had struck a chord.

But there were more than the books behind that wall.

The coffin. The stone coffin. The one in her dreams. No, the one in her nightmare. At the beginning of the nightmare? Or at the end? She couldn't remember. It was all too blurred.

Overlapping and mixing with memories of the life she had lived were others she couldn't quite remember.

Kenjins had found her, brought her into the town. But the coffin, why was he standing over the coffin? It sat in the middle of a clearing surrounded by trees with leaves that wept.

It forced its way to the front of Adie's mind and each time she focused on it, she drew a step closer.

She gasped, the lid was half open, but Kenjins still stood there, eyes solely on what lay within.

Stumbling in her steps dashed the images away from her mind. For a moment Billie's grip released and the thought to run screamed at her.

But Adie wasn't fast enough. Too much swam within her.

Billie grabbed her arm once more, lower down this time, almost to her elbow. There would be more bruises. With a jerk of her arm, Billie pulled Adie onward.

She needed more time to damn well *think*.

The soles of her feet stung anew with each step. The cold hadn't lessened, but her body had adjusted to the temperature. The hard packed earth, littered with small, jagged rocks, dug into her skin as she moved.

The light continued to pulse.

Dark and light.

Dark and light.

While the dark no longer blinded her, the lights illuminated more details of the path in front of them. Adie wished they hadn't.

They weren't rocks that cut up her feet. The white irregular shards were too bright, too white. The white of bones, not yet fallen prey to the dirt and the darkness. They came in and out of the pulsing veins.

Dark and light.

Dark and light.

It was a heartbeat. The knowledge came to Adie without hesitation or doubt. She knew it. The knowledge was as real as anything she had ever known, any words she had ever read in any book she had picked through.

The latest pile of skulls and discarded bodies lit up in the light of the pulse. Bright in horrific detail and then plunged into shadow once more.

It was smaller, and not quite the even pyramid of the previous shapes of devastation.

It had not yet been completed.

But it wasn't just the size that made Adie's throat clench. The shape on the top of the half-formed triangle was a head, not a skull. The tangle of blonde hair made Adie shiver.

She heard the sob float back to her. It was an endless sound of anger and pain that came from in front of her and Billie. Tala's wail was a nightmare all on its own.

Despite Adie's desire to keep her eyes on the darkness, she turned to look at the face of the head as Billie dragged her past the unfinished triangle.

Standing beside it was the ethereal body, head attached. A transparent version of the necklace she still held in her hand rested against Diana's chest, hanging from the thin silver link chain. The silver wolf's head glowed bright against her ethereal form.

"She isn't worth mourning. She did harm to my town. She

was nothing but an enemy to Openfields." Mr Kenjins' nasal voice was close, too damn close. They had caught up, but she had been distracted with the revelations in her mind.

Tala had slipped from his grip and knelt beside the tower of skulls. Her back was arched and her shoulders shook. Hands that trembled held her. Diana's ethereal hand gently stroked Tala's shuddering back. Adie's heart threatened to break at the sight.

Mr Kenjins seemed unmoved by Tala's collapse and display of emotion. His gaze passed through the spectral image of Diana. If he *did* see her, he was a vastly superior actor than his daughter.

"I didn't think there was anything wrong with the article," Adie snarled.

"She called us a cult, like we were some kind of frauds." Mr Kenjins sounded so much like Billie had. Both petulant children throwing tantrums. Both far more dangerous than Adie had ever imagined.

"You aren't a fraud. You are most *definitely* the leader of a cult," Adie spat. "Just like so many other murderers."

Kenjins turned to Adie, and in that moment, she saw a fear flicker behind the cruelness of his eyes.

A fear Adie would use to her advantage, the moment she understood how the pieces fitted together and once she had the answers to the questions.

CHAPTER
SIXTEEN
ADIE

"I am the saviour of this town." Spittle flew from Kenjins' mouth as he spoke. "I am faithful to the magic *and* to Openfields."

As though he realised that he was getting too carried away, Kenjins reeled himself back in and waved at the half finished tower of skulls. The movement of his hands dismissed the brutal reality of his actions. "Their lives were meaningless until I granted them a purpose."

"You are so clichéd." Adie's skin trembled beneath her clothes, but she let out a mocking laugh. She was impressed her words showed no signs of the quivering she felt inside. "You going to say we'd be nothing without you? And what of the Goddess? Just a fiction of your own creation to justify your villainy?"

Another look flashed across his face. Unreadable, but it twitched the corners of his mouth down before he turned away from her.

"Take care of this one." He waved that hand again, toward Tala's still mourning form. "I'll keep going with Adeline." His words were clipped and as unfeeling to Billie as they had been to Adie.

Billie barely nodded, letting her grip on Adie's arm drop as she moved to stand over Tala's sobbing form. As Adie stepped past, running her hands over Tala's shoulders, she felt the strength of tensed muscles beneath the coat and material beneath.

The tears were real, of that Adie had no doubts, but there was also anger. It wound itself in the shoulders and held so much more power with the grief that Tala embraced with her tears.

"Lead the way," Mr Kenjins poked a hard finger between Adie's shoulders. "And head to the very end." His words were too relaxed, too sure of himself. And the sneer took on the mocking tone of someone who thought themselves very clever.

"And why should I?" Adie tensed her shoulders against another inevitable jab.

"Because you want to know what's down there." The jab didn't come, but the hot breath washed over her ear, stinking of arrogance and, was that blood? No. It wasn't quite right. But there was something old and rotten.

"I know what's down there," Adie replied, hating that his words had been on point.

"Good, now let's see if you're correct. Get moving." The jab came now, and an involuntary groan escaped Adie's lips as she stumbled forward a little.

"No." She righted herself and pushed her shoulders back once more.

Mr Kenjins lifted his hand and Adie's feet left the ground in time with his movements.

With a thud, she hit the wall of the cave. For a moment she stayed, pain encasing her where she hit the dirt. Then she landed hard to the floor. She was now on the opposite side of the tunnel to Billie, Tala, and the pile of skulls where they still remained.

Pain radiated through her right shoulder like a streak of lightning. It raced up her neck and smashed itself against her skull, like a police raid using a battering on a druggie's front door to gain access.

She sagged in the darkness, alone and powerless once more.

In the moments of silence, the air itself seemed to hold its breath. As if it wondered who would make the next move and from which direction it would come.

Adie used the moment to think once more.

No one resident should ever have as much strength and power as Mr Kenjins had just displayed. The transfer of power rotated weekly to avoid that *very* thing. That had always been the reason they'd been given for the change and switch of recipients.

But he had tipped his hand, and *so* early. Adie knew she could use it against him. She just had to figure out *how*. She'd never heard of the magic being used as a weapon. Not physically. The magic was based in nature; protective and life giving.

"You're a conduit." Adie knew it wasn't entirely correct, knew it was barely the tip of the iceberg to understanding, but she had to start somewhere. She hadn't read all those books for pure entertainment value, and a life of reading was a life of learning.

"A conduit who never shared the power with the town." Adie pushed as Kenjins remained silent. She searched for a trigger that might set him off once more.

"No, I'm a *leader*. I'm granted what I need to keep this town *perfect*." He strutted over to where Adie lay half bent against the wall.

"The private transfers," Adie scoffed and had she had the

physical strength to do so, she would have slapped herself in the head. "They get sent to you. And we all think we're the only one."

Adie laughed, biting her cheeks to keep back the hysteria and the exhaustion that wanted to overtake her.

"You aren't special, Adeline. Just a little orphan suitable for my purposes. You're lucky you ever got a taste of the magic. I simply took what was mine."

"You can't be a conduit, can you? The essence doesn't work for you." Adie couldn't hold the smile back. The incredulous amusement of just how far this man had gone to steal what didn't belong to him.

"Not anymore. I learned a long time ago that there is a finite amount any one person can consume." Mr Kenjins growled, scowling down at his shoes, heavy black boots splattered with mud and darker purposes.

"That makes it sound like you don't steal the magic," Adie mocked. Her head pounded and her shoulder screamed for attention. But she had to focus. No matter what, this man could never be allowed another single day to commit any more of his horrifying acts.

"He was going to take the beast with him. He spoke about the entire world needing a touch of the magic. But here, we could make our town perfect, instead of spreading it too far and too thin. I use it for the betterment of our town. Now get up and get moving."

He? What exactly was Kenjins talking about? *Who* was he talking about? Now wasn't the time to ask. She had to keep playing along. She had to finally put it all together, find those answers that kept her just that little bit disconnected from everything else. Because it had never been just the nightmare.

For some reason, she had never found the thread that linked the nightmare with the knowledge that sometimes came to her. But she knew they were linked. That knowledge filled with truths she hadn't remembered learning. The precognitive visions that she ignored more and more as the years rolled on and turned into one massive blur of sameness.

But just as the knowledge itself came to her mind, *this* information snuck through the breaking mortar between the brick wall splitting her mind.

The coffin.

Adie got up, Mr Kenjins at her back. A few more things fell into place as more mortar deteriorated, allowing bricks to fall away, causing holes in that mental block in her mind.

She hoped Tala had enough strength and wits left in her to deal with Billie. She had to trust, and that alone spiked fear within her.

"Okay, so I'm going to die, obviously. Tell me what the hell this is all about."

"Like I'm some kind of villain in those stupid movies?" Mr Kenjins snarled, just like one of those very villains.

"Well yeah, kind of. Book or movie. Either or really. But you've still got me on the tablets. I don't have contact with the magic, and the least you can do is tell me what is *actually* going on."

'Please don't know about the tablets. Don't turn around, don't show him your terrible excuse for a poker face.'

"I'm not the villain," Mr Kenjins said. "I'm the hero. I'm the reason this town didn't disappear into oblivion when the gold ran out."

"The gold in the mines ran out long before you were born. Sorry to tell ya, but you had *nothing* to do with saving this town from oblivion."

She heard his scoff behind her.

Adie had always felt so stupid around him. She'd always

been the last to know everything in Openfields. But she *wasn't* stupid. It had all been by design.

He jabbed her in the back again, keeping strong and not giving up his heinous reasons or plans. Every now and then he would prod her as her feet shuffled and she tried to slow the progress toward every nightmare, toward every hell, she had lived through since stepping foot into this town.

They were moving further through the tunnel and toward the cave. She knew she had to face the beast. She had to face the darkness and the nightmare that had been trying for so long to lead her here. And she wanted to face them, to find those answers. But still she feared the walls and the cave.

"You know what, I actually don't care." The truth of the words surprised Adie as she voiced them. Turning on her heel, she faced him. She let him see the truth in her eyes. "Whatever psycho reason you have for this, I don't care. You're nothing more than a murderer. And for what? To keep a town beautiful? You're seriously cracked."

Mr Kenjins smiled, a cruel jagged line that didn't reach his eyes. "I am not cracked."

His hand barely moved, but the power he wielded whipped against Adie's cheek, splashing her blood onto the dirty ground. "Enough of your delaying tactics."

"Why not just kill me?" Adie didn't *want* to die, but delaying walking into that cave really was all she could focus on at that moment.

"You're a conduit. Any conduit can replace the beast. They're needed to keep the magic flowing through our town. Your pills will run out and the magic will return. You will finally do your part to keep this town alive. We have harboured you and your selfishness long enough."

"You're lying." Adie smiled. "I can see it in your eyes."

"The beast will die. And you *will* take his place," Kenjins snapped.

A sound somewhere between a groan and a gasp escaped her mouth. That's what he was planning.

She would be trapped, chained to the walls and used to pass the magic through to those in Kenjin's good graces. A fear she had never before found the words for illuminated in her mind.

Caged. She would be nothing more than a caged animal.

Tears stung her eyes, and it took a moment for her to realise she actually mourned the beast's fate as much as her own.

It made no sense, though it made perfect sense in a way she didn't yet understand. The beast, the one that had *terrified* her nights for years. Why should she mourn the creature? She wanted to believe it was her own fate replacing his, but it was more than that, she knew it. She felt it.

She had let the beast suffer down here. She had turned away from the nightmare, from the fear, to protect herself in a world she had never even felt safe in.

Anger, at Mr Kenjins, at herself, built like Lego inside her, building up brick upon brick until she felt like she would gag on the emotion.

"Why do you think I'll help you?" she hissed.

His smile flickered in the light and for a moment, Adie saw teeth sharpened to points and terror dropped cold acid on her spine. Like the portrait of Dorian Gray, the darkness revealed the true nature behind Mr Kenjins' face.

"You don't remember where I found you. There have been times when I wondered." He smiled and nodded. "But *you* never did. Oh, I was so close to giving up, so near the end of hope. After two-hundred years, the magic was thinning out. It was barely keeping this town alive. But then I found his kryptonite. The beast has never retaken his human form, even then, but the ward against his mind lifted and I saw *you*. All those years, asleep in the forest."

'What is he talking about? Two-hundred years?'

He walked toward her, and she stepped back instinctively, shuffling her bare feet on the bone riddled ground.

"Cracked was too kind a word for you, wasn't it?" she scoffed.

Without warning, his hands came up and he pushed with the palms of both against her chest. There wasn't enough time to strengthen her stand and hold her ground. She stumbled backward, the breath rushing from her lungs even as she twisted mid-air to see the ground rushing up toward her.

With reflexes faster than she'd ever known, her hands were out, slamming down to the dirt floor in front of her. Her elbows locked just in time to save Adie from crashing face first into the rough ground.

Sharp rocks stung her palms, but the pain was minimal and overall irrelevant. Without moving she scanned the surroundings. She had fallen further than she'd expected and now she understood why.

Face down, arms trembling to keep herself aloft, Adie lay inside a deep recess in the ground. An imperfect circle that, as she followed its curve with her eyes, led to an end of the tunnel, a thick solid wall. The tunnel had bulged out and become more like a cavern, round and swollen. Bigger than even the town hall where it had started.

The size of the space threatened to overwhelm Adie's senses. Something felt wrong about the shape, beside the fact that there was a huge Goddess damned *cavern* beneath the town. But the thought flew away as her eyes were drawn to the dark mass across from her, stood in front of the far wall.

A noise rumbled from the darkness. It vibrated up through her hands and shook her heart in her chest.

The scene washed over her like a tidal wave. Everything was similar to what she had seen night after night in her nightmares, but not quite the same.

What was it? What was so wrong about it? The size? The shape? Both.

That was it. They were *both* wrong, because something was missing? But as the beast snuffled and snorted across the open space between it and her, her mind gave up all other thoughts.

The beast was real.

"Get up!" Mr Kenjins' nasal whine barely got through the roar of blood in Adie's ears and the thump thump thump of Adie's heart trying to break free from its rib shaped cage.

The beast snarled, and Adie closed her eyes dropping her chin to her chest, away from the nightmare in front of her. She swallowed over a raw lump in her throat.

She wanted to get up, turn away and run. With the adrenaline rushing through her, she could imagine pushing her way past Mr Kenjins. She could even imagine herself winning the chase and attack he would undoubtedly follow her with.

But what was the point? The nightmare was in her mind just as much as it surrounded her now. And if she started running, she would never be able to stop.

If Kenjins screamed at her, threatened or blustered, she didn't hear it. Not against all the thoughts in her head, swirling and building like one of those tunnel tornadoes she saw on tv shows and read about in books all set overseas. She wasn't even sure Australia had them. But there was no doubt they existed in her mind, as thoughts that never let her rest.

In the centre of it, in the calm within the chaos, she breathed a sigh of relief. More than any of the lashing winds that surrounded her, she knew she wouldn't run, even if Kenjins *wasn't* there.

She wanted to look into the face of the beast and find out the power it had over her. Why it scared her so much that she feared sleep, and what lay in the depths of those uncontrollable hours. Adie opened her eyes. With her head still bent and the distance between the two of them, it took a moment for her eyes to adjust, and her mind to register what it was that she saw.

Hooves. Stained hooves. The sight made Adie's breath catch in her throat. The hooves moved as the beast snorted and snarled once more. They were rubbed raw and bare of fur, sending up clouds of dust and dirt as they stamped into the ground, over and over again.

Adie let out a slow, icy breath between pursed lips as she stood, every inch of her body ached from being thrown against the wall earlier. Regardless, she got to her feet, and she would *not* whimper on the ground in front of an enemy she didn't even understand and knew nothing about.

Taking a deep breath, registering a few uncomfortable points on her back, undoubtedly results of being thrown against the cave wall.

She raised her head, and lifted her chin, stealing herself against the sight in front of her.

For the first time, she would face her nightmare with confidence.

CHAPTER

SEVENTEEN

ADIE

Adie tilted her head slightly as she stepped closer and focused on the beast.

It loomed large and solid, pacing as best it could, back and forth in the small alcove of the cave. The roof above him sat slightly lower than the rest of the large space. Adie hadn't noticed the ledge the beast stood upon when she first saw him. Now it was impossible to ignore the small space he was confined to.

She moved closer to the beast. Each footfall she took caused a puff of dust to rise up in small clouds, coating her bare feet, tickling the outsides of her ankles.

His hooves shuffled at the lip on the other side of the indented circle. Adie froze staring at the incomplete replication of her nightmare. His movements were limited to drastic measures by the thick chain that attached his back hooves to the wall. Even though she had seen him thousands of times, with his wild eyes and canine grin, the sight of him sent a new kind of fear that tried to liquefy her bowels. Even as the curiosity inside her rose to overshadow that fear.

She counted her breaths, each inhale and exhale, until the sound of her racing heart quietened enough for her to hear his snuffling and shuffling in front of her.

She took in every detail of the beast. Details she could never focus on in the nightmare, because her subconscious never allowed the counting. Never allowed her to gain control over her body or her mind.

The beast's matted dirty fur gave hints of a lighter bronze colour that might still exist somewhere beneath the years of captivity. She imagined how beautifully it would have shone in the bright light of day, had it been washed and brushed and taken care of. But as it was, giant clumps stuck together, matted with a black tar like ooze that Adie could *smell* even from this distance.

It was a stench that made her gag. A mixture of faeces and blood. Empathy for the beast's condition filled her, and the shock caused a hitch to her carefully measured breathing.

But a bigger shock waited. Adie lifted her head higher as she examined the beast, and she froze when her eyes met his. The fire she'd always seen, always known, in those eyes had been dulled by the film of milky cataracts. Adie stared, unable to pull her eyes away from his gaze. As she stared, the eyes cleared, just a little, just enough to *truly* see her.

And for her to see him.

The kindness and the pain radiated toward her. She ached inside for the beast who had once traumatised her nights. From the corner of her eye, something moved, something else that was never in the nightmares.

"Lisa?"

Lisa's hands were handcuffed in front of her. She knelt on the rim of the recessed floor, a cut above her brow dripped blood over her swollen left eye.

"I'm sorry, Adie." Lisa's voice slurred slightly.

It reminded Adie of those late nights when work had been harder than normal, and they had shared a bottle of wine. But the sweet smile that accompanied those nights was nowhere to be seen now.

Adie looked between Lisa and Mr Kenjins.

"Sorry for what?" Her top lip twitched as though she fought her body's urge to snarl the words. She didn't want to hear that the one person in town she'd trusted was also in on the murders.

Was Lisa involved in the control her mother and this monster had over Adie? Not the beast, but the monster who still stood behind her, his gaze boring into her back.

"Mum and I were looking into something. Something to do with you. I should have told you."

"Yes, you should have. But that's not really the issue right now." Adie's words were softer and gentler than she expected them to be. "Are you okay?"

Lisa let out a small laugh that held no humour, but she nodded in that way that never meant yes, but knowing there was nothing anyone could really do to help that.

Mr Kenjins chortled and shook his head as he pushed past Adie. "How very sweet. As if you *actually* care for each other."

Adie's face didn't hide her surprise fast enough as Mr Kenjins stood in the middle of the recess. His arms were at an angle away from his body, elbows straight turning as though it were the centre stage of a circus tent. And why not? He certainly wore the arrogance and cruelty of a ring master well enough. The term was so accurate a description Adie wondered why she hadn't thought of it before now.

He flicked his gaze from Adie, to Lisa, and back again. And in true arrogant Mr Kenjins fashion, he misread it, believing he knew all there was to know.

"I know everything in this town, Adeline. That's what

makes me a veritable God. And I control everything. Do you really think it was Lisa's idea to have you work in the library? She's been my little messenger mouse from the first day you started working there."

'Just like a villain in one of those stupid movies.'

Kenjins couldn't let any of his masterful movements be seen as someone else's choice. *'He. Adie. Remember the 'he' Mr Kenjins mentioned. Knock him off balance, he'll reveal all, he can't help himself.'*

"So, you told her to fuck me?" She raised her left eyebrow, hoping it looked nearly as impressive as Tala made it so effortlessly look.

She silently begged that Tala had taken care of Billie. Adie wouldn't mourn long over Billie's death. She was certain Billie wasn't involved in the actual murders but did that matter? She hadn't done enough against what she knew, to deserve anything less.

"I told her to do whatever was needed for the greater cause, for this town." But his eyes flicked with a dark glare toward Lisa.

"So that would be a yes, but she never told you what that entailed, did she?" Adie laughed, a small sharp noise that felt like a stranger's.

Adie felt alive and electric, the warmth inside of her comforting amid the cold air surrounding them. With it came a sense of hope, that sense of being far more than just a pawn. And there was a rumble inside her chest. But she was too tired. Too sick of feeling used and abused.

She looked to Lisa, unsure if it was a wink or Lisa trying to flick drops of blood from her eye. Adie wasn't sure it mattered now. She wasn't sure *much* mattered at all, not in the ways she thought they once had.

People had died. Human beings had been murdered. Lives that mattered.

Despite the weight in her limbs. Despite how she felt. It wasn't over until her heart stopped. There were too many questions still left unanswered. She needed to know; she needed to be sure. If she had to die to stop this nightmare coming real for anyone else, she would. But she would go to her death knowing the truth, having the answers that itched at her.

The building pressure of the town's storm pushed against her head, against every memory and thought she could remember. It relieved Adie to hear that she wasn't special. That she was just there. But she couldn't just let it happen. She couldn't let it *keep* happening.

"Who is the man?" Adie's voice quivered like a small child's. Everything ached. Her cut feet and hands, the throbbing of her shoulder and neck. But the rumble in her chest was insistent.

She was so tired.

But she couldn't stop yet.

She had to find *him*.

That had been what was missing. That was the rumble in her chest. It was him. And he called to her.

There was no man here, she couldn't hear or feel him. In her memory she saw his angled eyes and face, his anger and exhaustion. He was present in every nightmare.

But there was nothing in the cavern. No man, and no coffin.

"What man?" Mr Kenjins hissed as he stepped closer to the beast, then stopped more than two metres away. Adie looked down at his boots, at the earth that cradled them.

Had Lisa felt him? Did Lisa know? Was it a wink after all?

The beast stopped pacing and collapsed onto the ground in

a thud against dry packed rock. Adie saw its ribs through drooping skin covered in scars. A fresh wound lay across his back legs and her heart wept for his pain. He wasn't well, he wasn't the true beast of her nightmares.

The nightmares were not her own, they were the man's and the beast's. They had been calling out all these years, screaming for help.

And she had never listened. But she was listening now. She just hoped it wasn't too late to matter.

"What man?" Kenjins' shrill scream didn't force her to answer. Not like it had in the past. There was less power in his voice, though his face didn't seem to understand how his power wavered.

Adie pushed her shoulders back and moved forward, closer to the beast. Everything ached.

She wasn't sure Kenjins needed the answer more than he needed her alive. But if he wanted to kill her it would be on her terms. She might not have lived on her own terms but come hell or high water, she would die on them. She pushed the thought aside and focused on each step.

Adie walked closer to the beast, raising her arm and opening the fingers of her hand. She reached out as though to pat him. Is that what she was planning on doing? Even she wasn't entirely sure. Too many things clashed and boomed inside her mind and her chest.

Kenjins screamed for her to stop. She didn't. She kept moving forward until her hand rested on the side of the beast's marked hide.

The images swept over her in a rush.

Kenjins stood in front of the beast. Behind the two of them, man and apparent monster, a scene of beauty filled the world. There was an underground waterfall, shining with a light that bloomed beneath the froth. The waterfall roared with a clean perfection, filling Adie's ears and chest with a calmness that let her take a full breath, inflating her lungs to capacity. She had never felt such freedom and life within her before.

Yet it felt so familiar, and so safe. Safe had never been a word she had considered in relation to her life.

The walls of the cave were veined with rainbows of colour that fed into the water. Drops of the clean crisp pool flicked back and captured the colours in iridescent diamonds.

The beast stood strong and healthy, his shoulders risen and his head held high. And his eyes, oh those eyes were filled with such gentle kindness.

But as Kenjins walked closer to the beast, Adie saw the shift in them. Kindness and gentleness still permeated, but at the edges hovered a touch of fear and a little more than a bit of anger.

Kenjins' fingers were ghost white with the strength he gripped the handle of the whip. It glistened with blood on the tips of spikes that ran down half its length. With a flick of his wrist the whip lashed forward hitting the beast with a savage snap in the air that cut lines into his hide. The beast roared and tried to run toward Kenjins. Chains pulled him savagely, dragging him back toward the waterfall where he stumbled and then fell. His blood dripped into the pool of water.

"You will give me the magic." Kenjins' voice held the nasal quality Adie had always been familiar with, but with it carried a youth Adie found hard to reconcile with the old bastard she knew. "You will help me make my world perfect again."

The beast snorted a hot puff of air from his nostrils. Kenjins' face reddened and he flicked his wrist again. This time the beast had been expecting it, and he didn't roar or move. He stood still, that hot puff of air continued to echo over the rush of the waterfall.

It took a moment longer for Adie to realise Kenjins was being laughed at.

The beast paid again for his insolence.

The blood dripped from the beast's body from the open wounds a dozen whips had torn open. Kenjins caught the blood in small vials. He tucked the glass jars filled with the stolen liquid into the inside pocket of his jacket. There were enough of them for Adie to notice the bulge to his previously smooth suit.

Adie watched at first with curiosity and then horror as time sped by. It moved on from that moment of torture and theft. The waterfall's glow receded, followed by the water itself. The pit of earth grew smaller and smaller until all that remained was the recess she now stood at the edge of.

Kenjins visited over and over again. Sometimes during light moments, where sun streamed through cracks and holes in the walls and ground above them. Other times the darkness was lit solely but the pulsing veins of the earth itself.

Every visit, Kenjins held that whip in his clenched fist. His cruelty highlighted by his inconsistency. It took its toll on everything the beast had once been. No visit could be predicted. But there had only ever been one monster in these memories, and it wasn't the beast.

Sometimes the man, the real monster, would begin thrashing at the beast the moment he stepped close enough. He didn't bother asking a single question. The vials were all filled and still he would continue to flick his wrist; the smile widening across his face, his eyes gleamed with his pleasure. *Those* moments were hard for Adie to watch. But she respected the beast like a physical throb behind her heart causing a dull ache and sadness. She wanted to turn away, she wanted to run. But she knew that this creature deserved to have someone acknowledge the extent of his torture.

Time continued to speed by. People were on their knees, so many people, with their heads bent forward, over the indent in the earth. Their hands were bound behind them and Adie felt the tears slip from her eyes and down her cheeks as Kenjins' knife slit their throats. She tore her eyes away at one point and saw her own pain and sorrow mirrored within the eyes of the beast.

They both watched as Kenjins, covered in the creature's blood, whistled. He actually *whistled* as he sawed through their bones. He ruthlessly ripped the skulls from the rest of their bodies and took them one by one back into the dark tunnels with him.

Adie's breath was heavy and loud as the visions of the past slowed to the present day. There were *still* questions.

Kenjins continued to scream at her, but he had yet to take a single step closer. Adie didn't know what stopped him. In the past he had ruthlessly strutted around the entire cave, the ring master in his perverted circus.

'How long have you been here?' Adie asked in her mind, her hand still touching the coarse coat of the creature.

Each moment she lingered gave Kenjins another moment to plan or to work out what she was doing. But Adie was more than happy to bet on the unknown.

Her fingers shook where they lay against the creature's side while her heart raced. Still better than the devil standing behind her.

'He is older than he looks. He has lived more than three lifetimes when he should have only lived one.'

The words were a relief and a horror. Adie's eyes stung as they widened.

Lifetimes he had been chained and beaten, deprived of the sun and the feeling of the cool breeze brushing past and through his fur.

'I'm so sorry,' Adie projected. *'What do I do?'*

'I cannot tell you. I don't control humans or their actions.' His voice was one Adie could imagine being soothed by. A grandfather reassuring her back to sleep after a nightmare. She wanted to laugh. Not from humour, but the ironic horror of it all.

'Are you a God?' she asked, her mind spinning the pieces she had picked up over the last 24 hours into places she wasn't yet convinced fit.

Adie moved her hand, gently stroking the beast's fur. The muscles beneath her touch rippled. Whether with enjoyment or fear she wasn't sure. The voice hadn't sounded afraid in her mind, but she didn't know. The fur itself was gritty and hard beneath her faintly stinging fingers. She had forgotten about the cut from the morning. She turned her hand to see the cuts stuck together, but not quite healed.

How were they starting to heal already? The wounds had been deep, she felt it and she saw the splash of blood over her doomed breakfast.

"Get back from him. You will not touch the beast any longer." Mr Kenjins commanded, his voice touched with panic.

"If you want to stop me, then come and get me." Adie called his bluff.

Kenjins' face paled.

'Yes, child, I am a God.'

An old god. Adie nodded; she didn't need to ask.

"Who are you?" The information had overwhelmed her thoughts. Too many rushed together fighting for the front seat and she could no longer maintain the strength to ask the questions inside her mind.

Kenjins sneered at her. Of course he would think she asked him. As though he were the only important life in the cave.

CHAPTER

EIGHTEEN

ADIE

Adie looked over her shoulder and narrowed her eyes at Kenjins.

"You aren't the one that matters. You're hardly even a man," Adie said.

'*My name was lost and burnt away. But you once called me Pha. I am just one of many who keep the land, the animals, and the waters in harmony.*'

"Tell me of the man!" Kenjins' scream was so loud Adie wondered if dogs were now reacting somewhere above ground.

"Oh, would you just shut *up* already!" she yelled and turned to face him front on. Her hand no longer touched the beast but the warmth that had wrapped her up at the touch lingered on her skin.

"How dare you." Spittle flew from his mouth as though giving his indignation more emphasis.

"How dare *you*!" She screamed back. She was so sick of the pathetic little man and all the games he played, as if those other people's lives didn't matter.

But while she had lingered, searching for answers to questions she barely knew to ask, he had done exactly what she knew he would. He had pondered on words that had been spoken and actions taken since they stepped over the couch in his office.

"What do you know of the man?" His voice, still filled with arrogance, carried far less of the omniscient air he carried everywhere with him.

"Pha, his name is Pha! And he is so much more than a man."

Adie knew the truth as the words poured from her mouth. They had come from within her, not from the beast's mind, that link severed though the warmth he had lent her remained over her skin. There were many more truths that lingered in the shadows, almost knowable as their outlines became clearer.

She met the beast's eyes and tried to find a name. Because Pha, Pha wasn't the name of this beast. Her heart raced in her chest but not with the fear she'd felt all evening. Hope filled her chest and made her heart pump harder and faster in her veins.

Pha. Her mind repeated the name over and over in her mind. Fighting to latch on to one of the shadows stepping forward from the dark corner of her thoughts.

Her head filled with many versions of Pha. Each of them moved together as they changed, like those books with the stick figure in the corner that runs if you flip the pages fast enough.

She turned back to Kenjins as fear and excitement crashed within her chest. They were waves beating against the rocks of a cliff. There was too much power, raw, untrained and uncontrolled as it vibrated beneath her skin. Sparks, like a fire trying to be lit with flint and stone, leapt from the tips of her fingers.

Memory of its warm caress flooded through her veins. The fear had come later.

Adie watched the sparks and heard Kenjins' intake of breath. She lifted her head to meet his wide eyes and smiled. The pull of her expression so wide it stung the edges of her lips as the skin cracked just a little.

She raised her hand and flicked her fingers in Kenjins' direction. She watched the man, still wide eyed, screaming as he flew through the air, hitting the wall of the cavern with an audible whhhooopphh.

Adie's hand trembled as she looked at it, fighting with something inside of herself that had the urge to pick up the unconscious man and throw him again and again against the rocks until blood poured from him. As much blood as he had stolen from everyone and everything he touched.

Lassoing her fear, she reigned in the adrenaline only to look up and meet Lisa's gaze. The fear almost took over once more, but Lisa's lips trembled up at the sides, a smile as wide as she could give with the exhaustion that filled her eyes.

Adie blinked back tears as this strong woman she had adored looked back at her with pride. Lisa had never feared her, and even now there wasn't the faintest hint of it in her gaze.

Even when Adie had feared *herself*, and part of her did again, Lisa never had.

She wanted to see Kenjins' brains and body, everything that made up this cruel and vile human, shattered and broken. It could be smeared over the walls of this great cave and she would still want to find a way to hurt him *more*.

He deserved it.

He deserved so much *worse*. But *she* didn't deserve the guilt or the nightmares.

She balled one hand into a fist and focused on the beast's body as it shook beneath the other.

"I won't hurt you." But as she spoke, she realised her error. He wasn't shaking out of fear. He shook with *laughter*.

It was then she heard the second laugh, the sound of a man's weak chuckle. She couldn't face that, not yet. It was too much. In her thoughts she cheered at now understanding so much. More than what even Kenjins knew, but she couldn't face it yet.

"Did the magic turn Kenjins into this?" She spoke the words aloud. Her head pounded at the temples. Her own fate plagued her. Would the magic turn her into that dark shadow she had run from every time she caught a glimpse of it as it lurked in the periphery of her vision?

'*No, the magic is neither good nor bad. His nature always held this possibility. It is the same possibility found in all living things, not just humanity.*'

"He doesn't see the man. I haven't seen the man since we got here. In my nightmares, I thought you two were the same, but you aren't, are you?"

She sensed the head shake and while she wanted to ask more, she could feel his breathing more laboured beneath her hand. Her fingers trembled and tears built in her eyes.

"Is he dead? The man?" Adie looked around as though she may have simply missed him sitting casually against one of the walls of the cave. "Where is he?"

'*I am not done yet. I have something for you.*' Exhaustion washed over her in a wave, and she wanted nothing more than to curl up, listening to the grandfatherly voice as it told her story after story until she fell asleep.

"For me?" Her voice slurred at the edges.

'*A memory.*'

Adie swallowed over the lump in her throat as her mind

was taken away once more from the here and the now. This time, there was no cave.

Adie lay down on a slightly raised patch of grass, leaves and the odd twig. She looked up. Smiling, she caught snatches of the blue sky as it played peek-a-boo between the gaps of leaves in the forest canopy.

"Why must I go to sleep, Pha?" she asked as the man scooped her up in his arms as though she weighed nothing more than a discarded feather of a parrot.

"Because there is danger, and I must find Marcell." His arms were strong and his skin tanned golden. Despite his apparent strength, he was gentle and kind as he lay her down in a space too small for her liking. "I must make sure we are all safe. But you must sleep until I return."

Adie closed her eyes and felt the warmth of the sun leave her skin. She shivered as darkness crept over the light that pierced through her closed eyelids. Her breath caught and tears slipped over her temples and were lost in her hair. She opened her eyes and took in the smooth grey cement slab that now covered her. Pinpricks of light slipped through irregular gaps where the cover and the sides didn't quite meet.

She reached up with her hands and touched the cement. They were small hands, that of a child. The cement wasn't nearly as smooth as it had first appeared. She brushed her hands over the cover. The bumps and imperfections tore at the pads of her fingers, leaving them sore and bleeding. A small sob escaped her young lips as she opened them to call out to Pha. But before the word, the plea, could leave her mouth, the darkness became complete, and pulled her out of that small space and away from the memory.

The images faded, and Adie returned to her present-day self.

"I was entombed?" She didn't want to ask, but she had to. She had to know what had happened to her.

'Yes. For as long as I could keep you. For your safety'.

"Why?"

'To stop you from being stuck here as well. Will you release me, child?'

"Yes." She nodded, trying to force herself to think about something other than that coffin.

Squaring her shoulders, Adie stood tall against her fear. She didn't want to live like this, drained of all her power, trapped. The word was a lump in her throat.

She had lived years in the world above ground, where her claustrophobia raised its head at the most inconvenient of times, but she could almost ignore it most of the time. Living down here, she would never be able to escape it. And it sure wouldn't be living.

But could she live with herself if she turned and left him here for even longer than what he'd already suffered?

She didn't think so.

But the beast wasn't Pha. Pha was the man who had tried so hard to keep her safe. Where was he now? Her mind couldn't quite put the pieces together, even now with so many more pieces to work with, she still couldn't see the full picture. The beast was separate to Pha.

'Is it true? Any conduit can release you?'

'No.' She sensed the chuckle.

'But I can?'

'Yes.'

Adie shook her head as she spread her arms wide to encompass the death of the landscape around her, and Kenjins who pulled himself up to lean against the pulsing wall.

"Are you Marcell?" she asked. The beast lowered his head in a deep nod. "Did Pha die? Was he here before you? Is that why you have his memories? Why you can pass them back to me?" She couldn't hold back the need to know. Not any longer. She would do what was required, the thing that only *she* could do. But she had to know. What happened to her Pha?

'*You haven't yet figure it out?*'

"No. I guess I'm not as smart as you thought. I'm no more deserving of the magic than any of us."

'*It was never about deserving. The magic and the powers will be able to go where they belong if you release me.*'

"Okay." She could have sworn she heard the crack of her heart inside her chest. Her questions would never be answered.

'*Oh, you will know everything soon enough.*'

"What do I do?" she asked, speaking out loud, her voice quavering only a little. He hadn't lied as far as she knew, but still she doubted her curiosity would ever be sated.

However, she wouldn't go back on her word. Perhaps she would get used to the cold that made her tremble.

'*Step toward the wall. You must see beyond it.*'

Her feet fought against the movement. It was one thing to be dragged into her nightmare, but this would be different. This time she would be *willingly* stepping inside of the darkness, claiming that very nightmare as her own.

Her mouth was dry, too dry. The cold seeping once more beneath the warmth Marcell had provided her earlier. She failed to swallow over the lump in her throat and instead left a puff of cold mist out of her mouth.

Adie would sacrifice her existence. She would suffer to give him relief, she would suffer this price for exchange of his freedom. She would pay the retribution for all he had endured. It wasn't something she'd ever thought she could *possibly* do. She'd never thought of herself as selfish, but selfless wasn't on her cards either. A life she would now never experience flashed across her mind, similar to the images she'd seen of Pha's life. No, Marcell's life. *Friends and family, a Christmas tree she could lie beneath and fall asleep under, a dog snoring on her feet, dinners in restaurants where no one knew her name.* All these possibilities existed for the briefest of moments, before they were gone an instant later.

But she knew while these possibilities had never really been any closer, she was now taking away any hope that one day they *might* be.

She stepped again, pushing those wishful images aside.

The air tingled against her skin and the world warped around her. Turning back toward where she had just been, she watched the beast as his feet clawed at the dirt floor, kicking up dust as he shook his head and kept stamping.

With another cold ribbon of breath streaming from her mouth, she turned back and gasped. In front of her the man, Pha, hung limp against the wall. Around him were human statues. The statues didn't face him. Instead, they faced the coffin that sat in the middle of the space.

Her coffin.

NINETEEN

ADIE

That's what had been missing. With everything else going on, she had forgotten the statues.

Adie took them in, one by one, pressed around the edges of the cavern. One ring, pressed shoulder to shoulder with their backs against the cavern's walls. But there were now more than could fit, creating layers, the inner ring with their backs to the outer rings' fronts.

Some of the statues were crumbling, collapsing in large chunks around the newer ones.

How had she ever blocked them from her memory? A glowing red throbbed behind the black stone within each and every statue. Even those that had crumbled continued to pulse with the same ruby red. And all of them beat in time with the veined colours in the walls.

"Are they the hearts of the dead? The hearts of the bones and skulls that lay out there?"

"Yes." Pha's voice was gravel scraped back with metal. But even with the unused pain lingering there, Adie couldn't deny it being the same she'd heard in her mind.

The links she'd put together in her mind as she and Marcell spoke connected with bright white clarity. She hadn't been conversing with Marcell. Marcell was Pha's familiar, a fact Adie knew without ever remembering being told. He'd been a channel for Adie, allowing her to open her mind enough to speak to the man.

But he wasn't just a man, despite what she saw in front of her. Adie knew all about looks being deceiving.

Pha looked like nothing more than a frail, limp excuse for a man who had used up all of his living. With hair like ragged seaweed, dirt and stubble on his face bled together with no definitive mark of where one stopped and the other began. He was the personification of the surprise character in every pirate movie she had ever watched as a kid. That starved, half-drowned person who had been chained below, in the prison of the ship, the entire time the other characters acted out their own adventure.

But Pha's eyes were alive and strong. They held a darkness that filled Adie with safety but also the steel look that promised pain and revenge on those who had wronged him.

She shivered.

They had been speaking through the beast, but now they looked at each other face to face. Adie's heart pounded in her chest. In the vision Marcell had sent her. No, *Pha* had sent it. In that vision, Pha looked nothing like he did now.

"You, you're Pha," Adie dry swallowed as best she could over another lump in her throat. "My father."

"Yes, Child. I am."

"Why?" Adie's voice cracked on the question.

"Why?" He tilted his head and light seemed to radiate from his movement.

"Why are the hearts in the statues?" She couldn't ask what she truly wanted to. But this question needed to be answered as well, and for now that would have to be enough.

Pha coughed, thick and heavy as though his lungs were giving out on him. He took two deep breaths, his face contorted in pain.

Adie gave him the space to take the time he needed.

"*He* learned," Pha finally began, "that once the waters were gone, he needed human blood and the power of the triangle to keep us here. To keep us alive. I brought the souls in here with me so he could not find a way to abuse *them* as well."

"And my... my coffin as well?" It wasn't quite the question she'd wanted to ask, but it might bring enough courage for her to now ask it.

"Not a coffin, but a stasis chamber. I did not imagine you would be trapped in there all these years. I felt it when he touched the blood against the lid. He woke you. But time stole your memories. I took the chamber before he could return for it."

She'd heard enough, *seen* enough. She had seen too much. Her fill of horrors had well and truly overflowed. Although she knew they were nowhere near finished yet. Because he was still trapped, and she, she wasn't.

"Can he see us?" Adie asked as she looked over her shoulder to see Kenjins pulling himself to his feet, using the wall to help him.

She turned back and stared at Pha. Waiting for his answer.

He gave the smallest shake of his head.

"Why can I see you? Why can I see them?" Adie jerked her chin toward some of the more crumbled statues.

"You see everything because you have my blood."

"The blood of the Gods," Adie mumbled as this reality wrapped fingers around her mind, gentle for now. "I'm a Child of the Gods. But who was my mother? Another God, or a human?" Adie couldn't even be sure she asked the questions of the man still shackled to the wall.

But Pha smiled and nodded his head as though having expected the query. And why shouldn't he? They were questions anyone thrown into such a reality of strangeness would ask, surely.

She could see it now, even behind the stretched skin and dirt, the familial relationship between the two of them. Features she had previously only ever seen in the mirror.

She had hoped, and imagined in her more ambitious moments, of finding someone reflecting back her features, once she escaped this town. But she had never let her mind dream about finding them here. Let alone finding them here, beneath her feet, literally all this time.

"How long had it been? Since you, since you put me to sleep? Since Kenjins trapped you?"

"Two-hundred years. Or there about. It's hard to keep track of time when light and liberty have been kept from you."

Almost two-hundred years she'd been asleep.

Two-hundred years he'd been abused. Tortured by Kenjins.

It was all too big. Too much for her to take in and really focus on. Her mind seemed ready to split open with all the lies revealed. That angry fire within her cracked and spat as it grew large and wild.

She focused instead on the man in front of her. Tears burned her eyes as she blinked them back. This hardly seemed the meeting of any childhood fantasies. Of finding family and a sense of belonging somewhere.

But this was her father!

With a shaky breath, Adie forced her eyes away from Pha and looked again at the statues.

"Are any of them still there? Can they go back?"

"They are there, but trapped just as I am. They are not able to be returned to their old lives, but when I am free, they will also be free to move forward." He shook his head as he spoke, such heavy weighted sadness in the movement, in the deep rumble of his voice.

"What do you need?" Adie wasn't sad; she was *well* past that. She felt a wild fury, and for once she no longer cared how angry she was, or how close the darkness inside of her was to coming out.

The fire that burned felt right for the first time.

Her hands remained still, her heartbeat had eased to a steady and even pace.

"Water." The word was barely audible, his head lolled forward as though the minimal conversation had drained what little energy he had.

"Oh, of course." And as simple as that, the darkness receded just enough for her humanity to remember the pain and imprisonment this God had suffered. Her father had suffered.

His bones were so close to his paper-thin skin. She could see each rib and every breath. She found the water bottle in her backpack and pulled it out. Unscrewing the top, she held the metal cylinder up to his mouth.

Pha gulped it down and the hearts surrounding him throbbed a little brighter.

"Where did she go?" Kenjins shrill voice interrupted Adie's joy.

Her and Pha turned their attention toward the raging nasal fury of Kenjins as he beat clenched fists into the body of the beast.

"I can stop him." Adie wasn't certain she could, but she felt the power surge beneath her skin, and she suspected she was stronger than she knew.

The fire returned in full force, and she was looking to burn with some revenge.

"No." Pha's voice still sounded like a rusting robot, but there was a hint of strength now. "Marcell is no longer in pain; I have removed him from that body."

"I'm so sorry."

"He is my guardian, my conduit, and my familiar. Above all, he is my friend." The God's voice was thick and slow, no hint of the fire that was burning hotter and hotter inside of Adie's chest.

Adie shuddered.

He couldn't be ready to give up the fight. Her sacrifice could not be in vain. Adie would not leave him here while he still had breath in his lungs. Time pressed against her. "How do I release you?"

"You already have. All I needed was one of the triangles to be destroyed, and water in my veins again." His arms fell limp beside his body and Adie ran to help him as he pushed against the wall to help him stand up.

She noticed the marks on his skin then. They were the identical copy to the whip lashed scars that were on Marcell.

"How do I get you out before I take your place?"

"Take my place?"

"Yes." Adie forced her shoulders back and gave her head a strong single nod up and down. Her insides were a contradiction of roaring power and quivering fear. But this was her father, and she would not give into the fear, not now.

"Oh, my sweet child." He chuckled, a container of pebbles being shaken by children's hands, and he pressed the rough skin of his palm against her cheek. "You came to me; you helped release me and all this time thinking you would have to replace me?"

She nodded, unable to speak over the lump in her throat.

"No, this town needs to end. I might have been caged, but I still have my claws. I can send you away, you do not have to see any more horrors."

"No!" Weight sloughed from her shoulders. She had given up on the fantasies of a future, of a life outside of tonight, outside of the cave, outside of Openfields.

A spark reignited inside her chest, and the quivering fear was pushed away. She would stop the nightmares of this town, and she would find a way to stop the arsehole himself, somehow.

She would not turn away, tail between her legs. Not now, not ever again.

She would see this end and know first-hand what happened to the town she loved and hated in equal measures. Her life was not as important as that. But she would fight and hope for life. If she lived, she would hunt down the answers to the questions that continued to scream for answers.

"Ah," he cried out as his legs buckled beneath him.

Adie grabbed the man, the God, her *father*, to stop him collapsing completely to the ground. As he leaned on Adie, pulling himself back onto his feet, he gasped again. She felt him inside her mind. All the horrors her life had been since she'd felt the magic, since she became a conduit. The fear that wrapped around her when Kenjins held her down and siphoned the magic from her body. The private transfer he said was normal, he said was part of the *Goddess's* wishes.

"I'm sorry, child. So very sorry. My gifts were never meant to torture you." Pha's voice cracked with fresh pain.

"I never understood what was happening. I never understood the nightmares you sent me; what you were trying to tell me. But I'm here now and together we can end this."

They shared a smile and Adie gasped as the God glowed, a shimmering golden aura around him.

"You really are a God, glowing and all, just as important as all the stories tell." Adie stared as the frail and weathered man in front of her seemed far less of either.

"You have an aura yourself. You glow with the strength of your power." His head cocked as he stared at her. Thoughts danced behind his studying eyes. Adie wasn't sure she ever wanted to know what those thoughts were.

"I have strength and power?" She smiled, though her voice betrayed her as it leaked the awe and doubt of herself.

"Yes. You have far more than you realised. You have survived horrors, and a misbelief that you are nothing, that you are unimportant. But importance doesn't come from our blood or lineage. Importance comes from our actions."

Adie tucked the information away. It was too heavy for her to think about now. She scanned the cavern that could not see her.

"He has Lisa."

Pha turned and faced where Adie's eyes rested on the broken form of her lover. "Then come. It is time for this to end."

He grabbed her hand, and she felt the fury and the fire burning within him. She felt relief and an angry pleasure as his fire helped to build her own higher, with greater heat and intensity.

"Concentrate on the veil."

She saw the glimmer of the veil waver in front of Kenjins as he kicked Lisa to the dusty ground.

"Where's the man? Where did that little *bitch* orphan go?" Kenjins' voice was shrill as he asked again.

The fire continued to build within both father and daughter. The veil wavered and crackled with the pressure of heat against the cool of the hell beyond it.

Kenjins grabbed a fistful of Lisa's hair, yanking her back to her knees.

She yelped in pain.

"Answer me, slut."

"You really should have done your homework before you fucked around with a God." Lisa looked up at Kenjins. Her smile was little more than her lips curling back from blood covered teeth.

Her eyes left Kenjins and met Adie's through the veil.

Adie sucked in a breath. Lisa could see her, see *them*. Lisa winked before turning back to Kenjins and spitting a bloody wad of saliva at him.

Before Kenjins could retaliate, Adie squeezed her father's fingers hard. His return squeeze was all she needed.

The veil cracked open in a rain of frozen shards. The cold blasted away from them, their heat raging and roaring through the cavern. Adie and her father stepped toward the shimmering air between their reality and the ravaged world.

She controlled the fire once more. She felt the darkness, dove into it and gasped for breath.

Her father's hand gripped her fingers tightly, not letting go but neither controlling nor demanding she control what raged within her.

Kenjins turned and stared. His face a drooping mask of confusion. Ice shards melted around the man that caused such rage within him.

And there the man stood, hand clasped with the very orphan bitch Kenjins had so recently been screaming about.

CHAPTER

TWENTY

ADIE

The confusion didn't last long, nor did it make him release Lisa's hair. He turned and dragged her along behind him. Her head now pulled so far forward, she had no choice but to bend her neck and look down at the dusty ground he dragged her over. She struggled to keep up on her knees.

What Adie wouldn't give to meet Lisa's eyes again. To let her know it would be okay, that she would save her. Adie *would* rescue Lisa, the way Lisa had been rescuing Adie for all these years.

But the grip Kenjins had on her kept Lisa's face turned downward.

Adie studied the woman. Her shirt had been ripped open and bright, fresh blood soaked through the tears into the material that remained. It took a moment to realise what had shredded her clothing and her flesh beneath just as equally. Adie's attention had been so caught up on Lisa herself, she hadn't noticed what Kenjins carried in his other hand. Not until he raised it once more over Lisa's sagging back. That bloody spiked whip. Kenjins held it up, ready for another strike against Lisa's already torn flesh. It had just as much effect as pointing a gun to Lisa's temple.

The rage it inspired made Adie's lungs burn with the heat boiling within her.

Lisa looked up, Kenjins hand now untangled from her dirty and knotted hair.

Adie could see better in the dark than she did previously.

And as clearly as she met Lisa's eyes, she could also see glistening beads of aorta blood dripping from the spikes and the black leather between them.

The blood, so fresh shifted as the whip moved higher in the air. The drops landed with thunks on to the thirsty earth.

The ground soaked it up greedily.

Lisa turned her eyes from Adie and looked directly up at the spikes that drew closer to her.

Kenjins grabbed her hair again, pulled her head back further, and forced Lisa's body to arch upward to meet the whip that whistled through the air and hit Lisa's chest with a meaty thud.

"No!" Adie screamed and stepped forward. But her progress was stopped by the grip of Pha's fingers in her own.

Lisa laughed. Adie recognised the hysteria in the sound. Pain lanced Adie's chest as she failed to stop more pain being inflicted upon Lisa.

She looked to Marcell, now still and lifeless, and then to Pha. She gasped as she saw the fresh cut across Pha's chest. The long line gaped as blood welled along the top of the raised flesh, cut open by a whips lash.

"You're linked with Lisa?"

"Yes."

"How? Why?"

"Lisa is hiding in her mind. Marcell's body was about to give out. I transferred him to share with Lisa. We are linked mentally, but the bodies we inhabit are influenced by that. Hurt one, the other hurts, too." The gravelled voice sounded smoother, water and purpose having softened the friction between stone and metal.

"Move away from her." Kenjins' voice rose as it echoed with force across the swollen cavern.

"He has used up the last of the magic he has taken into himself. He never learned moderation." Pha mumbled. Adie picked up traces of a dark laugh beneath.

Kenjins laughed in turn and lowered his arm. Lisa cringed, but her eyes locked onto Kenjins before shifting back to Adie's.

Lisa was still there, but behind her eyes lingered something darker and far older.

Adie smiled, touched her fingers to her lips and blew her fiery breath on them.

Kenjins screamed. Lisa broke through and sobbed.

All eyes in the cave watched as Kenjins' arm was wrenched from his body in a thick tearing sound before it flew across the cave, the whip handle still clenched in his fingers. The blood was warm and hissed against the coldness that surrounded them. The arm and whip landed by Adie's feet. She stepped on the wrist until the inert fingers released their grip on the leather handle.

Clutching uselessly at the stump left where his arm had once been, Kenjins screamed abuse and worthless threats between agonised sobs.

Pha let go of Adie's hands and stepped toward Kenjins. The very air vibrated with Pha's fury and pure intent of revenge. A new scream of terror, or pain and horror ripped from Kenjins' throat and bounced against the rock walls.

"Mercy." Kenjins words came out on the next scream as his hand was pulled from his body. His eyes widened his wrist ended in tendrils of frayed nerves quickly covered with blood.

"My daughter was too kind, taking an entire limb in one go."

"Mercy, Pha." Kenjins sobbed as he fell to his knees. Another screamed ripped from his throat as he tried to catch himself falling further, and pressed the stub at the end of his arm into the ground beneath him.

"The same mercy you showed Me?" Another sound of tearing flesh filled the cave as Kenjins lost his right leg above the knee. "The same mercy you showed Marcell, or my daughter?"

Adie watched as pleasure danced with her darkness. Kenjins' body was slowly and painfully pulled apart. His threats and abuse turned quickly into more screams of mercy. The last of his other arm joined the one still whole on the ground at Adie's feet. Three pieces, crushed and broken before having been discarded.

Tears streamed down Mr Kenjins' face, wet and thick. "Please, I only ever did what was needed. And not for me. It was for the town. I only ever did what the town needed. What they all needed to survive. They were insatiable and they kept demanding more and more. I had no choice."

Pha snarled as he stepped closer, towering over the bleeding stump that remained of Kenjins. "You had choices. A plethora of them."

Kenjins' remaining leg snapped beneath him, bones breaking and piercing through flesh, before being ripped from his body with invisible forces he couldn't fight against.

His screams echoed and bounced around them.

The God grew in size and light as his anger and revenge rebelled against his years of captivity. Behind him, the statues crashed to the ground, throbbing orbs of red rushed at high speed out of the cavern. Some rocketed down the tunnel, while others buried themselves directly into the ground above them, creating light shafts and breezes of fresh air.

The darkness faded. Adie no longer needed to tap into her powers to see the reality of the surrounding decay.

Her heart broke just as her anger built, as she thought about the difference between the desolation down here and the stolen beauty that continued above. But not for long. She would not allow the magic to be stolen and used any longer.

"Adie."

The word, her name, brought Adie back from the darkness. She had been mesmerised by seeing, and feeling, the pain and the anger Kenjins suffered. It wasn't enough, it would *never* be enough, but it would have to do.

"Adie, please help me." That voice. Adie's memory of that *beautiful* voice finally snapped the hold the darkness had taken control of within her.

Adie turned away from the torture and breathed out a whimper. It was the happiest sob she could remember expressing, the perfect sound to her relief at seeing Tala trying to lift Lisa's unconscious body from the ground.

"Help me with her, she's barely breathing." Something new burned behind Tala's eyes.

Maybe not new. Maybe it had always been there, and it was Adie's sight that was now new. Either way, it made Adie smile. She knew she could trust this strange but beautiful woman. Adie saw more than what her human sight had been forcibly limited to.

"Give her to me." Adie lifted Lisa into her arms, smiling at how easy it was to take her weight.

It was a heady sensation. One that she knew she had to be careful with. Power and strength did not come without their own issues and struggles. She had no idea of her true power or strength. No idea of the potential within her. But for the first time since she could remember, she looked forward to finding out.

Tala helped wrap Lisa's arms around Adie's neck, making sure she wouldn't fall with any sudden movement on Adie's behalf.

"We must leave now," Pha said, his breath heavy as though he had just finished the Olympic triathlon.

Kenjins' sobs continued to echo around the cave.

Pha's skin was golden, his bones no longer visible, but he was still far too thin and frail to look upon.

"Stay close, Tala." Adie moved to follow her father, but he turned, eyes sad and frightening.

"She cannot join us."

"Fuck you!" Would Adie be punished for swearing at her God? Would her father punish her? What punishment was there for the Children of the Gods? She needed to tread carefully. "She comes with me."

"She cannot." Pha seemed unconcerned about Adie's outrage.

The disregard only fuelled the anger inside her. Adie shifted closer to Tala, until their shoulders brushed together.

"If it weren't for her, I wouldn't have even found my way down here. I wouldn't have known a thing about it even if I *had* finally managed to stumble my way here." Well, so much for treading carefully. "So, I don't give a shit what you say. Tala is coming with us."

"Not me, Adie. He knows me; he wouldn't leave me here, even if I *had* done something to deserve being abandoned." Tala spoke quietly, but that did nothing to lessen the impact of her words.

"He knows you? What the hell?!" Adie snarled; her defence of Tala dropped in an instant as she lashed her words out angrily.

"I'm a Child of the Gods. He can feel my blood, just as I can feel his, and yours. We all have eyes that bear witness to the history of our people."

"You knew this whole time? You *knew* I was one of The Children?"

"Yes, and no." Tala grimaced. "I wasn't sure. Diana was better at that part. Yes, I could feel your blood. It called to me the way blood of The Children call to each other. But I couldn't be sure if it was some of the *stolen* blood, or even those stupid bloody pills."

Adie blinked rapidly, trying to rush through some kind of processing. They both spoke so simply, as though everything they said had always been so obvious. But then the other meaning to Tala's words, the things she *didn't* say, sank in.

"Wait, you want me to leave Lisa? No, I'm not leaving her here. She deserved better," Adie snarled.

"She's gone." Pha's voice was sad, but there was no arguing with it. "Marcell is keeping us both alive. The final act and power of a familiar. It is his right to go out as he desires. He is sharing his life essence with me. I have asked him to save himself, but he will not. It will take all our strength combined to get us out of the cave."

"Why can't we go the way we came?"

"Listen to the earth, Adeline. Listen to the call and rumble of the world above us."

Adie couldn't bring herself to close her eyes, but she looked down at the dusty earth and tried to do as Pha suggested. It didn't take long. The earth was rejoicing, the magic was free and the two danced together, weaving around each other as though they were attached to a maypole.

"The earth is happy."

"Yes." Pha spoke patiently but there was a panic hidden

deep beneath the calm. "But push beyond the emotion, push to see and feel it *all*."

"You can do this." Tala's hand squeezed Adie's shoulder.

Adie did close her eyes this time, and the world rushed toward her. The world that was taking back its magic. The souls had pushed through the earth, creating instability and chaos.

"It's falling apart."

"Yes. So, we have to go another way. And we don't have the power or strength to bring her as well. We simply aren't strong enough."

"I'm strong. Stronger than you think. We can do this."

"No, we can't." It wasn't Pha who answered, but Tala. Her words hit Adie in the chest, but she believed the truth in them and her heart broke.

"Lisa." Adie sobbed and held the small frame tightly to her chest.

"She fought against him. She revealed nothing," Pha spoke softly, a gentle caress to soothe over Adie's pain. "She could see me, clear and complete. She had received a lot of my blood offerings, though I know she had no idea of the truth behind the magic. She died well."

If Adie thought she would be punished for swearing at a God, her thoughts of slamming a fist into his face would undoubtedly be frowned upon. But no one ever died well. Death wasn't something people did well or poorly. This death, the way she had died, was something Lisa hadn't deserved.

"Diana will guide her." Tala's hand was gentle and warm on Adie's skin. The touch made the tears flow. Adie's head fell forward as she looked at Lisa in her arms and finally noticed what the others must have already realised. Lisa's chest had stopped moving in and out.

Laying Lisa's body down on the desolate and dusty ground

hurt deep within her. But she couldn't deny the relief that also washed over Adie. The decision had been made. Lisa's life had been given in its own way, in *Lisa's* way, to save them.

Adie's life had been filled with fear of the darkness inside of her, but now she saw there was also light. A lightness that more importantly, she could feel. The relief was the taste of fresh air on her skin.

Inside there was still a breakable heart that remained soft, warm, and caring.

"I did love her."

"I know." Tala helped Adie back to her feet and together, fingers entwined, they turned toward Pha.

"We must go." His voice still held a little of the rough and raw edges, but his authority was absolute.

Kenjins remained a limbless stump in the dirt, his whimpers gurgled. All but ignored by the others. But Adie couldn't ignore the way the man continued to linger. The sounds travelling up her spine and making something inside of her twitch.

"He's still alive?" Adie asked.

"Yes." Pha nodded. "The stolen blood is keeping him alive. He will linger until the last of the magic in him is returned to the earth.

Adie couldn't help the sadistic smile that spread across her face as she saw the moment Kenjins registered that he would be left behind to linger in agony before the mercy of death would be granted. His screams resumed and doubled. A blood curdling horror would be his fate. Despite Kenjins deserving his fate, Adie couldn't reconcile the pleasure she had taken at seeing Pha enact his revenge. He did deserve it, there was no doubt about that, but Adie still felt nausea in her belly at anyone suffering so horrifically. Even Kenjins.

"Close your eyes," Pha commanded. He looked at Adie and

the softness at the edges of his eyes was enough for Adie to push down the bile wanting to rise up her throat.

She did as commanded, closing her eyes and held tighter to Tala's hand.

Behind her eyes she saw Lisa's limp body, cut and bruised and damaged at the hand of their own Town Leader. She saw the waterfall he had murdered and the piles of skulls, each representing a life that was stolen and used against its will, even in death.

She wondered if she would ever close her eyes and not see these things, waiting in the darkness to find her.

"Will it hurt?" Her voice was a whisper of breath.

"Did it?" Tala's hand was gentle on her cheek.

Carefully, Adie opened her eyes and turned to look over at the town as it rumbled in the darkness, shapes darkening against the dawning sky.

They stood, the three of them, near the edge of Dedo Rock, alone in the greying darkness.

They could all feel the beginning of the new day. And they could all smell it.

CHAPTER
TWENTY-ONE
ADIE

A soft breeze picked up. Adie shivered in delight at the feel of it brushing against her skin. Gingerly she sat down, the aches and pains of the day catching up, felt even through the adrenaline of the night.

Swinging her legs over the ledge of the rock, she breathed in the fresh air.

The man, the God, her father, remained standing. His eyes and concentration focused almost laser-like on the Town Hall.

Adie watched, her fingers spreading out as they pressed against her thighs, only for her to pull them back to a fist and repeat the sensation. It felt good below the hem of her shorts. It was something tangible. Something that reminded her that she still lived. That none of this had been her own subconsciousness twisting and forming a new dream while still trapped in that old living nightmare.

Tala sat down beside Adie, their shoulders brushing against each other. She took Adie's other hand in both of her own. The touch made Adie's eyes water, but she gulped the fresh air, forcing back the tears.

"We don't have to stay, or to watch."

"I think it's what *I* need to do." Adie leaned heavily against Tala's body.

"Then that's what we'll do." Tala's breath brushed Adie's hair, and she smiled sadly as she noticed the darkness that lay over the town begin to break apart, patches of light bursting through the dense cloud.

The rumbling from below them built in intensity until, with a crack like thunder that made Adie jump a little, the Town Hall collapsed in on itself. The entire building had been nothing more than a house of cards, and now it had been toppled.

Adie couldn't seem to stop her mind from hearing the screams of the people in the town. But she knew those screams were imaginary, and she knew that with certainty as the wind blew in the wrong direction.

But still, she knew the screams would come if they weren't already filling the town already.

They would be woken by the earth's tremors.

But there wouldn't be any time for them to take in the extent of the danger before it was too late.

She hoped, at least for some, that they would never wake. They would never experience the horror of *knowing* what was to come.

Those would be the lucky ones.

The town, building by building, collapsed in on itself, crushing the barren waterfall beneath them. They had stolen its life and beauty for the themselves. It only seemed right that it would end with it all being returned.

Adie didn't know how many of them knew the truth of the magic. She should care. The innocent ones were dying for the sins of the rest. But she was too broken to spare a thought for any of them right now. Perhaps she would care in the morning, or next week, maybe next month, or even next year. But she was too depleted of emotions and had nothing left in her for what she should be doing or feeling. Then again, maybe she would never care. Not a single name came to mind as she worried about the innocents. They all knew, at some level, that things weren't right. But they craved the magic, the power of that drug more than they wanted to know the truth.

The noises finally ceased to reach them as the sun completed its rise above the horizon.

"It needs to burn, Adie," Pha spoke as though the words were being pulled without consent from his mouth.

"Okay." Adie nodded, wondering at the tone and what it meant.

"Adie?" The force of her name was softened by the care around the edges.

Adie looked up to meet Pha's eyes.

His eyebrows raised, waiting for her to understand what she had failed to grasp thus far.

When clarity alighted upon her, Adie's mouth dropped open.

She shook her head, demanding she be spared *this* horror on top of everything else. But his eyes pierced through her and gave her no such relief.

She had the power. He'd given it to her. Given back what had been stolen. In her mind, the last few bricks of the wall collapsed, and the world opened to her once more.

She was one of The Children of the Gods.

Tala's hand settled over Adie's hand where her fingers had stopped curling in and out against her skin.

"You've got this." Tala's deep voice soothed the hardest of the edges around Adie's panic.

"Okay," she said, nodding. "Okay, okay." She repeated the word as though they were blocks building up her confidence.

Taking a deep breath, she focused on where the library had been and sent her energy there. It was pulled from her, not unlike the night her magic had been siphoned by Kenjins. But this time there was no horror or theft. She gave the magic *willingly*. She felt the soft tug and tear from inside of her. A heavy weight pulled at her arms and her heart. There would be nothing left to remember Lisa. No books with her handwritten chicken scratch in the margins, no colourful decorations she made in her spare time, during those nights alone in the house with the stained carpet.

It was necessary, but it didn't make the feeling any lighter or make any of this any easier.

She knew the flame existed. It was a part of her, and it came to life under her guidance. It snatched at debris, teasing and tormenting items nearby until it finally caught onto enough of the town to roar.

It took a while longer before the smoke and the fire were visible from where the three of them watched. The magic felt right and pure, for the first time in her life.

Her shoulders dropped, her energy spent, and a small hiss escaped her lips.

Tala's hands moved over Adie's skin, and soon the pains and aches eased.

"Is that better?" Tala murmured.

"Mmmhhhmmm," Adie barely managed to mutter as she leaned her head against Tala's shoulder. "Thank you."

"You're welcome." Tala's voice a gentle whisper.

"You have questions?" Pha's voice was soft and tender.

Adie had almost forgotten he stood behind them.

Her father.

The idea was beyond surreal, but that, like the regret for the innocent lives lost, was a problem for another day.

She looked up, forcing her tired eyes open once more. Her

heart sank as their eyes met, and she saw the truth in his sadness.

"I can't save you," she said. The pain and the weight gripped her insides too tightly. She couldn't breathe, she couldn't find the words or the time to know what they were like together, what they could be as a family.

"No." He shook his head slowly, but his eyes remained locked onto hers. "Marcell has held on long enough."

"All these years, I could have helped you. And it was all for nothing."

"It was for *everything*." Pha smiled. "But now is my time."

"You're dying." Adie didn't bother holding back her sobs. She wasn't sure she would have been able to, even if she'd wanted to try.

It had all been in vain.

Dr Simms was dead. So were Lisa and Diana. The bones of hundreds of others who had been killed for Kenjins' and his power-hungry greed.

What had they *actually* achieved?

"I am, as must all things when their day arrives. But I'm dying free, thanks to you."

"How can you die? You're a God."

"It is merely a word, an old word. We are but a race. A race that is dying. We once populated this world in greater numbers than humans. But we didn't know how to fear, or how to be cautious, until it was too late. Now, I know fear, and I do fear that there are now less of us than there have ever been. And with men hungry for power, more of us die, more of us are used for what is our nature."

"More of your people are trapped?" Despite the exhaustion, this realisation sparked some unknown depth of energy that lingered inside of her. She lifted her head from Tala's shoulder and straightened her back.

"*Our* people, daughter." He nodded, his eyes dimming as he sat down, taking deep breaths as he lay on the grass, a smile on his face.

"Daughter." The word tasted foreign on her tongue. "You never answered me before. Who is my mother?"

Sadness deepened Pha's eyes and made them glisten, reflecting the flames that licked at the town below them.

"When we came to this town, we were fearless and helpful. When the town leader stole Marcell and trapped me, I put you in the stasis chamber, and I put a spell on Kenjins to forget. He'd already drained so much of my blood by then, and my strength was not at its greatest. He forgot me, but he did not forget Marcell. You forgot as well, you forgot everything in the length of years between going to sleep and rising; an orphan, or so everyone thought. I'm afraid soon you will be. Your mother was the first victim of his cruelty. He killed her slowly and took her blood. But her blood was the strongest I had ever known. Despite his desire to hide the Goddess from every one of those humans, she spoke of her love and her strength, her desires, whenever he let down his guard. She called to me and on occasion, I rested behind his eyes, and I saw our child becoming more like her, and tortured by the same beast."

"I'm so sorry. I thought we had gotten to you in time."

"Do not be sorry. Without you, I would still be a captive. Now we can rest." His finger vibrated warm against her cheek, wiping gently at the fallen tears.

"How do we find them?"

"The sisters know." He shook his head as he remembered, sadness creasing his face. "Just the one sister now. Stay with her, help each other. There are more Children than you know. But they hide in fear and confusion. Find them and our people, find the other Gods."

Adie and Tala said nothing. They sat, frozen in the brightening light, and silently witnessed the death of a God and a father, of a race that had been twisted and warped for humanity's own gains.

'*A member of **my** race.*'

The thought washed over Adie, too large for her to truly grasp. Adie stopped crying. She simply couldn't cry anymore. Breathing had never been so easy. Only rubble remained of the wall in her mind and the air flowed through her, crisp and fresh.

"You and Diana are part of a group, a group of The Children?"

"We *were*. We broke away from The Children years ago. They were too scared to stop the abuse. Too scared of what powers they might be capable of wielding. Some we know are too afraid to discover they haven't enough God in them to wield anything."

"How did you know? That my father was here?"

"He called to us, and we told The Children. A year ago. We were sick of sitting back and doing nothing."

"What happened to Billie?" Adie asked in a rush, only now remembering who had also been in that tunnel with them.

"I killed her." Tala pulled Billie's bloody torch from one of her pockets and laid it on the ground beside her.

Adie nodded. It would take time for her to really come to terms with the Firey darkness within her that knew Billie deserved it. Worse, it wished she had suffered longer. If their past friendship hadn't already been tarnished by the lies and the treatment since she lost the magic it would hurt more. She had already grieved their friendship.

"I don't expect that to endear me to you. But I'm on my own now, and I plan to keep searching for our people, our race."

"Our race." Adie's smile widened. Just moments ago, she'd

wondered if she would ever be able to smile again. "I can still feel Kenjins. And if I focus, I can hear him screaming."

"He deserves it."

"He deserved worse," Adie agreed. "But that doesn't mean I wanted this, or that I'm okay with it."

"And maybe that's why we won. I don't have the humanity, the *mercy* you have."

"Maybe you just need to be reminded of your human side as well?"

"Maybe. If I had someone to show me?" Tala's lips quirked up on one side.

Adie threaded her fingers with Tala's as she nodded her assent. She could only imagine what she looked like. Hair wild, skin dirt-smeared and eyes so black she could sleep for a week, perhaps more.

"So, what next?" Adie asked with a yawn.

"We find our people," Tala shrugged, "and I suppose we kill any arsehole who gets in the way."

"Okay, sure." Adie nodded and then smiled, "But maybe we can find a town that has a hotel room with a hot bath and some food first?"

Tala laughed and nodded. "Sounds like a good idea to me."

"Pity we can't teleport like we did out of the cave." Adie flinched, she couldn't talk about Pha, about the cave, not yet.

It would take time. She didn't know if there would ever be enough time for her to talk about the family she found only to lose it. And even less sure she would ever be okay to discuss the hunger for blood and the enjoyment of seeing Kenjins suffer.

"I can't teleport or relocate, as the Gods seem to call it." Tala yawned and covered her mouth with the back of her free hand. "But I *do* have a car."

"A car?" Adie turned to Tala. "It didn't happen to be parked down *there*, did it?"

"No." Tala laughed. "I'd never risk something as silly as actually parking where I need to be."

"Right." Adie smiled.

Tala stood and offered a hand to Adie. She took it and together they turned away from the town as it continued to burn, falling into the emptiness below. Buildings collapsed, and lives were taken, and there were no more witnesses as Hell finally claimed Openfields.

PART TWO

CHAPTER
TWENTY-TWO
TALA

Metal scraped against cement in a cacophony of chaos.

"Adie!" Tala screamed as her feet stamped against the accelerator, the side of the car torn up as it sparked along the cement barrier beside the road.

"I'm okay." Adie's voice trembled.

Tala gripped the faux leather steering wheel. Her fingers turned white as she yanked it and the vehicle to her right, away from the barrier. But the barrier had become the least of their problems.

No amount of foot stomping or manoeuvring could get them clear of harm. Not now. The barrier gave way to tall mountains that closed in on them. Tala flicked her eyes to the side mirrors. The vehicle she had sped from wasn't there.

Don't be in a blind spot, you bastard.

How could she have been so *stupid?* Falling for such an amateur trap as being herded. She would have made a baa-ing sound if she could see any humour in the large white truck that filled the end of the ravine's natural tunnel.

Too fast. It bared down on them. It can't have been the

same truck, it can't have gotten in front so easily, and without being seen.

Of course there wasn't just one.

Tala pushed away the self-recriminations

Time for a non-approved tactic.

Tala swung the wheel. She stamped down with both feet on the brakes and turned the car so it's side now faced the vehicle baring down on them. The greatest risk would be the vehicle flipping, but she had never opted for the safe road.

Adrenaline pumped through her veins, and she smiled as her muscle memory took over. Diana would be...

The ache of missing her sister smacked her in the chest once more. No, now wasn't the time to mourn her sister, even as she heard Diana's mantra repeating in her mind.

You are strong, stronger than most, use it to protect the others. Do whatever needs to be done to save them.

Tala would protect Adie, no matter what the cost. The woman had suffered enough, and The Children protected each other. No matter what the elders said or thought, or the rules they slapped up on a wall and barked on and on about.

Maybe it would have been worth at least letting them know about Openfields. She had gone in blind, too concerned for Diana to think about her own safety.

"Tala?" Adie's voice called from the back seat.

Tala flicked her eyes to the rearview mirror. There was an intriguing beauty to Adie. She wouldn't consider it traditional, but something had pulled at Tala, fizzed beneath her skin, the first time she saw her. Tala closed her eyes. She would have liked to have gotten to know her better.

"We going to die?" Adie's usually expressive voice was now a robotic sort of functioning.

Tala turned her head to look through the side window of her door. She could see the man's face through the windscreen of the truck, snarled lips and thick eyebrows. She wondered if he hated her for the right reasons.

"Hold on!" Tala called back to Adie, meeting her eyes once more in the rearview mirror. "And keep your head down."

Adie's face drained of colour as her hands gripped the belt that pressed her to the back of her seat. She dropped her head, and Tala turned back to look at the driver's side window. It burst into a rain of glass that stung her face.

The car's door slammed into her half-turned body as the truck hit, buckling the metal. A painful silence filled her head before it erupted into voices and screams. Acrid metal coated the back of her tongue while a coldness made the hairs on her arms stand up.

Ouch, what the fuck?

Despite the pain radiating from all corners of her body, the sharp prick at the bend of her elbow elicited the words.

Panic pulsed at her temples in time to the headache. She had to make sure.

Make sure of what?

"Tala, it's okay. It's going to be okay." Adie's voice floated over Tala.

Oh, that's right.

Adie was okay.

That was good. That was right. She'd see Diana again.

She'd find her way back to that hell and find Diana's ghost.

They'd be together and it would all be alright.

Adie had been freed, and retribution had been given to those who had stolen from Pha. The world moved on and the blackness lulled Tala with a rocking of the waves, into oblivion.

CHAPTER

TWENTY-THREE

TALA

Tala forced one foot in front of the other. Dust scuffed up from the dirt road as her feet slipped more than stepped along the path away from Openfields.

She needed time to heal and to process. The physical and emotional toll of freeing Pha weighed on her shoulders. But she couldn't stop yet.

Tala rubbed her fingertips over the palms of her hands, not quite curling them into fists, but her skin continued to feel roughened and sticky, as though blood that hadn't touched her skin, might never leave it.

A lump formed in her throat, emotion pushing up from her chest and fighting its way to freedom.

Diana. How could she go on without her sister? She missed her sister with each unknown step.

The path Adie had led them to was little more than a gap between snarled branches, the ground thick with untrodden scrub. Tala had to lead them single file as she was the only one who knew where the car was hidden.

"Are we there yet?" Adie's voice broke into Tala's thoughts from behind her. A smile, even now, in her words. "I need to sleep for a week after I shower for a month."

"We haven't even gotten to the car yet." Tala flicked a look over her shoulder.

"How long until we get there then?" Adie poked out her tongue before smiling just long enough to meet Tala's eyes. When her head dropped, her shoulders curled inward, hunching forward as dust billowed around her feet.

It had to be more than exhaustion, but Tala had no way of knowing. Her own heart struggled to understand everything they had gone through.

But Adie had smiled, small and sad but present.

Tala couldn't have forced herself to do as much, and it hadn't even been her father trapped and tortured all these years. Her entire world and knowledge of herself hadn't been turned upside down.

The strength of Adie radiated from her, pressing into Tala's spine, stiffening and straightening it.

I shouldn't be the one leading, but there's no one else. I'll do it for now, for Adie.

Tala's lips jerked, as though mimicking a smile that wouldn't yet come. Diana would be insufferable if she knew how concerned Tala was about a near stranger. She imagined a new comment from her sister, oscillating between angry and amused with each kicked-up step.

'*Diana's not angry or amused, she's dead.*'

Tala closed her eyes, the scream pushed against the back of her clenched teeth. It wouldn't be fair to lose it now.

Did she *really* care about fair anymore?

No one played by the rules.

Anger hadn't been a stranger in her life, but it hadn't been this swirling pit of raging darkness that scraped the insides of her rib cage either.

Just stop then.

The words were her own, but she struggled to grip onto what she wanted to stop *more*. The moving, or the caring.

Does it even matter?

Tala shook her head as she stepped past a bend in the makeshift path. Through the leaves and branches, dark paint glinted in the light of the morning sun.

"Hello Beauty." Tala's shoulders dropped and she lifted her feet with more purpose as she revealed her car.

"You named your car?" Adie asked.

"Oh no," Tala turned to face Adie and her wide eyes. "Attitudes against Beauty are never allowed."

"But you named her Beauty? Does that make you the Beast?" Adie's smirk brought a smile to Tala's lips and a lightness to the air.

"You're welcome to walk alongside." Tala opened the front door; a wave of heat smacked her in the face. "Unless of course, you're willing to grovel. Then she might let you slip into her."

Adie laughed, her mouth opening in a strange o shaped smile. Only then did Tala understand what she had said.

A small groan escaped her lips as her cheeks flushed.

Stale air wrapped Tala in an uncomfortable embrace as she got into the driver's seat. She caressed the cracked faux leather steering wheel, soothing her palms in a way her fingers had failed to.

"She's wonderful," Adie whispered.

"Yeah." Tala nodded.

Adie took her time to slide into the front seat. "Will she kick me out?"

"Depends on how nice you are." Tala turned the key; a sigh escaped her lips as the engine purred to life.

Dirt and dust kicked up in the rearview. Tala rubbed at her chest with one hand as she guided Beauty away from the nightmare she had lived.

"What's it like?" Adie asked once they were on the highway heading south.

"What's what like?" Tala flicked her a quick look. The woman's face gave nothing away as she stared ahead.

"Being part of The Children of the Gods?"

"I'm not sure I remember." The words slipped easily from Tala. Ignoring the panic simmering in her lower stomach, she leaned into the ease of truth that came with talking to Adie. "It's been so long since we separated from them."

"But Pha didn't know you were separated from them. Yet he knew about them?" Adie's face scrunched as she asked.

"They're just a race." Tala shrugged as she overtook a couple in a car who looked as though they had forgotten they were driving, arms flying from both driver and passenger as they spoke. "The Gods have power and knowledge humans don't understand, but they've never been omnipotent."

"Ok, fair enough," Adie said, nodded slowly as she blinked. Tala could swear she could hear the woman's thoughts swirling inside her head. "So, you separated from them, but we're heading to them now, why?"

"I need to tell them about Diana. Jonah and Xand deserve to hear it from me, in person."

"Jonah and Xand? They're other Children? Other umm, family?"

"Yes." Tala's newfound smile dropped.

Oh hell, how was she going to tell Jonah and Xand?

"And me? Will they be okay with you bringing me?" Adie pulled on threads at the hem of her shirt. "Outsider and all."

Tala took a deep breath and pressed her lips together tightly. She focused hard on the road, though it presented little obstacle or challenge. "We aren't like Kenjins. The Children aren't like Kenjins."

"Why did you and Diana separate from them then?"

"Me." Tala swallowed the lump in her throat. "*I* parted ways with the Elders of The Children years ago."

"And Diana?"

"Technically she was still running them."

"*Running* them?" Adie's voice squeaked.

"She ran our Clan."

"The one you left?"

"Yes."

Adie didn't respond. Not even Beauty's engine filled the space enough to ease Tala out of the tension bunching in her shoulder muscles.

"I left because of the Elders. They stopped bothering with the magic and started caring primarily about finding stronger blood. Diana never separated from our Clan. Not really. Except on the papers Jonah sent to the other Clan Elders."

"Why is everyone so damned obsessed with blood?" Adie's voice rose, a rumble on the distant horizon.

"Elitism, basically." Tala felt the snarled lift of her lips. "Some of the Elders, the ones in charge of the Clans, started ordering other Clans to stop recruiting."

"But why? It makes no sense."

"I know. Diana and I were furious. Basically, they only wanted Children who presented strong enough with their gifts, who had a high percentage of the Gods' blood active in them."

"So, not everyone, every Child, is strong?" Adie asked.

"Everyone is strong in their way, Adie." Tala gripped the steering wheel tighter. "The Elders only see *one* strength, and that's active power. Sometimes it's dependent on their parents, the blood, other times it's just the way it is. Either way, it's a load of bullshit. Percentage of blood, even active powers mean *nothing* on their own." Tala smiled over at Adie.

"So, you're still a member of The Children?"

"More like an ally instead of a member. I don't stay at the Clan houses; so, I don't fall under their rules. According to the other Elders, I'm banished. Diana was stripped of her Elder status." That lump in her throat made itself known once more.

"And it's been just you and Diana ever since. I'm sorry you've lost her." Adie slipped her hand onto Tala's thigh, just above her knee. Tala's hand rested on top.

"You've lost your whole town, Adie. You don't need to worry about me."

"I was lonely long before you came to town."

Tala clenched her jaws.

"I didn't want that to be how it ended. I didn't come to your town to destroy it." Tala put her hand back on the steering wheel. "Would you have preferred I stayed away?"

Calm down. Your anger is not with Adie.

"Of course not. I--," Adie's mouth gulped silently at the air. "I didn't mean it like that."

Cloying silence wrapped around Tala. What were they but strangers, after all, pushed together by murder and horror?

"I wasn't alone or shunned. And it was never just me and Diana. Openfields is a kind of hell I've never seen before."

"Oh great, nice to know we were the worst of the worst."

"Maybe, maybe not." Tala shrugged. "My best mate, Xand, she's still entirely under Jonah's protection. She's told me about some other towns who have hoarded the magic. I don't know the details though."

"She's your spy?" Adie asked. Tala heard the smile and chuckle beneath the words.

"I guess so. She's like our other sister, a third sister. She's our pixie sister." The smile quirked up Tala's lips, but she didn't feel it. "I need to let Xand know about Diana. I don't know how I'm going to tell her."

"Everything is so screwed up. I should have known earlier. Understood what was happening and saved them all."

Tala pushed a tape, an honest-to-gods, old-school cassette tape, into the deck of the car. Rocket Man played and Adie laughed.

"No dissing Sir John either."

"I would *never*." Adie removed her hand from Tala's leg and pressed it against her chest.

Kilometres slipped beneath the wheels of Beauty, and Sir Elton John entertained them as they kept council within their own heads.

"What's Xand like?" Adie asked.

"Xand is my co-conspirator." Tala smiled, though the laugh didn't quite break free. "She was Diana's last recruit. No one ever believed that Diana could *actually* be two months younger than me. By the time we met, she was already running half the agility and strength classes for The Children's training. And then I rock up, a total screw-up of a kid. Twelve years old and already kicked out of every school in the area. Mum was at her wit's end, not knowing what to do with her freak kid."

"How had you two never met?" Adie's face was alive with curiosity. It might have annoyed Tala at any other time, but despite the pain, talking about Diana eased the edges of the jagged hole left in her heart.

"Same dad, different mums. Didn't even know I *had* a sister until I got sent to the Clan."

"That's a trip. And I don't think you're a freak. Twelve-year-olds mature enough to run classes of training? That's not the standard you should *ever* be comparing yourself to."

"*Half* the training." Tala smiled. Though it sat stiff on her lips, she couldn't deny how nice it felt. "There was a -- a situation before I arrived. The second Elder of our Clan had been killed. Diana was the only logical choice, seeing as Jonah had trained her since she was three."

"Wow." Adie's lips were open slightly as she stared out of the windscreen. She shook her head and leaned back further into the seat. "And you didn't even know you had a sister."

"No idea." Tala's smile danced on her lips. Memories flooded her mind in fast-forward. "I thought it was bullshit when Mum told me. But it didn't matter. As soon as Diana and I met, we knew the truth of it. Blood calls to blood and all that. I never cared that she was my superior in all ways."

"When did she recruit Xand?"

"We were fifteen. Diana was already *such* an adult."

"And what about you?"

"Me?" Tala flicked a look to Adie and met those eyes. For a moment the world disappeared. The horn of a passing car made Tala realise just how stupid she was being. Stupid and open. "I was still a kid. Angry and pissed off at the world."

Tala's shoulders lowered. Adie gave Tala the freedom to talk about herself. She didn't understand, and couldn't explain, but as much as she wanted to hold back, the relief of sharing pulled at her. "But then Xand came, and the world got a little bit brighter." Tala laughed, shifting in her seat and stretching her back as much as the seat and the belt would allow. "I had been hard enough, but us two together. We were thorns in Diana's side, every chance we got."

Silence settled over the car at Tala's words. The lightness sharing had given her slipped from her grasp. The reality now so much heavier as it sat on her shoulders.

No wonder Diana rarely laughed. No wonder she always seemed so angry. Tala could never take on the troubles of so many others, guiding Children and helping them come to terms with who and what they were.

"This is going to be a long drive, isn't it?" Adie shuffled in her seat, pulling her legs up to her chest and pressing her back against the passenger seat door.

"A few more hours," Tala said.

"Mind if I sleep?"

"Be my guest. I have all the entertainment I need." Tala lifted the armrest between the seats to reveal more than a dozen tapes tucked neatly into hand-labelled cases. They floated on a sea of half-spooled tapes, denied the dignity of a case or a proper burial.

Adie smiled. Lines creased the skin at the corners of her eyes.

Tala missed the ease of talking with Adie. But soon Adie's breathing changed, and the pull of sleep relaxed her face and lowered her shoulders.

The rhythm of the wheels over the bitumen mixed with the songs she knew by heart. Tala relaxed into her seat, focused on the road that slipped beneath them. But despite her determination, her mind had other ideas.

They were headed back to The Children, and despite her reassurance to Adie, Tala couldn't be entirely certain what kind of reception they would receive.

If only she'd known they were never going to reach *that* particular destination.

CHAPTER

TWENTY-FOUR

TALA

FIFTEEN YEARS EARLIER

Tala saw only the black target in front of her. The world around her disappeared as she beat the heavy sand-filled punching bag.

Right, left, right, right, left.

Blood seeped through the white wrappings around her knuckles. Sweat tickled her forehead and dripped down over her eyes. She shook her head and blinked the drops away, never missing a punch. The chains, holding the bag in place from the top and bottom of the large gymnasium, rattled as they strained to keep the bag attached.

"Tala." Diana's voice snapped from the other end of the room. Her call bounced off the brick walls and polished floorboards. The mats and few squares of cut-off carpet did nothing to soften the echo.

Tala didn't stop, didn't hesitate in her rhythm.

"Tala!"

"*What?*" Tala threw one more right-handed punch and

wheeled around, full force glare like only a teenager could manage, ready on her face.

But Diana wasn't alone.

Next to Tala's sister stood a kid. A short smiling blonde. Not a strawberry blonde like Tala herself, but a natural dusty blonde, with waves down to her shoulders.

"Who are you?" Tala asked, ripping the wraps from her knuckles. Her shoulders moved up and down as her muscles pulsed beneath her skin, vibrating as her blood sought to cool her body down.

"I'm Xand." The smile got bigger, and Tala tilted her head and narrowed her eyes in her best attempt at disgust.

Xand laughed and shook her head.

"Wanna see what *I* can do?" Xand stepped forward and touched Tala's arm before either Tala or Diana could stop her.

"Oh, my Goddess." Tala pulled back, she didn't know how to explain it, not even to herself. Something akin to the sensation of fingers as they brushed hair from your forehead, but with a zap of static electricity, beneath the skin. All teenage angst left her face as she stared wide-eyed at Xand. "What was that?"

"My power." Xand's smile reached her eyes and twitched up her nose. She bounced on the balls of her feet and let out a small laugh. "You did feel it, didn't you?"

"Yeah, I felt it." Tala's smile stretched across her face. But it didn't last long, it drooped as Diana's sharp voice cut in.

"You never show your power."

"Why? I know we're like superheroes and can't show off to the normals, but we're like family now, right?" Xand flicked her grey eyes back and forth from Tala to Diana.

Tala blinked at this young open child. Where *had* Diana found her? Normals?

"No. Family or not, powers are sacred. You keep them to

yourself unless you have no other choice. No one should know what you're capable of."

"But, why?" Xand's light dimmed slightly.

Tala loved Diana and hated her half the time. Right now, she had never felt more like telling her to shut up. She also hated that she understood it now better than ever. Ever since ... no, nothing good came out of thinking about that.

"Because anything known can be used against you." Tala recited.

"Even from family?"

"*Especially* from family," Diana said.

"D." Tala hadn't used her begging voice on her sister since she'd turned fifteen, three months, and several lifetimes earlier.

"Tala, you need to start training Xand." Diana pinned Tala's eyes with her wolf stare. Diana's ease with the beast they both had within their blood, thanks Dad, caused an answered howl within Tala. She shoved back at her own beast, barely keeping the thing from taking over. "And be nice."

"Why?" Tala's voice hardened. The beast should have been warning enough. But Tala wouldn't be cowed by another one of the psychotic wolves that tried to run her life. Despite that ice-cold chill that spilled down her spine.

"Just do it, Tal."

Tal? That got her attention more than any snarling wolf could. Tala opened her mouth to get more information, but Diana turned and stalked away. The click of the gymnasium door boomed with the finality of Diana's words.

"I didn't know." Xand's lips scrunched together as she bounced harder on the heels of her feet. "I'm sorry you got stuck training me. I'm not the fastest learner."

"Which Clan are you from?" Tala asked, resigning herself to the frustration and pain she knew was to come.

"I'm not from a Clan. My, my mum died. Like that wasn't fucked up and shit enough, but then this guy I've never seen before rocks up and says hey I'm your Uncle Jonah and *bam*, here I am. This is far more terrifying than exciting. Books and TV have a *lot* to answer for."

"Do you always talk so much?" Tala's arms dropped at her sides, shoulders pulled down from her ears.

"Pretty much, and I talk too fast. I do everything too fast, except learning. That's sort of the problem. Mum had to home-school me because I kept getting into trouble."

"But no Clan?" Tala tried to wrap her head around the idea. It sounded a little like bliss.

"No Clan." Xand pressed her lips together as though stopping more thoughts from flying out.

"Fuck me, I didn't know there were any of us who *could* fly under Jonah's radar. I mean the Elders' I get, their heads are all stuck so far up their arses, but to have Jonah miss it?"

"I guess I'm just not powerful enough." She didn't entirely stop moving, though the motion carried far less sunshine to it than it had before.

"What? Who the fuck told you that?"

Xand's cheeks pinked and the bouncing took up speed once more, the colours surrounding her lighting up the starkness of the gym. Besides, Tala had a pretty good idea who had wormed their way into Xand's mind. And that shit didn't fly, not in their Clan.

"Your power is *wicked* cool."

"Really?" The pink in Xand's cheeks darkened as Tala threw an arm across her shoulders.

"Really. I could actually *feel* your fingers under my skin. It was crazy. What can you actually do with it?"

"I have no idea, not really. I mean, if I press or push too hard, or squeeze, it can hurt people. But I don't do that."

Xand's hand flew back, and forth as though scared Tala wouldn't believe her. "I'm not sure exactly what I'm capable of, I was kind of hoping I might get a chance to figure it all out, now. Mum just told me to hide it."

"What happened?"

"Cops came, told me she died. They won't really tell me much more until I'm old enough. It was a car accident, apparently. Just more things to hide."

"That's shit," Tala meant it more than Xand could understand. "We shouldn't have to hide."

"I was kinda hoping I wouldn't have to anymore."

"Well, I won't tell if you won't," Tala smirked and gave Xand a quick wink. "So, how old are you then?"

"Thirteen."

"Cool. I always wanted a little sister. Come on then, pixie. Let's start this training."

CHAPTER
TWENTY-FIVE
TALA

Tala's heart raced as Adie's scream echoed in the enclosed space.

Adie thrashed in her seat, her belt the only thing keeping her locked into her seat.

"Adie." Tala flicked another glance over. Adie's eyes were still closed, the screaming downgraded to an indistinct whimper but the thrashing remained.

Tala flicked the indicator, eyes darting to the car's side mirrors, the rearview mirror, and back again on a loop. She forced Beauty onto the shoulder of the road, her breath too fast and warm over her parted lips. She jerked the car to a stop, yanked on the hand break and twisted in her seat.

"Adie, it's okay, you're safe." Her tone, rough and raw gave voice to her thoughts. What had Adie endured in that hellscape? She placed a hand on Adie's bare arm, her own fingers trembling.

No, she couldn't let the real beast out. Not so soon.

Adie's thrashing weakened. But the whimpering lingered, interspersed with intermittent gasps.

Tala waited and watched Adie's chest as it finally shifted into smoother, longer breaths.

Tala's breath bounced around the inside of Beauty, too loud in the quiet space.

Quiet? When had the music stopped? Had she pressed stop, or had the tape ended? Did it matter?

Tala rolled her eyes and flicked the indicator to get back onto the freeway.

Thirty minutes later Adie still slept, and Tala had little choice but to stop again. She pulled into the green and white service station, shiny clean panels welcomed cars, and their exhausted drivers.

Waking Adie felt cruel, but Tala couldn't risk the fuel indicator dropping any lower. As quickly as she could, she filled the tank and raced inside. The aromas of oil and salt filled her mouth with saliva and sent her stomach growling. At the counter she grabbed some drinks and hot box food, grabbing too much as she had no idea what Adie liked and didn't.

Electricity raced beneath her skin.

Not magic.

The beast within slept easily, satiated from its recent activity.

This something *other* caused Tala's heart to race like nothing had before. Exhaustion pulled at her, as the panic tugged in different directions.

She had once consumed far too much caffeine in an attempt to replicate Xand's energy levels. She hadn't even come close.

Pressing her free hand to her chest, the pulse of her heart made that experiment look like a lazy day.

Loaded with a cardboard tray of food, drinks tucked

beneath her arms, Tala stepped out of the service station. Not two steps from the door she met Adie's eyes through the dirty windscreen.

Her skin pulsed at her wrist, a hard and heavy thud.

Tala's boots slapped hard on the black bitumen as she ran to the passenger side of Beauty. Adie's face was white, her eyes large. Tala's concern however, focused on Adie's hands, where small blue flames flickered in and out of life in her open palms.

"What's happened?" Tala dropped to her knees, ignoring the pain of the hard surface as she dumped the food beside her and placed her hands over the flames. Her magic sizzled against them.

"We, we." Adie shook her head and swallowed audibly.

Had Kenjins survived? Had they been followed by one of his sycophants? Was Adie having a heart attack?

"Adie." Tala's voice trembled.

"Oh no." Adie's hand flew to her mouth, covering what else might have come out, but Tala didn't hear anything but Adie's heavy breathing.

"Hey," Tala whispered despite the dull, steady thump in her chest. She grabbed the food from the floor. "It's okay. Take these. We'll get going. Food'll help."

Tala stood, forcing her body to slow as she handed the food to Adie. Fingers trembled as they touched, and Tala couldn't tell whether it was her own or Adie's.

Sliding back into the driver's seat, she rubbed her lips together as she started Beauty. The petrol indicator rushed in an arc to the F on the gauge. They'd make it without needing another stop.

They were back on the freeway before Adie broke the silence. "We have to go west."

"What?" Tala asked, concentrating more on the road as she

floored the accelerator and squealed into a gap between a sporty red convertible and a Holden, painted old gold.

"We need to head west, Tala," Adie's hand rested on Tala's thigh. Tala's body tensed against the shudder that raced through her body. "Please?"

"What's happened?" Diana had trained her, and she'd be proud of her questioning, even though the wrongness of questioning Adie fired along her veins in a spark of power.

Adie stared out the passenger window and Tala rubbed one hand across the back of her neck. She had to get something, some kind of answer.

"Why west?" West wasn't exactly a destination. They could make it to Forty West as easily as they could make it to The Children. But Tala had to know what she was heading *toward*.

"I had another dream, another nightmare." Adie pressed the button and Beauty's passenger side window rolled down just enough for the taste of cool fresh air to kiss Tala's cheeks.

"Is there danger if we head south?" Tala's fingers tightened on the wheel.

"No. It's not about going somewhere else it's about going *there*, going west. Something bad is happening, and I'm not going to ignore it this time."

"Adie, taking you *toward* danger isn't exactly what I had in mind when we left Openfields."

"What exactly *did* you have in mind?"

Tala felt Adie's eyes boring into the side of her face. It was a reasonable question; one Tala didn't have an answer for.

"I know you want to protect me, Tala. I know I'm damaged beyond repair." The self-deprecating words filled Beauty. "But I'm not delicate or weak. I've never been delicate; I wouldn't have survived any of it if I was."

Tala forced the lump down her throat. "Was it like Openfields? Is there another God trapped?"

"No, and yes." Adie let out a puff of air from her nose. It reminded Tala of the horses in summer, when the flies would be too much, and the horses were over them as much as everyone else. "It's not a trapped God. I don't think anyway. Someone is in danger. And the feeling, yes, it's like Openfields. And it wasn't a dream."

Tala let the words float around in her head. It caused an obnoxious cacophony in her thoughts. One that mixed confusion and mourning like an ill-fated cocktail.

"I think you're a seer, Adie." It explained a lot, including Tala's pull toward her.

Adie laughed. "Aren't they all old blind women?"

"You've watched too many movies. You'll like Xand."

The silence from Adie twitched Tala's eyebrows together, but she didn't know what it meant, how to read this stranger she'd gone underground with, had killed for without hesitation.

"West?" Tala asked, turning to glance at Adie as she flicked the indicator and slipped into the fast lane, overtaking several of the middle lane vehicles.

"West."

"Nothing more specific than that?"

"Not yet. I'm trying to figure it out." Adie rubbed her temples with the tips of her fingers. "What the fuck does it even mean?"

"Okay."

"Okay?" Adie asked.

"Yeah." Tala nodded, to herself as much as to Adie. "I've got some calls to make, and then we'll head west."

"Phone calls?"

"It's always best to give them a heads up when I'm heading their way," Tala smirked. "Last time I showed up unannounced, things got a little crazy."

"Good crazy?"

"Of course." Tala smiled, and for a moment she forgot. But Diana's memory never drifted far enough. Tala grabbed it back to her, holding it close, letting the smile drop. "They'll need to know about Diana. It might as well come from me."

"Children of the Gods?"

"Yes and no."

Adie remained silent as though waiting for more. She deserved to know more. She deserved to know everything.

But Tala didn't have the right to burden her with her and Diana's paths. They'd been up to many things. Tala didn't know if she would, or could, keep going now. Not without Diana. The hard decisions always landed on Diana, and they rarely made sense to Tala.

She couldn't make them. Tala would not be the one to take on the Misfits. They needed someone who knew how to lead them. She could try, but she would fail them, in the end.

"Can you tell me anything more than that? It'd be nice to know what to expect," Adie asked.

"Sure, once you tell me about the nightmare."

"Why do I get the feeling you aren't going to let it go?" Adie pushed her lips to one side, but she couldn't hide the smile completely.

Tala laughed lightly and shook her head.

Despite not needing fuel to get to Forty West, Tala would top Beauty up half an hour out. She would call from there. It would give them plenty of time to prepare for Tala's arrival.

Dirt and rust clung to the fading signs of the service station they pulled into. The signs advertised sales and deals, no longer valid as the petrol prices were less than a dollar. Tala might even have thought the place shut down, or at least closed, if there weren't a half dozen people around. A young man walked into the doors, which surprisingly opened with sensors, while three other vehicles lined up at petrol pumps, one with a yawning older woman pumping gas.

"See if they have anything with an expiry date within the last year." Tala handed Adie her wallet and headed off toward the side of the building where a row of public phone boxes sat.

The first box held nothing but the smell of stale urine, while the second box missed the handset of the phone inside.

"Lucky number three," Tala muttered as she nudged open the last phone box. The door squealed its objection to being opened, but inside the phone at least looked intact. Dust covered every surface within, but she only needed the phone to be serviceable.

The loud dial tone was melody to her ears as she pinched the handset between shoulder and ear. It had been a while since she had punched in the numbers. They had been on speed dial on Diana's phone. Tala never bothered to get one of her own.

"For fucks *sake*, stop wanking and answer," Tala muttered as the dial tone continued to drill into her ear. The message box picked up and through gritted teeth, Tala left a short terse message.

She slammed the handset down and dialled the next number on her list. A list she would never write down, even if such things were natural to her.

This time, the call was picked up after two rings.

"Pour another one."

"Thank the Goddess, Jake." Tala smiled. The dirt might as well have been fairy dust, the kind that put a person to sleep in a moment, with the way she leaned heavily against the side of the booth.

"Tala?" Jake's voice rose over the obnoxious sounds in the background.

Tala imagined him shoving a finger in his right ear as he

pressed the phone harder up against his left. Like she had seen him do a million times or more. The familiarity created another lump in her throat.

"Yep. Some bad shit's gone down. On my way to you now. 'Bout half hour out."

"You and Diana?"

"No. Me and a new Misfit." Tala forced herself to stop at that. It would be easier to answer the questions and fix the half-truth when they got there.

"Okay, half an hour." Jake didn't ask for more, but she knew that tone.

"Can you keep track of us?" Tala asked, knowing it would ramp Jake's worry to the next level.

"Anything specific?" His worries might as well have become an item on the bar's menu. It travelled down the phone line, coating Tala's tongue with the thickness of it. Just like Jake's gravy, without the delicious taste.

"Not sure. Just not liking how things feel right now." She had liked them even *less* since Adie woke from her latest vision.

"No worries. Give me your location and I'll find you. You in Beauty?"

"Always." Tala smiled. "Thanks Jake."

Tala closed her eyes and pressed the hang up tongue with her finger. There was a benefit in having a locator as a friend. One of the best she'd ever had. Locator *and* friend.

She lifted her finger and tried Jonah's mobile number again. Since when did Jonah not pick up? The thing was glued to his bloody ear.

Should she mention Diana? No. Not unless he actually answered.

He didn't. After leaving a second message, less snippy and more concerned, she finally tried the last number. That one was destined to be the hardest of the calls.

After five rings, Xand's upbeat voice cut in with a recorded message. A strangled sound, somewhere between a chuckle and a sob, escaped Tala's mouth before she hung up without leaving a message.

The feeling she had mentioned to Jake grabbed onto the two unanswered numbers and woke the beast within Tala.

She shook her head, the rumble of her beast vibrated warmth through her chest. Now wasn't the time. If she went off beast crazy every time things unsettled her, she would have been dead many years ago.

Instead, Tala squared her shoulders and stalked back to Beauty, where Adie leaned against the passenger side door, her eyes trained to the western sky. Clouds dotted the crisp blue, not dark but no longer white.

"Ready to get going?" Tala asked as she pulled open the driver's door and slipped inside.

"Yeah." Adie followed into the passenger's side. "But wanna tell me where we're going?"

"Depends." Tala shoulder checked, surreptitiously sneaking a peak at Adie before driving out of the station. "Wanna tell me about the nightmare?"

Adie let out a deep shuddering breath, as though she had been holding it unawares until Tala's question.

From the corner of her eye, Tala saw Adie close her eyes and lean her head back against the headrest. Adie pulled her legs up into the seat, crossing them as she gave a single heavy nod.

Tala drove while she listened to the horror that had awoken Adie.

CHAPTER
TWENTY-SIX
TALA

NOW

Sweat and blood mixed as they dripped into her eyes and stung the other cuts that covered her face. She had been beautiful once. A lifetime ago, before *he* came. She should have known better; she should have felt the black anger that she now saw clearly, swarming around her. How had he hidden it from her? Why did she care now? She just wanted to live.

He shimmered in the half-darkness of the room. No, not a room, a metal box of some sort, with ridged walls and a tinny echo when she spoke.

"You don't have to do this," she whispered.

"Shut up." He stepped back, hiding himself in the shadows of the corner once again. The warning had been clear, it vibrated in the very air, but she couldn't let that stop her, not now. Not after seeing what he had done to Michelle. Her name had been Michelle, was it *still* Michelle? Oh god. Becky let out a small sob before taking a deep breath.

"My name is Becky Angels. I won't tell anyone I promise. Please. *Please* don't do this."

"I said shut *up*." His voice thundered low and dangerous, a storm building on the horizon.

Becky's bare feet weren't quite flat on the cold cement floor of the dark room. Her arms were pulled up over her head, and her wrists were bound, attached to something above them. She twisted her wrist, hissing against the pain of the rope as it dug into her flesh. She just needed to get them far enough apart. She would teach that bastard a lesson. The next time he stepped out of the shadows. She just had to create a gap, just a small gap, tiny even. It was all she needed. She could channel lightning for fuck's sake. She would not let this psycho get away with this. *Any* of this. Once she broke the locks, freed her hands to move how she needed them to, he would learn the price of his villainy. She hissed as sharp strikes of pain lanced from wrist to elbow.

Exhaustion weighed on her as the mental grip on her anger slipped. Fuelled by pain and fear, she gave in and let it have control.

"Too scared to face me, you coward? They'll be looking for me, and when they find you, *you'll* be the one begging," she screamed at the corner.

A shuffle of feet, and the man, the *monster*, stepped into the light. He was tall and wide, with a face that might have been handsome without the scowl or the shining silver scar that tracked down over his right eye. It raced across his chin, and down his neck until it disappeared beneath a stained shirt. Even with the scar, on a glance, he wasn't someone she would have avoided on the street. However, a longer look at him, and the black darkness that shimmered around him, would instantly have her reevaluating that opinion. When he stepped further into the light, around his edges she could see right through him.

What he looked like barely mattered now. Her focus fell entirely on the stains that covered the blade he clenched in his fat meaty fist. The sharp metallic tang of blood filled the space, and she lost herself in the bright red and rusting brown smears of blood. Old and new. A shiver ran up Becky's spine.

"Find you? It's been a week Becky, and no one has started looking. So, don't push me, Becky *Angels*." He spat her last name. "Hardly. You're only here because they grew weak, rutting with pigs in the mud."

"Screw you. *You're* the weak pathetic excuse of a man." What was the point in holding her tongue now. She was going to die, and she knew it. "Having to tie up a woman half his size to beat her. Is that what you need to feel like a man? There is *nothing* manly about you. You're nothing more than a powerless, *dickless*, coward."

The man lashed out, the silver of the blade moving faster than she could follow.

"Argh!" The scream, guttural and uncontrolled echoed and reverberated in the small space. Pain radiated around her wrists. Bright flames of light burned behind her closed eyelids. She collapsed to the ground, the chains around her wrists slipping off through the blood, without hands to keep her there.

"You've had more than enough warnings, especially for a disgusting half-breed like you. You're the reason I have to do this. You have to die, accept your fate. After the eclipse it will all be right again. I'm not about to let a little *bitch's* sobs stop me from getting what I deserve."

New beads of perspiration covered Becky's body as a chill raced over her skin. Forcing her eyes open, she looked over to where her dismembered hands lay in a pile of her blood. She shook her head, noises babbled from her mouth without any cohesive words joining the sounds.

"Enough." The man flicked his hand forward, as though shooing away a fly, and pain turned into a raging inferno. Becky pulled the stumps on the end of her arms toward her chest and stared as they burned, the flames cauterised the wounds with the man's power.

Becky turned her head just in time to save her lap from the vomit that splashed onto the metallic floor. When she finished, she wiped her chin with her forearm and turned flinty eyes onto the man.

"I'm going to see you burn in hell before I'm done." Becky's voice was low and cold.

The man's laughter filled the dark windowless room.

-

Adie shuddered. "I can still hear his laughter."

She had retold the details of the vision with her eyes closed. Her hands clasped together in her lap by the time she finished the tale. Her mind caught on the description of the bad guy. Snared and bleeding, like a hangnail.

"What makes you think it's West?" Tala kept her eyes on the road and the building traffic beside them. A small hand popped out of a 4-wheel drive back window, making airplanes with the wind. Where were they off to? A family on vacation? Heading to the grandparents? Or maybe a play date with friends?

"I just know." Adie's voice brokered no arguments. "There's something in the air. When I woke, I knew it was West." She stopped and let out a heavy sigh. "Look, I know it sounds crazy. So did my nightmare of the beast and look how well that turned out."

"Adie." Tala rested her hand quickly on Adie's upper arm. "It's okay. I believe you."

"Really? Just like that? What if I'm wrong?"

Tala laughed. "And *now* suddenly you're questioning yourself?"

A small sound, one Tala couldn't interpret, but she suspected she might understand. "Please don't do that. You don't have to question or justify any of it, not to me. You never should have had to. Not ever. Not to anyone."

Adie turned and looked out the window. From the corner of Tala's eye, she watched as Adie lifted her hand and wiped at her cheek.

"I'm so exhausted, Tala." Adie's voice was thick and rough.

"It's no wonder. Your sleep wasn't exactly restful. Lean your chair back and try again."

"I'm scared." Adie spoke so softly that for a moment Tala wasn't sure she had spoken at all. "I'm scared of myself."

"You have a great power, but what you did was necessary. You're untrained and yet your control is amazing. I don't think for one second that has to do with your power, but with who *you* are."

"You really believe that?" Adie's voice was laced with the same self-deprecation.

"Absolutely," Tala said. "Now lean back and get some sleep. I'll wake you when we get there."

Tala told Adie how to lean back the passenger seat, as more kilometres slipped beneath Beauty's tyres. Tala slipped a mixed tape into the deck and let herself be carried away into her past. She should tell Adie, maybe it would help her, but Tala had her own processing to work through first.

Diana was big on keeping the Misfits hidden, and there

was no point burdening Adie with things she didn't need on her shoulders. But for the first time, Tala had a burning desire to tell someone everything; about herself, her life, her powers, her fears.

No, not a desire to tell *someone*.

She wanted to tell *Adie* these things.

And none of that would be fair, on either of them.

CHAPTER
TWENTY-SEVEN
TALA

Tala found Diana two hours after the meeting had been scheduled to end. A meeting of Elders and their proteges. She hadn't seen Diana or Jonah leave the meeting house.

Her sister had been predictable from the moment they first met.

Diana liked order and discipline. The perfect candidate for the next Elder of the Children. She was everything the Elders wanted. But lately, the solid ground Tala had always felt beneath her feet when she followed Diana's lead had felt less secure. And now, not being able to find her, sent a torrent of concerns through Tala.

Xand had been just as worried, and after searching for an hour the pair had split up. Xand currently searched the youngest recruits' quarters. It was a likely assumption that Diana had been needed, to help one of the younger ones adjust.

She never had been *just* Tala's big sister.

Tala watched, unsure if she were relieved or more unsettled at finding Diana slamming bare knuckles into one of the heavy black canvas punching bags in the large auditorium.

"D," Tala called out. The rhythm of flesh against bag continued uninterrupted. This time she called louder. "What's happened?"

"I can't stay here anymore, Tal." D's head shook back and forth, her fists still pummelled the bag. She hadn't even bothered to look over her shoulder at Tala.

"What?" Heat rushed up Tala's chest and squeezed her throat.

"They are cutting off *all* help to recruits."

"But, you thought that would be the case?" Tala spoke slowly, hoping her thoughts would catch up, but she sensed there were too many links on this chain that she now missed.

"Not exactly. I mean yes. I thought they would retract assistance, but they are forbidding *any* new children be recruited, Tala. They're enforcing a ban. Whether the Elders help or not, no one is allowed to recruit another Child. I argued, and they laid it out very clearly." Diana's fists punctuated each word.

"What does that mean? We find loopholes all the time. We can find them this time."

"I know. But I'm *sick* of the loops and the jumps. Maybe there really is something in your whole expect the worst from everyone attitude."

"Hey, weren't we paired up so your good behaviour would rub off on *me*, and not the other way around?" Tala smiled, forcing out a laugh.

"You've never been bad, Tala."

"Did they say why they're cutting the fund?" Tala ignored

Diana's comment, pinning it for over-analysis another time, when alone.

Diana finally stopped hitting the punching bag and turned to Tala.

Tala stepped back as her eyes met Diana's. The deep grey of Diana's beast pinned Tala to the spot. They hadn't always known each other, but Tala had never seen Diana give such control to the blood of the God that ran within them both.

Diana dragged her hands through her dirty blonde hair. But they weren't hands.

Tala stared at the paws. Had that always been possible?

"They are cutting it all and enforcing the ban because they aren't worth our protection or training. If we can't find them through the Elders, then they aren't worth finding," Diana hissed. "The elitist *fucking* arseholes. Without training, more people will die."

"Motherfuckers." Tala clenched her fists together. Her beast paced back and forth within her. It dragged its claws along her ribs like a prisoner with a tin cup. Her being its warden made her shoulders itch, but not half as much as letting it out made her shudder.

Diana's magic and strength had always been stronger. At least when it came to the beast. And while Tala's water magic had always been hers and hers alone, she never envied the power Diana had to fight against from her own beast.

"I've been their perfect soldier, Tal. I've always done what they've asked, even when it felt wrong. But I can't do it anymore. There's so much more that matters. I'm done. I'm leaving."

"Okay." Tala shrugged. "And I'm coming with you." It was a no-brainer.

"No, Tal." Diana's eyes cleared of the beast and that beautiful water colour grey returned. "I can't ask you to leave this place. It's the first time you've ever had a real home."

"It's only home because of family." Tala took Diana's hands in her own. They were hands once more. Had they really been anything else? Maybe she'd only imagined the shift.

"Xand is your family as well," Diana argued.

"*Our* family." Tala rubbed her palm on the back of her neck. "So, what do we do?"

"I don't know," Tala said. "What will you tell Jonah?"

"I don't know."

The sisters looked at each other with mirrored smirks.

"Well, we better think of something, because if we just leave, we will break bridges and all kinds of trust." Diana sighed and sat on the gymnasium floor, legs crossing in a fluid motion.

"And what happens if we tell them?" Tala sat beside her sister, aware of her own clunky movements in comparison.

"We end up breaking hearts as well." Diana looked into her lap.

Leaving without a word would most likely be nicer for them all in the long run, but Tala couldn't bring herself to entertain the idea.

"When do you want to leave?"

"I'll need a few weeks to get everything sorted. Plus, I don't want to ruin Xand's birthday."

"Her birthday." Tala coughed out the words. She hadn't forgotten about it, but it was weeks away. Plans weren't even on her schedule yet.

"Unless you want her to come with us?" Diana asked.

"Maybe." Tala smirked. "Planning on inviting Jonah as well?"

Diana laughed.

Tala needed it more than she would admit. More than she could. Without Diana, she had no idea where she belonged.

CHAPTER
TWENTY-EIGHT
TALA

"Happy birthday, little pixie." Tala tickled a feather beneath Xand's nose.

"Piss off, dickhead." Xand waved her hand at the air, missing Tala and her feather by at least a foot.

"Oh, you get old and suddenly you've a mouth like a sailor, ey? Come on. I already let you sleep in." Tala laughed and pulled the blanket off Xand. "It's time to go have some fun."

"Real fun, or Diana fun?" Xand asked with one eye cracked open.

Tala laughed and left the room, Xand's blanket still bundled up in her arms.

Five minutes later, Xand bounced down the stairs, her bedroom door banging closed when she was almost at the bottom of the flight.

Tala sat in the chair by the front door.

The townhouse, their townhouse had been a Goddess send. Three bedrooms upstairs and the shared living downstairs.

When Diana had turned 16, Jonah had given her permission to act as guardian to Tala and Xand. Technically just Xand, but no one fooled themselves about the reality of the situation. Jonah often popped in unannounced to catch them out or quell his own worries. Not that he would ever admit to either. His visits were cloaked in pretences of urgency. Most often about training. Sometimes he changed it up to be general Elder matters, but it fooled no one.

She would miss this place the three of them had called home. Shaking her head of the thought, Tala focused on the day, and beamed her best smile as Xand landed on the floor, having jumped the last three steps.

Tala's legs lazily draped over the polished wooden arm of the chair. Nearby on the couch no one ever sat on, she had unceremoniously dumped Xand's blanket on one side.

"You mentioned fun?" Xand asked eyeing the couch and its contents. "That better include getting out of this house."

"Yep." Tala's smile eased into something more natural.

"Why at the crack of dawn?" Xand planted her hands on her hips, backward, Janeway style.

"Because we are getting out of here before Diana wakes up."

Xand smiled. The wide one. The one that lit up her entire face. It turned her already grey eyes into smoky clouds that promised a refreshing deluge.

"Slow down, pixie. You don't even know where we're going." Tala struggled to keep up with Xand. Despite her shorter legs, Xand's energy could not be contained and rarely kept up with.

"I'm just waiting up here." The call came like birdsong through the trees. Light and high as it floated down from somewhere to the right and up ahead of Tala's current position.

Tala slowed her steps and pressed her hand into her side. The mountain walk had seemed like a good idea when she'd thought of it. She hadn't been aware that Xand's physical strength and stamina had already increased so much from their last adventure away from the rest of the Clan. Tala's strength and stamina weren't inconsiderate, but as she struggled to match Xand's pace, she mentally reshaped her fitness routine to focus on both for the coming week.

Tala had been itching to let Xand know about her and Diana leaving. She wanted to rip off the bandaid, as much as she dreaded it. When she thought about leaving, she thought about all of the recruits she'd trained since Xand first bounded into their lives.

She'd taken over all of the training since Xand arrived. Diana had been kept busy on far more important tasks. But Tala had overheard a heated discussion between Diana and Jonah. She hadn't understood it at the time, why Jonah would be keeping Diana away from the training, but it had all fallen into place now.

Training had effectively become redundant; *Tala* was now redundant. Seeing as they were forbidden to bring more into the Clan. Who exactly would Tala be training?

She would have been relieved to be given something *other* than training to occupy her time. The newer recruits had all bored her. Those who knew about their heritage were savage, trying to prove themselves beyond their skills, blood lust raging in their eyes. The few, like Xand, unaware of their bloodlines, were far too timid. They were little mice scurrying around, too afraid to find out what they were truly capable of.

"Xand?" Tala's breath sped to a level she didn't know existed.

She'd turned the corner but the track that spread out in front of her held nothing but fallen leaves and a small bush turkey that scurried away at her call. The path's edge was a sheer drop down the side of the mountain. A drop to make even the most daredevil adrenaline junky baulk.

"Boo." Xand jumped out from behind Tala.

"What the *fuck*," Tala snapped.

Xand's smile dropped; her eyebrows furrowed.

"That's not funny, Xand," Tala hissed out as her short nails bit into the skin on her palm. "It's dangerous up here, I thought you'd slipped and fell."

"Tal," Xand's smile peeked around the edges of her lips, but her eyes were half-lidded. "I'm not going anywhere. You don't need to keep looking out for me. I'm not a child anymore."

Tala took a deep breath. Her lungs shuddered out the air, still recovering from the unusually faster pace.

"I'm sorry I scared you." Xand took a step closer.

"It's okay. I know you're not a kid anymore."

"I've not been a kid for a very long time."

"None of us have." Tala looked down as she scuffed the toe of her boot into the debris scattered over the path.

The silent melancholy blew with the breeze, teasing Xand's long curly hair and Tala's shaggy shoulder-length cut.

"Alright, enough of that shit. We have somewhere to be." Tala smiled and met Xand's eyes.

"Really?" Xand bounced on her feet once more. "There's more than just the hike?"

"Ahuh." Tala shuffled the stuffed backpack further up on her shoulder and took the lead again.

The crunch of slate and rock shifted behind her. It calmed Tala's breathing and helped her pulse return to a manageable pace. She smiled at the sound. For each of her steps, there were several behind her.

She'd give the kid credit; no, she wasn't a kid, Xand had been right about that. However, Tala would still give Xand the credit for not complaining as they kept at Tala's pace. The extra steps would be Xand twirling, or taking steps backwards and forward again. She'd seen her do it when they'd followed Diana anywhere.

Diana approved of the friendship between Tala and Xand, *most* of the time. They were no longer trainer and trainee. Xand stood beside Tala during training sessions more often than she did in front of her these days.

They were nearly there, and Tala still hadn't decided exactly how the day would work out. Would she finally tell Xand about her and Diana's plans? It wasn't exactly the birthday gift she was hoping to give her best friend, but then again, the lying had been eating at her for weeks.

Tala stopped and Xand shuffled up beside her. They looked out beyond the drop that lay only two steps away from them.

"Close your eyes," Tala said.

"Are you kidding me, this view is amazing!"

"OK, press your back against the rock face and close your eyes."

Pink crept into Xand's cheeks and Tala groaned internally. Tala had never seen Xand as anything more than her pixie sister. She knew it was different for Xand. The way she looked at her when she thought Tala didn't notice. Tala could be ignorant at times, but she wasn't completely blind.

"I need to set something out, ok?"

"OKAY" The cheeks deepened a darker pink, but she nodded, shuffled back until the heels of her sneakers touched the wall behind her and closed her eyes.

Tala nodded and quickly pulled off the bag. She unzipped it and found the birthday breakfast she'd planned. She lay the blanket from the top of the bag down over the path and quickly pulled out the egg and bacon rolls that she'd made before waking Xand, bottles of water and juice. Last, she pulled out the small tubs of cubed cheese, crackers, and berries.

"Come on Tala, you're taking forever," Xand whined.

"And it will be worth every second of the wait. Now shut up; I'm almost done."

Xand laughed.

After a quick flick of her eyes to check that Xand truly wasn't peeking, Tala pulled out the pièce de résistance. The cake.

"Alright." Tala stood up and splayed her hands out toward the food at her feet.

Xand opened her eyes and then kept opening them.

Tala laughed and waved Xand over to sit. "Come on, the rolls are still a little warm."

"Oh my." Tears blurred the stormy sea of Xand's eyes. "You did all this for me?"

"Of course." Tala shrugged. "How often does a person turn sixteen?"

"Twenty-three times if you're Sandie." Xand fell to her knees on the rug next to Tala.

Tala laughed and nodded. "OK, fair point. But you're Xand. Best mate and partner in crime."

Xand smiled at Tala and mumbled a small thank you before starting in on the food. It had been quite a while since Tala had seen Xand so quiet. But she supposed shovelling food in her mouth had that effect.

Most of the food containers lay empty on the rug behind them as the two sat on the edge of the cliff, legs dangling off into open air.

Xand regained her chattiness and Tala's shoulders relaxed as the pair returned to their usual programming; Tala listening and Xand chatting away.

"So, what are you hoping for your birthday this year, Xandia?" Tala lay back on the blanket, hands under the back of her head while she studied the building clouds in the sky. They were fluffy and white in their centres, though grey outlined the edges. Tala closed her eyes, ignoring the hint of a storm to come.

"Urgh, Xandia? Really? I'm still mad at you for sneaking into Jonah's office and finding out my full name."

"To be fair," Tala yawned, "I didn't mean to find it out. I didn't even know you weren't just Xand."

"I *am* just Xand."

Tala chuckled. "True enough."

"I'm stuffed."

"*And* stalling." Tala's lips twitched and she could sense Xand's glaring at her, but she didn't give the birthday girl the satisfaction of opening her eyes. "Come on, what do you want more than *anything* else?"

"More than anything else? I want something I can't have."

"What makes you think that?" Tala was used to Xand's self-deprecating and self-depriving ways, though she made every room light up and would perpetually preach about the happier, more fun experiences of living.

"It doesn't matter," Xand huffed.

"Of *course*, it matters. Haven't you figured out how much you matter yet?"

"I matter?" The incredulity jabbed Tala beneath the ribs.

"Now try it without the question."

"I matter."

"Better." Tala smiled; eyes still closed. Sleep pulled at her, but she kept it at bay. "Now, what do you want?"

The sound of shuffling made Tala's eyebrows crease, but the warmth of the rising sun kept her eyes closed, while her full belly encouraged a nap.

"I want a kiss." Xand's words brushed Tala's mouth a mere second before her lips pressed against Tala's.

For a moment Tala reacted on instinct. Then her mind caught up. With both hands on Xand's shoulders, Tala gently but firmly pushed Xand back, breaking the contact with their lips.

"Oh, sweety no. I'm sorry, I love you, but no, not like that." Tala opened her eyes and sat up as she spoke.

"Of course not." Xand sat back on her heels and looked down at her hands as she twirled her fingers around each other. "No one ever wants me like that. So, of course, you wouldn't."

"Xand. You will find her, I promise."

"Don't make promises you can't keep."

Tala's chest ached and she fought the urge to rub circles in it. "I'm not."

"So then, what's wrong with me?" Xand looked up and a sheen of watery unshed tears blurred the pain Tala could still see.

"Nothing is wrong with you," Tala spoke each word slowly and with force.

"But you don't want me." Tears dropped onto the rug as Xand dropped her head once more.

"I'm really not worth it."

"Don't," Xand scrubbed at her face, "*don't* do that. The it's me, not you, don't give me excuses. I'm not good enough for you. I've always known it."

"Stop that *right* now," Tala snapped; anger boiled to the surface faster than she could stop it.

"Why?" Xand met her eyes again, the hardness in them scared Tala more than anything else.

"Because it's bullshit and you know it. You're being a wallow party of one."

"And heaven *forbid* the 'pixie' ever be sad."

"That's not it at all." Tala softened her voice as much as she could.

"So, then what was the point of all this? Make me think you were going to spill your heart out to me, just so you could knock me down? Thanks for a really memorable birthday." Xand got to her feet, hands brushing ruthlessly at the seat of her pants. As though dirt on her bum would be the most embarrassing thing that could happen to her.

"I was going to spill my heart, but not feelings I don't have, Xand."

"Then *what*?" Xand's plea made her sound fourteen again.

Tala pushed the unkind thoughts aside. "This." Tala grabbed a half-drunk bottle of water, unscrewed the cap, and tipped it upside down.

"Sto..." The word died on Xand's lips as she collapsed back down beside Tala. She watched the water from the bottle pour into Tala's hand as though she held an invisible globe. The water poured in, curling around itself to form the perfect circle. "Wow." Xand stared at the water as the circle shrank, growing smaller in size and turning opaque. Water filled the inside of the shape to make it seem solid.

"You're my best friend, Xand, and I hate seeing you so unhappy with Jonah's rules about keeping our gifts a secret."

"It doesn't make sense." The words were ones Tala had heard before, but the distant awe in Xand's voice made Tala smile. "Can I touch it?" Xand didn't take her eyes from the water globe as she asked.

"Sure, why not?" Tala expected nothing less.

Mere centimetres away from brushing a fingertip along the surface of the water globe, the sound of heavy footsteps made Tala jump, the water ball lost integrity and spilt over her hands, splashing to the ground.

The group of hikers broke through the foliage and stomped past with red faces and sweat drenched shirts.

"Sorry." Tala scrunched up her nose.

"Don't be." Xand laughed, the light back in her eyes, her energy fizzing in her movements. "Thank you. You have a beautiful gift."

"So do you." Tala bumped Xand's shoulder.

Despite her joy, Tala's skin itched as Xand's hurt and feelings of rejection still lay thick and raw in the atmosphere.

———

"When Pha stood against the Goddess Nulla, he was ruthless and gave her no freedoms. The others followed his lead and agreed to her banishment and exile. They knew the only way to live on, for their people to live on, was to evolve alongside the human race. Nulla was furious. She threatened Pha, promising him he would be sorry. They would all be sorry for aligning themselves with the lesser beasts of humanity. But her words fell on deaf ears, and none of the other Gods listened to her xenophobic vitriol as they covered the tomb with dirt and magic." Diana's voice filled the small room with tonight's lesson.

Tala and Xand sat with crossed legs on the foot of the bed while Diana replaced Tala's pillow, while it lay on the floor.

Side by side, laughing and drawing on each other's knees, Tala and Xand didn't even pretend to listen to the lesson they'd heard more times than they could count. Tala still sensed the distance that remained between them, a wedge that left them at odds with each other. Xand's wanting and Tala's not, but the punishment for sneaking off to the hike without leave had helped close the gap enough for now.

"Would you two *stop* it. For shit's sake." But Diana's eyes twinkled, and she fought a losing battle against smiling.

"Please D, can't we just take one night off?"

"And skip learning about the bitch of the night?" Diana smiled and held up a small book with a black cover, the title Goddess of Night embossed on the front.

"Fine," Tala butted in, "But then I get to take the birthday girl out for ice cream."

Diana's face paled, and she muttered a curse beneath her breath. Xand and Tala knew they'd won.

"Fine, we can learn more about Nulla tomorrow. Happy birthday, Xand."

The two didn't wait to be told twice.

Xand threw a thanks over her shoulder as Tala grabbed her hand and pulled her out of the room.

"Thanks, T."

"I told you, Xand. You mean a lot to me."

They squeezed hands and didn't stop until they reached the ice creamery.

CHAPTER

TWENTY-NINE

TALA

MOMENTS EARLIER

Undimmed high beams of the vehicle heading in the opposite direction on the highway burst into her memories, bringing Tala back to the present.

"Arsehole." Tala's voice wasn't loud though it boomed around the interior of Beauty's relative quiet. She turned the music down low enough to be nothing more than a soft rumble.

"Everything ok?" Adie asked.

She struggled to sit up, trying to adjust the seat though her belt was still buckled in. After a third try, she unclipped the thing, causing a ting ting bell to ring in Beauty. After sitting back up and adjusting the seat she slammed the buckle back into place.

"Better your majesty?" Adie scowled at the dashboard.

"Now play nice, you two." Tala smiled.

"She started it." Adie poked her tongue out.

"It's okay, baby, she's just grumpy 'cos I woke her." Tala put on a playful voice as she stroked the wheel.

"Didn't much like the dream I was having, so that's fine. What's up?" Adie shook her head as though she could shake away whatever had tormented her unconscious mind.

"Just some idiot who didn't turn down the high beams," Tala answered.

"Urgh, I hate when they do that. Usually city folks too."

Tala laughed. She nodded along because truth be told, she couldn't argue with the assessment. She had noticed it more than once over the years as she travelled the country with Diana.

"Are we far? Did I sleep very long?"

"Not far away now. You slept a few hours."

"Holy shit, is that really the time?" Adie pointed to the clock on the dash as the digits turned over to 03:02am.

"Yeah. I would have had to wake you soon, but I'm still sorry I woke you like that."

"It's okay." Adie breathed in deeply through her nose and slowly out of her mouth.

"How often were you having the other one?" Tala flicked her eyes to Adie and back to the road again.

"The other one?" Adie asked, knuckling sleep from the corner of her eye as she yawned again. "You mean the nightmare?"

"The premonition," Tala corrected.

"I don't know if that's what it was. I mean, you weren't with me when I went underground in the nightmares. No one was with me."

"Whatever it is, it's more than just a nightmare. This one as well."

"Yeah, it's why we're heading West."

"About that." Tala smiled. "I was planning on heading West anyway."

"What?" That made Adie chuckle and the tension in Beauty lifted a little. "And yet you made me justify it all."

"Yeah." Tala rubbed one palm along the back of her neck, fixing her eyes on the road ahead. "I wanted you to tell me. You shouldn't have to carry these on your own. I saw your face when you woke up."

"Oh."

"And the flames."

"Flames?" Adie's eyes bored into the side of Tala's face.

"Yeah."

"Why the *hell* did you let me go back to sleep? I could have hurt you!"

"Nah, it's okay. You needed it," Tala said, but the tension showed in the grip she had on the steering wheel.

For a moment they drove with just the music keeping them company.

"It came and went." Adie's voice was soft, but Tala heard it easily enough. "So much was suppressed by the drugs, more than I even realised. I don't know if the nightmares were as well. I have no idea who I really am, or what I'm even capable of."

"Of course." Tala nodded.

It was hard to believe Adie was so new to this. To know about the magic but have such a screwed-up knowledge of her power. Tala had trained enough that did and didn't know their heritage. But nothing like Adie. No one at all like Adie.

It didn't matter. She had to follow what she knew, and Adie would be an incredibly powerful recruit and ally. But would she want to be another Misfit? It was Tala's job to offer it to her.

Adie pulled her shoulder-length hair back with both

hands, sighed and then let them fall down, hair spilling out around her face once more.

"Glove compartment," Tala said.

Adie looked over to Tala with a raised eyebrow as Tala chanced a quick glance away from the road.

"Hair ties." Tala smiled in response.

Adie pulled open the glove compartment and found an array of items. "Why would you have hair ties?"

"My other, less often on the road but enough for me to keep them stocked partner in crime. She's forever losing them." Tala smiled.

"Xand, right?"

"Yep." Tala felt the heat in her chest again. She missed Xand, but how she dreaded telling her this news. And she still hadn't called back. Tala lifted one hand from the wheel and absently ran her palm along the back of her neck again.

"The three amigos, huh?" Adie whispered, as though afraid to raise her voice, afraid to mention anything to do with Diana.

The pain stole through Tala, but she wanted to talk about her. She didn't want her to disappear into the void of grief.

"Diana would accuse us of being more like the stooges, at least me and Xand. We always found a joke in everything."

Adie laughed as she pulled her hair into a small ponytail high at the back of her head.

"Can you tell me about her?" Adie asked as she leaned back into her seat, pulled out the hair tie and retied it at the base of her skull.

"Who?" Tala asked. Talking about Diana in context was one thing, but could she dive that deep yet?

"Xand."

"Oh." The nervous laughter spilled out of Tala before she could stop it. "You'll meet her soon enough. Once we get to Forty West, I'll get Jake to try and reach her again. Jake knows we're on the way, and I left a message on Jonah's mobile. But Xand didn't answer when I tried to call her."

"Forty West?"

"Yeah, Jake runs the pub and hotel in the town."

"And Jake is?"

"He's one of our Misfits."

"And the Misfits are?" Adie lifted her hands and let them fall back into her lap.

"Sorry. The Children we've recruited since we left the Clans."

"You've been recruiting," Adie smiled. "Of course, you have been. So why were you taking me to The Children and not to Jake?"

"Because of Xand."

"Oh." Adie turned to look out the passenger window.

The thrum of the wheels over tar lulled along with the music that hummed through the car.

"Apparently, this eclipse is going to be a big deal," Adie spoke softly, still looking out the window.

"Huh?" Tala rolled her eyes at herself. Her articulation needed some work.

"The signs." Adie tapped gently on the passenger side window.

Tala had seen the banners flying but hadn't bothered to read any of them. As they drew closer to the bridge, the banners fluttered from every second light pole.

"Oh." Well, that proved her vocabulary.

Exhaustion pulled at Tala. She couldn't wait to be done with the flickering lights of the city. The road looked like spilled ink beneath them. Her eyes stung and the weight in her chest, squeezing at her heart, grew more intense with each kilometre they travelled.

"She deserves to be told in person." Tala hadn't formed the

words yet. She wasn't sure she would ever be able to. "If she gets my message she'll meet us there."

"Sorry?"

"Xand. That's why I wanted to head back to The Children. She needs to be told in person; she needs to have her comforts around her when she finds out, about Diana. But Forty West has become a second, or fifth home of sorts."

"Shit," Adie mumbled. "Here you are, stuck with dragging me around because of my father. Stuck in your responsibilities as much as I had been."

"No," Tala shook her head, stealing a look at Adie, not bothering to hide the horror on her face. "It's nothing like that. You aren't a burden, and you weren't given responsibilities you were given orders and demands. You were a prisoner. I've *chosen* this life, and I've *chosen* to bring you with me." The beat of silence rushed thoughts through Tala's mind. "I didn't ask. Fuck, I'm so sorry, if you don't want to..." Tala felt her heart racing beneath her chest as her words faded out. Well, at least she found *some* of her articulation.

They drove on as the city lights became fewer and further between. Tightly packed houses turned into yards and then stretched into fields. Soon trees hugged them on both sides as they drove through the middle.

"No." Adie finally broke the silence as she carried on in a rush. "I mean. Yes, it's terrifying, don't get me wrong. But I wanna stay with you."

"Staying with me is terrifying?" Tala squinted and jerked back in her seat as another car passed them, not bothering to dim the high beams of their front lights. "Damn it, people this far out West are supposed to know better. All that country charm bullshit."

"Are you ok?" Adie asked once the vehicle had passed. "And

it was a truck. Normally they're a lot more considerate, even more than us country folk."

Tala scoffed. Her own experiences with truck drivers hadn't had them being considerate at all.

"Well, the ones that came to Openfields were some of the nicer visitors to the town."

"You're right." Tala withered slightly under Adie's matter-of-fact tone. "A few bad apples don't ruin the whole tree."

Adie laughed.

But before Tala could join in, light flooded the interior of the car. This time the source wasn't in front of them but from behind.

"What the fuck?" Tala flicked the rearview mirror down so the beam didn't hit directly into her eyes.

"What's going on?"

"No idea." Tala pressed her foot down harder on the accelerator and moved into the left lane, hoping the arsehole just wanted to go faster than the posted speed limit and was making a point of it.

Drive past, drive past, drive past.

The arsehole moved up to next level bastard in Tala's mind as he followed them into the left lane.

"Mother fucker."

"What is it?"

"Still no idea, but it ain't good." Tala watched the speedometer creep higher as she indicated moving off of the highway and onto the exit. Mr high beams followed.

"Yeah, *really* ain't good."

"Shouldn't we slow down?" Adie asked, her hand now gripped onto the bar above the window as Tala took the turn off too fast.

"Beauty knows what she's doing."

"That's great. But do *you*?"

"Yes," Tala growled and planted her foot until it touched the floor of the seat well.

Adie fell silent as Tala took the turns with reckless abandon. She changed lanes until the vehicle started to fall behind. After a count of ten, the lights no longer filled the interior of Beauty, and she eased a little from the accelerator.

She didn't like it, any of it. But she hoped it kept them away long enough to get to Jake. "They've fallen back."

"Yep," Adie said, her breath coming in short gasps.

Tala turned and met her eyes. They smiled at each other, but before the laugh could bubble out of Tala's mouth, Beauty jerked forward, forced by something from behind. The steering wheel jerked out of Tala's hands.

"Shit." Tala stopped the wheel spinning and took back control of Beauty.

"One lane." Adie's whisper was more powerful than a gunshot in the dark.

"Fuck." Tala cursed again as the road cut in sharper than she expected. A metal railing missing its reflective strips sparked as Beauty scraped along the side of the road.

"Adie?" Tala called as she pulled Beauty away from the metal railing.

"I'm okay."

"Tala, is that another vehicle with high beams about to come over that hill?" Adie's voice came out husky and low.

The hair on the back of Tala's neck stood up and her fingers tightened on the wheel.

The road, which was generously called a highway, had become a two-lane wide bitumen strip cut out between tree-covered mountain ranges on both sides. Even the space along the shoulders of the road had vanished. It wasn't a long stretch, but long enough. Too long. There was nowhere to go and right then Tala wished for nothing more than to get off this road before another vehicle met them in this tight-squeezed section of the highway.

Tala didn't believe in coincidences.

The lights, too bright, crested the hill. The vehicle roared down on them.

"Adie, get in the back."

"What?"

"Sit in the seat behind you and buckle up, as tight as you can. Please, just do it." Tala didn't ask, she gave the order. She could apologise later. If there were a later.

Adie grunted and shuffled. A bare foot pressed against Tala's shoulder, and she wanted to smile, or maybe run a finger along the sole to see if Adie was ticklish, but the lights were getting closer.

Please be safe, Adie. Please be safe.

Tala slowed as much as she dared. Pinpricks of other lights showed in her rearview mirror. If she stopped, they would get caught in the onslaught as well. But she had to minimise the damage, she had to act on instinct.

"Tala!" Adie screamed from the back seat. At the same time, the vehicle, another truck, swerved into their lane. It didn't slow, it gained momentum.

"Adie..." Tala hoped the word said all the things Tala had never found to say, all the things that danced on the tip of her tongue. She braked and pulled the steering wheel sharply to the right. The vehicle moved into the other lane, baring down toward them again. Trying to avoid it wouldn't work. Time for another tactic.

"We going to die?"

"Hold on and get your head down."

Tala swung the wheel to the left, adrenaline pumped through her veins, flooding her mind with muscle memory and training. Tala looked up in the rearview, already pointed into the vehicle, to meet Adie's eyes as Diana's voice rang in her mind.

You are strong, stronger than most, use it to protect the others.

But Tala didn't need Diana's words in her head for this. She would protect Adie, no matter the cost.

The sweet relief of blackness teased as memories, disjointed and sepia coloured, played her into oblivion with a sigh of release.

CHAPTER

THIRTY

TALA

NOW

Adie's voice filled Tala's ears. She called out words, important words. But Tala couldn't make any of them make sense. They were distant and distorted. Her mind fought to breach the water of haze and confusion.

"Adie." The name clawed out of Tala's throat; she pushed everything she had behind the word. But she couldn't hear anything.

She reached for Adie in the darkness. Something pinned her arm down, held it in place. Pain lanced across her stomach and punched into her shoulder. Not just her arm. Something pinned her entire body down. The urge, the *need* to fight raced adrenaline through her veins.

Tala's eyes flew open.

More pain washed through her. Pain and continued confinement. Her breath sped and with each inhale her chest tightened further. What had she gotten them into?

Sounds clashed together in her head, marching along

with the pain. The taste of metal lingered at the back of her tongue. If she were dead, she had some issues to bring up with management about this whole pain thing, that's for sure.

Tala cringed as she breathed in, calling on the power within her blood. She focused as best she could despite the pounding at her temples. The worst of her pain radiated from her cracked ribs. One had been broken, most likely more than one, she assessed.

The agony continued, and she whimpered as she tried a second time to reach for her power, to manifest it through healing. The surge of strength, the comfort of her power, remained lacking. It was there, she could feel it, but she just couldn't quite reach.

She had no doubt now that she lived. No *way* death could be this damned painful.

Disappointment blended in with her exhaustion and landed like a brick in the pit of her stomach. She didn't want to die, she knew that, but the mere thought of having to keep going filled her with dread.

Stilling her body, though it barely moved as it was, she disassociated from the pain within her physical body. It was one of the first skills Diana had taught her. It hadn't been in any of the books, or the strict guidelines for training. Still, Diana had taught it to her, and she had, in turn, taught it to Xand.

Use only the amount of pain you need to get the job done.

Sounds filtered through as she blocked out the pain. It had nothing to do with magic, which she still couldn't seem to grab hold of. Somewhere close by, a light breeze brushed chimes together. They were too soothing, and too far away. Nothing like the breaking glass she'd heard smashing before everything stopped. Further away she heard hushed whispers, but far more disturbing was the slow steady breathing of a sleeper too close to not be in the room with her.

She forced her eyelids apart only for them to flutter shut again, refusing her orders to remain open. She didn't fight her body, not that she could have.

For that second of sight, she knew the room was bright, but *not* a hospital room. Relief washed over her. Authorities meant nothing but trouble. She respected them well enough, but they had no place in her world. They weren't equipped for her world.

Unless you are imitating them to get into towns like Openfields. Her mind unhelpfully supplied.

True but not the point. When the *real* authorities, the human authorities interfered, they only ended up getting themselves hurt. Tala shivered at the memories of such events. She could do without more blood on her hands.

The sound of Billie's nose cracking beneath her pounding fist punctured her mind like a bullet.

The thoughts were loud, too loud and she forced her eyelids back again. A fierce pillar of light through Venetian blinds stabbed into her eyes and burrowed into her still-clouded mind. Even the room fought against her.

But she'd been still for too long already. How long she didn't know, but her body itched to move. Action, she needed to get back to doing things, anything.

There were too many questions and laying on her back wasn't going to give her the answers.

Breath scraped up her throat, a garbled, pitiful sound that barely managed to push its way past her lips.

"Tala?" The word, soft and far away, lulled a calm within her.

"Diana." She sobbed.

"No."

No.

Memories of Diana's ethereal form loomed behind a tower or skulls.

No.

"Tala. It's Adie. You're safe." Adie's voice, not Diana's.

Tala forced her eyes open, shifting her head just enough to avoid the shaft of light. Adie's dishevelled hair, framed her face. Bruised and cut. Her eyes looked down as Tala tried to meet her gaze.

"Adie." Tala tried to smile; she wasn't sure if her mouth cooperated.

"Hey you." Adie looked at her between lowered lashes.

"Adie, you're okay, than-" The words were rough and hard to force out.

"Hang on." Adie disappeared. "I'll get you some water."

A warm strong hand cupped the back of Tala's head and raised it slowly until she half sat. Pillows were quickly shoved behind her back, and she leaned into them with a sigh. A straw brushed her mouth, and she clamped her lips and teeth down, taking a small sip. Ice-cold water flooded her mouth. Bit by bit, she allowed the cool liquid to slide over her raw throat.

Painful clarity and flashing lights swam in her head.

The crash, the truck.

"Where are we?" The words hurt, but they came out this time.

"We're in Forty West."

"Forty West," Tala repeated. Her shoulders relaxed. They'd made it. She could have cried. When had she last cried?

"Yeah, very imaginative founders. Apparently, it's forty kilometres west from the previous township."

"Not a township." Tala laughed and cringed; cold drops of water splashed down over her chin.

"Sorry," Adie said.

Everything swam—her head, the room, Adie.

"Do you remember what happened?" Adie asked.

"The truck."

"The driver died."

"Oh." Tala felt the anger and disappointment. She would have enjoyed making the bastard talk, finding out who had orchestrated the attack.

"Jake showed up and the next thing I know we're bundled up here and he's taken care of everything apparently." Adie didn't look pleased by the turn of events.

"Jake." Tala squeezed her eyes closed.

There was something else she was missing, something that made her chest hurt and her breath shorten, but Jake hadn't let her down, hadn't let *them* down. He had kept tracking them. Tala could kiss him, despite neither one of them being attracted to the other.

"You saved me Tala." Adie's thick words broke into Tala's thoughts. "But now you have three cracked ribs, a concussion and, you look like the night sky."

"Night sky?" Tala asked.

"All black and blue." Adie waved in the general direction of Tala's body, colour darkening her cheeks.

"Well, you aren't exactly pastel-coloured." Tala smirked and then cringed as the movement of muscles in her face sent shards of pain through her head.

"It's all superficial." Adie slipped her fingers into Tala's. "Thank you, but next time," she shook her head back and forth, "I'll kill you myself if you scare me like this, again. I thought you were dead."

Tala smiled, remembering just in time to keep her head from moving as well. "I'm sorry I scared you."

"It's not like the books," Adie muttered.

"Huh?" Oh good, her articulation was back in sparkling light.

"I read all these books about adventures. They aren't like this. The fear is *so* much worse."

"I'm so sorry."

Adie's smile was soft and shy while Tala took another gulp of water from the straw. It stuck out of a clear plastic bottle with ridges in a band about two thirds up. Tala found this more interesting than she ever would have before the crash. Maybe everything was more interesting when you almost die. Was it more interesting because Diana had? Adie was right, the books had nothing even remotely on these feelings.

"How long have I been out for?"

"Three days, on and off."

"Three days?" Tala tried to stand up and was unceremoniously pushed back by her shoulder.

"Jake suggested taking you to a hospital might not be the worst idea, but the closest one is back East." Adie's eyebrows pulled in together. Tala could only imagine the horrors she currently relived inside that mind of hers. "I promised him I would keep you from doing anything overly stupid."

"Overly?"

"Well, he does already know you." Adie winked and Tala felt heat rush through her cheeks.

What the hell? Was she eighteen again? The number stuck in her throat. She coughed away the memories. Too many memories invaded her mind, unbidden and unwanted since Openfields.

Tala carefully scanned what she could see of the room, keeping her head from moving. The room sported a second bed two whole feet away from where she sat. Straight ahead of her, past the lump of blankets that covered her feet, sat a small kitchenette. It boasted two empty bench tops, a microwave on a third and a bar fridge tucked beneath. The closed door hid the bathroom she knew would be there. The only other furniture was a small desk-table-surface half covered in papers and pamphlets. The relief washed over her with an audible sigh.

"We're in a room above the local pub," Adie said, her eyes watching Tala in her surveillance of the room.

"Pour another one." Tala smiled. "He could have at least given us a suite, the beautiful bastard."

"It's all full up."

"Good to know business is going strong. Diana and I helped him buy the place when the old owner died. A lot of Misfits know to come here if they ever need anything."

"So, he's like a hub," Adie mused.

"Yeah." Tala smiled.

She caught the furrowed brows of Adie and carefully reached her fingers out and touched the back of Adie's hand.

"What's wrong?" Tala asked.

"Xand."

"Jake got through to her?"

"He hasn't said so."

"Damn it." Tala closed her eyes and felt her weight sink into the mattress beneath her.

"I was hoping Xand could come here, and we wouldn't have to go to The Children."

"Because they would have been able to tell my heritage?" Adie asked.

"Jonah is the only elder in our Clan, now. He wouldn't force you to go see the others."

"But I'm powerful enough to be worthy of training and recruiting?"

"Most of the Elders can sense the strength of the magic in others. They all preach at us to keep our strength and power secret, even from each other, but they always know if we're holding back."

Adie smirked and raised her eyebrows. "That sounds more like a cult than a Clan."

Tala opened her eyes, and they locked with Adie's.

"I should know, after all," Adie said. "Now be a good patient, move the blanket, and let me check your stomach."

"My stomach?" Tala's eyebrows rose, opening her eyes wider.

"You got a few nasty cuts there. The um, the door of the car folded in and buried itself into your stomach." Adie's face paled.

"It feels fine actually. Our blood lets us heal pretty quickly. You might not know just how much, with the tabl—"

"I've noticed." Adie cut her off. "But you aren't *that* good a liar Tala. I've learned your tells."

Tala smiled and lifted her arms just enough for Adie to pull the sheet down to her lap and reveal Tala wore only a crop top. The movement of the sheet scratched her bare legs. For a moment her breath caught. Bare legs? What else was bare? She let out a slow breath and shifted slightly. She had underwear on. At least that was something. She'd never been ashamed of her body; she had worked hard over the years to hone it into sleek lines and strength. Still, this wasn't how she had hoped Adie would see so much of her skin.

Tala closed her eyes and tried not to hiss when something sticky, tape perhaps, ripped from her stomach and the warm air touched uncovered wounds. The wrongness washed over her. Three days. She should have been up and running, not still flinching in a bed, limbs heavy and head pounding. What was going on with her powers?

"No sign of infection, thank the Gods," Adie muttered.

"Since when did you believe in more than one?" Tala smiled, grateful for the distraction.

"I guess, since I found out I came from one?"

Okay yeah, fair enough." Tala shifted and ground her teeth as Adie finished poking and prodding the wounds, redressing them with sticky gauze patches.

"It'll be alright. We'll figure it out." Adie's voice came out strong, filled with conviction.

But Tala saw the concern in her eyes, they mirrored her own.

CHAPTER

THIRTY-ONE

TALA

Two days passed and Tala finally managed to get up and move around freely, without her head spinning and her legs going from beneath her. Stiffness made her grunt and pout. Snappy responses to Adie's every question made her feel like a child, a spoilt one at that. But Adie shrugged, often laughing at Tala's childish grumblings. The sound both annoyed and somehow amused. She didn't want to find Adie so adorable. Things were already too complicated, and emotions were filled with grief and other feelings that swirled, but Tala couldn't yet name.

"You aren't used to having to wait for anything are you?" Adie smiled from her sitting position on her bed. She rested against the headboard, reading a book that looked tattered and worn. At the end of the bed, near her crossed feet, sat a stack of newspapers.

Tala had read them all several times. A grainy picture of a missing girl, Rebecca, smiled from the front page of the pile. Tala pulled her eyes from the paper, there was nothing positive in them, and there were enough dark thoughts in her head without the news adding to it.

"Where did you get that?" Tala asked, nodding at the book in Adie's hands.

"Jake." Adie's smile radiated warmth, and Tala dropped the pout and collapsed onto the edge of her own bed once more.

"He can always find whatever someone needs." Tala smiled, remembering moments far more cheerful than now.

"Is that his power?" Adie closed the book, her index finger jammed between two pages, keeping her place.

"Probably one of them." Tala shrugged.

Adie cocked her head and furrowed her brow.

"We don't restrict anyone from using or sharing their powers, but we don't pressure anyone to show us either. The whole point of the Misfits is to allow autonomous freedom. As long as they aren't hurting anyone, with or without their powers, we're here for what they need. Within reason." Tala smirked and rolled her eyes at her unintended innuendo. "Very few of us have just one power. Our main goal is to help everyone understand their powers, and how to control them."

"You're so perfect," Adie muttered.

"Sorry?" Tala had misheard, surely.

"The Misfits." Adie's face coloured slightly along her sharp cheekbones. Tala couldn't help hoping she had meant more than that. "Why would anyone side with The Children under all the harsh conditions when the Misfits are the perfect kind of group?"

"Oh." *'Of course she didn't mean you, you moron.'* The blush was her feeling stupid once again. That town was let off easy for how they'd treated her. "We aren't perfect. And we aren't there to compete with the Clans. If the Clans had kept their doors open, the Misfits wouldn't be needed."

Tala rubbed the back of her neck. "But the Clans do have

better resources. And not everyone appreciates that Diana doesn't let the powerism exist."

"Powerism?"

"The elitist bullshit and arrogance."

"How does that work?" Adie's expression was mixed with amusement and genuine curiosity.

"We don't let individuals fluff their egos. We don't let anyone act better than anyone else. It's not perfect, Adie, and for some not being able to lift their noses at 'lesser' Children is their own kind of hell. Plus, some people need more structure and less freedom than the Misfits have. Some people need to be told what to do and where; they need a hierarchy to know where they stand. And then some need the badge to say they belong. Misfits are scattered. We allow the freedoms of individuals and don't require total control or monitoring."

"And what happens if someone breaks the rules?

"Children or Misfits?"

"Either." Adie shrugged as she obviously gave up keeping her place in the book, throwing it on top of the bed cover near her feet. It landed with a soft thud, almost knocking over the pile of papers.

"The Misfits haven't had many, but we have had to kick a few out, tell our safe places not to let them back in." Tala shuddered at the mere memory of the *last* Misfit Diana had to turn away. Sam. The things he had done...

To this day, Tala had never seen Xand vibrate with such anger.

"But the only ones we've had to remove hurt others. Diana always managed to tear down anyone who tried to stomp on who they believed were less powerful. They went back to the Clans. But they're welcome anytime, if their attitudes change."

"I still think it's pretty perfect," Adie said.

Tala nodded. She didn't fill the silence. A thickness lay in the air, as though Adie still held the space, but unsure what to do with it.

"Am I a Misfit now?"

"If you want to be." Tala wondered when the question would come up. "I've already reached out to the safe houses and told them to let you in and help if you ever need it."

"What? When did you do that?" Adie smiled.

"On one of your many free jaunts outside in the world while I've been stuck in here."

"You can go jaunt, but I doubt you'll make it downstairs before you huff and puff and head back to bed."

Tala smiled. It felt false on her lips and Adie saw it.

"What aren't you telling me?" Adie asked.

"What do you mean?"

Adie stared at Tala, eyebrows disappearing beneath her fringe.

Heat rose up Tala's neck and she could have been fifteen again with Diana catching her with her hand in the metaphorical cookie jar.

"The truck." Tala swallowed the lump and forced the words out. "It wasn't an accident."

"Yes," Adie's face burst into a smile, but the worry remained in her eyes. "I did figure that much out. I hadn't imagined they had corralled up into that canyon by accident."

"Yeah, alright. But something else is going on, something more than pissed off truckers."

"Why do you say that?" Adie shuffled, putting her legs down on the floor between their two beds and facing Tala.

"How did they know we were there?" Tala asked slowly.

Adie opened her mouth and then closed it again.

"I made three phone calls, Adie." Tala held up three fingers. "Only three. No one else knew where we were heading." Tala sighed, rubbed her neck again. "And of the three, only one of them answered."

"You called Jake."

Tala nodded.

"Why would he help if he had betrayed us?" Adie asked.

"I don't think it's him. I don't think it's any of them." Tala shook her head. "Someone who shouldn't know, somehow knew. I'm thinking someone's tracking their phones."

"All three of them?"

"No." Tala shook her head and had no idea how people functioned with pain and headaches. "Yes?"

"Well, that clears it up." Adie laughed, and Tala appreciated her attempt at lifting the tension in the room.

"I left messages with the other two. Not a lot of detail but I did tell them we were heading here."

"Alright. That's *not* such a good thing." Adie's brow furrowed and Tala was mesmerised by the expressiveness of this woman. "Just to be clear, you trust all three that you called?"

"With more than just my life." Tala didn't hesitate in answering.

"Alright, so not them. Leaves the questions, who wants us dead? And why?"

"I don't know." Frustration leaked into Tala's words. "I should have thought about it right away. They could have tried again. You shouldn't go out alone anymore." Her head wasn't clear enough to put the pieces together, to understand what it all meant.

"Who else did you call?" Adie asked, her voice gentler this time.

The names were on the tip of Tala's tongue when a bang sounded outside their door. It repeated several times but it took Tala a moment to work out it was most likely a fist slamming against the wood.

"Tala!" A female voice. It stirred everything inside of Tala's head and stomach into a whirlpool.

"Who's that?" Adie's eyebrows hid behind her fringe once more as she looked from the door to Tala and back again.

"Xand." Tala smiled.

Xand wasn't a snake in the grass.

"You called her." Adie lowered her voice.

"Yes. One of the messages I left was for her. She would never do this."

"Are you sure?"

"If you ever trusted me, then trust me now." Tala stared at Adie, feeling more exposed than when Adie had changed her bandages.

"Alright." Adie nodded, jumped up, and opened the door.

THIRTY-TWO

TALA

"Oh shit, you aren't Tala," Xand said as the door she'd been pounding her fist against opened.

"No." Adie laughed and shook her head as she stepped away and to the side revealing Xand's flummoxed expression.

"Hey pixie," Tala called as she stood up from her bed.

"Oh, my hell." Xand rushed in as soon as their eyes met. "Woman, you have *got* to stop scaring the shit out of me."

"You're a damn good sight for sore eyes, Xandia Jackson." Tala wrapped her arms around Xand in an embrace that almost caused tears to well up in her eyes.

Warm arms wrapped around Tala's waist and despite the painful pressure on her ribs, she gave into the familiar feeling and smell. Sandalwood and vanilla filled her senses and brought home along with it.

Xand pulled back when Tala couldn't suppress the cringe any longer.

"You're a bitch." Xand smiled, though her eyes were watery. "You are also a sight that causes very sore eyes indeed. I guess the serious shit Jake was on about wasn't an exaggeration." Xand ran long fingers through shoulder length, wavy blonde hair that bounced around her head.

"Yeah, yeah, I've missed you too. Now sit your arse down so we can talk."

Xand looked back over at Adie, who had closed the door but remained standing, half leaning her back against the grain. Xand stared at Adie, and Adie stared right back. Tension rippled along Tala's skin, if she weren't so broken and raw, she might even have enjoyed the sensation or laughed at the ridiculous way they sized each other up. But those days, care-free and filled with the adrenaline of adventure, were long gone. They were swallowed up in grief and a new-found posi-tion of responsibility.

"Xand, this is Adie, Adie this is Xand." Tala sat down on the bed once more, back pressed against the headboard, a mirror to Adie's previous sitting position.

"Hey." Adie smiled.

"Yep, back at ya." Xand pulled her eyes away and perched at the end of the bed facing Tala. Her right leg jiggled on the floor while her bent left leg was tucked underneath her. She pierced Tala with her gaze.

"Now tell me, what the hell has happened?"

"No one has told you about the crash?" Tala asked, feeling her brows pull together.

"That's all I've *been* told. Jake called me and told me to get my arse over here because you're broken, Diana is nowhere to be seen, and the world has gone to hell. I spent almost a week hitching to get here and he's not even downstairs to let me abuse him about his *abysmal* taste in music. You never mentioned how busy this backwater town is."

"It's not usually this busy, and you hack on his music and he's not likely to forget it."

"Good. It's about time that scrawny little bastard moved out of the sticks and brought his ears with him."

Tala laughed and then hissed in a sharp breath of air.

Xand's right leg bounced a little harder.

"I'm ok, Xand."

"Yeah sure. It's been almost a week, and you're obviously still hurt, that's not alright. You know it and I know it. And I'm thinking even this Misfit here knows it. So, what gives?"

"The truck wasn't an accident," Adie said before Tala could speak.

"The truck wasn't an accident." For a moment Xand stopped all movement as she repeated the words more robotic than Tala had ever heard her speak.

They *definitely* had the woman's undivided attention.

"Someone knew we would be there. They were following us. There must have been a few of them all in contact, but who the fuck knows, the bastard died when he hit us."

"Who did you call?" The bouncing resumed as Xand asked the question as though it were an order.

"Jake knew we were coming here. I spoke to him."

"Jake wouldn't do this." Xand was adamant, head shaking back and forth. The leg jiggling apparently not enough to release the energy., Xand stood and started pacing back and forth at the feet of both beds.

"I know." Tala's tongue thickened as the words in her mouth felt wrong. "I left messages for you and Jonah."

The silence, heavy as a weighted blanket, smothered the air in the room.

"You think *I* have something to do with this!" The lack of question punched Tala in the chest.

"No."

"Then *why* would you mention it?"

"Xand, come on." Tala met Xand's eyes and despite the

moments of tense silence, Xand finally closed her eyes and nodded, though the light in her face hadn't returned. "You know I trust you, but I need to know who has access to your calls, and to Jake's."

"What are you thinking?"

"I'm thinking we have a rat in the nest. And there are too many things that aren't right."

"Definitely not right." Xand nodded.

All Tala wanted to see was that radiating smile again.

"Any idea why there are so many people downstairs, or where Jake is?" Tala asked. Her brain couldn't focus and the darkness that loomed between her and her magic continued to grow.

"The eclipse." Adie spoke up. "People are here for the eclipse. Apparently, it's going to be easier to see out here. As far as Jake said."

"Here?" Tala threw Xand a look, only to see her own questions written on the small creases of Xand's face.

"I guess it explains why we didn't get put in a suite." Tala closed her eyes and took as deep a breath as she dared.

"How does she know, and you not?" Xand cocked her head.

"I haven't been downstairs. I haven't talked to Jake yet." Tala blinked then turned to look at Adie. Hurt emotions radiated within her chest. How had Jake not come to visit her? He would have come if he knew she were awake.

"I've told him, Tala," Adie said with a tension so tight Tala imagined an over wound guitar. "He promised he'd come up when he gets a chance."

"Why didn't you tell her how busy it's been?" Xand snapped at Adie.

"I *mentioned* it was busy," Adie snapped right back. "How the *hell* would I know what's normal and not?"

"Please tell me what's happened." Xand sounded like she

was 14 again, and Tala wanted anything but to have to tell her what had happened. "*Where* is Diana?"

Tala looked down at her hands in her lap. Xand stopped pacing and squatted down beside Tala's bed, grabbing Tala's hand and squeezing as though she'd forgotten Tala had bones.

"Please?"

Before she could reorder them, edit them, rethink telling Xand, the words spilled out of Tala's mouth. Once they started, they wouldn't stop. Not until the story had been told.

"So, I was right, you *are* one of us." Xand looked at Adie.

Tala sat up straighter, stiffened her back, and prepared for battle. As much as she could when everything still hurt. "Only if she wants to be, Xand."

"Yeah, I guess I am." Adie spoke as though Tala hadn't opened her mouth. As though Tala was no longer even in the room.

"You helped save her life? Twice? And you made sure Diana's murderer died?"

"I'm not so sure how much was me. Without Diana's guidance and Tala's help, I wouldn't have gotten out of Openfields and Pha would still be underground."

Xand jumped up. Tala tried to grab her arm, but her fingers were easily brushed aside. She was a mosquito. Annoying and present but no match.

Adie stood still, back pressed as far as she could go to the closed door.

"Xand!" Tala called.

Xand ignored her. She stepped forward and wrapped Adie in a bear hug that caused an audible oomph from the surprised woman.

"Thank you. Thank you *so* much."

Tala breathed and let her shoulders sag.

"For what?" Adie asked with a bemused smile. She locked eyes with Tala over Xand's shoulder.

Tala shrugged in reply, a laugh on her lips as Xand finally let Adie go.

"For saving my blockhead best friend over there."

"Hey." Tala laughed.

"You know it's true. You act all tough but you're a big dumb blockhead at times."

Adie laughed and walked to the kitchenette. She filled and then flicked on the kettle while Xand returned to the bed.

"Xand, what's been going on? Why didn't Jonah answer his phone?"

"It smashed," Xand said, eyes not meeting Tala's.

"Since when did *that* stop him?" Tala's smile slipped from her face as Xand's light dimmed, her eyes clouded as she looked up.

"We've been trying to reach Diana for a few days now. We hadn't heard what happened in Openfields, we've been busy with our own issues."

"What issues?" Tala felt the cold rush over her body. A cold that came from within. It was a relief to know her instincts weren't entirely dormant.

"All the Clan leaders, all the Elders, have gone missing. Jonah was one of the last. His phone was left, smashed to pieces."

"What the fuck?" Tala asked through clenched teeth. The wolf inside, the one passed down by the Gods' blood inside her, lifted its head.

"And there have been deaths." Xand spoke softly.

"What?"

"Our people are going missing. We don't even know how many." Xand's eyes were glassy as she spoke. "Only a few bodies have been found since the disappearances. Well parts of bodies."

"*Parts?*" Adie faced the bed where the two sat, her face whiter than Tala had seen it.

"Yes, all drained of blood, the ends cauterised."

Adie slid down the bench and sat on the kitchenette floor, legs pulled to her chest. "No, not again. Not again."

Tala wanted to go to her, wrap her up and save her from this. But her own confusion and denial took precedence.

"This is ridiculous," Tala snapped. "And it's not funny."

"That's what we thought at the start." Xand didn't even react to Tala's words. "I mean. Who would be strong enough to go up against the Elders? *All* of the Elders? The leaders get challenged every so often, sure, but not like this. And then the deaths."

"Do we have anything to go on?" Tala asked.

Xand shook her head.

"How long was it between Jonah knowing about our people going missing and him being taken?"

"A few weeks."

"Why didn't he call Diana? Why didn't he tell us?" Tala clung to the anger. It was far easier to swallow than the despair that tried to overwhelm her.

"He *did* call Diana," Xand said. "She said you would both head home as soon as you were finished with Openfields."

"Oh." Pain squirmed in Tala's stomach.

When had Diana taken the call? When she'd already headed back into Openfields? That would explain why she hadn't told Tala, but she could have called the hotel room. As an explanation Tala knew it didn't sit right. Diana wouldn't have burdened Tala with anything she didn't need to.

She would have told her when she got back, maybe. Well,

she needed the information now and the anger that increased as it ran up Tala's back made her shift uncomfortably.

THIRTY-THREE

TALA

Tala and Xand caught up as best they could under the weight of fear and grief. Food had been ordered and brought in, and the walls closed further in on Tala with each breath.

"I need the fuck out of this room." Tala broke the silence.

"So, what can you do, Adie?" Xand ignored Tala's latest outbreak.

"Xand," Tala warned.

"What? Why can't I know? I bet you've told her what *I* can do."

"No actually, I haven't," Tala shot back.

"You haven't?" Xand blinked a few times as she looked at Tala.

"No." Tala shook her head, glad the headaches were nothing more than annoying throbs. "We haven't talked about the magic, not in detail."

"I can channel fire, and I dream premonitions or the past, or hell knows what," Adie interrupted the two friends. "I wish I could control the fire, but I was lied to, drugged and controlled." Adie's voice softened as the words ran out.

"Bastards." Xand shook her head. "The shit you've been through, it's so much worse than what happens to the rest of us. We just get ignored and treated like we're crazy; disbelief has it uses I guess."

"Well, it did feel a little like being ignored and definitely felt like I was crazy." Adie laughed with a hard bitterness Tala hated hearing.

"I'm sorry. I don't have a sensor button." Xand's face squished, and Tala smiled at the familiar expression.

"Is that your power?" Adie's laugh was genuine and kind this time, and Xand joined in.

"I can feel people's bodies."

Adie raised a single eyebrow and Tala felt her lower body clench.

"Oh shit." Xand laughed. "I didn't realise how that must sound to someone who has never known what I can do. It's been a while. I'm just so used to everyone knowing."

"I thought you weren't allowed to tell anyone?" Adie asked.

"Yeah, well lucky me. I became the nurse of the Clan when they realised that I could feel what was wrong with someone who was sick or injured. I'm the most accurate x-ray you'll ever get. Their rules only apply until they can use you."

"Sounds familiar," Adie muttered.

Tala watched as a look and small smile was shared between the two women. Images of the two of them getting to know each other swirled in a turmoil of confusion inside of Tala. They would be good for each other. Xand's optimism would help Adie work through her darkness. But the swirling didn't ease. It made Tala feel nauseated.

"So, what do you feel?" Adie asked.

Xand smirked and Adie's face flushed red.

"I pinpoint anything that doesn't feel right. It's been a pain in the arse having to learn biology like I was back in high school. But people got sick of me saying things like, the wiggly bit up above the swirly lump is wrong. Sometimes I need to touch the person. Sometimes, if I know the person well enough or have felt their bodies before, I can tell just by being near them." Xand turned to Tala. "Like right now, I know Tala's ribs are still cracked, they haven't even *begun* to heal. Her head is pounding and for God's *sake* Tala, why haven't you just asked?"

"What do you mean they haven't started healing?" Tala ignored the question, hoping Xand got the hint.

"Ask me, Tal."

"No."

"I have more than enough, you know I do."

"I won't hurt you." Tala shook her head back and forth with her words.

"I can help you, Tala. I can't stand you being in this much pain."

"What's going on?" Adie asked looking between Tala and Xand.

"I can transfer some of my energy. I have far too much. It's part of my skill set, apparently. The Clans and the Elders don't know. Tala and Diana are the only ones who do."

"You can help her heal?" Adie's eyes sparkled and Tala groaned.

"Great, now I'm getting ganged up on all over again."

"Please Tal, let me do this," Xand said.

"Why isn't it healing? Everything else has been healing, the cut on my stomach will leave a nice scar but it's healed."

"I don't know. But something is blocking you." Xand moved closer. "May I?"

"Fine. But no energy, just find out what's stopping me from healing."

"Stubborn mule," Xand snarled.

"Pushy jackass," Tala replied.

They smiled at each other, then Xand pressed her flat palms against Tala's chest, enough above her breasts to stop it being trés awkward. It took little more than a minute before Xand gasped and pulled her hands away.

"You've been poisoned."

"*What?*" Adie and Tala said at the same time.

"It's fading, but it's still there, lingering. Your body is fighting *it* instead of healing you completely."

"How?" Adie asked.

Tala turned slowly to Adie. She felt the shift in her eyes a moment too late and Adie moved half a step back as their eyes locked.

"It's ok, it's just her beasty." Xand spoke on a small laugh, shoulders shrugging.

"Her beasty?" Adie asked, not stepping closer.

"Have you two talked at *all?*" Xand shook her head. "With the chemistry you two have, someone might think all you've been doing up here is screwing the whole time."

"Xand!" Tala all but screamed and Adie made a gurgled sound in her throat.

"Tala, someone has poisoned you," Xand reminded.

"Adie." Tala spoke, hoping the heat that flooded her neck and cheeks wasn't a neon red sign. "What *exactly* happened after the crash?"

"What do you mean?"

"Step by step."

"Um, okay, well," Adie flicked her gaze between Tala and Xand, "you stupidly sent me to the backseat and then turned the car into the truck. It hit you full on instead of sharing the load."

"Mhm." Xand shook her head and pouted.

"Yeah, okay, spank me later, can we move on?" Tala rolled her eyes at Xand.

Adie laughed and Tala's mouth hung open.

"Sorry," Tala said, the heat up her neck growing in intensity.

"You and I need to talk later, Adie. *That's* for sure." Xand winked.

Tala felt the muscles clench in her shoulders. "What happened when I passed out?"

"An ambulance showed up. I heard one of them pronounce the driver DOA while the other one came over to us. I told him I was fine and to focus on you first."

"Did you call me by name?"

"I was calling out to you, trying to get you to respond." Adie's face lost all colour.

"It's OKAY," Tala said. "What next?"

"The paramedic started looking for signs of life. A pulse at your neck, he pressed a stethoscope to your chest and then he gave you a shot of adrenaline to try and wake you up. By that time, Jake showed up, he came out of nowhere telling the paramedic he had it covered."

"Fuck," Tala said.

"What?" Adie asked.

"I don't think it was adrenaline. And there is no way an ambulance would have gotten there before Jake. He's a teleport."

"So, the paramedic poisoned you?" Adie's eyes were wide and glassy.

"Best bet, yeah."

"But, why?"

"*That's* the mystery my dear." Xand smiled and flicked her eyebrows up and down a few times.

"It's not a joke or a fun mystery to solve, Xand." Tala's

patience had reached its limit. "They tried to kill me, and someone we trust is to blame."

Xand stepped back; her face crumpled as though she'd been caught in the beam of a flashlight.

"Xand. I'm sorry," Tala said too late.

"You *still* think it's me."

"No." But Tala's voice didn't hold conviction. "Not intentionally."

"You think I would hurt you? You think I'm *that* stupid I would just let slip anything that could be used to hurt you or Diana?" Xand paced back and forth again in the small space. "I'm not a child anymore, Tala. I was *never* a child. Not even before I came to Jonah's Clan. You know that, and yet here you are, the moment of truth. I ran here to help you, because nothing is adding up. It's not like you and Diana have never been hurt before, but with the murders and disappearances. And still, it's not enough for you. I'll *never* be enough for you!"

"You think it's all connected?" Tala grabbed at the thought, why hadn't she thought of that? *'Gods' damned poison,'* she silently answered herself.

"Sure, why not? I'm the evil mastermind after all." Xand turned and pulled open the door. It swung into the wall, the handle lodging firmly into the plasterboard.

"Xand, I didn't mean it like that," Tala called out.

"Fuck you, Tala."

She left and Tala could do nothing but stare after her.

She didn't think Xand had anything to do with it. Did she?

The shadow of doubt tried creeping into her thoughts again, but no. She shook her head. Tala didn't want to believe any of her circle were capable of it, but it *couldn't* be Xand. Of the three, she trusted Xand the most.

Yet, she couldn't deny there was a seed of truth in Xand's anger. It wouldn't be the first time Xand had been accused of being careless with information, and it had never been fair, or true.

"I need to go talk to her."

"She's in love with you, and you just told her you didn't trust her. You might want to give her a minute or two to cool down first."

"What?" Tala stared, open mouthed at Adie.

"You didn't know she was in love with you?" Adie asked quietly, though the small scoff wasn't disguised.

"She used to have a crush on me when we were younger, but that was a *long* time ago." Tala stood and walked to the kitchenette, toddled would be a better description. She refused to acknowledge the warmth that stretched across her chest. "Another cuppa?"

"Sure," Adie said sitting back down on the bed.

With coffee in hand, and the first sips of caffeine taken, Tala took a deep breath. "How are you handling everything, Adie?"

At first Adie laughed. It didn't touch on mirth. "How am I *supposed* to be handling it?"

"No one handles things the same way." Tala sipped her coffee.

"And that's part of the problem."

"What do you mean?"

"I have never been outside of Openfields before. Not that I can remember anyway." She blew on the steam that rose from her own coffee. "There are so many people. And they don't look at me as though I'm scum on the bottom of their shoes."

"You aren't."

"I know." Adie closed her eyes. "But I've lived a lifetime of knowing where I stood, even if that was beneath everyone else. People don't know me; it's a very strange feeling. I should be happy to be out of that place. It's what I always *dreamed* of doing. Getting out and living in the world. But the world I thought existed, the ones in my books, it's not *this* world. This is something altogether foreign and it's exciting, and *really* terrifying."

Tala listened as she sipped her drink. She didn't want to interrupt again. Adie needed to get this out. And Tala didn't have that skill of knowing just what to say. Not like Diana.

Adie looked up from the cup in her hands and met Tala's eyes. A small smile jerked the corners of her mouth up but slipped away just as quickly.

"So, I guess that's how I'm doing, or not doing at all."

"I wouldn't handle it nearly as well." Tala's words slipped out, as easily as they always did around Adie. Too honest and too open.

"I think you're a lot stronger than you give yourself credit."

Tala barked out a hard laugh and indicated her ribs. "As shown here."

"You can't fool me. It wasn't Diana who saved me."

"You saved me, Adie," Tala said.

"Maybe we saved each other. And a little bit ourselves at the same time."

"I like that."

Tala and Adie sipped their coffees, eyes and lips smiling as they gave Xand the time she needed.

THIRTY-FOUR

TALA

"I'll be down in a second, I just have to pee. Go on ahead," Tala said, palm curled around the handle of the bathroom door.

For a moment Adie hesitated and then nodded. Tala waited for the door to close behind Adie before heading into the bathroom.

After taking care of the necessary things, Tala looked in the mirror above the bathroom sink. Questions circled in her head, and she wondered at the self-introspection she kept finding herself in. Herself. She scoffed at her reflection. Who the hell was she without Diana? Who the hell was she?

By the time she made her way slowly down to the bar, she was breathing heavily, her stomach and ribs ached, making her wince with each step. Was this how humans felt all the time? No wonder so many of them were angry at the world.

Despite the warning, the crowd surprised her. People filled all the tables and most of the bar seats held patrons from all walks of life. She saw Adie and Jake chatting at the bar, and headed that way, slowing as Jake continued to talk, his words loud enough for the wolf in her to hear.

"They don't control the Misfits, they just help those who want to understand, who want to be trained on how to use their powers instead of focusing on fearing them. They've helped so many people know they aren't alone. Given them places where we can always find a friendly and understanding person. Pour Another One never would have happened if it weren't for them."

Adie started to respond but Jake's eyes met Tala's, and his face broke into a grin.

"Speak of the devil."

Tala poked out her tongue, giving herself a moment to push the words she had heard away for later. She couldn't think about the Misfits and what they might want from her now. It had always been Diana's baby, Diana running the show. She couldn't compete with that. She sure as hell didn't want to either.

Jake poured her a beer while Tala slid carefully onto the bar stool next to Adie.

"To Diana," he said as he lifted his own glass.

"To D." The lump in Tala's throat made it too hard to say any more about her sister. "Have you seen Xand?"

"Not for a while. She dared question me about my taste in music. I think I liked her better as the fun disembodied voice over the phone."

Tala laughed and nodded.

"How are you doing?" Jake's question instantly stole the humour from the conversation.

"I'll be back, gotta go to the ladies." Adie made a classy exit.

Jake and Tala watched until she slipped into the crowd.

"Honestly?" Tala turned back to Jake.

"Well, no, of course not. I want you to lie." Jake rolled his eyes.

"It's surreal. Did you hear what happened in Openfields?"

"Well, I don't even know how to begin processing it. The world that man had created. Cutting off people and using them as conduits for a magic he had no right to, to magic he *stole*." Tala sipped at her drink and shivered.

Jake's plucked-to-perfection eyebrows rose so high she expected them to disappear under his swept across fringe.

"The coldness, Jake. It seeped into my bones. And the place underground." Tala shook her head pushing away the desire to let it all out, the way she would have with Diana. But she couldn't hide the shudder as the memory of the cold rocked through her.

"I need to do some inventory notes but talk to me Tala. It's not good to bottle it up."

"How about, you do your boring arse work, and I see what kind of gays you've managed to recruit to this backwater town."

"You're lucky you drink with me girl, or you know—" He held up pathetic excuses for fighting fists, "we'd have to meet in the carpark."

Tala threw back the last of her drink, leaned over the bar and poured herself another one. She didn't manage the perfect rich head on her second beer and the thought made her chuckle to herself.

Of course, Jake was better at head.

Jake had already opened the book he used for notes. Whether they were pub notes or Misfits notes she had no idea. With his left hand he scribbled with a half-used lead pencil that might once have had patterns of a unicorn on it. Down by his leg, where none of the crowd would be able to see, he opened and closed his right hand, blue filaments of lights turning on and off as he did.

Tala swivelled around and watched as the pub slowly filled. She poured herself drinks with a nod to Jake each time, hoping he would be keeping tally for her bill, and knowing that he wouldn't. It wasn't until the third, or fourth, perhaps the fifth glass, Tala noticed the alcohol swimming too loose in her head. She was far more intoxicated than she should be. But the effect was a blissed out blurring of the confusing thoughts. The temptation to dive in and be swept away under the alcohol, tapped at the back of her skull.

As the thought solidified, it swiftly vanished as the hair on the back of Tala's neck prickled. The double doors to the pub exploded open with the excited babble of three women who looked like they were taking a break from the heat on a very ill-advised road trip. They all wore tailored slacks, heavy jewellery, and faces full of makeup. The false colours on their skin threatened to drip from the tips of their chins. The blonde, the only blonde of the three that looked like it might be her natural hair colour, stared a little too long at Tala. The prickle on Tala's neck turned into a full spider run of sensation as it made its way down her spine. It didn't feel threatening; it was something else.

"Hey, Jake?"

"What's up?" Jake looked up, his mind still on his notes for a moment before he focused fully on Tala.

"Those three, I'm guessing they aren't natives?" Tala turned away, still feeling the blonde's eyes on her back.

"Nah, not natives," Jake looked over at other patrons using the bar to slump in their misery, Tala assumed to check they weren't interested in the conversation, "but they come through on their monthly slumming it weekend. The bottle blondes like to torment me by trying to make me blush."

Tala laughed and patted Jake's hand in sympathy. "And how is Miki coping with the new influx?"

Miki looked no more than eighteen years old, but Tala had attended her twentieth birthday party three, no four years ago. Even now the girl skipped between tables, taking orders and collecting up dirty cups and plates without skipping a beat. There was the smallest energy of Gods' blood in her, but it was enough. Tala wasn't even sure Miki knew that, but the girl had showed up on Jake's doorstep on her eighteenth birthday and had proved herself a better worker than Jake had ever had.

Despite the noise level and the crowd, who ignored them as if they were a single entity like the Borg, one mind all having decided that the two of them were of no interest, Jake leaned over the bar and lowered his voice.

"Miki takes it all in stride, just as always. But Mia there," he jerked his chin toward the natural blonde. "She's a good mate." He slowed the last two words.

"Oh." Tala locked eyes with Jake, nodding her understanding that she was one of them, and breathed a little easier. It made sense her spidey senses were tingling. With the combination of the lingering poison, and the alcohol, no wonder she didn't recognise it for what it was.

"Still no sign of Xand?" Adie asked as she returned and slipped onto the stool next to Tala. Her eyes slightly puffy around the edges and her hair wet back.

"Nope. She's most likely gone for a run. She creates so much energy. The girl could run marathon after marathon and still have enough left over for a hike."

"She's not a girl, Tala." Adie smiled briefly before looking over at the city slickers.

"I know," Tala said, not knowing what else she could say.

"Well," Jake smiled, "next time you see her, tell her my

country ain't no western shit. She can turn off my music over my dead body. That woman, needs some educating."

"Right?" Adie smiled and nodded to Jake, her head bobbing along to the current song, barely audible over the crowd.

"Oh, I like this one, Tala." Jake gave Adie a wink. "Maybe you can help me convince Tala she can lay down roots and still do this job," Jake's voice softened. "Even without Diana. Help me make an honest woman out of her."

Adie smiled and looked at Tala from the corner of her eyes, eyelids half batted.

"Of course, she can do this job. If that's what she wants to keep doing."

Tala laughed at Jake's pout. "That didn't quite go according to plan now did it?"

"Fine, you're both impossible. I give up." But the smile danced over his lips. He pulled a premixed drink from the fridge behind him, flipped the lid and slid it over to Adie.

"Thanks." Adie smiled, tapped Tala's glass with the neck and took a drink.

Tala turned to see Mia heading outside. She locked eyes with her and the beer at the back of Tala's throat turned to ash. Was this really the spider sense of someone recognising the power in a fellow Misfit?

'Unless you really are losing your power, and it's not just the poison.' Tala's mind unhelpfully offered.

"Tala?" Adie's hand was cold and hard on her upper arm.

"What was that?" Tala asked as a zap of static electricity mixed with the taste of ozone at the back of her throat coincided with Adie's touch.

"What was what?" Concern furrowed Adie's brows.

"You didn't feel, or taste anything?" Tala swivelled back. Mia had disappeared into the world outside of Pour Another Drink, no darkness lingering in the door frame.

And now you're going crazy, well done. Her mind was a royal bitch tonight.

"Nothing." Tala shook her head and stood up. "I've got to go find Xand."

"Be nice." Adie smiled, her fingers lingering in Tala's hand before dropping and letting her go.

THIRTY-FIVE

XAND

Xand stalked through the pub. Jake tried to catch her eye, but the energy within her pressed against her skin, making everything inside vibrate. If she stopped, if she met his eyes, she didn't know what would happen. Although, she had no doubt it wouldn't have been good.

Tala had called after her, but Xand hadn't been able to turn around. She couldn't face this, not again. Being treated like a child, untrustworthy or worse, stupid. It didn't matter that she came here, that she took the initiative and acted. She'd brought the information directly to Tala as soon as she could. She'd already been on her way out of town when the message came through. She'd been heading toward Openfields at that point. Heading there in the hopes of catching up with D and Tal along the way.

Angry grief washed over her face as she pushed through the lull of strangers' voices, the shuffle of chairs, and the clink of glasses.

Finally, she made it to the closed double doors of Pour

Another One, she pushed one side open with flat palms. The smack against the wood echoed through her body and damn if it didn't feel right.

How she yearned for the punching bag at Jonah's. She'd learned to channel the rage and the extra energy into beating the damn thing up. They had to replace it regularly due to her near daily usage.

The night air brushed along her arms, cool and crisp, sizzling against her fury. It filled her mouth with a welcome chill, and for a moment she stopped, bouncing on her tip toes, being as still as she dared.

The carpark to her right brimmed with dusty cars and utes, with spotlights casting ominous shadows that leered and loomed. People milled around, straightening their clothes and checking their hair and makeup inside mirrors, before they greeted each other with air kisses and minimal contact hugs. Xand couldn't believe, even here, people could be so concerned about how they looked, how surface their relationships were. More cars pulled in vomiting their passengers out to repeat the same inane actions.

"Is this the whole bloody town?" Xand muttered as she pulled her head away.

To the left, the veranda sat in relative darkness. There were no lights on the rail of the veranda or any decorating the bushes beyond the steps that Xand could just make out. She couldn't stop and just bounce any longer. Despite her unfamiliarity with the town, she needed to let it out. All of it. The fear, the anger, the pain, the grief.

Unlike Tala, she'd never been here before, but it wasn't like home. Elders and Children hadn't been going missing here, so familiar or not she was going to run.

She'd heard of Jake; she'd even spoken to him a few times

over the phone, even before the panicked call that made her change direction and rush to this dusty side of civilisation.

The foreign smells and air pressed down on her. She took one full breath, filling her lungs to capacity, and then she ran. She'd just do the block a few times, work the edge of energy from her skin. The block was bigger than the ones back home. She passed a field with llamas beside another with horses. It still took three laps before the vibration in her skin receded enough for her mind to start kicking in again.

Tala trusted her. She hadn't accused her. If anything, Xand had accused herself. Diana and Tala knew her past, knew about the shop lifting and the other nefarious deeds she'd done while on the streets. The things she'd *needed* to do to survive. Her mother had been there, but she'd been useless, consumed with her own grief at the passing of Xand's father. When her mother died, relief had washed over Xand, making the hard seed of guilt grow and lodge within her chest. Everyone in The Children of the Gods knew her past, but Diana and Tala were the only ones to ever get past it. Jonah tried, but she saw the sideways looks from him, whenever something had been reported missing, or found broken.

Sweat cooled on Xand's skin and she shivered in the cool breeze. Turning the corner, she eased into a soft jog. The bar stood the same and the carpark remained filled with residents, same or different she couldn't have told. They were in varying degrees of inebriation hiding in and out of the shadows.

Xand wasn't ready to go back inside, not yet.

She'd used enough energy to ease the pressure against her skull but the energy hadn't entirely drained. It so rarely got *entirely* drained. Her mind sometimes made her feel like she had to at least try, or she might explode, or go truly insane. The rest that still lingered in her now, swirled in her mind like a building tornado. It collected her fears and pain along its destructive way. Her thoughts overlapped and crashed together.

Diana had been murdered.

Tala had found another Misfit. The energy between the two of them created a force Xand knew all too well.

She'd long gotten over her feelings for Tala, so why did it hurt? And what had happened to the Elders? That *should* be her biggest concern. That *should* be all she focused on, but who was she kidding? If things weren't okay with her and Tala, if she no longer had Diana, what would all this be for?

She wanted it to stop, the upheaval of her world. She wanted to go home, but what the hell *was* home? *Where* was home? The townhouse hadn't felt like home in years. Not since Tala and Diana had left her as their little spy. She didn't mind the work. It thrilled her to always be kept in the loop despite never being offered to come on the road with them.

Turning her back on the carpark, Xand walked to the darkened end of the veranda. Three wooden steps lead down onto a path that disappeared into pure darkness. Though Xand couldn't stop her mind imagining that the thick shrubs on either side were actually devouring all that stepped beyond where the light touched. With all the horrible things she had seen in her life, the damaged and the broken bodies of those who needed her skills, she supposed seeing the horrible in the beauty around her was all just part of the job.

Her feet jiggled on the bottom step as she sat on the top one, and she let out a harsh bitter noise that might have been mistaken for a laugh in an alternate universe. It sailed off into the darkness.

A gasp came back from the darkness, swallowed by bushes. Xand jumped back to her feet.

She pulled at the energy beneath her skin, just like she and Diana had practiced. She could have *helped* if only they'd taken her with them to Openfields. Her power was no longer passive, she'd trained enough to make it active. Diana knew that, even if Tala didn't.

The energy built and anger, grief, and power coursed through her.

"Sorry." The voice was warm and seductive. Not quite rough or deep like Tala's. Thank the Gods, Xand tried to convince herself Tala was the last person she wanted to speak to.

Her subconscious laughed, mocking her even as the owner of the voice stepped into the light. She had long blonde hair with large curls that bounced past her shoulders. As opposed to Xand's nearly white shining hair, the stranger's was a dirty blonde, with sneaks of light brown strands in the mix.

"I'm sorry, I didn't realise anyone was out here," Xand said.

"I won't tell if you won't." The woman lifted her right hand to reveal a half-burned cigarette between her pointer and middle finger. She looked sheepish, teeth together in a smile that told Xand that her smoking was a big no-no in her world.

"Your secret is safe with me." Xand laughed. She let go of the heat, the energy drained from her in a wave of spent adrenaline. She collapsed back down onto her top step and dropped her head in her hands.

"Hey," the woman spoke. "Are you OK?"

"Yeah." Xand looked up. "Just frightened me, I guess."

"Likewise," she pointed at the step next to where Xand sat, "mind if I join you?"

"Not at all." Xand leaned heavily on the upright of the steps, shuffling her bum enough to allow the woman to sit without being crowded.

"I'm Mia." The woman smiled.

"Xand."

"That's nice."

"It's okay." Xand laughed. "It's odd."

"Mmm, I would say unique, in a very good way. I used to like Mia; I thought it was unique once. But it turns out, so did lots of people and now there are all these mums screaming my name out at the shops, and it's never me, and it's never in a fun way." Mia looked sideways to Xand.

Xand might not have gotten out of the hometown often, but she knew when a woman flirted with her.

"Well now that's a real shame." Xand leaned into the smile, tilting her head forward slightly and looking at Mia from the top of her eyes.

"I think so too." Mia took a drag from her cigarette and blew the smoke out slowly.

Oh my, how Xand could get lost in those lips. "Got another one?"

"Sure, but they're inside, tucked away safely in the lining of my handbag."

"Ah." Xand nodded, though she wondered how that made any kind of sense.

"But we can share." Mia smiled.

Warmth washed through Xand's chest; her fingers brushed Mia's as she took the offered cigarette. Pressing the end between her lips, Xand tasted sweet wine and lipstick. She breathed deep of the vice and blew it out just as slow as Mia had.

"So, what brings a woman like you to a place like this?"

Xand laughed as she handed back the cigarette.

"Ah you know, a bit of this, a bit of that and what the hell, let's throw in some stuff as well."

"Oh, I see, going the enigmatic route, are we?"

"Not really." Xand leaned forward, resting her forearms on her knees as they jiggled up and down once more.

"You really are quite unique."

"Yeah," Xand leaned back and twisted slightly, her back to the upright railing, her eyes resting happily enough on Mia, "So people keep telling me, but then they get too scared to take me out and play with me."

Mia burst out laughing and only then did Xand realise what she had said.

The heat rose from her chest and up her neck. It had been a long time since she had managed to be embarrassed by her own words. It had been a long time since she let words slip out without realising the double meaning behind them.

"Oh Gods, please ignore everything I've just said. Exhaustion and a foreign place apparently do weird things to me."

"Gods? Plural?" Mia asked with eyebrows raised as she brushed out the butt of the cigarette on the step between where they sat and where their feet rested.

"Sure, why not?"

Mia smiled, a smile that both heated Xand's lower belly and ran a chill over her skin.

The coolness of the air made Xand's breath blow out in puffs of white. She blinked. At the sound of Mia's laugh, she snapped her head up at the woman. The eyes that had been a hazy blue were now dark. The eyes of a God's blood.

"You're doing that?" Xand asked with more puffs of dragon breath.

"Yep," Mia said.

"That's amazing. How strong is it? Does it cool everyone in the vicinity? Can you do ice?"

"One question at a time." Mia laughed and wiped a bead of sweat from her brow. "And damn, now I'm out. That was me being stupid and totally showing off."

"You didn't have to go full tilt to impress me."

"Really?" The vulnerability in Mia's eyes as they shifted back to that piercing blue, caught Xand's breath in her throat.

"Really." The word came out hoarse, as though she desperately needed a drink of water.

They leaned closer and Xand could smell the sweet wine on Mia's lips. The kiss began tame and tentative. The sweetness of the touch and the taste made Xand moan into Mia. Sweetness slipped away. Tongue and teeth teased open Xand's mouth, the nip on her bottom lip sent a spark of pleasure to her core.

The world faded away and the darkness wrapped around the two as they shifted closer together, legs slipping between the others, while hands found warm skin beneath shirts.

Xand's short nails gently dug into Mia's back, scraping upward. Mia pulled her mouth away gasping at the sensation.

"Sorry." Xand spoke quickly.

"Hell no. Don't be." Mia captured Xand's mouth with her own once more.

Their heated make out session ended abruptly when a group of people barged their way out of Pour Another One.

"Oh shit." Xand pulled away, her breath coming in short bursts.

Mia leaned back, her eyes twinkling and a laugh escaped despite the pressed line she pushed her lips into.

"Why do I suddenly feel like a teenager?" Mia wiped fingers over her slightly swollen bottom lip.

"Because we're acting like teenagers."

The laugh escaped Mia's lips and Xand leaned forward for another kiss. A mere brush of lips before Mia moved back again.

"I think your friend is looking for you."

Xand shifted just enough to see the familiar outline of Tala as she stepped out onto the veranda.

"I'll see you later, Xand." Cold lips pressed to Xand's cheek. Xand took in a deep breath.

"I'll be in town a while," Xand replied.

"Good." Mia smiled and slipped back into the shadows.

"Xand?" Tala's voice reached Xand in her relative darkness.

"Tala?" Xand stood and stepped into the light. "What are you doing here?"

"Funny, thought that was my question."

CHAPTER

THIRTY-SIX

TALA

"Xand?" Tala heard Xand's voice from beneath the shadow of the tree at the end of the veranda. The sky had darkened, though streaks of orange and purple were just now fading behind the hills in the distance.

Then Tala picked up a second voice, one she didn't recognise.

"Tala?" Soles of boots shuffled on the wooden deck moments before Xand emerged from the darkness. "What are you doing here?"

"Funny, thought that was my question." Tala knew Xand's guilty face, darkness and shadows notwithstanding. "Who were you talking to?"

Xand narrowed her eyes. "Oh, you know, just some big bad evil. We were just working out how best to kill you."

"Xand..."

"Tala. We have been best friends for the better part of twenty years and suddenly you don't trust me? Is it Adie?"

"Adie has *nothing* to do with this. She trusts you, though

she also thinks you're in love with me, so you know, her judgement might not be the best."

"She's perceptive, isn't she?"

"What?" Tala stared at Xand.

"Oh, *breathe* you moron." Xand shook her head. "I will always be a little bit in love with you, Tala. You were my first crush."

"Oh." Tala took a deep breath.

"So, you and her, huh?" Xand smiled.

"What? No."

"Oh come on Tala, she's absolutely electric for you."

"No, it's not like that."

"And why the hell not?"

"She's lost her whole life, Xand. She's got enough shit to deal with. She doesn't even know what I'm really capable of."

"Oh my Gods. Tala, stop overthinking it. Since when did you start being all think before you act?"

"Since Diana died."

"Yeah well, I lost her too." Xand's eyes were wet and glassy. "Don't take it out on Adie. She's lost enough. Let her have a little spark in her life."

"Yeah, I know all about you and your little sparks." Tala raised her eyebrows, a smirk curling the corner of her mouth.

"If you can't be with the one you love, honey," Xand sang as she winked at Tala, "have fun with the one you're with, but hon, that's not you and her, trust me."

A noise from the shadows made Xand jump, and Tala narrow her eyes. The wolf looked between the shadows of the shrubs. Residual energy lingered; energy that left a black ooze behind.

"The wolf is back," Tala said, relief washing through her as the poison finally lost some of its strength over her power.

Xand's fingers clamped tightly around her arm. "I met someone, she's one of us. Can you see her?"

"She's not there anymore, there's a black trail." Tala leaned a little closer to the darkness. "Fuck, there is a softer trail, beneath, it's faint but it's definitely one of ours. It looks like she's been taken."

"Oh shit, Tal. What has her?" Xand's voice was a nail, sharp and hard.

"Xand."

"What?" Xand asked, leaning closer to Tala.

Tala felt Xand's racing pulse in her wrist as it pressed against her skin.

"Something else is wrong," Tala furrowed her brows and cocked her head, "inside. Listen."

Xand stood silent for a moment. "I don't hear anything."

Xand and Tala's eyes met and the reality of what she'd said hit as hard as the truck had.

"I don't hear anything," Tala said.

Xand nodded, eyes wide, her hand gripped tighter on to Tala's.

The mesh of drunk voices and music had floated out to the veranda as a low lull, a background noise, easily forgotten until its absence became a yawning mouth. Black and ready to swallow you whole.

"What do we do?" Xand asked as she bounced on her toes. "We need to find her, Tala. She was nice. And you know I don't find just anyone nice."

"I'm sorry about your friend. We *will* find her, but right now I need you with me in there. Please?" Tala stared at Xand, begging her friend with everything inside of her.

"I'm always with you Tala. Are you ready for this?" Xand asked, taking a deep breath.

"I'm ready to stop being on the back end of all this shit, that's for *damned* sure," Tala growled rough and low.

"There's my pissed off partner," Xand said, a determined smile on her lips as she let go of Tala's hand and shook out her fingers.

Tala knew Xand's tell for preparing for battle. Better yet, she could feel Xand bringing energy to the surface of her skin. Damn it was good to have her powers back, and none too soon.

Tala used both hands and pushed open the double doors, as though they were in an old Western movie. Together Xand and Tala entered Pour Another One.

Darkness greeted them.

"Sorry folks." Jake's voice broke the black silence as the lights flicked back on. "Just a tripped fuse. All fixed now."

Noise washed over them as people started talking once more. Nervous laughter and mocking guffaws filled the space.

"What happened?" Tala asked as she and Xand approached the bar slowly. Beneath the calm demeanour, Tala's heart raced. The poison had definitely lost its effect. Black ooze floated around Jake and Tala swallowed once, twice.

"Miki plugged in an old blender I hadn't gotten around to throwing out. Tripped a fuse, nothing to worry about." Jake smiled; a cold heartless grin Tala had never seen from her friend before.

He, no, whatever had taken on Jake's visage, called them closer with a jerk of its head as it dried a glass with the dish-towel that usually hung on Jake's belt. Fuck, was it possession or copying? Tala had to focus. She looked over to Miki who stood several steps away from Jake, beads of sweat dotting her forehead and confusion furrowing her brow.

She refrained from nodding to Miki, but how she wanted to reassure her. She couldn't, not yet. The darkness that glowed from Jake also swirled around her in the shadows that lingered. She couldn't pinpoint where it originated from, not in the crowd.

Was it the poison or the alcohol still affecting her? Whatever they poisoned her with had an awfully long shelf life. It outlived anything she'd experienced before.

Just like Adie.

She hesitated. What the hell, how did her mind even jump at that one?

Xand gripped her hand and the energy rushed into her. She tried to stop Xand, tried to pull away, they would both need their energy. But it was too late. Xand's energy rushed through Tala. It sloughed off the last effects of poison and alcohol alike. The darkness almost glowed with the return of her wolf's full strength.

Jake's smile dropped at the corner.

"Where's Adie?" Tala asked.

"Bathroom." Jake smiled again, brittle like snapped off toffee.

"Well, what about some music?" Tala had to buy herself some time. Her mind was finally clear, but there were so many things it needed to catch up on.

"There's enough noise in here for now. Don't you think?"

This wasn't Jake. If she'd had any doubts, they were quickly extinguished. So, what did it mean?

*Focus, get out of here first. Get out of here **alive**.*

Xand and Tala stepped as one. Closer to the bar but with no move to sit down. Jake pulled an overly heady foam of beer with his right hand. Tala looked at Xand and warmth spread through her. The comfort of being able to read those eyes washed over her. Xand saw the signs as clearly as Tala did.

"So, you haven't been here long, that much I know." Tala forced her shoulders forward, to slouch, a misdirection to the coiled muscles beneath her skin.

"What do you mean?" A bead of blood burst into life at the corner of Jake's lip as he stretched the smile wider, a hungry crocodile convincing the land animals that he would take them across the river unharmed.

"What she means," Xand answered, "is that had you *been* here longer, you would know that Jake is a meticulous barkeep, who is left-handed."

"And he would rather die than be without his music," Tala added with a shrug.

Jake laughed and the screams surrounding them pulled the air from Tala's throat. The black ooze solidified into tendrils that wrapped around the patrons, and in the blink of an eye, their screams were cut off in gurgles of pain and heat. Bodies dropped around them. Sizzling sores and angry marks covered their flesh. Faces warped in their last moments of agony. The tendrils slithered away from the corpses and headed, in a leafy whisper toward Tala and Xand. Tala used a stool as a climbing tool as she clambered onto the bar top. Instantly she put her hand down and helped Xand up beside her. Xand nodded her thanks and turned toward the oncoming rush of slithering darkness.

Not-Jake's sudden grip on Tala's ankle felt like a vice. The hint of panic fled in the moment of anger. This wasn't her friend, but she knew, as she looked at the scarred flesh on the back of his knuckles, a lifetime of burns cooking at the grill, that she would never see him again.

It was his flesh, his scars and marks and bumps. Somehow, she knew it, she could smell him, beneath the stench of decay that radiated this close to their enemy. Jake was gone. Red washed over her vision. Guilt and anger were ready to kick the snot out of this bastard. Leaning all her weight on her trapped ankle, she raised her other foot and slammed it directly into his face. The heel of her boot crunched the cartilage of Jake's nose.

Silently, Tala begged the body of her lost friend for forgiveness.

"You *bitch*!" His scream was guttural. The roar of the real monster hiding behind her friend's face.

"And you're nothing but a coward."

"Tala!" Xand called from beside her and stopped Tala before she could jump down onto the other side of the bar.

She looked back to see Xand, tendrils wrapped around her, pinning her hands to her chest. Fear slithered up her chest, coiled around her throat and threatened to strangle her. She shook her head, fierce and hard, and clenched her teeth together.

"Quit hiding and come out and face us, you prick." Tala turned and screamed at the open space in front of the bar. She bellowed into the darkness that had settled over the dead faces that would undoubtedly haunt her for the rest of her life. Tala just hoped that was longer than a few more hours.

A laugh from the open door pulled Tala's focus and attention. From the corner of her eye, Tala saw even Jake stiffen and pay attention.

Interesting.

In the frame stood a silhouette, her features washed out from the darkness behind her. Yes, her. The laugh, and the figure, were most definitely female.

"Mia?" Xand said, face contorted in pain as she resumed wriggling against the dark grip.

Tala's attention shifted to her friend and in that instant, in that quick look, she knew her error. The tendrils dropped Xand and slammed with all their strength into Tala's chest. Wind forced from her lungs, and she gasped for air in the moment between her body breaking against dozens of bottles from behind the bar and the darkness washing over her.

CHAPTER

THIRTY-SEVEN

TALA

Tala woke with her thoughts spinning too fast to grasp and her stomach roiling. It wasn't a slow awareness but a gasp of instant consciousness. As though her body had been begging for her to wake long before her mind complied.

Before the idea of drinking herself into oblivion came to mind, her thoughts slowed, and a flood of memories filled her already aching head.

Memories in blinding technicolour realness. Openfields and the murders. The fight with Billie. The sound of her neck breaking beneath the beast's paws. The flames and Adie.

Crash.

Pain.

Xand.

Jake.

Wetness on her cheeks tickled. She took a deep breath, demanding the salty tears, *actual* tears, to stop. The smell surrounding her tormented her gag reflex. It was still better that than tears.

Her next breath inflated her lungs to the barest necessity.

Sure, throwing up would be preferable to tears, but doing both seemed beyond the nightmare she already found herself in. She prepared for the pain that had become so familiar over the week. Nothing happened, no sting or protest from her ribs. She remembered Xand's grip, and the energy she forced into Tala.

Oh Xand. Where are you?

Tala tried to rub her hands over her face, to scrub clean the whirlpool of thoughts and banish the tears. But her hands wouldn't obey. Confusion added to her jumbled mind of memories. Mentally tracing the length of her arms she found her hands bound, shoulders lifted over her head. Her temple pulsed. Pain both physical and mental pounded out the rhythm. Cold shards shot up her legs and she shuffled, her bare feet grazed against a metal floor. Where the hell were her boots? She had liked those boots, worn in just the right amount.

Enough!

She shook her head, both regretting the sharp pain and grateful for the clearing of her head.

Time to figure this shit out.

She looked up to gauge the quality of the ties around her wrists and winced at the brightness coming through a circular hole in the metal roof above her. She had to have been out all night, and *well* into the morning.

What the hell had that bitch done to her?

She really did have to stop waking up feeling like death. And this time, she was tied up.

"What have you gotten yourself into now?" Her voice was rough and hoarse, unused for too long and in need of some liquid.

"Yes," a voice, like a hyena, high-pitched and racing, came from a darkness outside the spotlight of the skylight, "you are *finally* awake."

"Who the fuck are you?" This wasn't the woman she'd seen in the doorway, and it sure as hell wasn't Jake, no matter the familiar shape in front of her.

This not-Jake that wore his face, couldn't dream of being a fraction of the man Tala had known. Burning bile rose to the back of her throat. She pushed it back and focused on her captor. Was he in charge, or just a guard? Had Tala's head not been filled with fireworks exploding in unprecedented ways, she would have laughed, perhaps even mocked the figure that stood in front of her.

"You aren't Jake," she growled out instead. Anger finally dried any more tears.

"Is that all you have figured out? This is even better than I'd hoped." He clapped his fingers, his palms stayed together. The action triggered some memory in the back of Tala's mind, but it remained vague and out of reach.

"Well, seeing as I'm tied up in a windowless room, I'm leaning toward you're the murderous arsehole I've been looking for."

"I'm *not* a murderer." Rage so foreign to Jake's features filled his once beautiful face.

Huh, not a murderer, nice trigger point there. If only I knew how to put the Gods' damned pieces together.

"I'm the one who will save us all."

"So, you're what, a hero?" Tala scoffed.

"Yes!" There was no trace of his earlier high-pitched laughter or unique hand clapping now.

Stepping closer to Tala, his dark eyes glinted with traces of her friend beneath.

Please don't let him still be in there, please don't let him be trapped and suffering.

"Stop being him." She forced the request out.

"I'm far better than that *imbecile*." Not-Jake giggled.

"Stop. Being. Him." The beast flared in her chest, burning her from within. She had to change tact, for her own sanity. She had to stay calm. "Where is Jake?"

"Oh, you really are so stupid. Jake is dead. He was nothing more than a tool. Unfortunately, tools get used up. He is nearly finished now."

"So, you *are* a murderer," Tala snarled.

"He's dead, but I didn't say I murdered him."

"STOP BEING HIM." *'Nice and calm, that certainly worked, good one Tala.'* Tala bit back the power that dared to lash out over her tongue. She tasted it, swished it around her mouth. Did he know the drugs, the poison, had stopped working?

Hold your cards close, no matter what you feel. Diana's words seemed to echo in this small metal room that reeked of death.

Tala had to prove she'd listened. Had to prove all the time and effort Diana put into her and her training had not been in vain. Even if it were too late to show Diana now, too late to make her proud, she still had to do it. For herself, if nothing else.

Movement beneath Jake's skin bubbled unnaturally, distorting his features and colour. Blood dribbled out of rips in the skin as the larger bulk of the man within the Jake facade pushed his way through. Soon another man faced her, where the not-Jake once stood. He breathed heavily with a snarl on his face, scarred flesh prominent on the skin. At his feet were the tattered remains of her friend. She closed her eyes and moved her face away from them.

"Better?" he asked.

"Can I have some water?" Tala managed to say, hating the weakness in her voice.

"Do you really think I'm that stupid?"

"Please?" She looked down, toward the corner of the room,

making sure not to see the shredded flesh again. She couldn't risk him not believing her poker face.

"No water!" he screamed.

"Okay." Tala's head split with the sound of his yell.

Keep them talking. People are self-centred in general, and they love to talk about their own brilliance.

Tala bit back a sob as Diana's voice filled her ears rather than her memory. Maybe it was just wishful thinking, but she would take whatever advantage she could get.

"Where's Adie?" She wanted to know but she also didn't.

She didn't want to hear that Adie had died alone and scared. She didn't want to hear that she'd lost her when she'd only just found her. She'd wasted time with Adie, holding back her feelings and desires. And for what?

"Oh Adie," Sam's voice softened, interrupting Tala's thoughts, "she is so untrained and angry. But she needs to be punished for her actions."

Is so untrained? Needs to be punished? Is was good. Needs was even better. Present tense means alive. Tala breathed a sigh of relief.

Silently she hoped Xand couldn't hear her, silently begged forgiveness for what she would imply. But she had to focus on keeping him talking, revealing without realising what he said.

"What did you do to convince Xand to join you?"

Tala let her mind trail off in thoughts that processed far better when she wasn't trying to force them to any one track. Thanks to Xand's own quick thinking and transfer of energy, Tala had more strength now, more energy than she'd had since the before the crash.

She couldn't let it go to waste.

"Xand?" His eyebrows, like fat furry caterpillars that wriggled together in question.

"The pixie," Tala seethed. How dare he not even know her name? What had he done to her? "The one who was with me."

"Oh," there was something weighted in that word that made Tala's stomach churn. It carried the same judgemental arrogance that had been one of the driving forces in Diana and Tala separating from the Clans. "I wouldn't let a passive skill like that anywhere near us. Xandia was of no consequence. Just another pest to be rid of."

Xandia? Tala's brain caught on the implication immediately. *This bastard actually knows us.*

"But you could be useful, if you stopped being so damned stupid."

And then the penny dropped. His voice splashed ice cold water over Tala's skin, raising small goose pimples over her flesh. With teeth chattering, Tala narrowed her eyes. Hope faded as she took in the finer details. She saw the face hidden behind age and anger.

Time had not been kind. But nothing could disguise the darkness in those eyes.

"Sam?" Tala asked as memories of the boy slammed into her as though he'd curled his fat fingers into fists and punched her.

He'd been young and angry. Too young to already be treading so far down that dark path. Despite how much Diana had tried, it hadn't been enough.

She saw him once again clapping at the horrors they'd found. The horrors *he* had called his artwork.

"Sam? Is that you?"

"I'm better than you and Diana *ever* were. You feared my power, and you tried to make me fear it as well. But there's nothing wrong with me. I'm stronger than both of you combined. *She* is the only one who ever believed in me, and she showed me how to use my power properly." That high pitched giggle escaped his lips once more.

"So, you're doing someone else's dirty work. Sounds about right. Why aren't they helping you?"

"Oh, they are." His smile sent a shiver up Tala's back. "*All* of them are. Turns out there were so many eager disciples. However, I make sure I get to do the *special* ones."

"Special ones?" Tala had pushed back against the sharp tang that had filled her nose since she woke, but now she couldn't deny it's horrid familiarity.

"Oh, your precious Elders. They were hardly even a challenge. They caved *so* easily." He spoke dreamily, his eyes glazed over to a past Tala never wanted to know the details of. "They think they're the most powerful of what has been left behind. Yet, I have defeated them all. *I* have defeated you all. The last will fold. I've trained *all* her rightful followers in my ways."

"Rightful followers? What makes you a rightful follower?" Tala knew the moment the questions slipped from her mouth that they were too direct, too eager.

"Now," he ignored her. "You and that sanctimonious *bitch* sister of yours will know real fear. I will find her. By all means, hold out as long as you can. I like to take my time. But you might remember that."

She remembered it, she remembered *him*. Despite how much she'd tried to forget.

Sam.

They'd *had* to kick him out. He was a sadist. The torture he'd inflicted on his fellow Misfit still haunted Tala in the grey moments between sleep and wakefulness. The rest of his words finally found their way to the front of her mind.

"You want to find Diana?" Tala laughed. At first it filled the metal room with a hard sarcasm. Too soon she lost what little control she had on it. Her lips trembled, teeth still chattering, as tears slipped from her eyes once more and ran over her cheeks. Lifetimes passed, stars birthed and died, and inside her head Tala screamed over and over, trapped within her pain.

She closed her eyes and sobbed with hysteria.

A cold wetness touched Tala's top lip with a shock that sprang her eyes open again. Had she passed out? She teased her tongue out and touched her bottom lip.

Oh, sweet water.

Tala opened her mouth, tongue searched desperately for more of the sustenance.

Sam dribbled the liquid into her mouth. Each drop sparked a relief inside her, but it was short lived and not enough. There would never be enough. Still, the relief flooded her veins and flicked on a light within her mind.

Her shoulder sockets burned, the twist to her arms above her head unnatural, but movement might soon be possible, if she could just concentrate hard enough. If she could focus and somehow stop him from noticing it.

"Why have me strung up here, Sam? Why not just kill me?" Tala couldn't wait, now would have to be soon enough. She might not get another chance, and like most bad guys he would expect her to wait.

"I told you—"

"Yes, yes, you *aren't* a murderer, so then what happened to the others?"

"What do you know about the others?" Sam's smile glinted, the sharp edge of a knife's blade.

The water built inside her. Her shoulders continued to ache, but the pounding in her head receded and thoughts began to run smooth once more.

Pity her mouth decided to keep running as well.

"Who actually killed them, Sam?" *Who you cowardly snake?* "What's in all of this for them? And for you? I mean besides the whole sadistic torture thing?" *Careful Tala.* "You were never really smart enough to be in charge of much, so who is pulling your strings, *puppet?*"

Well done, round of applause.

Anger raged within his narrowed eyes. Tala laughed until the back of Sam's hand stung her cheek and cut the skin.

Tala licked at the blood. "So, what's the plan then, big guy?"

And her mouth just *kept* on running.

His smile widened, and Tala thought of the Joker from Batman.

"You think you're so smart, how come you haven't figured it out yet?"

"Well, let's be fair. Being poisoned had something to do with that. Which of course is a *coward's* way out."

"I'm *not* a coward," he seethed between clenched teeth.

Tala had been so focused on the depth of darkness in his stare that she hadn't noticed his knife. Not until the light pouring in from above glinted off the blade. He lifted it up and wriggled it back and forth in his hand. Despite the meagre drops of water he had dripped in to her mouth, Tala struggled to swallow as her eyes followed the blades every movement.

Sam lifted it up to his face, his eyes sparkling. Without words, Sam moved forward. Tala tried to shuffle back, tried desperately to shift away. But what little strength she had couldn't begin to compete against the chains and the freedom of unrestrained movement he had.

Searing pain followed the slow draw of the blade.

"X marks the spot." He giggled as he cut into Tala's chest.

She screamed unable to hold it back. It wasn't so much from the pain, but the knowledge of what he was capable of, the memory of how he had left his fellow Clan member.

His giggle was replaced by a low hum. It terrified Tala more than any psychotic laughter could.

Sam smiled as he stepped back and surveyed his work. The control of his movements, in the way he examined Tala's bleeding flesh with an expression of such thought, caught Tala's breath in her chest.

A loud bang stopped Sam as he lifted one foot as though to step closer to her. The instant frown on his brow got Tala breathing once more. A reprieve from his scrutiny at the very least.

Without a word he walked to the closed door, white light leaking around the edges.

"I won't be long." He turned to the door and smiled. In any other context it might have been mistaken for loving. It sent a cold ripple over Tala's skin. "Hang in there, we don't have long to wait now."

The door clanked shut. Tala winced as something outside, a handle, a bolt, or a lock slammed into place. It didn't matter what. All that mattered was the sharp crack of pain and lightning the sound sent through her head.

"She's worse than him." A squeak of a voice came from Tala's left.

Unconsciousness threatened to overtake her, but Tala bit her lower lip, hard enough to taste blood. The shift of pain from her chest forced awareness back upon her, at least for now.

Little by little, she pushed the tips of her toes against the cold cement floor until she faced the corner where the voice had come from. Squinting into the shadows, she could only just make out a lump, slowly moving with a breath she had been too distracted to hear earlier.

Adie's vision, the newspaper. They slammed together and

she inwardly cursed herself for not noticing the connection before now.

"Rebecca? Becky?" Tala's voice sounded like a stranger's as it bounced around metal walls. "Is your name Becky?"

A sob answered, and for a moment Tala thought it might be the only response she would get. It was her nature to worry and care about others. Maybe not nature, but it sure was a lesson she learned from Diana's nurturing sisterly ways. But she had to focus on escape. She couldn't help Becky if she couldn't find a way out of the chains. All before Sam came back.

A shuffle and a groan joined the irregular sound of sobs. Becky had smiled broadly from the picture in the newspaper. The person who slid into the light looked as though she might have never smiled once in her entire life. Tala wasn't sure if she would ever smile again.

Her clothes were torn and ripped. Becky's arms and legs all ended in stained gauze wrappings that barely covered the stumps beneath. Blood stained her skin that peeked beneath the edges of the tattered cloth. Her nose sat at an unnatural angle and her left eye all but disappeared beneath skin too swollen and darkened to be seen. There were so many bruises that covered her face that Tala couldn't swear this was the same person from the newspaper.

"I'm so sorry." Tala slumped; pain yanked at her wrists as she made them take her weight. She had failed already. She had failed before she had ever begun. Everything Diana fought for would now die with Tala.

<Just promise me the fucker will pay.>

The words slid into Tala's mind. Tala's head snapped back up and met the woman's eyes.

<Yes, I'm Becky.>

And Becky was a Telepath.

Becky's eyes widened, and a fresh wave of panic lashed at the room as the door scraped opened again.

Tala pressed her lips together and forcing her expression into stillness as the door let in enough light to tell her nothing more than what the skylight had already made sure she knew. It was bright out there, no hint of anything beyond the light to give her hope or strength.

"Oh good, you met our little Becky. She's a bit *littler* now." He laughed as though his joke was amusing but he needed to be humble about his own genius.

He was met with nothing more than the heavy breaths of the two women.

"Do you know what she tried to do?" Sam chatted as he lifted the knife and trailed its tip over the cuts on Tala's chest. She hissed in through her nose but would give him no more satisfaction than that. He would have to work for every fucking scream he tore from her.

"No?" Sam flicked his eyes to Becky and then back to Tala. "She tried to get me to kill her before the eclipse could start."

Tala wanted to make sense of what he was on about, but truthfully, she didn't care. The only thing she could focus on was the pain.

"So, I had to teach her a lesson. None of us, not a one, can go on as we have, in this perverted way and *not* be punished. But our little Becky showed *such* impatience." Sam's mocking words were punctuated with the closing of the door. It shut with a finality Tala didn't want to think about, she *couldn't* think about.

She didn't care, but she knew she had to. She wasn't dead yet. Diana fought beyond the grave. Tala would *not* give up. Despite how much she wanted to escape the pain.

What had he said? The Eclipse?

Adie had mentioned it. The reason for Pour Another One

being so busy. And there had been the waving flags as they had driven over the gateway bridge. She hadn't taken enough notice of the date at the bottom; it had seemed so far away. Lifetimes away. Hadn't it?

She couldn't remember. Being hit by a truck seemed to be messing with her sense of time.

Tala nodded gingerly and Becky's shoulders shuddered before she slid back into the darkness.

"Good little rat, scurry back to your corner." Sam laughed before he slipped into the shadowed corner opposite where Becky huddled once more.

The sound of steel scraping against something that fluctuated between hard and soft, tensed every muscle in Tala's body.

<She's still alive.> Becky's thoughts rang inside Tala's head. It hurt, the pain that filled Becky's thoughts.

"What?" Tala said, shock momentarily forgetting her need to keep her mouth shut.

"Shut up," Sam growled from the corner.

<He doesn't kill us. Becky's thoughts continued inside Tala's head. *She does. She takes our blood first. He cuts parts off us, and she takes them, I think she drinks the blood.>*

"Why?" Tala didn't have the luxury to keep herself quiet, screw Sam. She needed the answers.

"Because I told you to shut up. Ask Becky what happens if you don't listen."

<Just think, I can hear you.> Becky thought.

Well, that's not creepy at all. Who is still alive? Is it Adie?

<I haven't heard or seen anyone called Adie, but they've talked about her.>

Then who's still alive?

<Her name is Jess. She was already here when Sam took me.

He's been slicing her up. I hoped she would be dead by now, but I can still hear her. She's screaming inside her mind.>

I'm so sorry, Becky. Tala thought. *So, you're a Misfit, yeah? Do you know who I am?*

<No.>

My name's Tala. The silence in Tala's head told her Becky knew her name as well. *I **will** kill this bastard, if it's the last thing I do. But I need to know everything you know. I need anything you know that can help me. About how to get out, about what the hell is going on.*

<He talks in riddles, I don't know why she's draining us, but she doesn't mean to kill us. Every time one of us dies, she sends him off to take another. Please, I just want to die.>

I'm so sorry for what he's done.

<Don't be sorry. Just make sure you kill him. Kill both of them. I don't know how many others there are. Those two are the only ones who have hurt me. But I can hear Misfits screaming sometimes when they are both here.>

Tala shuddered. The slice of metal on soft, and hard, then scraping on stone bounced off the metal walls.

<I'm not going to last much longer. But I will hold on, as long as I can, if it means those fuckers will die.>

The silence chilled Tala. Small sparks of light flicked from the opposite corner, hurting Tala's light sensitive eyes.

Becky?

<Yeah.>

What have you learned from him? Do you know how I can fight him?

<No, I don't know. He does keep talking about how Adeline, Adie, is the key. How it'll be a waste to lose her, but she can't be allowed to go unpunished. I guess if you figure that out, it might make some sort of sense.>

The bubble inside of Tala's chest was ready to pop. Like

when her ears blocked on a plane flight, and she'd struggle to keep herself together as she waited until equilibrium would unblock them once more. Her equilibrium seemed so close, closer than it had in days.

Her limbs ached. Too soon the weariness washed over her again. Her head fell forward, and with a jerk she lifted it again fighting against the exhaustion and pain.

The desire to give into the warmth promised by oblivion proved too strong. Her head fell forward slowly and as her chin rested against her chest, she escaped the chains of this living nightmare.

CHAPTER
THIRTY-EIGHT

XAND

The crunch of boots over broken glass woke Xand faster than smelling salts had ever managed to achieve. She had been on the veranda with Tala and then?

Then!

Waking more clearly, her head pounded worse than any previous fight or hangovers to date. She barely remembered the fight. Except for a few threads of memory that slipped through.

With a start she sat up, swatting at her body, the tendrils still so vivid in her mind that she could feel them wrapped around her. They stung and made her twitch. Taking a deep shaky breath, she blinked away the visual memory and saw what remained. Where the tendrils of darkness had touched, blisters, raw and red, remained on her skin.

The crunch of boots came again. They hadn't been part of any dream. Hair rose on the back of her neck, muscles stiffening even as she forced herself to relax. Tension only worked in a fight if you could control it. Diana had taught her that. Slowly Xand stood and turned around.

The dark cavernous space of the pub loomed before her. Tables were tipped over and chairs lay in splintered ruins. Two of the three pokie machines were dark, glass skirting around them. The last machine seemed even more macabre in its brightness as it continued to encourage people to try their luck.

"Well shit."

Had something woken her after all, or had she simply swum to the surface? What she wouldn't give to have another battle on her hand, something other than this isolation. Scenes from the multitude of apocalypse movies she watched flashed across her mind's eye. They overlaid on top of the dark destruction around her.

Xand jerked her head to the right, knots in her neck cracked, and then to the left, more cracks echoed around in the silence.

The walls began to creep in. Closer they pressed in as her vision blurred.

"No," she forced through clenched teeth; eyes squeezed tight. "No, I can't do this. Not alone."

Sinking back to her knees, Xand held her head in her hands.

"I'm so sorry, Tala." The whispered words echoed off the walls of the pub.

There hadn't been many moments, not since she met Tala and Diana, where her fears and past collapsed in on her.

Diana's reaction to her show of powers, Tala's reaction to their one and only kiss, her fear at hearing Tala's voice so unlike her best friend's down the phone line.

She had only told Tala a few years earlier about her ability to transfer energy, but she had kept the rest close to her chest. Guilt warred with relief, Tala couldn't reveal what she didn't know. This part of her power had never come in handy before.

"Until now," she answered no one as she straightened her back, breathed deep and loud into the space and stood back up.

The isolation within the room could only make her feel alone if she let it. The truth was, she was never truly alone.

She didn't transfer energy often. It had been easy enough to explain the pain of draining herself in a sweep, and while it did hurt, she had never drained herself to actual exhaustion. Not ever.

It had always cost more than that to transfer the energy.

Inside her mind, Xand focused on the points of light. They glowed and connected like a fluorescent silk spider wed. Every single person she had ever transferred energy to was represented by those points of light. As far as she could tell, they were the parts of herself she had willingly given to others as she transferred some of her overflowing energy.

Only one had ever gone out, and that was with her death.

Following the florescent lights; she searched the points for the latest transfer.

There. She smiled and admired the way all five points that represented Tala, one for each transfer of energy Tala had received from her, gravitated to each other and orbited the latest one.

"She's alive." Xand kept her eyes closed though a few tears broke through, wetting her eyelashes before their journey down her cheeks. Before Xand could overthink it, she raced upstairs. She grabbed an unfamiliar backpack, flung some water bottles in and a few other items before throwing the straps over her arms and heading back downstairs.

She might not have left the Clan much, but she'd never forgotten how she grew up. Before Jonah and Diana had found her, she'd been nothing more than a street rat; fending for herself while her mother wallowed in her pain and misery stuck with a person.

One last look around at the debris, she headed out of Pour Another One and left Forty West. She didn't know how far it would be, but she wouldn't stop, she couldn't, not until she reconnected to that point of light. The one she had given to Tala without hesitation.

"Well fuck."

Xand's top lip curled as she looked over the wasteland of storage containers before her. She hadn't been able to see them from the front of the place. They were stored down the hill from where she stood.

It hadn't been nearly as far away as she'd feared. She'd walked past the front fence made in the same crosshatched wire that encircled the containers below. The name of the yard was emblazoned on a rusted sign and her imagination had conjured up many things. The sign announced their storage containers were both for sale or hire with *great rates. Delivery and collection all taken care of.*

But the images she'd conjured up in her head had nothing on the sheer immensity of containers that lay in front of her. A muted haphazard rainbow of metal boxes spread out all the way to the fence, stacked two and sometimes three high. Weeds and dust waved between rows and rows of the bloody things.

"Guess I'm really not in Kansas anymore," Xand muttered as she shuddered, thinking a little too much about the small space within each container.

Taking a fortifying breath, as though that would hold back the claustrophobia, Xand focused on the landscape. It reminded her of something post-apocalyptic. Not quite visual, the energy that surrounded her breathed in and out, a throbbing pulse beyond what her human sight could see. Feeling over fact.

"I'm coming, Tala."

Pebbles slid, clattering down the steep hill, as Xand made her way over the dusty slope. Blood rushed in her ears. Drawing closer to flat ground she no longer needed to keep her eyes on the shifting dirt beneath her feet. As she looked up, her breath caught as a dark ominous presence swelled around containers at the back left corner of the fenced yard.

The sun beat down from above as it approached midday. Despite the muted heat of the winter sunshine, sweat dripped down Xand's back, tickling her spine. She stepped into the path between two towers made of containers and wondered if bugs felt like this all the time. The containers loomed over her, threatening to topple down if she stepped on the wrong spot. She fought her desire to reach out and run her fingertips over the waved metal. If a step near the boxes felt dangerous, surely a touch was an even stupider idea.

Muted voices filtered around the corner to her right, and she slipped backward, into a small gap between two rust-coloured containers. These ones had pinprick holes and warped sides. Rusty metal flaked onto Xand's fingers as she used the solid walls to keep her breathing flowing in and out. To keep her standing upright.

'Well so much for the danger of touching them.'

She rubbed her fingers together and the similarity between what now stained her fingers and old blood wasn't lost on her.

"Let me go, you arsehole." She recognised the voice that spat out the words.

"I can't do that Adeline. You're special. I mean, she's still going to kill you, but you will help make us both stronger. Your blood is unique, apparently." The voice was male, more a boy's than a man's.

Others laughed as Xand heard something that sounded far too much like flesh hitting flesh. She cringed and clamped her teeth together.

Don't go in half cocked, you'll get killed, and Adie as well. She knew this voice as well. It wasn't Adie's and it sure as hell wasn't coming from outside of her mind. Whether it was truly Diana from beyond her death or Xand's own wishful thinking didn't really matter. It had the same effect. Xand rolled her shoulders backward and waited, still and strong. She channelled her never ending energy into strengthening and coiling her muscles, in preparation for a fight.

"My father helped me destroy the last person who tried to use my family's blood. You'll all die, and I won't hesitate to have *your* blood on my hands."

Xand didn't need any special powers to hear the quiver that overtook the last of Adie's words. If there was a response, fists or words, from Adie's captor Xand didn't hear it over the laughter and the shrill scrape of metal against metal. She made an educated guess that it was the sound of a door being opened. After a few beats, the scrape came again and the clang of a lock echoed around her.

"Hurry up, she'll be here soon, and Sam wants to make sure we're all ready and waiting."

Sam? *No!*

The stillness Xand had been forcing into her limbs became easy as the cold truth washed over her. She remembered all too clearly what the sadistic arsehole had done to her friend before he had killed her. It had him banished from the Clans, and the Misfits. But it wasn't enough. Nothing would *ever* be enough.

Footsteps faded away and Xand remained still, caught between action and reason. She wasn't stupid enough to think she was invisible. She conceded that they might even know she was lurking, and this could all be a trap. But she didn't have an option she could live with. Trap or not, she wouldn't let Adie stay in there, alone.

The thought sent shivers up Xand's spine. No one deserved this, not even someone in love with the same person as her. Of course she was still in love with Tala. No one else had ever meant anything to Xand more than a simple stress release. How could they, when her heart was still Tala's?

No one deserved what Sam could do. Xand could only imagine the horrors that would be done to Adie. Taking a deep breath, Xand stepped back around the side of the container, heart pounding.

She forced each step forward as her shoulders brushed the two containers on either side of her while fear coursed through her veins. She finally reached the front, facing the gap between this row and the next row of containers. Carefully she stuck her head past the sharp corner and looked out. Nothing and no one looked back. The small hairs on her body stood on end but she couldn't let that keep her from moving.

Fear and Time warred with each other.

The sun warmed the back of her neck, where her ponytail didn't quite hang low enough from her head to cover.

"Shit," she groaned.

Being alone sucked. Having to make decisions with no idea what she would find had her energy bubbling uncomfortably beneath the surface. She wanted to run a few laps of the container yard, but she wasn't that fast. Quicksilver would still run rings around her.

She stepped out onto the path between rows and moved to the front of the container she had been certain they'd shoved Adie into.

The sound she'd heard wasn't a lock, at least not one that

needed a key. It was some strange arrangement of metal poles interlocking that kept the doors closed and locked for anyone inside.

Before she could talk herself out of it, she pulled up the handle, following the path of the metal poles, and then yanked the door back. With a hollow clunk and a soft scrape, the door opened. Xand's heart raced as she anticipated someone coming to inspect the sounds at any moment. As soon as there was a big enough gap to slide her frame through, she stepped inside. The hit to her head had such force behind it, that her body flew forward and into the depths of the container. Sheer force of will, or perhaps the end of her luck, managed to keep Xand awake.

'A mother fucking trap! Of course it was a trap. How stupid was she?'

"What the ..." she couldn't finish the sentence, her energy already pulled from her speech and into her head that now had a marching band playing out of tune. The drums going one way and the trumpets going another.

"Oh, my Gods." Adie dropped beside her. Whatever she'd used to concuss Xand fell with an ear shattering clang to the floor.

"Hey Adie," she murmured.

Whatever kept her awake, finally gave up.

"Please, please wake up Xand. He's going to come back." Adie's words were distanced by the pain of having her shoulders being shaken.

"I'm awake." Xand tried to say but the words were slurred, still Adie stopped shaking her, so job well done either way. "They didn't tie you up? Are they fucking stupid?"

"We have to get out of here before he comes back. Oh Gods, Xand. They're crazy. They're all *fucking* crazy."

"Have you seen anyone else? Any on our side?" Xand sat up and scooched her bum back until it hit the wall of the container. In the centre of the room, in a round circle of light lay a tangle of ropes, the ends blackened from fire. At least that answered some of the questions Adie had failed to answer.

Swallowing against the wave of nausea in her stomach, she closed her eyes and focused on keeping down the contents.

"No one alive," Adie said.

Xand opened her eyes again to look at Adie. Her voice had been filled with such sadness and pain. Her face reminded Xand of the old Greek statues. The serious expression she wore enhanced the striking features.

"I'm sorry." Xand reached up to Adie's cheek, where a split of skin leaked blood. "May I?"

"Um sure, okay?" Adie said and gave a sharp intake of breath as the energy Xand pressed into the wound and knitted it up in moments. Blood remained, but there would be no scar. Adie opened her mouth.

"What's happened?" Xand asked, cutting off the usual barrage of questions a healing would produce.

"They keep going on about Pha, about my father, and I have no idea what the hell they are talking about." Adie's legs were a tangle, one tucked beneath her while the other was bent, her knee pulled to her chest.

"Did they talk about anyone else? *Anything* else?" Xand asked, leaning her head back against the wall.

Her energy was hard at work fixing the pounding in her head and the concussion Adie's whack had undoubtedly caused.

"I'm not sure." Adie's wide eyes held so much Xand didn't understand but she knew that look, and it wasn't one of happiness. "They all get scared and silent when one of them mentions she or her. I don't know who it is. I don't think I *want* to know." Adie shook her head back and forth and sat back on her ankles.

Now her head no longer felt three times the size, Xand blinked against the dim light and looked around. Chains hung from the walls, and blood-stained wooden beams made a cross in the centre. Leather straps hung from the ends.

Bile burned at the back of her throat.

"Have they hurt you? Other than your cheek?"

Adie followed Xand's eyes. "No. Not yet. Why are they doing this?"

"I don't know." Xand pressed her hand against the wall of the container and forced herself to her feet.

"You shouldn't be standing up." Adie grabbed her arm.

"We don't have a choice. They've taken Tala."

"*What?*" Adie's gripped tightened on Xand's forearm. Adie was all but vibrating. Xand got a snippet of an idea of how she must look to people. Everything moving and twitching, no part of her able to stay still.

"They took Tala," she repeated.

"Why?"

"I have no idea. They talked about Sam, like he was a leader. If it's the Sam I think it is, he's a psychopath. And right now, I don't care why he's running a torture cult, all I care about is getting my family back and getting the hell away from this place."

"I can help."

"Good, because I'm seeing three of you."

Adie's laugh was light, but a choke stopped it soon enough.

"Let's go find our girl, huh?" Xand smiled.

Adie smiled back when their eyes met.

Both women nodded and moved to slide out of the door of the container.

"I didn't feel that going in." Xand shook her hands from the electricity that had zapped her as she reached for the ajar door.

"They've put up a magical barrier." Adie sighed. "I tried to leave but couldn't even get as close to the door as you already have.

Xand looked at the door, to Adie, and then back to the door.

"Do you trust me enough to help get us out?"

"How?" Adie's eyebrows knit together.

"It's going to hurt, but I promise, it won't be long and I'll make it all go away as soon as we are outside the doors."

Adie's hand rose to her cheek that Xand had healed earlier. She brushed over it, silence filling the space.

"Alright."

"Hold on." Xand offered Adie her hand. "Squeeze as tight as you need. You won't break anything."

Xand focused on the magic sizzling in the space around the door. A strong magic had been used, but done clumsily. There were holes, and Xand almost let a sob out as she found one close to where she stood.

Mentally reaching out, she gripped the hole and pulled at it. Her breath caught and her muscles tensed.

"What's happening?" Adie's voice held pain even as she fought to hold it back.

"I'm punching a fist through the wall and using their own ineptitude against them."

"Well," Adie said. "Glad that clears it all up."

Xand chuckled, finding Adie's humour exactly what she needed to fight through the clinging threads of the magic. She pulled as much pain from Adie as she could bare while keeping the hole opened and her body still moving forward.

By the time they had taken the three steps required to

break through the wall of magic, Adie and Xand were both puffing, sweat streaking their clothes.

"You've got to teach me how you do that." Adie's knees wobbled as she let go of Xand's hand.

"I wish I knew more of how I did half the shit I do." Xand smirked.

They both turned back to the container. The heaviness of knowledge surrounded them. The containers were torture chambers, and Adie had almost become a victim. But neither could let themselves worry about that now. What they focused on was stopping anything similar happening to Tala.

That's assuming it hadn't already.

CHAPTER

THIRTY-NINE

TALA

Tala came back from a dream she couldn't remember to a world of pain and agony.

Sam stood in front of her, his blade glinted with beads of her bright red blood. She looked up and met his eyes.

"Awake again. Good. I prefer a screamer," Sam purred. He leaned forward and pressed the top of his blade into the soft flesh above her collar bone.

She clenched her teeth together, but the pained groan slipped out with a muttered "Monster".

"Oh, I'm not a monster," he held up a clear plastic bottle, about half filled. "See?"

Sam dipped his weapon of torture into the bottle, water washed over the silver sharp blade, making remaining water inside turn pink. Drops landed with loud pings on the floor of the container as he pulled it back out.

"You wanted water, I'm *happy* to oblige."

With slow movements he sliced again across Tala's chest. It cut through both her tank top and bra, slicing into the flesh beneath. The water, as it touched the new wounds, stung. The blade nicked the edge of her nipple, and her scream bounced around the room.

Sam laughed and turned back toward the bottle, dipping the blade once more. But the scream that had escaped Tala wasn't nearly as filled with pain as Sam assumed. The water on the blade, though it stung against the new cuts, seeped into her veins, the moisture flooded her body quicker than a drink ever could have.

Her mind raced, and then she coaxed it into the background and let her instincts and training kick in. She had *one* chance.

As he drew closer, she looked away from him. *'Come on, you arrogant prick. I know how you like them to watch what you do to them.'*

His fingers dug into her cheeks, and he yanked her jaw around, making her face him again. She let the power that had been building roar into life. Diana wouldn't come to save her, no one would. She had to save herself. And she damn well would.

With all her strength she jerked her head forward and smashed her forehead into Sam's nose.

Music, in the sound of the knife clattering to the metal floor filled Tala's ears. Sam screamed as blood rushed over his mouth and down his chin.

"No, not the blood. I need the blood. No," he screamed, slurping at the blood, scraping what he could into his mouth, licking at his coated fingers. It told Tala more than she could process right then. She had to focus on survival.

Tala lifted her knees to her chest; *'see Diana I was right about the pole dancing lessons.'* Agony ripped through her wrists as they took her weight, her head fell back between them as she tilted a little more. The wrong angle of her shoulder blades and the pain would be worth nothing if she hesitated. If she got this wrong.

'*Please,*' she silently begged, as she struck her feet out. They made contact with a thick meaty slap.

Sam didn't have time to scream. Not even a shocked oomph escaped his lips as he sailed back from the impact of Tala's feet that had landed square in his chest. He disappeared into the surrounding darkness.

"No matter how much blood you steal arsehole, mine will *always* be stronger."

The sound of objects clattering to the cement floor bounced around the dimly lit room. The sun had moved passed midday while she had escaped into unconsciousness.

Tala lowered her legs slowly, ignoring her wrists as they screamed for her to hurry up. As soon as her toes touched the ground, she let out a sob.

"Becky?"

Silence from the corner.

"Becky, if you want to see outside this box again, get out here and get me out of these things before he wakes up and starts slicing more from us."

A small sob replied. It was better than nothing.

"*Now* Becky," Tala snapped.

Tala pressed her lips together fighting the desire to scream at the traumatised woman and wondered where that demanding self-assured voice had come from. It hadn't sounded like Diana, but it had done the job just the same.

Becky's eyes focused on Sam's still body as she shuffled into the light.

Tala caught her breath, seeing again the deformed result of Becky's torture. She was still alive, and yet here was Tala making her fight more than she already had. She wanted to apologise; she wanted to tell her she would find another way.

It wasn't fair, Tala knew it. She *also* knew there was no other way.

"Can you break the chains?"

For a moment their eyes locked, and Tala felt the pain and emotion welling up inside of Becky. It was all too much. Too much pain and loss, suffering and anger. No, not Becky's pain and anger. Tala could feel her *own*. Tala would be willing to kill the entire world, if she thought for just a moment that it would give her any kind of peace and clarity. Any kind of relief.

"I can't, I only used my hands. I need my hands," Becky sobbed.

It pulled Tala out of her darkness.

"I can't channel the energy," Becky continued.

"Yes, you can. You don't need your hands." Tala hated herself as much as she hated the world and its pain right now. No, she loathed herself far more. How did Diana do this? How did she make the hard decisions and *still* have that pure light inside of her? Tala already felt the darkness creeping into the edges of who she'd been.

"How?"

"Channel it into your eyes, Becky," Tala said.

"My eyes?"

"Yes. All your power is still in you, Becky. No matter what he's done, what he's taken. He can never ever take *that* from you."

"I -- I can't."

"You *can*." Tala met Becky's eyes and nodded.

She watched as Becky's energy welled, like a drop of blood pierced with the tip of a knife, slowly growing in size and colour.

Becky's sharp intake of breath filled the space as her eyes focused on Tala's once more.

Tala didn't need the confirmation of what Becky saw. She

already knew, already felt the restless beast in her rising to the surface.

Her wolf guided Becky, her own eyes shifting and changing, channelling her power. Her body had never been so disconnected to her mind before. She had shifted her eyes without even realising it, but the blood knew, and it showed Becky what to do.

Fear gnawed at the edges of her mind and she swatted it down like a buzzing mosquito.

Becky's eyes began to change colour. To deepen and darken as she tapped into her own blood of the Gods.

Tala smiled and nodded.

Hope bloomed and exhaustion fought against the desire to live beyond this nightmare. She had already spent too much energy. She had fought beyond what she would have ever imagined herself capable of. Her eyelids began to droop, they were so heavy. She couldn't hold them open. Just for a minute, she could close them long enough to catch her breath again.

"*Tala!*" The scream came from outside of the room, somewhere close by, outside the realm of Tala's pain and power.

Unless of course delusions were starting to come a-knocking. To be honest, she couldn't rule that out entirely.

"Adie?" Tala asked the darkness. Her eye ached as she blinked them open.

"Tala, are you in there?" The banging on the door grew louder and harder.

"Adie. Adie we're here." Tala's head pounded as though Adie were knocking directly into her skull.

"He's there?" The waver in Adie's voice splashed Tala's mind with the cold water she needed.

"Unconscious. Becky's here, we need to get out."

"Okay."

Sounds and shuffles from the outside, a clang of something heavy and hard hitting the walls.

"No," Adie screamed.

Other voices joined in, but Tala couldn't pick out any of the words.

"Oh Gods," Becky sobbed.

Tala followed her eyes to where Sam was writhing. Waking with shuffles and groans.

"He's waking. Adie, we need out, NOW!" Tala turned to Becky as she screamed the last word.

Becky's shoulders rose and fell with heavy breaths, but Tala saw the determination, the gathering of strength in her features. She nodded. Becky could do this, but they both needed to believe it.

Tears streaked down Becky's cheeks and a moment later, a bright burst of sparks and debris fell from above Tala's head. Her hands dropped hard and heavy. She crumpled to the ground, open palms catching her just in time. Pain flared as fizzy agony raced up and down her arms, originating from her elbows.

"Look out." Becky's voice was weak but urgent.

Tala turned to see Sam, eyes raging as he got to his feet. Her throat thickened, thoughts of calling to Adie fled her mind as quickly as they came. Her attention *had* to be on Sam, completely and utterly on Sam, and on her own survival.

Adie screamed from outside. Tala couldn't help her unless she got this bastard under control. The knife, the one that had simultaneously hurt and healed her, glinted in the slits of light that filtered into the darkening hot room. Tala reached for it, but Sam beat her to it. Dwarfing the handle, Sam lifted the blade in his thick meaty grip.

But Tala's hands were free.

She had never needed them to control her magic. Lesson

101 had always been, the power is always inside you. Her power fuelled her, waking and relieving her like cold spring water pressed at the back of her tongue. She silently promised her body a real holiday, once this was all over, as long as it didn't give in now, not yet.

"Seriously, how stupid must you be, to think poison would keep me down?"

"I'm not stupid," Sam slurred.

It was petty, but it gave Tala a little bit of joy to know he endured some suffering from her attack. That's what she needed more of, action. Diana had always been happy to wait, to work things out so mistakes wouldn't be repeated. But it had also cost them at times. That had never been Tala's way. Not naturally, despite how well she'd learned to follow Diana's lead. She'd had enough of waiting. Time had well and truly passed for this *bastard* to be put down.

"No, you're just a cheating coward."

"I'm *not* a coward."

"So just a cheat? I guess it's worked for you though. You're bigger, and you've got a knife, so I'll most likely die. Pretty basic concept. Now, tell me *why*."

"You always were too *stupid* to pay attention. We were in the same classes, but you never remembered a thing," Sam spat at Tala.

"Get to the *point*, Sam."

"Nulla."

"Nulla?" Tala blinked; the name did ring a bell. A very distant and distorted bell.

The door opened with a squeak, followed by a bang as it hit the wall with force.

"That would be me." The silky voice came from the doorway.

For a few seconds the woman was little more than a

silhouette, all superhero-like with her jutted out hip, hands wedged into her hips, and head cocked to the side. Tala's eyes adjusted and she recognised the woman, the one who had made a similar appearance in the pub. Right when everything started going to hell. What had Xand called her?

"Mia, wasn't it?"

"Oh, that's just this skin. I quite like this one, but you humans are all so fragile."

Oh, I'm so sorry Xand.

"I'm *not* human."

"Hmm," she stepped into the room and surveyed it as though the stench of old blood, piss, shit, and fear were not a disagreeable aroma. "Enough of *you* is."

"What do you want?" Tala asked.

"I don't like repeating myself."

"Huh?" *Very articulate, Tala.*

"Just a moment. They won't be long." She looked at her nails, as though there were nothing more interesting happening in her afternoon.

True to her word, moments later Nulla-Mia, whatever the fuck her name was, moved aside. She revealed Adie and Xand standing in her vacated place. Tala's heart beat a staccato of relief, before the two women fell forward. They were pushed from behind by big hands. The man who did the pushing looked half familiar. Someone from the pub most likely.

This woman would have had to have spies everywhere. No wonder they knew Tala and Adie had been on their way. Was she also responsible for the crash? Did that even matter anymore?

"Tala." Xand locked eyes with Tala for a heartbeat, then her eyes moved in search of everything written on Tala's face. A language only Xand had learned to read.

Tala nodded and tried to coax her lips up into a smile, but the movement hurt too much. She turned toward Adie, their eyes met in a completely different language, but one that had been easy to learn.

They were both okay. They were all okay. Cuts and bruises healed. Tala could do this. She just couldn't do it alone.

Her heart ached and roared with a fury she had long ago learned to tame. Her fingers shook slightly as she reached down and helped both Adie and Xand to their feet.

She kept her grip tight and entwined her fingers with theirs as all three women stood in a line and stared at their captor. Out of the corner of her eye, Tala noticed Sam shrink into himself. Her shoulders rolled forward as he slunk to the edge of one of the darkest corners of the container.

"Now would not be the time to play hero, Tala." The woman caught her in a gaze that pinned Tala to the spot.

"Who *are* you?"

"You already know." She winked at Tala. "Sam never was good at keeping his mouth shut but I do enjoy the formal introductions." With a flick of her head the facade slowly transformed, rips appeared across Mia's face.

All three women flinched and looked away, only to find themselves drawn back to watch as skin split and peeled. Beneath the flesh that had once been a woman named Mia, a shining presence, an outline too bright to look directly at. As it faded, a beauty queen Tala had never seen the rival of, stood with a smirk on her lips. Thick black strands of hair looked as though they floated around her head. More bells rang in her head, but they were all discordant and painful.

Sam rushed from his dark corner, holding up a black flowing dress. His eyes leered over her as he helped her slip into the clothing. If Tala wasn't so entranced by the woman's beauty, she might have scoffed at the dramatic vampiresque attire.

"What happened to Mia?" Xand breathed hard.

Tala's fingers had blanched with the strength of Xand's grip.

"I really do hate to repeat myself." The words were the

breaking of glass, slashing ribbons of Tala's thoughts and mind.

"Where *is* she?" Xand asked again, her words were strained but not backing down.

"You're the extra one, aren't you? The one the others put up with, pity, in your weakened state." Nulla looked like she'd swallowed something particularly disgusting. "The most human of the spawns. Well, fine, let me humour you. She's dead. You humans are such short-lived batteries."

Tala wriggled her fingers until Xand loosened the death grip enough for Tala to trace small circles on Xand's palm. The vibrations didn't stop, but the pulsing eased slightly, enough for Tala to focus on the God in front of her. Because she could be nothing else *but* one of them.

"Who are you?" Adie asked, her thumb running over the back of Tala's hand. The sensation relaxed Tala more than she could have thought possible given the situation.

"I," the woman bowed in a flourish of toned arms, black hair, and flowing material, "am Nulla."

"So, you're Nulla." Tala's words were dull even to her own ears. "Whoop de doo."

Diana's voice droned on in Tala's mind. Lessons from years gone by, when Tala was planning her and Xand's next adventure instead of listening to the history of her people. Nulla, Nulla, Nulla. The word repeated in her mind, but nothing else was yet forthcoming.

"I am. And I am quite the whoop de doo. At your service." Nulla winked and laughed. "Actually, you will be at mine."

"Okay, so who the hell is Nulla?" Adie's voice was soft, but in the confinement of the container it bounced around them; a stray bullet brushing strands of hair with its nearness.

"Oh, let me." Nulla smiled and flung her arms out wide. "I do love to talk about myself. I, am the last *true* God."

Tala clenched the hands in her own, willing them to remain still, unaffected by whatever words the silver-tongued God let slither from her lips.

"Well, that sucks to be you. You don't happen to have a blue box at all do you?" Xand asked.

Despite the fear that pressed down upon her, Tala couldn't hold back the small guffaw.

"Didn't I already tell you, human; *you* don't matter. Are you really so eager to die?" Nulla's eyes flashed with a fury that Tala found amusing. Perhaps not funny, but everything seemed coloured with an inappropriately humorous layer, like a can of paint splashed over a once beautiful canvas. A bubble of hysteria stretched inside her chest. She gulped back air. She couldn't fail them. They were together now; she would *not* let them down. She just had no idea how to do this, or how Diana had ever done this, so many times.

"If I didn't matter, you would have already strung me up and killed me." Xand's voice shook a little, but just enough for Tala to notice. She hoped.

"Ya know, the girl's got a point." Tala nodded and quirked her lips in agreement. "Why haven't you drained our blood like the lowlife bottom feeding vampire you really are?"

"Tala." Adie's voice was a mumble, obviously having learned from her previous whisper.

"So, you have me all figured out, have you?" Nulla asked.

"Nope, not at all." Tala shrugged.

"And I couldn't give a shit," Xand said. "Do you give a shit, Tala? Adie?"

Both Tala and Adie shook their heads.

"I liked Mia. She was *kind* to me," Xand snapped.

"She was *weak*." Nulla spat right back.

Tala blinked as a small puff of cold air followed Nulla's words from her mouth. It was just past the middle of the day.

Sure, it was winter but that hardly meant much in Queensland. Xand's fingers stilled in Tala's grip. What Tala would give right now to have Becky's skill set.

The tension in the air vibrated like an over tuned violin string, ready to snap at the barest brush. Tala wanted to reach out and find where Becky had hidden herself. Problem was, she couldn't remember what this God *could* do. She didn't dare move her head or her eyes toward the corner she last knew Becky to be.

Was Nulla a telepath?

"So, are we finished with all the interruptions? Because my story is far too interesting to be interrupted with the unimportance of a mere human's life."

A cocky response lit up and then died on Tala's lips. Now was definitely *not* the time.

No one spoke, no one moved. For a beat, no sound of anything could be heard.

"Excellent." Nulla beamed, clapping her hands together, the radiance of her presence undeniable.

It hurt Tala's eyes.

Nulla's gaze beckoned all closer. Her oval eyes the bright colours of a Venus fly trap to the curiosity of a spider. Her full lips pursed and the desire to suck the bottom one between her teeth caught Tala off guard. She remained still and tried to will her brain back into submission.

How she wanted to thank past-Diana for her insistent training. The repetitive drills that formed Tala's mental muscle memory, giving her a sliver of a chance against this God.

"As I said," she repeated, eyes boring into each woman in turn. After a small dip at the corner of her lips, Nulla continued. "I am the last *true* God. The last of my family finally died and now I'm free of their bindings. And about time too. Our precious blood has been so diluted through the years of rutting in the mud with the vermin. But I will put it all to rights."

"Pha," Adie said.

Tala turned her eyes to face Adie. She hadn't thought it possible just moments earlier, in rapture of this God's presence, but at the sound of Adie's voice, the spell that had bound her to Nulla had snapped. Tala flicked her eyes back to Nulla, to see the God's eyes narrowed at Adie.

"You know Pha. Did you get a gold star for that one?" Nulla smirked.

"I got a lot more than that." Adie spoke with a shrug.

"Sure." Nulla rolled her eyes. "Pha was the first and last to stand against me, but he really was nothing more than a nuisance with too loud a voice."

Tala knew the freedom from Nulla's pull now and found her mind clearing as she began putting pieces together.

"The rest followed him as though he knew what was best. And he believed it too. Believed he was somehow better than the rest of us. In the end, he was the weakest. The first to fall prey to you pathetic lifeforms." Nulla truly enjoyed hearing the sound of her own voice. "I mean, honestly, look at my kind. They're all gone. Even their memories have faded from this world. Now I'm the last and I *will* make this world mine once more. To think, he thought breeding with the humans would save us. Pathetic."

"You aren't the last," Tala spat. "The Gods aren't dead, we've just evolved, Nulla. You're the last of nothing more than a self-inflated ego."

Nulla stepped closer. Tala stiffened as she was unceremoniously sniffed, before Nulla reeled back.

"*Urgh*, you're one of Neha's. Goddess of the Wolf." Nulla mocked the title, a whiney voice that scratched inside of Tala's head. "She had far too many bastards to keep track of you all. But I can smell her spawns taint on you. They were all so fooled into their dear mother's views of humans. She was so *smitten* with Pha, but then she got this bright idea to actually fall in love with the *plague* of this earth. As though they were ever worth more than a fuck and a feast." Nulla chuckled. "And look where her and her spawn are now?" She lifted both hands, palms up and twirled around in true Diva fashion.

"Do you really think all the Gods are dead?" Tala spat out before an incredulous laugh followed. "You really are delusional."

"I am *not* delusional." Nulla's rage flared around her like a pulse of energy. It pushed against Tala, forceful but not nearly enough to truly fear. Not yet at least. "Of course they're dead. I wouldn't be here if they were alive."

"Unless," Tala spoke slowly, putting the theory together as she went, remembering dribs and drabs of lessons from her past. "You were freed by Pha's death alone. Maybe, all you ever needed was Pha's death."

"Are you *still* trying to play the hero?" Nulla laughed. "Oh, I've heard all about you and your need to be wonder woman. But tell me *half*-breed, why am I only free now, when Pha was killed many years ago?"

"He wasn't killed, you bimbo." Tala scoffed a mocking laugh. She was done with this bitch and her voice that caressed Tala in ways that both repulsed and aroused.

"Bimbo?" Nulla raised her eyebrows and looked over at Sam as though he would provide the answer. He remained mute, eyes cast down at the stained cement floor.

"Yes, you stupid airhead." Tala spoke slowly. "It's a good thing *you* didn't breed."

Nulla laughed. "Really? You think mocking me is going to

help you out here? Somehow you'll win through your acerbic tongue?"

"I haven't even *begun* with the acid yet, bitch." Tala hoped she knew what she was doing.

She wasn't Diana, she never could be, and never would be. But had anyone really asked her to be? *'No one but yourself.'* Tala silently scowled at her mind's unhelpful comment.

"I saw him die," Adie said.

"And how did you manage that?" Nulla huffed.

"I freed him." Adie took a step forward, but Tala gripped her hand, stopping her from taking another.

"*Lies.* No one as diluted as *you* could free a God."

"She's not the Lady of Lies." Tala finally remembered something solid from the lessons.

Nulla's moniker.

"Ah, I do so *love* the old names. They save so much time."

"If our blood is so weak, why are you drinking it? Why are you and your sycophants all so desperate for it?" Tala asked. She had to bide more time, learn more and find a crack in the game.

"This one is weak, but he does have his uses." Nulla pouted and walked toward Sam. His flinch was not subtle when Nulla raised her hand and petted his head as though he were a dumb dog. "The Gods' blood is addictive, even to you half-breeds."

"Sure, I get puppet boy's habit. Even the addicts out there," Tala jerked her chin upward, toward the door that now stood unguarded. Please get the hint. She squeezed both hands. "But you. Why do *you* need our dirty blood?"

"I don't *need* it. I simply enjoy it." Nulla's voice held no defensiveness.

"Lady. Of. Lies." Xand spoke the words, slowly.

Nulla laughed and shook her head. Her black hair moved more like rivulets in an inky starless sky.

Tala blinked and shook her head. The light in the container had dimmed during Nulla's rant about herself. It couldn't have been any later than 2 or 3 in the afternoon. But the shadows had lengthened and continued to. They were too long and growing longer too quickly.

"Urgh, the eclipse." Tala hadn't realised the words had slipped from her mouth until Nulla stopped moving. She stood as though frozen, glaring at Tala.

"Think you're so clever, do you?" Nulla smiled, her cheek bones sticking out as she dipped her chin down. Tala felt the desire to swoon, but the wolf growled, and the urge receded as she looked closer. She warred with the beast often enough, but she knew when to let it out and when it could be soothed. It receded as she focused on the God. Nulla, the only one who refused to accept being called a Goddess. Tala had kind of liked that part of the story, but this bitch wasn't the feminist Tala had imagined.

Hiding just beneath the angry flirtations, was that fear Tala spied?

"Definitely not." Tala laughed. She was so tired, so sick of all the games and the bullshit. She wanted it over. What *it* was, she shied away from knowing. "I'm a shit student, but sometimes things stick no matter how little I listen."

"I remember!" Xand spoke.

"Oh, how sweet, you learned about me, too." Nulla pouted. "But enough. This grows tedious. Besides, the eclipse has started, and so has the countdown on your lives. Be excited, you're pivotal to a whole new age of this pathetic planet."

"Yes, I learned all about you," Xand ignored Nulla's dismissal of the topic. She pulled her hand free of Tala's and stepped right up into Nala's face. "All about your lies, and your weaknesses."

Nulla hissed, but Tala's jaw all but fell open when Nulla

shuffled a half step back. She stopped moving and lifted her hand. Xand went flying, her back hitting the far wall of the metal box.

A beat, and then Tala screamed, running full force toward Nulla.

CHAPTER

FORTY-ONE

XAND

Xand's rage vibrated inside her chest as pain radiated up her back. She took a deep breath, logging the damage and the pain. There was nothing a few minutes and some focus couldn't cure. She forced her energy into the muscles that throbbed and mended the blood vessels beneath her skin that had burst. She would be sporting bruises tomorrow.

Hopefully.

The memory of Mia's lips on hers, as she watched this woman, this puffed-up *God*, talk as though she had been nothing. Mia had been *everything* Xand had needed. And not even realised. She was a ray of sunshine, brief but blinding. Just when Xand's own light wilted beneath anger, pain, and grief.

She couldn't focus, her mind kept returning to those precious moments she'd spent with Mia, the real Mia. What was she missing? Why couldn't she focus on saving the lives of those in the room with her right now? But her mind kept returning to Mia. A near-stranger whose death now pulled her heart apart in ways she couldn't begin to understand. She wasn't sure she ever wanted to.

It wasn't until she saw more dragon breath puff out of Nulla's lips as she laughed, that something shook loose. Nulla easily blocked Tala's attacks, but that didn't deter Xand's best friend from throwing fists and legs in the God's direction.

The God continued to laugh, even as she shuffled back ever so slowly toward one of the dark corners of the box.

"Argh!" Adie screamed.

Xand turned in time to see Sam push Adie to the floor. The edges of his clothing smouldered and as Xand followed the trace of magical fire, she saw the origin on the tip of Adie's fingertips.

'Way to go Adie!'

Xand blinked back the unshed tears.

'Focus, you aren't the extra! Argh, so remember then, you idiot.'

Another cool thread of breath flowed from Nulla's lips. If she noticed she gave no indicator of it.

An image of darkened steps and her own dragon breath floated in to Xand's mind. The penny dropped. She held back a gasp only just in time.

Pieces fell into place.

She left Tala and Nulla to their fight. Adie had gotten up and held Sam back, a large ball of fire in her palm this time.

Nulla, Nulla, Nulla.

She remembered it all. Nulla was Pha's greatest threat. She believed in the purity of the Gods and had assumed Pha would be on her side because he'd joined with a fellow God, and not 'lowered' himself to the human race. But he'd called her out on her xenophobia, and his mate started calling herself Goddess. And both had fought back.

<Good, now keep going.>

Xand froze, the energy within her coiling in preparation to fight. *Who are you?*

<Becky. I can help.>

Good, we need it.

And then it all flooded back, what once didn't make sense, now made too much.

'Oh Shit.' She knew her own voice, and this time it was mercifully alone. "I remember," Xand said aloud.

"Good for you, but also, too late." Nulla's hand was wrapped around Tala's throat.

"You stole her life; you took her body, but you couldn't read her mind, could you? Just like Sam couldn't know Jake's quirks and beauty."

"Beauty," Nulla scoffed, throwing Tala to the ground. Xand's heart stuttered inside her chest for a moment, then Tala moved. Slowly she pushed herself back to her feet. Xand breathed and her heart resumed its rapid thud against her ribs. "As though I would want to be inside any of your minds. Primitive base thoughts in the best of you."

"Mia controlled the cold," Xand spat.

"So?" But Nulla's voice vibrated like it hadn't earlier.

Fear or fury? Xand had no way of knowing, but she had to follow this road. What other option did she have? She couldn't wait for Adie and Tala to catch up, but she hoped they understood soon.

What Xand found herself betting on was little more than a theory, and a history written by unnamed hands from unknown sides.

"You aren't as strong as you think you are," Xand said.

"Says the tiny insignificant human," Nulla scoffed.

"You know what I worked out," well this would be interesting, Xand was just as curious to find out what words would follow. "The more people tell me I'm weak, or passive, or tiny the more I realise they fear me. The more they worry I just *might* realise the truth."

"Fear you?" Nulla laughed and it sent icicles down Xand's back. "And what *truth* is it you think you know?"

"No one is insignificant," Xand said. The words were an icicle of strength within her.

"Really? *That's* your big weapon?" Her face twisted, in confusion and mockery. Which would win out was anyone's guess.

"Not a single person you've inhabited, taken over and used up, is insignificant. Not a drop of blood from those you've drained is useless."

"Yes, yes, you *all* have something to contribute." Nulla rolled her eyes and her hands, as though the movements would give her back the power Xand felt building up within herself. "Humans and your need to believe you are somehow important."

Tala's hand was comfort and warmth as it interlaced with Xand's fingers once more. There was a strength in the touch; as her friend, as the first person she ever loved.

"Jake, he was stronger than you and your little minion combined." Tala's voice was rough and dangerous, a dirt track with sharp turns and unsuspected obstacles. Dust that lodged in your throat and crusted at the corner of your eyes. It couldn't simply be brushed away.

Xand felt her chest swell. They were still connected; best friends who knew the words the others didn't say.

The deep laugh from Sam came from the closest corner, too late for Xand to realise just how close he was, as he stepped forward and grabbed her arm. With a sharp bend backward at the elbow, he broke Xand's arm.

"No!" Tala screamed and caught Xand by her other arm as her knees gave way beneath her.

"They are still in them," Xand gasped, hoping Tala heard, and no one else did.

If Tala understood she made no hint at it.

"What the fuck do you want you psycho? You want our blood, why? What are you waiting for?" She screamed at Nulla.

"I like to take my time."

"Bull*shit*," Tala replied. A growl underlying the word. The wolf was so close, Xand could feel it. Tala returned her attention to Xand, as though the God was of little consequence and zero threat.

Pain radiated from Xand's elbow, clouding her mind and what she'd finally managed to brush her mental fingers against.

What was it?

"The eclipse." Xand squeezed her eyes shut, nodding as she forced the pain back just a little further, just enough, "Nulla is the Goddess of the Gark. She had no power in the light, but night is still forbidden to her, by the power of Pha's blood."

"Pha is dead." Tala's words came quickly. "I saw him die Xand; there's no way he's still alive."

"But his blood still runs." Xand had to make sure Tala understood. She forced as much energy as she dared into the broken limb. "Where's Adie?"

Over Tala's shoulder, Xand met Adie's eyes, half crumpled to the ground where Sam had thrown her. With the smallest of head nods and the twitch of lips, Adie turned from Xand and looked at Nulla.

"Do you know who I am?" Adie asked as she staggered to her feet.

"You're the stronger one Sam told me about. Stronger, but not strong enough." Nulla waved her hand as though Adie were nothing more than a mosquito, but Xand watched the God's eyes as they grew flinty.

"I am the reason Openfields is a smouldering hole in the ground."

"Interesting, isn't that what *you* just claimed?" Nulla's lips curled up in an arrogant snarl as she turned her attention to Tala.

"Why is it all the pretty ones are so stupid?" Xand rolled her eyes at Tala.

"Because they think they know everything. They think they're stronger than they are." Tala shook her head sadly.

Xand smiled despite her arm still throbbing.

"Oh, back to this are we?" Nulla's arrogance slipped into frustration that creased lines into her otherwise smooth forehead.

Xand and Tala shrugged at each other, and Adie's lips twitched. Xand eased out of Tala's grip and stood on her own.

"Alright, *enough*," Nulla said.

"You're finished talking about yourself already? How is that even possible?" Xand scoffed.

"I've said enough," Nulla said between perfect white teeth that pressed so hard together Xand almost expected them to crack and snap from the force.

"Then kill us already." Tala turned her body toward Nulla, back straight and head up. Xand knew her own pose was a weak imitation, but she stood beside Tala, like she always had.

"She can't, Tal. The eclipse needs to be at its peak. Until then, she's no stronger than a child."

"Huh. So, you mean she just has to wait." Tala laughed.

FORTY-TWO

TALA

"Oh, you'll be begging for death before I reclaim my true power. Pain is a beautiful thing." Nulla's words were cruel and dark.

"You really do love the sound of your own voice don't you. God, my arse," Tala scoffed. The beauty that had drawn Tala's eyes the moment she shed Mia's form shattered a little more as her eyes bored into the God.

"I am the *last* God."

"Oh, look around you," Tala scoffed as she lifted her arms and turned in a circle. "We are *all* Gods. You're weaker than all of us. How many are trapped in these containers, how many have you had to drink from just to keep that body firm? Vanity, the real reason for the Gods' demise."

"I have killed more of your kind than you have ever *met*; I am the one blessed to bring my kind back to its full power. I am the mother of —"

"Delusion? Yep, I'd say so. Back to this last of the Gods rant and bullshit. You aren't. We are everywhere. And you, you're nothing more than an old, wasted husk. A parasite with no power of her own."

Nulla's arm rose. The energy surged from the God's hand. Tala shoved Xand away from her, as she dove in front of Adie. Scrabbling, she moved them closer to the far back corner, opposite where she had pushed Xand. She had created a large gap in the middle of them. Separating them. With just enough time to hope the gap was large enough, before the force of Nulla's strike slammed against the back wall of the container. Sparks lit up the corners, and for a moment time stood still.

Tala took in the small wooden bench covered in cloth and blood; the torso of a once human being writhed on top. Still alive and in agony. What was her name? What had Becky called her? On the floor, limbs lay in pools of blood. Bile rose at the back of Tala's throat. A hand, strong and warm pressed against her back.

"We have to get out of here." Adie's eyes were fixed on something behind Tala. Tala turned to see the back wall of the container ripped open, flames licked at the edges of the torn metal.

"Xand," Tala called but silence met her. She turned back searching the flame flickering darkness.

"Go," Xand called out, not turning to meet Tala. Instead, she stood in front of Sam. The two glared at each other.

Only then did Tala remember who Sam had tortured in the Misfits. The one who sent his arse into the arms of the deranged puffed-up God, Nulla. She was a friend of Xand's. Tala had never found out if they'd been *more* than friends.

"He's not worth your life, Xand!" Adie called before Tala could utter something similar.

"My friend is dead because of him, Adie. This monster tortured her." Xand didn't move her focus from Sam. Sam laughed and made a show of turning his hands into fists.

"Don't leave me, *please* Xand." Tala finally found her voice and let everything inside her fill the words. She held nothing back.

"Argh." Xand shoved a hand out and Sam crumpled with a scream as he clutched his stomach. "I hate you, Tala."

"No, you don't." Tala laughed, the relief washing over her as Xand pushed through the flames first, out into the eerie darkness of the half eclipse. Tala followed, turning quickly to see Adie rush through.

"What now?" Adie asked.

"The eclipse." Xand pointed at the sun, slightly dipped to the west. The moon, touching its edge. "Looks like we're on a timeline."

"You knew I'd be able to piss her off enough for her to lose her temper?" Tala asked, already knowing the answer.

"Who else?" Xand smiled.

"OK, no time for more compliments. Since when could you harness your energy to become an attack?" Tala asked. She put a pin in the pain of being left out of Xand's power, for now.

"For a while now," Xand replied.

"Are you drained?" Tala asked.

"Not even close." Xand's words came out in a laugh.

Tala felt a surge of pride, and a little concern. "Adie?" Tala turned as she asked.

Adie's hands moved and the flames copied like a dance routine well-rehearsed. The hole Nulla had created in the wall of the container, was now an entire wall of fire.

"They aren't in there. They got out the other side, and they've headed toward the back corner."

"Okay," Adie breathed, lowering her hands, the wall of fire already beginning to lessen.

"And Becky?" Tala asked.

Adie took a sharp intake of breath.

"She passed, before Nulla exploded," Xand said quietly.

"Oh." Tala couldn't find the words.

"I failed her," Adie said.

"No, you didn't." Tala spoke with the authority of a leader, whether she felt like one or not. "We need a plan, so what have we got?"

For a moment the only sounds were the crackles of the dying flames as their projections danced pale on their skins, barely visible in the afternoon light.

"Mia is still in her. Mia was sending a message to me with Nulla's cold breath."

"Maybe," Tala didn't look convinced.

"Did you notice the waver? Nulla's insubstantial form?"

"I--" Tala turned and locked eyes with Xand, glad for the distraction, the pull from the evidence of torture. "I thought it was just the light."

"No." Xand's voice was strong and fierce. "It was more than that. I can feel them, Tala."

"OK, say you're right. Can we bet on that?" Tala hated to burst Xand's bubble, but she had to think of more than just them now. She had to think about *all* The Children, and what about the Elders? Had they really all been killed?

"We're stronger together, Tal. We always have been." Xand gently brushed Tala's arm as she spoke.

"I can't lead like Diana. I don't know what she would have done." Tala's fear and frustration filled her voice. It had plagued her since leaving Openfields. But she was so tired, and so sore. She couldn't hold it back any longer.

"No one is asking you to lead. We do this together," Xand said.

"We aren't strong enough, Xand. *I'm* not strong enough." Tala hated herself for the confession, but their lives meant more than her embarrassment and shame.

"Not just you and me. All of us. Even human history books tell us that. And we *are* strong enough, together. Our blood sings to each other. Can't you feel them?"

"No Xand. That's your power, not every—"

"I can feel them," Adie spoke up, cutting off Tala's words.

"Are either of you going to let me finish a sente—"

"Probably not," Xand said.

Adie laughed as she and Xand looked at each other. Tala joined in because she trusted them enough to believe in them, to know they felt it, even if she couldn't.

"It feels a little like home." Adie brushed her fingers along her temple.

Xand nodded. "They're here, Tala."

"But who are they?" Adie asked.

"The missing," Xand said.

"All of them?" Tala asked.

"I don't know." Xand worried her bottom lip with her teeth. "There are so many, and they all want to be heard. She's killed so many more than we know about, more than Sam realises."

"Well, that wouldn't shock me." Tala smirked. "But how does it help us?"

"If I can reach them, that could help us."

"They're ghosts, what could they do?" Tala asked.

"Mia made her breath cold, Tala. I don't think they're *just* ghosts," Xand said.

"I've got nothing better, so." Tala shrugged. "I distract while you appeal?"

"We need the others first."

"Which others? Isn't that what we're trying to do?" Tala's head swam. The sun slipped further behind the moon's dance.

"The ones still in the containers, the ones being tortured," Xand answered as the wall of fire finally died out beside them.

"Guess it's time to get to work then huh?" Tala nodded.

"I think we have our plan." Adie smiled.

"Alright fire girl, let's do this." Xand winked at Adie and Tala felt the world might just survive this eclipse after all, even if they didn't.

CHAPTER

FORTY-THREE

TALA

The shadows between the containers shrunk as the sun continued to slip further behind the moon. They stepped past the destroyed container and moved slowly. Tala didn't need to see to know which was the way to the back corner of the fenced off yard. It pulled at her, a hook that had caught her by the ribs and planned to never let go.

"We have to split up," Tala whispered.

"Seriously?" Xand stood with hands on hips, head cocked, and eyebrows raised. "I know I've taught you better than that. Did you not pay attention to any of those geek nights I forced you into?"

"I know," Tala said. She wanted to be able to see the world the way Xand did. Always so positive and sure of herself. "But we don't have time."

"Tala?" Xand asked.

"I know we shouldn't split up, but the full eclipse is almost here, and it won't last long. I'm guessing when it hits, Nulla's going to do something rather unpleasant."

"The old wipe out the world ploy?" Adie asked with a quirked-up grin.

"I like her, Tala." Xand laughed low beneath her words. "When this is over, you better not fuck it up. But for us to all survive. There is NO splitting up."

Tala felt her face heat and watched a small blush creep up Adie's neck. Rubbing her palm across the back of her neck Tala nodded. "Fine, but we have to hurry. Where do we start?"

"Right here." Xand stepped forward, unlatching the door of the container they stood in front of. Before stepping through she looked back at Adie. "Any chance you could help a gal out?"

Adie smiled and nodded. With a flick of her wrist, and a click of her fingers, small lights hovered above Adie's fingertips. She cupped her hand as though a ball sat in her palm. Her eyes were alight with the dancing blue fire.

Tala led the way, Xand and Adie barely a step behind.

The light flickering behind her shoulder didn't quite illuminate the entire container. Thank the Gods for small mercies.

What Tala *did* see made her legs wobble, air leaving her body with a heaviness worse than deep sea diving. She couldn't take her eyes from the clumps of flesh and cloth that littered the ground of the container.

"What the hell?" Tala choked and took a half step back.

"Stay with me Tala." Xand's voice helped ground her.

"We don't have time to open them all up," Adie whispered.

"We don't have to. I can feel the ones with the living in them."

Tala looked over her shoulder and met Xand's gaze. Without a word, she turned her body to the side, stepped back and stilled until Xand took the lead. Xand nodded, not stopping as she passed.

"Talk to me Xand," Tala wanted to convince herself that she needed information, though she suspected her own fear and disgust played a larger part in her demand for conversation. "Tell me what you remember, about Nulla."

"Diana told us so much about her, so much more than any of the others. The Elders must have known this was at least possible." Xand spoke through deep breaths through her mouth as she continued. "She needs to sacrifice a blood child during the eclipse to become whole once more. I'm guessing she's draining the Gods blood to keep herself here, instead of becoming incorporeal, or moving on or going back to wherever the hell they came from."

"A Blood Child?" Tala asked.

"Or any of the other minions," Adie supplied.

"How many are there? How many have you both seen?" Tala asked.

"We've seen a few. But who knows how many there are? Look at all these containers," Adie answered.

"She will sacrifice him, maybe she plans to sacrifice them all," Xand said.

"At least one of us listened to Diana." Tala smiled, sad but selfishly comforted in knowing she was not alone in her grief.

"I had to prove my worth somehow." Xand's voice dripped with self-deprecation.

"Nulla doesn't know you, Xand," Tala said.

"It doesn't matter now. We just have to stop the bitch." Xand smiled, and it brushed a light in her eyes. Not a full spark, but it was a start.

"If she becomes whole, what will it actually mean?" Tala asked.

"Assuming she goes back to her original plan," Xand swallowed audibly over the lump in her throat, "she will kill anyone who is pure human, and enslave those with God blood. There aren't any other Gods to fight her down this time. No one to stop her."

"Except us," Tala growled.

"They're still in there, you saw it too, right?" Xand asked, eyes pleading, "You believe me now?"

"I've always believed you, Xand. But how do we get them to fight against her?"

"By pissing her off, she seems hella vain. The cold air came out every time she got angry," Adie answered with a shrug.

"You're definitely a Misfit." Xand laughed.

Adie's face paled.

"It's a compliment." Tala smiled.

"Do you two always approach certain death with a laugh?" Adie asked with a small huff of shocked amusement. The pull up of her lips taking away any sting the words might have carried.

"Basically?" Tala asked. She locked eyes with Xand and they both replied together.

"Yep."

Adie nodded with a roll of her eyes before the three moved together and with purpose. They were only a few containers away from the now smouldering wreckage of the prison they'd escaped from when the sounds of voices, both male and female could be heard. The three pressed their backs against the rusting wall of a container and waited.

"Scream all you want, no one will find you. Sam might hear you, and *then* you'll be begging for us to come back." Other voices joined in on the laughter and mocking as the clang of a door being bolted cracked into the air, like thunder.

"I hate them," Adie whispered from around the corner. Her hands were balled into fists.

Tala slowly wrapped her own fingers around one of Adie's hands. She lifted the clenched knuckles to her lips, pressing a soft kiss on the skin. "I know, but don't let their darkness turn you."

Adie's small smile was punctuated with a nod and a pushing back of her shoulders, despite the glassy look in her eyes.

"Alright ladybugs," Xand said, popping her head out around the corner of the container and pulling it back in half a heartbeat. "Time to get moving, they've gone the other way."

"So, what's first?" Adie asked, her voice low but strong.

"We open those containers; our people will not suffer in cages any longer," Tala answered.

"And what about those like Becky?" Adie asked.

"We help as best we can," Tala answered.

"We have to work on a way for you to distract Nulla, while I reach out to the souls she has stolen." Xand spoke as they moved toward the container the minions had just locked.

"So, start brainstorming."

The first three containers they opened held Children and Elders, all baring different levels of torture and abuse.

"Please, kill me," a boy no more than 16 begged from a wooden cross, his eyes were missing, and his body was covered in open wounds. His wrists and ankles were lashed to the wood behind him, keeping him outstretched in a perverted X marks the spot.

Tala watched as Xand stepped forward and placed a hand on the boy's shoulder. He jumped and then relaxed into her touch. Xand muttered words too low for Tala to understand. After a few minutes, the boy sagged forward.

"What did you do Xand?"

"I released him." Xand's face was streaked with tears. "They poisoned him, Tala. They poisoned him. I couldn't cure him; he would have died within the week. I couldn't let him suffer any more."

Tala cursed as Xand left the container. She exchanged looks with Adie.

"Makes me almost wish for Openfields." Adie's voice was flat as she spoke.

"Something far worse is going on here." Tala nodded in agreement.

"Exactly." Adie reached for Tala's hand and together they followed Xand out of one hellscape and into the next.

They had opened three more containers and made two emergency detours to avoid followers of Nulla. Now, Tala stood frozen in the doorway of the next container. Without any verbal agreement, the three of them had fallen into a pattern of taking turns opening the containers.

"Fuck." More light shone into this container as it revealed similar signs of torture, but this container also revealed two people chained up just as Tala had been.

"Jonah." Xand pushed Tala out of the way as she raced inside.

The cuffs holding Jonah upright burst into shards. Tala turned to see Adie standing there, blinking at her hands. Xand caught their Clan's Elder and lowered him to the ground.

"It's okay, Jonah." Her words were thick with unshed tears.

"Xand?"

"I'm here."

"It's Nulla, she's been freed." Jonah struggled to get the words out.

"We know. It's okay. We have a plan."

"Good. The rest of them. We need to free them."

"All part of the plan, J," Tala spoke. She coughed, the roughness in her voice threatened to expose the emotions she couldn't process. Not yet.

"Tala. Good. Where's Diana?"

"She was killed." Tala crouched beside Jonah, a globe of water materialised in her palm and slowly she let drops fall onto his lips, and into his mouth.

The silence washed over the container.

"Tell me the plan." Jonah's voice was stronger now.

"We free everyone. And then we show that *bitch* what we're really made of," Tala said.

"Vague but I like it." Jonah tried to smile and decided the half grimace would suffice.

Seventeen containers opened to reveal Children, Misfits, and Elders. Only nine stood with Xand, Tala, and Adie. There were so many of their people unable to help, barely holding onto their lives, while others relaxed into their deaths with the relief of freedom.

"Where are the rest of the Elders?" Tala asked Jonah. He'd recovered much of his strength during the search.

"They went into hiding." Jonah wouldn't meet Tala's eyes.

"Fuckers," Tala spat, she only wished she were more surprised.

She'd deal with that later, but it left them with a problem. Her plan had relied a little on there being enough Elders to help keep Nulla distracted. Now, there were barely enough to fight. And definitely not enough to win.

FORTY-FOUR
XAND

Xand overflowed with anger at what she'd seen. Worst still were the deaths that now stained *her* hands. Mercy deaths were still deaths.

She would end up being useless in the fight. Her energy had never been drained. She hadn't known if it were even possible, but the more she healed, and the more she helped pass on, a pull weighted down her limbs and dragged her energy. It still fizzed, but a muted version to what she had always known.

She still didn't like that in the end they had split up. But what choice did she have? There was so much to do, and the time slipped past with the darkening of every shadow. Her thoughts raced as she slowed her steps. She paced along the dusty corridor at the edge of the container yard. A chain-link fence topped with barbed wire would hardly stand against their power.

However, while she waited, there was no harm in creating a plan B escape route. She had to believe they would need a way out, that they would survive this war. Giving into the fears of not getting out alive wasn't an option. She'd seen the doubt in Tala's eyes, it gnawed away at Xand's hope. Without hope she would've still been on the streets, dead or drugged up to the eyeballs just to get some reprieve from the constant pain of the world.

Adrenaline spiked and washed away, like a receding tide. Her energy worked on rebuilding, but too slowly. Wanting a fight to be over had never been a thought for the previous fights and battles she'd run headfirst into. But how she wished this one to be over now.

She looked up to the sky, only half the sun remained uncovered. It would start soon. As though they'd heard her, the commotion began, two corridors over.

Dust floated up around her feet as her boots slapped against the ground. Shadows lengthened, and every tuft of weed became a lurking enemy. Adrenaline spiked again and blood boomed in her ears. Turning a corner, she skidded in the dirt. She'd barely stopped in time to avoid running into the crowd before her.

"Is this the cavalry?" Nulla laughed over the shoulders of Tala, Adie and two other Misfits. They'd been some of the first rescued, but she couldn't remember their names.

"I'm just here to see the show," Xand said.

"All good?" Tala asked as Xand stepped up beside her.

"Always." Xand winked.

"How touching," Nulla drawled.

"So, where's the fatted up minion?" Xand asked.

"Sam." Nulla called out and Sam stepped from behind the container next to Nulla. The knife he had used on Tala gripped in his meaty hand.

"Oh, he doesn't look so good," Xand said.

It wasn't just for dramatic effect. Sam's large body shuddered in the dim light. Blood stained the front of his shirt and the scars that ran over his features were highlighted against his ashen skin.

"You can't honestly care what happens to him." Nulla's top lip peeled back, an angry dog ready to attack.

"Not at all. He's a brutal sadist, but if I get off on his torture, makes me no better." Xand shrugged.

"You *are* no better. Five dirty half-breeds against a God in her power. You don't -"

"Almost," Tala interrupted.

"What?" Nulla snapped.

"You are *almost* in your power." Tala shrugged. "I mean, sure you have almost stopped waving around like a flag, but you aren't in your power *yet*, are you?"

"I am *stronger*." Nulla narrowed her eyes.

"Even without him?" Xand scrunched her face as she asked, making it clear she didn't believe the God.

"Without who?" Nulla looked around.

"Jake." Tala's voice floated around them.

Nulla's single eyebrow rose in question.

"Jake," Adie said a little louder.

Nulla's face crumpled in confusion.

"Jake," Xand said, loud and through clenched teeth.

"Who the fu—"

Sam's scream cut through all words and thoughts.

Xand looked and a smile spread across her face as she met first Tala's eyes and then Adie's.

"Jake." The Misfit with the pixie cut black hair said his name with a spark of energy that seemed to dance from her tongue.

Nikki, Xand thought her name might be Nikki.

"Jake." The other Misfit all but screamed over the chaos that roared around Sam.

The chant began, voices floated from behind containers.

The rest of the missing joined in with their voices. Jake's name grew louder and louder. Magic floated on the word, floated from mouths that had recently screamed in pain. From hearts broken by what had been taken from them. There were more than 12 voices. Those clinging to life, waiting to give their last breath to the fight, screamed out Jake's name, magic crackling the air.

The voices grew and Xand felt her body swell with the energy coursing around her.

"Jake, Jake, Jake." The name repeated, more voices joining the Mass.

In a slow circle Xand turned, dropping Tala's hand—when had they grabbed hands—and saw the mangled and ruined bodies of the tortured as they drew closer. The stronger helped the weaker and all of them with fire in their eyes.

"Mia." Xand's voice was drowned in the torrent of the others, but the taste of energy on her tongue—like sweet wine and lipstick—reached its mark.

"I am *not* some fatted up pig. She's gone," Nulla snarled.

"Then why do you look so scared?" Tala's voice roared from beside Xand.

Fingers interlocked with her own once more.

"Jake?" Xand asked Tala. Panic raced up her neck. She felt the heat and fear at her ears.

"They have it covered," Tala said with certainty.

Tala and Xand's eyes brushed quickly, before narrowing in on Nulla, not giving her long enough to retaliate.

"Mia. You're stronger than her, together we're *all* stronger." Tala spoke clear and loud, her fingers squeezed Xand's as she spoke.

"Your little coup won't help you. All it will do is piss me off, and trust me, I can make the pain last lifetimes." Nulla threw out her hand, anger raging in her face.

The energy hit Tala like a punch to her chest and sent Tala flying. Her fingers, still gripped in Xand's pulled Xand along for the ride.

"Tala?"

"I'm fine." Tala spat a wet bloody wad onto the darkening dusty ground.

"Mia," Xand called. "Help us." Unshed tears stung Xand's eyes and the throb in her arm rose to levels of cold numbness.

"She is *dead*." Nulla scowled.

"Mia," Tala and Xand called together.

Another wave of Nulla's hand, but the two were ready. The rip in Xand's cheek stung like a knife's blade, another sharp pain roared from her arm, but she was stronger than that, she had to stay focused.

"I know you can help," Xand continued. "You were amazing. I would have found you again, I would risk a cold just to taste your lips once more."

"She is dead!" Nulla screamed, a rush of cold air raced from her mouth, a tinkle like the sound of shattering glass.

"She wasn't talking to *you*, bitch," Tala screamed back.

Xand smiled, the tears falling from her stinging eyes. The world blurred as she watched Tala race headlong toward Nulla. Nulla's movements were slow as though she were stuck in quicksand. No, Xand's mind amended, she's frozen from the inside out.

Screams and calls, the meaty slap of fist on flesh, pulled Xand's attention back to what was happening behind her. Sam stood, holding his ground against the onslaught from both inside and out. Jake fought within while the two Misfits ducked and weaved, dodging Sam's blows, landing their own in between. In the distance Xand heard slapping feet on dry dusty ground.

Other faces, rough and dirty from the weather, joined them

on the battle ground between two towers of containers. Xand's eyes bounced back and forth as Nulla's minions came head-to-head with her own people. Xand hesitated unsure who to help.

"I've got this." Tala laughed as she slammed an elbow into Nulla's nose, blood flowed over the God's chin as she wavered a little more in the darkened light of the eclipse.

They were winning, but Xand knew luck could turn in a heartbeat. She pushed memories from her own life away and the indecision snapped like a flag in a gale. Turning toward the larger group, Xand winced as she forced her broken arm down beside her body. She'd pay for that later. Right now, all she wanted was to ensure there *was* a later.

"Sam!" Xand screamed as she stormed toward the mass. Others turned, stepping out of her way, either feeling the fire raging inside of Xand or simply having their survival instincts still intact.

Sam turned slowly; knife raised in his grip. Rips covered his body, blood leaked from his wounds, and oh how his eyes were filled with just as much pain as they were fury. Xand shook her head as she took a gulp of air. It was his blood, splashing down onto the hard packed dirt, that would kill them all. No, not his blood. The blood of all those he'd tortured and drained of their own power and magic.

He deserved this and more.

But as Xand stepped closer, her heart shattered. She looked at the metal, blunt and tarnished with levels of pain Xand couldn't take in, not yet. Not if she wanted to see through the afternoon, see through the fight.

Over Sam's shoulder, Xand's eyes met those of a Misfit's. She nodded and the Misfit ran, shoulder down and barrelled directly into Sam's back. He didn't fall over, but he stumbled forward, catching his footing as his hand lost its grip on the knife. Xand grabbed up the blade, before Sam could register all that had happened. It hadn't exactly been the plan, but she'd work with whatever she could right now.

"Was this yours?" She pointed the tip toward Sam.

"Give it back bitch," Sam growled. The pain in his eyes overtaken by the feral fire of the sadist.

"Your wish." Xand ran forward. Sam called on powers that were not his own. The magic vibrated around him in a barrier of protection.

Please, stop him. We have you. The voice soft and familiar in her ears might have made her halt in her steps, if she hadn't already known what to do.

"No more suffering, Jake," she whispered, already missing their conversations over the phone.

The wall of magic, Sam stood so confidently behind, dropped like a curtain as Xand rushed through, knife ahead of her. For a moment Sam's eyes widened and mouth gaped. The metal slid easily into his throat and he fell back against the dirt, gurgling.

"I should let you bleed out, feel what you have done to so many others, but then I wouldn't be any better than you." Xand's voice was hoarse as she pulled out the knife.

Bile rose in the back of her throat as she knelt beside him. Her fingers prickled as she gripped Sam's head. The blood continued to spurt from the wound she'd inflicted. Memories of finding her friend beaten and bloody, the things she'd imagined doing to Sam to get even. And then finding her friend's suicide note years later, when she could no longer live with the nightmares and memories.

Xand closed her eyes and with what strength she could muster, she gritted her teeth and yanked with both hands. Her broken arm and voice screamed together, in agony and release. The snap was inconsequential to the cacophony of sound around her.

The fighting continued; Misfits versus Nulla's minions.

Tears covered her cheeks, tickling and dripping to the ground, mixing with the blood. She moved from Sam's still body. Energies and lives dripped into the earth. They fed the dry ground with a release of fear and pain. It would prove more potent than the salting of Carthage.

Her arm lay, heavy and useless beside her as she collapsed to the floor and pushed her back against a container wall. With her one working arm, Xand pulled her legs to her chest and leaned her forehead on her knees.

She sobbed as the moon hid the last of the sun's light.

FORTY-FIVE

TALA

"Who do you think you are?!" Nulla screamed as she pressed a hand to her nose. The stillness that had allowed Tala to land two solid blows to the God's face was weakening.

"I'm no one important, remember. Just a dirty half-breed." Tala slammed another fist into the God's cheek, sending her head to the right.

"Killing you will be the highlight of my day." Nulla spat a tooth, mixed with blood and saliva, to the ground.

"What are you waiting for?" Tala spoke between clenched teeth.

"You can win as many battles as you find, but you can't win this war. I'm waiting for you to break and beg for my mercy. It's just a matter of time."

"You're the last God, isn't that what you said?" Tala tilted her head mirroring Nulla's movements as the two circled each other.

"I *am* the last God. By the time I'm done, you will beg me, on your knees, for your death."

"Ahh," frustration seeped into Tala's words. "Your time is over you old has been."

"You know the disrespect from you Children will be the first thing to go."

"You're too late, Nulla. You were stupid and careless. Any of our blood would have sufficed but you had to go and take the Elders, you had to go so large that even the humans started to notice. Stop this *now*, and embrace the evolution of your kind, of *our* kind." Even as Tala spoke, she knew it was as useful as tits on a bull.

"Weak," Nulla spat out as the freeze within her shattered and she sent another push of energy toward Tala. It cut across her shoulder. The sting of a knifes blade. Tala winced but didn't look down. She forced herself a step forward shrinking the arc of the circle.

"Bow." Nulla sent another shard of energy out. It slammed into Tala's stomach and before she could stop herself, her knees bent, and she crumpled.

Raising her head, Tala saw the smirk and hard eyes of Nulla looking down at her.

"You're too late." Nulla's hard laugh hurt her ears and made her cringe. "You're on your knees just like I said you would be. Now, *beg* me."

"No." Tala's word was barely audible to her own ears, the sounds of fighting continued around her. She heard Adie corralling the Misfits and Children into fighting against their captors. Xand's screams at Sam had been swallowed up in the roar of battle.

"Alright, then." Nulla let out an exaggerated sigh and raised her hand. More energy bristled along her fingertips, but there was an odd jerkiness to the movement.

Tala pushed herself back to her feet and watched as the energy moved, slow and cold, a shard heading toward her. Tala closed her eyes, her body rocked as the wolf came to the surface. Her eyes opened, and she saw with the clarity of the animal. The darkness of the eclipse meant nothing. Opening her mouth and thrusting forth her hands, Tala sent out a roar on a wave of power. The shard of Nulla's energy was pushed back and in the blink of a moment, it went from being in slow motion to speeding back toward the God.

Nulla screamed and fell backwards onto the hard ground. A whoomph of air expelled from her lungs. Tala wasted no time, she was on Nulla. Straddling her, punching her face; right, left, right, right, left. Blood spilled from Nulla's nose and mouth, from the cuts that appeared on her cheeks.

Nulla began to laugh. The sound held Tala's fist half-way to Nulla's face.

"What are you laughing at?"

"You're right, I will live on. Just feel the anger and hatred, the darkness that surrounds us. My blood lives on, and stronger in you than even the others."

Tala straightened her back. She could feel it, the anger, the hatred, the darkness. With a quick look over her shoulder, Tala saw Xand and Adie standing, ready to intervene should Nulla get the upper hand again. Memories flashed through her mind, Adie's tearful confession fearing her darkness, Xand's fight within herself to find the light again. Waves of darkness came from her friends.

"No," Tala got off Nulla, "I'm not like you. Darkness is a choice."

"I will hunt you down, I won't ever stop."

"I know, but that doesn't mean I have to become you."

"Tala, what are you doing?" Xand and Adie flanked her.

"I'm choosing my light."

Nulla laughed again and turned back to her.

"I am the last G—"

"No. You're not." Adie clicked and Nulla gaped at the flames that danced on her fingertips. "*I'm* a God. You would have learned that if you bothered to pay attention or let anyone else talk."

"Well, well. Turns out you *aren't* my legacy of darkness, Tala."

"She's the Child of Pha," Tala said.

"The blood of Pha." Nulla's smirk slipped from her lips, a slight tremble evident before the smile returned. "We can rule this world together. I'll even spare your friends."

"And what makes *you* think I would want you by *my* side?" Adie spat.

"Sam!" Nulla called, the smirk returned to her lips.

"Pay attention," Xand snapped.

Tala felt the pain and anger mixing with Xand's usual energy, though the darkness she felt earlier was cowering in a corner.

"What have you done?" Nulla screamed, her hands scrabbled on the ground as she tried to push herself up.

"We got over ourselves. We evolved, and we won."

The darkness washed over them, as the eclipse reached its peak. Around them the sounds of battle had dulled. Now, the heavy breathing of survivors, and the surrender of Nulla's minions echoed around them.

"I can still hurt you," Nulla screamed.

"Just stop," Tala said, the pain and exhaustion washing over her. "Your time is over."

The three turned their backs on the defeated God and walked away as a sliver of the sun broke free from the passing moon.

"*Never!*" Nulla screamed.

Tala, Xand, and Adie turned to see Nulla back on her feet and racing toward them.

"Nulla." Jonah stepped out from between the nearby containers.

His hands raised, Nulla's movements froze once more. Beside Jonah, two other Elders stepped forward, joining their strength to Jonah's. Tala had been little more than a child the last time she saw either of the other Elders. Their strength and imposing presence paled in comparison to her memory, but when she took all three in, her lips shifted into a tired smile.

"Let me go," Nulla sobbed.

"Jonah?" Tala asked, looking at the strain on his face.

"No!" the Elder to Jonah's right answered and sent out a burst of energy. The brightness in the dim light burned Tala's eyes. It hit Nulla and the God screamed in pain instead of defiance. Lava swallowed her up and quickly cooled, solidifying her into molten rock.

"We've got it from here. Take care of the others." Jonah nodded toward Tala. Bruises and cuts covered his face, arms, and legs. Blood seeped through the scrap of cloth that might once have been a shirt. When their eyes met, Tala saw the old fury, and her shoulders dropped a little.

"Come on. It's time to go home," Xand said as she took Tala's hand in her own.

"Where's that?" Adie asked.

"Wherever we want it to be," Tala answered.

"Cold, can we go somewhere cold?" Xand smiled and tucked herself closer to Tala's side.

"Sure." Tala laughed.

"Can we sleep first?" Adie asked.

"That's a given." Xand smiled over at Adie who held on to Tala's other hand.

FORTY-SIX

TALA

"How did it go?" Adie jumped up from the wooden table as Tala stepped into the kitchen of their small apartment. They had spent the last six weeks calling the place home, all be it temporarily.

"They agreed." Tala smiled.

Adie squealed and jumped up, wrapping her arms around Tala's neck. They looked at each other for a moment before gently moving in for a kiss. The kissing had taken a few days to get used to, but now it felt like home, even though every touch of Adie's lips still sent a tingle through Tala's body.

Breathless, Tala pulled away and smiled. The pull on her own lips, the smiles that were genuine and soft, were still foreign. Like so many things, she would grow used to this new world as it wrapped around her.

"When are we holding the memorials?" Adie's voice was soft and gentle.

"In two days. They agreed to include all the Misfits and Children as the same family. There are a lot of things that the Elders are still discussing, but no one is arguing with Jonah."

"Not yet." Adie smirked.

"True. No doubt time will wash away the edges," Tala agreed.

"From us as well?" Adie asked.

"Our edges are smooth," Tala said and kissed Adie once more. How she wanted to curl up in bed and explore her body again, take her time and spend days thinking about nothing else but this woman of her dreams who came out of all these nightmares.

"Where's Xand?" Adie asked half-heartedly looking around Tala's shoulders.

"She stayed. She said she would be back in time for dinner." Tala ran a hand through Adie's black silk hair. It still amazed her how lucky she was to be allowed to touch her.

"Why did she stay?" Adie kissed Tala again before untangling herself from Tala's arms and turning toward the kitchen.

"She didn't tell me," Tala said, following Adie, watching as she filled the kettle and flicked it on. "Despite what you think, we don't know *everything* about each other."

Adie laughed and shook her head.

"I don't want her to feel uncomfortable around me, Tala." Adie's smile filled with doubt.

"She doesn't," Tala reassured.

"Are you sure?"

"Yes." Tala pulled Adie back into her arms and kissed her again. The kiss began sweet and quickly built-in heat as she teased Adie's lips open with her tongue. Adie moaned in her mouth.

"We have a few hours to ourselves." Tala's smile stretched wide; suggestion smeared across her swollen lips. "Any idea how we can pass the time?"

Adie laughed. The kettle flicked off, ready and boiled, but Tala ignored it and led Adie upstairs to their room. As soon as they stepped into the room, Tala pushed Adie against the door, clicking it shut.

Home had always been an elusive concept to Tala. She'd tried to find it in the Clans, in the house she lived with Diana and Xand, she even tried to find it on the road. But she'd never considered home could be a person.

Her thoughts floated away as Adie's fingers slipped beneath her singlet. A palm pressed against her back, pulled her tighter against Adie, she gasped and pushed her head back, giving Adie access to her neck. Teeth and tongue teased the exposed skin and sent a bolt of lightning through Tala's body.

"Bed, now," Adie gasped.

Tala took her time laying Adie down on the bed. She couldn't imagine ever tiring of peeling clothing from Adie's body. She slowly revealed more skin as she slipped Adie out of her shirt, and then slowly pulled her pants from her legs.

"Please Tala," Adie groaned as Tala took her time kissing up the inside of one leg.

Smiling, Tala scooched back down and made another line of kisses up Adie's other leg, stopping before she reached Adie's underwear. Adie's bum ground against the bed as she groaned.

"My, my, impatient aren't we." Tala's voice was low and raspy. She knew precisely the effect it had on Adie.

"Oh god."

"Just the one?" Tala chuckled.

"Just you." Adie sat up, grabbed Tala's head between both hands and kissed her hard enough to bruise both of their mouths.

"Fantastic," Tala breathed against Adie's lips before slipping her tongue inside and pushing Adie back down on to the bed. "Now lay back and let me show you what this God is truly capable of."

"Yes ma'am."

Tala winked and moved from Adie's mouth to her strong jaw, nipping teeth along it and down her throat, lavishing them with small licks before sliding down to Adie's chest. The bra barely lasted a moment before Tala slid her hands beneath Adie, unflicked the clasp and flew the offending garment across the room.

"God you're beautiful." Tala straddled Adie's hips, slowly rocking her pelvis back and forth against Adie's hotness.

"I never would have thought you such a tease."

"Oh baby, this is how you like me," Tala murmured. She leaned forward, hips still grinding against Adie as she clamped her mouth around one breast.

Adie gasped out a scream, fingers digging into Tala's hair, holding her still as Tala sucked and gently bit the nipple. After lavishing it with her tongue, she moved onto the other breast. Adie's hips met Tala's in time to her rhythm, grinding against each other as Tala sucked and nipped Adie's sensitive breasts.

"Please Tala," Adie moaned as her fingers slid from Tala's hand and dug into Tala's back.

"Please what?" Tala asked, as she continued to show appreciation for Adie's breasts.

"Fuck me."

Tala groaned, a nipple in her mouth sending a shudder through Adie's body.

"Fuck me, *please.*"

"Yes ma'am." Tala gave the nipple one more soft clamp of her teeth before returning to Adie's mouth to kiss the already swollen lips.

She smiled as Adie whimpered when she stopped grinding and used her knees to lift her weight up off of Adie.

"It'll be worth it."

Adie's breath was hard and heavy, her head pushed back

into the mattress as she lifted her hips and helped Tala tug off her underwear.

"I love you, Adie." The words slipped out before Tala could stop them. They were out before she realised that they weren't just in her head.

Adie smiled and her eyes locked with Tala's. "I love you too, Tala."

Tala slipped one thigh between Adie's legs and soon their previous rhythm picked up. It gained momentum as they kissed, Tala's hands roamed Adie's body as though trying to touch every inch of who Adie was.

"I want you," Adie whispered in Tala's ear as she sucked on Tala's ear lobe.

"Good." Tala slipped her hand down between her thigh and Adie's. She cupped Adie's sex, the heat and wetness made Tala groan with her own building need.

She pressed the heel of her palm against Adie's clit and teased her fingers around her entrance.

"Can I be inside you?"

"Yes," Adie begged as she ground her hips against Tala's hand, Tala's knee giving more pressure to her need. "Please."

Tala didn't use words to respond. She didn't have to. She kept her hips moving, her own sex rubbing against Adie's lifted thigh. Her wetness soaked the clothes she still wore. Slowly she eased a finger into Adie, pushing as deep as she could inside.

"Fuck yes."

Withdrawing she added a second to the next thrust and was rewarded with Adie's nails digging into her back. She laughed and moved in and out of Adie. Adie's pants turned into screams and soon Tala's entire body moved in time with Adie's growing pleasure. Tala's body pressed as close as possible to Adie's as Adie's body shuddered and stiffened beneath her. Tala slowed her movements. Her fingers withdrew little by little as her hips circled slow and steady.

"Oh, oh fuck." Adie smiled as she sighed with her eyes closed.

Tala smiled and kissed Adie's swollen mouth. Adie kissed her back and relaxed into the mattress. Her breath had barely slowed before she gently pushed on Tala's shoulder and rolled her onto her back.

"Really?" Tala asked, one eyebrow raised, one side of her mouth lifted in a smirk.

"Oh definitely." Adie's eyes glimmered with mischief. "It's *your* turn."

"I can't say I hate the sound of that."

"Good. Now get those clothes off and lay on your stomach."

Tala did as ordered, not willing to admit aloud just how much she loved it when Adie took control. She had a sneaking suspicious this woman was already well aware of it.

"I love you, Tala." Adie said with each kiss of her lips against Tala's spine as she made her way down.

Tala let herself dissolve under Adie, as Adie showed her just how much she loved Tala.

"Ah, she's going to be pissed with me, I stopped you getting dinner ready." Adie opened the fridge and closed it, clearly unsatisfied again at what was inside. The sun had gone down while they'd explored each other's bodies.

"She's a big girl, if she's hungry she'll find something to eat."

"But if I wasn't here, you would have gotten food ready."

"Maybe," Tala caught Adie in her arms. "But we've never been each other's keepers, not even for food. Why are you so worried?"

"Because I don't want her thinking I'm taking you away from her."

"Trust me, she doesn't think that."

"But she's been so distant. Even you said so. I mean I know I didn't exactly have a great handle on who she was before but, something's happened and she's distant."

"It's not you, she doesn't think you're taking me away." Tala knew this but couldn't find the words to explain why or how she knew it.

"How do you know that?" Adie's eyebrows furrowed as she asked.

The squeak of the back door opened, and they both turned, arms still wrapped around each other.

"Because I think you're the best thing to have happened to my bonehead best friend." Xand smiled as she stepped through the threshold of the door. "Plus, I know what you two are like when I'm not here, so I brought us dinner." Xand held up a plastic bag filled to the brim with Chinese containers. Aromas wafted over to Tala and her mouth began to water.

"Oh." Adie's neck reddened and she lowered her eyes.

"Everything okay?" Tala looked at Xand, hoping to find a clue in her eyes. They looked tired, just as they had the last six weeks.

"It will be." Xand smiled.

Adie made cups of tea while Xand and Tala set out the containers, plates and cutlery on the small round table in the dining room.

"So, we can have the memorial together," Xand asked between bites of a spring roll. "Have they made any other decisions about allowing the living Misfits to be part of the family?"

"The memorial, yes, but the rest is all still under discussion," Tala replied before forking in a mouthful of honey chicken and moaning at the taste.

"And what about you? Will you still head up the Misfits?" Xand asked.

"Well," Tala almost chocked by the unexpected question. She looked from Adie to Xand and back again. "If the Misfits are still needed—"

"They will be," Xand interrupted, and then pressed her lips together. "Sorry."

"*If* they are still needed," Tala laughed. "I was thinking it's time to take the lessons from battle to heart."

"What lessons?" Xand's eyebrows creased together.

"That I can't do it alone. That I'm not Diana." Tala reached under the table and took Adie's hand in her own.

"Diana didn't do it alone," Xand said.

"Perhaps not, but I thought she did." Tala shrugged.

"What does that mean, Tal?" Xand asked.

"It means, we do it together." Tala smiled. "If you can stand me."

Xand smiled and nodded.

They chatted amiably for the rest of dinner and cleaned up as a family. When the last dish was put away, Adie hung the damp tea towel over the handle of the oven and wrapped her arms around Tala's neck and kissed her. Tala lost herself in the smooth lips and taste of magic and chai spice that was all Adie.

Xand coughed. "I'll leave you two to it."

"No." Adie pulled away and reached her hand out. Xand grabbed it and laughed.

"It's okay. I need a run anyway." Xand winked and let go of Adie's hand.

When the door closed behind Xand, Tala turned back to Adie.

"That would leave just us then." Tala looked from under batted eyelids to Adie.

Adie laughed and melted into Tala's arms.

FORTY-SEVEN

XAND

Xand stopped at the large stone as it sparkled under the warm winter sun. There were more names than Xand would have liked carved into the stone, but each one of them deserved to be remembered for their lives, not just their deaths. She ran her fingertips over Diana's name, Jake's name, and then lingered as she found Mia's. Tears pricked at her eyes, and she blinked, allowing just a few to ease down over her cheeks.

"Thank you," she whispered to the three insignificant letters that couldn't begin to explain how the five minutes with a stranger had changed her life in ways she still didn't understand, "for everything."

The memorial echoed around the open space of what was once the container yard. The Elders had purchased it, finally using their resources for something worthwhile.

"Hey." Adie's greeting was gentle, as though trying not to sneak up on Xand or scare her.

"Hey," Xand replied, wiping gently at her cheeks.

"I'm sorry about everything you've lost," Adie said.

"You've lost a lot as well. I'm sorry we couldn't get any of their names added to the stone." Xand replied.

"They didn't belong here. Even Pha. His death doesn't mean what it should. None of it seems to have really hit me the way it should."

"How *should* death hit anyone?" Xand asked, genuinely curious.

"With some caring, I guess."

"Just because you did what you had to do and would do it again, doesn't mean you don't care."

"I don't know if I feel anything either."

"Not knowing what you feel isn't the same as not feeling. You aren't broken or uncaring. You love Tala, and that's enough to heal both of you."

"I hope so." Adie smiled.

"Trust me." Xand winked.

"Okay, Guru Xand."

Xand laughed; a sound she thought would take more months to escape her lips again. "I like that."

"The memorial is about to start." Adie's words came out as though she were apologising.

"Then let's go."

The memorial didn't last long. Tears were shed, and words were spoken, but what words could any of them say to have the loss of their family make sense?

"Come on. Let's go home." Tala reached her spare hand out for Xand. Her other one entangled in Adie's fingers since the beginning of the service.

"I'm not going," Xand said.

"What?" Tala and Adie dropped hands, both staring slack jawed at her.

"I've spoken to the Elders, and they've agreed I'm the best person for the job."

"*What* job?" Tala asked.

"To take over Pour Another One." Xand swallowed audibly.

"You're staying in Forty West?"

"Yes. And I'm going to help liaise between The Children and Misfits. Maybe one day there won't be a distinction."

"But the Elders are still deciding?" Tala blinked as she asked, confusion furrowed her brow and scrunched up her mouth.

"On some things," Xand rolled her eyes, "on *many* things. But I convinced them this would be a good step. Plus, I'll be training whoever wants to work on their powers."

"Wow." Tala's smile was strained, the sadness in her eyes almost made Xand change her mind.

"I want to do this, Tala." Xand forced out the words before others took their place.

"I'm proud of you, pixie."

Xand laughed and let Tala wrap her in her arms. She breathed in the smell of her adolescent home, of her first crush, of her best friend.

"You better come visit me often," Xand pulled out of the embrace and wiped the tears from her cheeks. She looked at Adie. "Both of you."

"We will." Adie stepped forward, tentatively.

Xand wrapped her in a hug. "Don't let her get away with shit, I'll kick her arse if she fucks it up," Xand whispered into Adie's ear.

Adie laughed and nodded as she stepped back.

"Be safe." Xand blew them both kisses.

"You too." Tala said as she grabbed Adie's hand again.

"Now bugger off, I've got work to do."

They smiled at each other and Xand waved as Tala and Adie walked to the car the Elders had supplied them. Xand watched as they drove away.

The war might be over, but Xand's life had just begun.

ABOUT THE AUTHOR

Neen Cohen is an Aussie sapphic speculative fiction author. Her novel *The Void*, won the Page Turner Awards for best LGBT book of 2024.

Neen tries to take things seriously but thrives being the hyperactive bookworm who rarely stops smiling or laughing.

If she had to decide between never reading or never writing again she simply wouldn't. Rules were never her strong point.

When not writing or working at the day job, Neen loves nothing more than dancing, nerf wars with the boys, roaming graveyards and forests, playing the PS, and crafting wild and crazy things sometimes for the kiddo, other times simply because she can.

In her ideal world, Neen would spend her days wandering graveyards for inspiration before finding the perfect tree (usually within said graveyard) to lean against and write.

To keep up to date on Neen Cohen's adventures you can find all the links here:

neencohen.com/links or you can sign up to my email

Thank you so much for spending time in Adie's world. If you've enjoyed reading Children of the Gods, and you wouldn't mind popping up a review wherever you feel comfortable to, I would be so grateful.

Indie authors survive primarily on word of mouth and it means so much to me to be able to keep doing what I love.

Thank you

Be Safe

Be Brave

Be Kind

Neen x

COFFEE, CARS, AND NECROMANCY

Immortal days as a necromancer aren't what they are cracked up to be when Death is mad as Hell.

Stuck in a perpetual nightmare, Lily just wants a break. But a dead body stands in her way of a good cup of coffee and a day basking in the sun. As a necromancer, this job wasn't hers to take. But this time she can't turn away as the dead leads to the living—the one living person Lily never wanted to see again.

Detective Larissa Alanor has been a pain in Lily's existence. Ever since her baby sister died, Alanor has blamed one person and one person only, Lily. But the connections can't be denied, as the past and the present collide.

Will these two enemies come together to solve the real mystery? Or will they stick to their guns while more lives are at risk?

Coffee, Cars, and Necromancy is a portal urban fantasy novel, with a sapphic enemies to lovers romance thrown in the mix.

If you love slow burns with lots of paranormal action, this is the book for you.

https://mybook.to/ccandn